# THE LAST DAYS OF CAFÉ LEILA

Also by DONIA BIJAN

*Maman's Homesick Pie*

# The
# Last Days
## of
# Café Leila

A NOVEL

DONIA BIJAN

ALGONQUIN BOOKS
OF CHAPEL HILL
2017

Published by
Algonquin Books of Chapel Hill
Post Office Box 2225
Chapel Hill, North Carolina 27515-2225

a division of
Workman Publishing
225 Varick Street
New York, New York 10014

Printed in the United States of America.
Published simultaneously in Canada by Thomas Allen & Son Limited.
Design by Steve Godwin.

Excerpt from "Little Gidding" from *Four Quartets* by T. S. Eliot.
Copyright © renewed 1970 by Esme Valerie Eliot. Reprinted by permission
of Houghton Mifflin Harcourt Publishing Company. All rights reserved.

This is a work of fiction. While, as in all fiction, the literary perceptions
and insights are based on experience, all names, characters, places, and incidents
either are products of the author's imagination or are used fictitiously.

LIBRARY OF CONGRESS CATALOGING-IN-PUBLICATION DATA
Names: Bijan, Donia, author.
Title: The last days of Café Leila / a novel by Donia Bijan.
Description: First edition. | Chapel Hill, North Carolina : Algonquin Books of Chapel
Hill, 2017. | "Published simultaneously in Canada by Thomas Allen & Son Limited."
Identifiers: LCCN 2016043555 | ISBN 9781616205850
Subjects: LCSH: Mothers and daughters—Fiction. | Fathers—Death—Fiction. |
Iranian American women—Fiction. | Iran—Emigration and immigration—Fiction.
Classification: LCC PS3602.I368 L37 2017 | DDC 813/.6—dc23
LC record available at https://lccn.loc.gov/2016043555

10 9 8 7 6 5 4 3 2 1
First Edition

FOR MITCHELL AND LUCA

We shall not cease from exploration
And the end of all our exploring
Will be to arrive where we started
And know the place for the first time.

—T. S. ELIOT, from "Little Gidding"

# THE LAST DAYS OF CAFÉ LEILA

# PROLOGUE

TEHRAN, APRIL 2014

Zod marked time by the postman's arrival, usually by four p.m., quarter past at the latest, except on Fridays when he didn't come at all. Friday was the day of rest, when if anything, Zod grew more restless with every rigid minute ticking by. Waiting for the mail on Saturday, he spent the last hour watching the clock, and at half past three, he stood up to look out the window with his hands in his trouser pockets. A breeze sent flurries of wisteria into the courtyard. The trees had sprouted new leaves. You would never believe how lifeless they had been just a few weeks before, their splayed branches bare and brooding. Now it was April, true spring, each day warmer than the last, each bud becoming a frilly blossom. He observed a family of finches nesting in the eaves, touching down to pick up a suitable stick and then off again in busy bouncing flight.

Except for this pause in the afternoon, Zod didn't have much time to watch the world. Naneh Goli came in from hanging the wash to stand beside him, nudging in mock reproach for here he was again. "What on earth are you waiting for?" as if he didn't stand there every afternoon expecting the faint drone of the mail scooter and the puffs of dust from the alley. He pushed away from the ledge and crossed the hall to go outside, leaving his jacket on the peg and the old woman framed in the window.

Already he felt light-footed, less pain in his joints when he tested the first step with one shoe. He considered leaving his cane, but Naneh Goli was watching him and Zod didn't want to hear her fair warnings. Sometimes he deliberately prolonged the short walk to the garden gate, pausing to examine a chipped tile or tuck away the loose tendrils of jasmine curling forward from the brick wall. How far was the carrier from him now? Had he reached the traffic circle? It was best to approach the gate just when he arrived so as not to seem too anxious.

Letters from America took sometimes two to three weeks to arrive, and there had been no post at all the past month. Noor still wrote to her father and he kept her letters neatly bundled in his dresser drawer. Letters that lately spoke of nothing much at all except domestic matters, but it wasn't so much the content anymore as it was the thread that reassured him, that drew him into her life. A silence this long was unusual and he was afraid that something had happened. Children didn't even answer their telephones anymore and Zod couldn't stand speaking into the hollow space after hearing their recorded greetings. He still preferred a penned note. *It must be today, please let it be today.*

Yet whether a letter came or not, Zod greeted the postman with a warm smile. And today, when the carrier said, "I have something for you," Zod took the envelope from his hand and folded it into his pocket in a casual way and continued to exchange pleasantries, as if the man could be deceived into thinking that the envelope from America wasn't from Zod's daughter, as if it were a utility bill, as if his restless thumb wasn't twitching to part the glue. All in a moment, the waiting gave way to joy. The letter came alive in his grip, pulling him at once into two worlds: one on the threshold of Café Leila, where every day he listened for the sound of a motor drawing near, and another world in his pocket, with his children, where he had to curb a desire to run, to shout, to draw out the paper and wave it to and fro.

# PART ONE

# One

⁂

Noor stood at the sink with her sleeves rolled up peeling yellow potatoes and dropping them into a water bath. The long blade of her knife, sharpened without a scratch, gleamed on the chopping board. Her father believed that anything cut with a knife is tastier than mauling it in a food processor, so even in her modern San Francisco kitchen, she didn't own one and took special care of her knives. She liked to use her black cast-iron skillet to cook the onions with crumbled sage from the dried bouquets above her stove, cooking them in oil until they were quite tender before adding the sliced potatoes. Already the onions' sweetness wafted through the house, settling into the linens. She knew that her daughter would not like the pungent smell, so she closed her bedroom door and opened the tall windows to the cool morning air and the sound of a faraway lawn mower.

Most of her recipes came from her father, but Noor learned how to make the luscious potato cake from Nelson's mother. The recipe her mother-in-law had whispered into Noor's ear was the authentic one used by Nelson's great-grandmother. In its own unpresumptuous way, the Spanish Tortilla is an honest love omelet, and every bite must be suffused with fragrant olive oil—in this case, too much of a good thing is not a sin. Even when Noor was an amateur and the potatoes were sometimes raw, Nelson would say, "Oh my God! That was the best tortilla of my whole life!" Which of course wasn't true, but he was acknowledging the effort of peeling and slicing immense quantities of potatoes.

What she loved most about Spanish food was its lusty simplicity, so unlike the gastronomical somersaults of French cuisine or the complexity of the Persian food she grew up with. When she was little she could eat pyramids of saffron rice and rich meat stews, but she now associated the colors and perfumes of her husband's native cuisine with their courtship, with paddleboats and honeymoons and champagne in silver buckets, with flamenco and candlelight and little fried sardines with sea salt by the water. Her postcards were menus, smudged and wine-stained, saved from their meals, addressed to herself and read carefully like romance manuals.

With just two hours to prepare a picnic, there would be no time to get her nails done before going to work. It seemed a waste of time when she could better spend that hour layering rows of cured black olives with roasted red peppers. There were still cucumbers and radishes to slice, strawberries to wash. She thought about how Nelson would point at each bowl like a giddy child and speculate with excitement on what the food would taste like and then enjoy it all a hundred times more than painted fingernails. And when would they ever be as eager to celebrate as now, as today, their sixteenth anniversary, on a ferry over to Angel Island at dusk? They saw so little of each other lately that her heart was set on this annual tradition, which coincided with the first days of spring, when they would break away from work to escape to the harbor, leaving their patients in the care of their colleagues.

"There we are," she said to herself. "I just have the lemon left." She cut a lemon into eighths and placed it with sprigs of cilantro on a blue butter dish from a set they were given as a wedding present, then rinsed the knife under hot water, drying it with a dish towel before placing it in the drawer. From the cupboard she took a wicker picnic basket and put it on the kitchen island to begin the careful assembly of silver, two china plates and crystal flutes, each item nestled between linen-covered tiers. No matter how hungry they were, there was a certain slowness to unpacking the basket, to unfurling their napkins and popping the champagne, that made the afternoon last longer, allowing them more time to tell each other stories they had kept to themselves until now. It was as if before Nelson she had eaten in the dark, and when he came into her life their meals became as companionable and good as grilling sausages and peppers over an open fire under the stars.

On the counter lay a note for her daughter that she would be home late, with instructions on how to heat the veggie lasagna when she returned from volleyball practice. Lily had only recently become a finicky eater, vowing not to swallow anything that could walk, fly, or swim, but Noor felt safe with pasta. All that was left was to brew a thermos of black coffee and remove the tortilla from the mold before leaving for the hospital. She hummed and flitted about the kitchen like a moth in a kind of ecstasy, catching a glimpse of her flushed face in the glass oven door, her cheeks ablaze.

THE HOSPITAL BREAK ROOM was small and sparsely furnished with a watercolor painting and not much more than the necessities of a microwave and a refrigerator. Here the staff relished any indulgence, from party napkins and frosted cakes to the contents of their lunch boxes, which could be anything from barbecued chicken to carrot raisin salad—whatever added cheer to the drab decor and their long shifts. Thus they broke into a wild cheer with the appearance of flowers, especially from boyfriends and husbands.

The anniversary bouquet for Noor arrived just as she started her shift, and the nurses paused their lunchtime banter to tease her good-naturedly when she brought them into the break room. Noor took her flowers to the sink to clip their stems. She rinsed a vase and filled it with cool water, then carefully cut the thick ends of two dozen red roses with surgical scissors before placing them in the vase on the nurses' table.

There was an outburst of sympathy when Noor read Nelson's note out loud: "*Mi vida*, can we postpone our picnic? I'm so sorry, I have a surgery this afternoon." This had never happened before. She said nothing and sat down with her arms wrapped around herself. It was good how disappointment slowed things down so she could ease back into the chair with her coffee and look out on the spray of roses, letting the chatter continue without her. Amy took her hand and squeezed it as if they were thinking the same thing, but Noor was thinking about the basket in the trunk of her car beneath a blue-and-white checked tablecloth. *What about all that food?* she thought. *There's no sense in wasting the tortilla; he has to eat after all.* She would drop it off for him after work. With that, she went to check on her patients, who looked at her kindly and with renewed relief as if she had been gone for weeks.

Nelson was an in demand heart surgeon, though he rarely missed family occasions and even managed to coach Lily's soccer team. Noor would have walked to cardiology when her shift ended, but being on the other end of the compound, it was easier to drive rather than carry the food over. Her eyes were focused on finding a parking space until they were drawn to a familiar shape near an unfamiliar car. Nelson, in pale blue scrubs, stood in the parking lot at arm's length of a nurse Noor met once at a staff Christmas party. He leaned forward to tuck a strand of hair behind her ear and she smiled up at him. Noor had just pulled in, and without needing to see or hear more she knew the affection in this small gesture revealed everything between them. One glance told her what was lost and could not be mended. A little gasp of surprise escaped her lips.

Without thinking, she drove straight home and unpacked the picnic as if it had simply rained and there was a change of plans. She threw away the olives and the peppers, dumped the tortilla in the garbage, and poured the champagne down the drain. As she washed the Tupperware, she slipped her wedding ring off her soap-slippery finger and left it by the kitchen sink. Then, seeing the school bus across the street, she ran outside and startled Lily with a hug.

The separation was swift and Nelson had not resisted, infidelity being a genetic cliché he couldn't deny. His parents had been happily married for over forty years, but "women found Papa irresistible," he yawned, "like velvet." There had been others, he confessed nonchalantly—an attitude that served him well when he removed a broken heart and fastened a new one in a patient's chest. Noor, somewhat anesthetized, didn't see the point of demonizing him, sparing him Lily's judgment, although Lily blamed her and she could've at least bought herself some sympathy. It was as if Noor believed the odds of having a good marriage like her parents were so little that it was no wonder hers had failed.

There were no battles, no court dates—she couldn't stomach it, and Nelson didn't press the custody issue, agreeing to weekends and alternate holidays. Over the years they had had more impassioned arguments over a referee's bad call in a soccer match. In the process of splitting up they cowered in the corners of their bedroom, speaking rationally and not raising their voices, even going so far as apologizing for letting each other down, the conversation so cordial it made Lily wonder if their love had ever been real. They led her to believe that their fairy tale marriage—Nelson's pursuit of Princess Noor's hand, their wedding on a boat, a seven-tiered rum cake, their honeymoon in a castle near Barcelona—was all a spectacular fable spun in bedtime stories.

Noor was angry, but she was also embarrassed that she didn't know. That she was not prepared. Was she the only one not to know? *How stupid am I?* She thought this was something that happened to other people—not her life, not her marriage. So she did what she had to. She took Lily and left Nelson. She rented an apartment but when she reached the door, her daughter beside her, she didn't go in; she stood outside and looked around for Nelson to help her carry their suitcases. Of course he wasn't there.

Her father, who was born within crying distance of his family's café in Tehran, rarely left home, yet he had sent Noor and her brother as far away as he could when she was just eighteen. For months Noor expected him to come for them, and she would stand outside and look for him. She wrote letters begging him to let her come back, but his reply was always the same: this is no country for a child, Noor. She gave up eventually, just as she'll give up looking for Nelson.

When she was small, her father told her again and again the story of how he and her mother had chosen her name. For weeks, almost every night, they sat talking about it, trying a variety of boy and girl names, always choosing one and changing it by morning. Then on the night Noor was born, the power was out at Café Leila until the moment they brought their new daughter home. When the lights came on, a name popped into Zod's head. He said she filled their world with light. For years Noor imagined the house dimming whenever she left. *What vanity!* she now thought. To live into your forties thinking it was you who brightened rooms, because nothing of what you had seen so far prepared you for the truth: how small and inconsequential your so-called luster, how easily extinguished and utterly dark.

# Two

---ⵡⵡⵡ---

In a cul-de-sac at the end of Nasrin Street, quiet except at the hour when the kindergartners at Firouzeh Elementary were set free, sat a faded yellow brick building detached from its neighbors. Here, beneath a recessed sign, was Café Leila, its entrance framed in low-hanging wisteria in full bloom this late April. When the postman finally delivered Noor's letter, Zod brushed powder blue petals from his lapel with the envelope and, feeling grateful, insisted the mailman have a cup of tea. Afterwards, he stood watching the scooter disappear down the alley, then fiddled around in the garden and clipped roses for the café's tables. After weeks of waiting, he wasn't ready to tear the letter open. He had to ready himself for the first line that always moved him to tears: *My dearest, my Baba.*

With the dinner hour near, Zod would wait even longer. Karim, a young apprentice, was already fanning coals with a broom head in the courtyard, stationed there to call the names of regulars as they arrived, like actors to the stage—an impatient cast of doctors, office clerks, shopkeepers, engineers, and students who would soon duck through the gate. The boy was only thirteen but he had a manly way about him, having learned from Zod to recognize and greet guests with the purest appreciation. Hardly anyone came in that he didn't know.

From the original staff of Café Leila two waiters remained, both silver foxes hired in the sixties by Zod's late father. Hedayat and Aladdin still wore the same faded dark blue jackets with gold-fringed epaulettes, making them look like retired generals. Until his wife died, Aladdin wore aftershave and a white carnation in his lapel every day, but he gave that up and now had to be reminded to trim his mustache and mend loose buttons. Ala's barrel-chested younger brother, Hedi, a wrestler in his youth, lifted barbells in the courtyard every morning. At sixty-four, he still did all the heavy labor in the restaurant. Their cousin Soli worked in the kitchen. He had shown up one day after the war looking for work and Zod found him something to do. In a few weeks he had proven to be dependable and stayed on as an apprentice. Zod's own nanny, Naneh Goli, carried the full weight of her eighty-five years to the garden where she dug potatoes and radishes with one hand on her hip, the effects of time visible in the curve of her back. Like a family, so familiar to one another and their tasks, they hardly spoke. Early birds arrived to hear Hedi's grunting as he rearranged tables, Ala's deep sigh with every napkin fold, Soli calling to the young boy, his nephew Karim, to light the coals, and Zod's every command braided with endearments—incapable of asking Naneh Goli for a tomato without lavishing her with praise.

The days were growing longer now, but in the short days of winter the customers arrived sooner to leave the somber streets for the light in the café. Like children being called to dinner by the plume of smoke, a hand beckoning over the rooftops, they arrived one by one, two by two, their faces stung from the cold air. In the courtyard the heady odor of onions and grilled meat converged, and through the half open door they stumbled in like drunken sailors, bumping into one another to reach a table. If a regular didn't show up, Karim was sent to look for him.

For Zod, Café Leila was an ongoing opera where from his vantage point he felt privy to the secret lives of these men who loosened their shirt buttons and rolled up their sleeves to play a part in his theater. He lamented the absence of women, who came less frequently, finding the hejab oppressive and the watchful eyes of the gendarmes loitering the streets looking for an excuse to antagonize them prohibitive. Sometimes families came with wives and grandmothers and daughters and sisters, and when they did his eyes lit up like lanterns and he clapped his hands in the air like a wedding party had arrived.

The world changed around Café Leila, but the life that had gone on there since the 1930s continued. Where there were once merchants to their left and right, there now stood mostly uninhabited buildings gazing vacantly at one another. Dusty storefronts with remnants of their merchandise—a tennis shoe, cans of old film, a bicycle tire—told of lives that had moved on. The only ones who remained were the old doctor in the two-story house (his family long gone abroad), the grocer who sold Ala his tea and cigarettes, the kindergartners who went home at noon, and Zod in his tidy café with its marble floor and ladder-back chairs, opened nearly eighty years ago by his father, Yanik Yadegar, a Russian émigré who had once trained in the kitchens of the Hotel Astoria in St. Petersburg.

In the 1930s Yanik brought blinis and apple charlottes, beef stroganoff and *kulich* to Tehran, opening the first confectionary with a garden café. He came with his wife, Nina, who spooned cinnamon-scented ground beef and onions into delicate piroshkies and learned to cook Persian food by trial and error, nourishing her family and customers with a generous spirit, mingling delicately with neighbors, and learning to speak Farsi. To steady their leap across borders, Yanik changed his surname from Yedemsky to Yadegar, and planted a small orchard of pomegranate, almond, and mulberry trees that would shade the terrace tables. Year after year they blossomed, filling the air with their sweet smell, regardless of political turmoil or the events on the street.

Before a second story was built, before the children were born and the dream of an adjacent hotel was realized, Yanik and Nina slept like two stowaways in the storeroom, snuggling between pickling jars and burlap bags of rice and pinto beans, with their few possessions neatly folded in a cardboard box fashioned into a cupboard. There was no bath, so twice a week they set off by *doroshke* (a horse-drawn carriage) to the nearest hamam, where Yanik smoked *qalyan* (water pipes) in the men's section and Nina drank tea with the women after emerging pink-skinned from the steam room and the rough scrub-down by a dour-faced attendant. It was on the wooden benches of the communal baths that the couple endeared themselves to the locals; a gregarious Yanik grew an impressive handlebar mustache and sang Russian ballads to fathers and sons who welcomed him with a warm rumble of applause, and Nina brought tea cakes to grandmothers, aunts, and young girls already enchanted with this fair-skinned beauty. From them she learned how to haggle, how to make yogurt, when to pickle the eggplant and cucumbers and garlic the villagers brought to town on donkeys. When December brought snows and their street lost power, they learned about *Yalda*, the Persian winter solstice celebration, and they lit the café with candles, filled ceramic bowls with pomegranates, dried fruits, and nuts, and cooked enormous pots of hearty *ash reshteh*, a thick noodle soup stirred with whey. It was a night so cheerful and memorable, full of storytelling and feasting, that for years it remained a neighborhood tradition to gather at Café Leila for the solstice.

Eventually, brick by brick, living quarters were added, a porcelain pedestal sink and footed tub were installed, but Yanik and Nina continued to frequent the hamam and sneak into the café's storage room to grope and make quick love, finding comfort in their original nest, always cool and dim against the heat between them. It would not have surprised Zod to find out he was conceived on a bed of lentils. His parents once dreamed of a better life and Iran folded itself around them, offering sanctuary where they could raise their three sons and work and live with dignity.

In the old days when cities like Tehran and Kabul boasted cinemas and tennis clubs, Café Leila was home to intellectuals. The fifties and sixties seemed filled with possibility, and Yanik welcomed students from the university, writers, musicians, poets, and journalists, parties of guests who gathered here every afternoon and stayed long into the night. He envisioned the ambiance of the elegant cafés he'd seen in Budapest and Vienna and loved to sit in the glass-fronted cubbyhole that served as an office, watching his customers dig into his wife's baklava with a fork and knife. He bought copies of their books to display on the shelves and asked for their autographs, and if they liked a dish, he named it after them so it was no longer borscht, but Nima's soup or Forough's stuffed cabbage and Sohrab's cream puffs. Their regular visits sustained him—wanting more than just a restaurant, he created a cultural hub where his sons learned to play chess and backgammon with the patrons, to serve and sweep, to roll filo dough and fry blinis with rose petal jam under Nina's gaze.

Of the three, it was Zod, her middle child, who took to the alchemy his mother practiced in the kitchen. She was self-taught, relying on intuition to bring ingredients together and finding ways to honor them. Where Yanik insisted on his formal training, an acrobat expecting to be applauded for his skill, Nina improvised and laughed at her mistakes, which were often her triumphs. If she forgot to add mashed potatoes to the cutlet dish, the vegetables were folded into crepe batter for a thin potato cake she sprinkled with chives and fresh cream. Mostly, it was the way things were always new that kept Yanik and Nina open and purposeful—there was no end to their learning. They made a good life for their children in a country where they weren't raised and would never leave, but such a peaceful existence would not be a given for their grandchildren.

AT LAST IN HIS bedroom with the door closed, Zod sat by the window with Noor's letter in his lap, the sun sinking away behind the trees, an ice-cold hand seizing his heart. Somewhere, beyond the borders of the city, beyond the continent and an ocean, in a place his hands could not reach, his daughter sat in darkness with a broken heart. It used to worry him to think of his children as strangers in a strange land, but each time they asked to come home, he patiently explained his desire to give them a better future until they stopped asking.

Zod had always felt that when you first become a parent something happens that makes you see and hear as if you're a newborn, too. In the first year of his daughter's life, he found himself looking at the world through her eyes and living in it as if he didn't already know it, like they were both creatures with wide-open eyes and shaky limbs. Her every move was as new to him as it was to her, from the slow grasp of her rattle to her small sneeze. When she screamed, he screamed. When she hiccupped, he hiccupped, so that she would never be alone with her new sounds. How did he ever let her out of his sight?

# Three

—⊶⊷—

Noor was glad to see Lily bring a friend home from school. They had been living in the rented apartment in Pacific Heights for six weeks. Lily's bedroom was much smaller than her one at the house and Noor had worried that she wouldn't be comfortable having anyone over. From Lily's room came the ripple of girls' laughter and Noor smiled to herself as she prepared a snack of fruit and pound cake and carried it to them on a tray.

Laura's bright, open face, and the way she eyed the tray so eagerly, encouraged Noor to linger a moment and she bent to kiss the crown on Lily's head. Lily looked quickly over her shoulder, her dark eyelashes fluttering in distress. Undeterred, Noor lingered behind her questioning Laura about school.

"Mom! Enough already!" Lily said, exasperated. Noor felt flattened. She smiled a tight smile, mumbled to Laura how nice it was to see her again, and retreated.

What seemed odd to Noor was how she thought in these few weeks they would become closer, not slip apart. Just the day before, Noor's best friend Nassim—practically Lily's godmother—was visiting from out of town and Lily barely acknowledged her. All of Noor's offers of mother-daughter outings and special treats were thrown back at her, and all week she watched Lily willfully dump the contents of her lunch sack into the trash.

"Don't make me lunch," she cried, "You try to make it too fancy . . . I hate those stupid little fruit cups, all brown and mushy. I'm not three years old!"

Sparks of anger were understandable in a teenager, especially with her home turned inside out, and Noor was making every effort to maintain a sense of calm and security, to keep the channels open, but Lily's hostility was making it difficult.

When at last Laura went home, Noor asked Lily to come to the kitchen.

"What was all that about? What's wrong with me asking Laura a few questions? I've missed her," she said, leaning into the counter to study Lily.

"Because you're embarrassing me with all your questions!" Lily's hand flew up so abruptly that she knocked over a glass of cranberry juice and made no attempt to clean up the red pool gathering on the counter.

Noor straightened up and moved closer with a dish towel.

"Lily, I think it's okay for me to talk to your friends."

"Fine. But you don't have to ask them ten million questions. Can I please go now?"

"Not yet. Can you tell me why you were so rude to Aunt Nassi yesterday? You didn't even say hello. How could you ignore her? She brought you a lovely gift," Noor said softly.

"I don't want that cheesy bag and I can't stand her either."

"Why? Where is this coming from?"

"She's a phony, that's why, with her big hair and fake boobs."

*What put her out?* thought Noor. Lily had always adored her glamorous auntie.

"She's my friend, Lily. And yours. Listen, I know you're shy. I used to be shy, too—"

But Lily cut her off. "*I AM NOT SHY! STOP!* I just don't like her, okay? What do you want from me?"

"I want you to greet people politely! And please stop shouting."

Every day was hard. Today, harder still. Noor felt so hollowed out and tired she wished she could put her head down on the counter and leave it all for another time.

"Sometimes I don't like some of your friends but don't I still chauffeur them around and buy them birthday gifts and treat them to lunch? Huh? I'm still polite to them."

Lily turned her back to leave then changed her mind. "Then you're a phony just like Auntie Nassim . . . pretending to like people you can't stand." She seemed suddenly relaxed as if she'd finally succeeded in ridding herself of something lodged in her throat.

"That's enough, Lily. I think you've said enough." Noor clutched a damp, pink-stained dishcloth in both hands to stop herself from throwing something and Lily slouched away.

TWO MONTHS INTO THEIR stay at the apartment, the furnishings were still spare. Noor had planned to look for a condo once the divorce was settled, even though Nelson had offered to move out so they could stay in the house. Nassim suggested she at least take some of the good furniture, but Noor didn't want to clutter the small space with remnants of her old life.

One day, when she knew Nelson was at work, she did go back with a few empty boxes to collect some dishes and pots and pans. Standing in the kitchen, the bright light of a May afternoon streaming through the skylight over her old stove, breathing in the scent of a thousand meals she had prepared here for her family, the atmosphere was so rich with memories that she pulled open a drawer and reached for her knife to carve out her heart and leave it on the kitchen counter for Nelson, the heart doctor.

Instead she left empty boxes like coffins on the scrubbed tiles of the graveyard that used to be her kitchen. Wanting nothing to do with that place, she took inventory of all their possessions, remembered how much everything meant to her, and decided to leave it all behind, except for a moth-eaten navy blue sweater that had belonged to Nelson.

That night Lily said, "Are you wearing Dad's sweater?" Noor actually preferred her daughter's sarcasm to silence and sulking. She hadn't wanted anything else from that life, but the sweater reminded her of Nelson's warmth. She wasn't proud of it, but so what? It was just a sweater and she was always cold. "It's way too big, but it suits you," Lily said and Noor took one step forward with an urge to hug her, but Lily turned away.

How steep was the penalty for being a jilted wife? Noor was a good nurse, calm and meticulous, but since the separation there was a tight-lipped tension in the air at the hospital, apparent in the demeanors of the staff, the patients, and even their visitors. She could sense it. It was there—the humiliation, the pause to blink and look away, and now she counted her profession among her losses. To work at the same hospital as Nelson was untenable.

After lunch one afternoon, she went to the locker room and collected her extra pair of shoes, clean uniform, mismatched earrings and hairpins, tea bags and a coffee mug, photos of patients with their cats and dogs, and went into the break room to say good-bye. Seeing her standing in the doorway, her arms filled with her lamentable belongings, they gathered around her, and for one brief moment the indignity of it all washed over them. In the end she could not look into their eyes. What little she had to show after twenty years of nursing fit into one box.

Back in the apartment, she called Nassim. "What should I do now?" Noor and her best friend, both motherless, had long ago become each other's surrogate mom. They met in nursing school at Mills College when Nassim, a year younger, had arrived with a wild-eyed look Noor recognized. Dark and petite, she steered clear of the cafeteria and darted along the hallways pretending she was late for something, all the while checking her watch. One day Noor asked her to lunch, instantly becoming guardian and interpreter to this newcomer who sat safely squeezed in a booth with her new friend. They made it through those precarious post-hostage-crisis years by faking French citizenship and rolling their *R*'s, celebrating many firsts together—tacos and Thanksgiving and driver's ed. But while Noor groped her way through, Nassim would metamorphose, leaving nursing and losing her rich accent to become a television broadcaster in Phoenix, where she lived with her husband, Charlie, and their twins. Her very Iranianness, aside from her alluring eyes, uprooted and dried like dead thistle.

"I looked at all those people and it was awful how they pitied me," said Noor. "They all said how well I was looking, as if I'd been sick."

Nassim seemed relieved to hear that Noor had left her job. "Oh, thank goodness! Why should you work? Get a good lawyer and make that son of a bitch *pay*." She offered the names of some "hotshot" attorneys. "Don't let it go too long, Noor." She sounded disappointed that Noor did not want to go after Nelson.

Noor's voice broke when she tried to defend herself. "I don't know . . . I haven't thought that far." What lay at the bottom of her abyss was something else, something that could not be mended—not with money, not with vengeance.

One Saturday afternoon, upon returning home from the grocery store, the sight of her father's letter in the mailbox quickened her heartbeat. The staircase under the portico was empty, so she sat on the bottom step and ripped it open right there. She wasn't prepared for the wonder of it.

Noore cheshmam (light of my eyes),
You won't believe it now, but please trust me and the light that is inside of you.
Pack a bag for you and Lily and come visit your old father.

Until I hold you . . . one thousand kisses,
Your Baba, Zod

AT THE APARTMENT THERE was nothing for Noor to do except boil water for tea and drink it on the fire escape, where she perched on the ledge overlooking the marina, a view that had once lured her to San Francisco overshadowed by an eagerness at the thought of how soon she would see her father. Noor loved the city; she had experienced her first sense of a future here, but all happiness had seeped out, and from the moment she read her father's letter, Noor began planning their visit to coincide with Lily's summer break.

Now that she was leaving, the fog, the stale air that had made it hard to breathe these past few months, lifted, and she knew that when they returned to San Francisco, it would be as if they had never lived here, with the possibility of a fresh start. Once an amateur tour guide to its hilly neighborhoods, these past few weeks she felt like a tourist, taking snapshots of the Golden Gate Bridge and buying gifts and souvenirs for her father and all the people who kept Café Leila running.

Noor had kept her father's letters dating as far back as 1984, re-reading them to stem the gulf between them. Awful penmanship belied funny anecdotes about neighbors, customers, cooks, and grocers, failed stews and recipes. *Light of my eyes*, they began, *I have just taught Soli to make borscht! Yesterday I bought beets with big, glossy leaves still caked with wet soil. Naneh washed them in the tub until her arthritis flared, but she's promised to make dolmas with the leaves. After we closed Soli tucked the beets under coals and roasted them all night. When I woke up I smelled caramel and winter and smoke. It made me so hungry, I peeled a hot, slippery one for breakfast and licked the ashes and charred juices off my burnt fingertips.* Noor, bruised from betrayal, remembered borscht, remembered stirring sour cream into the broth and making pink paisley shapes with the tip of her spoon, always surprised by the first tangy taste, each time anticipating sweetness. Her mother had called it a soup for the brokenhearted.

She marveled at her father's enthusiasm for borscht, when for thirty years each day had been a struggle. Another man would've untied his apron long ago and left the country for a softer life, but not Zod. He would not walk away from his courtyard with its turquoise fountain and rose-colored tables beneath the shade of giant mulberry trees, nor the gazebo, now overgrown with jasmine, where an orchestra once played and his wife sang into the summer nights.

One by one they'd been sent away to safety and comfort abroad while Zod stayed behind to tend to his customers who still came, week after week, to the one place that remained standing, that swept its entrance, that kept its kitchen open and made soup and offered a respite from the hopelessness on the street. You caught a whiff of sweet simmering onions—almost visible—at the door, behind which they were treated with kindness. Sometimes they couldn't pay, often the plates were chipped and the wait was long, but the soup was always hot, and when there weren't enough spoons, they wiped them on their shirttails, rinsed them off in the hot broth, and shared.

Beyond the walls of Café Leila raged riots, marches, brutal arrests, crippling inflation, but Zod had stayed open through the despair, scoured the pantry for the last onion, dug up the yard and grew tomatoes, raised chickens, and if the streets became too dangerous to walk, his café became a makeshift hotel where he urged his guests to rest on cushions and blankets on the dining room floor while he circled through aisles of sleeping men like a nurse, offering tea and lozenges for the pepper spray that burned their throats and left their mouths dry. In his shadow they slept until dawn, when he lit the samovar for tea and sent them home before first light.

Noor found herself alternating between two worlds, being excited to see her father one moment and worried about going back no longer a child, but a single mother. Yet all the reasons why she should stay in San Francisco and find a new job and keep her daughter in clean comfort had lost their luster. It seemed the separation gave Lily more leverage, using it as a tool for sympathy, revenge, a ride, a new phone, an excuse for a failed test—playing her parents like chess pieces. When Noor attempted to push back against the advancing permissiveness—"Today it's a pierced nose. What's next? Tattoos? Cigarettes?"—Nelson winked at their daughter conspiratorially and rushed to her defense. "Ah, don't be a wet blanket, Noor." "A wet *what*?" She had to look it up.

When worry kept her awake, Noor wandered down the hall to Lily's room to gaze at a soft moon face nestled between piles of teddy bears, the curtain drawn on the theatrical roll of her eyes. She longed to tickle her and plunge her nose in the soft belly she used to sprinkle with talc. Sometimes, inching into a place on the bed to smell Lily's scalp still damp from a bath, she sniffed the part on her crown and found her daughter—*There you are, baby. There you are.* Then, as if hearing her mother's thoughts, Lily would stir and growl, sending Noor shuffling mournfully back to a cold bed. How would she ever explain this journey back to Iran?

NOOR'S FATHER HAD SENT her to America against great odds. At eighteen she had no desire or need to leave her widowed father, her friends, or familiar surroundings. But young and docile, she submitted to Zod's plan, wishing to please, unable to just say that she didn't want to go, too obedient to imagine that her life was her own business. A relative accompanied Noor and her brother as far as New York then helped with a connection to Los Angeles, where their uncle intercepted them and eventually delivered her to college in Oakland. And thus she was left to carve out a place for herself, to untangle English and make sense of its concealed meanings, to become a person of her own making.

For months, robbed of a familiar context—street, home, language, family—she carried a map, a calendar, and red markers in a backpack to remind herself where she was, how long she had been there, and where she had to go next, learning to numb her nostalgia until a letter from home would stir homesickness, reminding her that even if she stood out among people who all knew one another, she was nobody here and if she didn't go to class, no one would come looking for her. It was new being someone whom no one was waiting for.

Her father had scattered his children like seeds—her brother Mehrdad in Los Angeles, Noor in Oakland—hoping something evergreen would spring up to be pruned and shaped on American soil. The odds had seemingly paid off: his son had graduated at the top of his engineering class and married a pretty lawyer, and now ran a successful solar panel company, proud of his autonomy. They lived in a mansion with imported Italian marble countertops where their two children ate organic cereal aloft on titanium stools.

Noor knew a person assimilates without knowing it because one afternoon, after a difficult final exam, the scent of eucalyptus and the ocean's breath swept her outside to sit on a bench, and while she ate her sandwich a classmate smiled and stopped to ask her name. "My name is Noor. It means light." In that moment the prickly sensation of a first shoot felt like a pinch, the seedling starting to take root. Until then California had been a dream she stumbled into, but she woke up to find that the street where the neighborhood children had played tag and Mehrdad had beat a boy who looked up her dress, that their schoolyard, the details of her bedroom, were blurry beyond memory, and a new life opened to her.

Nursing may not have been her calling, but with a capacity for watchfulness, she took to it readily, its purpose clear and uncomplicated. She worked long hours and holidays, taking extra shifts her colleagues unloaded, coming home to a dark apartment to eat Pepperidge Farm Chessmen and drifting off to reruns of *The Golden Girls*.

Then, at the crisis age of thirty-one, when her candidacy as a bride had been discarded by Persian standards, came a serendipitous hospital romance. Her relatives stopped wringing their hands once she was engaged to Nelson. And with Lily's arrival, motherhood allowed her to construct a world for their child out of the glistening miniatures of her own childhood—the simple bliss of a swing set beneath the shade of two pomegranate trees that would grow tall, bear red fruit, and send out roots into a new neighborhood. Yet still, after thirty years, she was at best a tender sapling with shallow creepers easily plucked.

Now all Noor felt was free. It was a strange relief knowing that nothing would ever be the same again, that she could make decisions without consulting Nelson, though she did need his consent to take Lily abroad. When she asked Nelson, he looked past her into the long hospital corridor.

"Ah," he drew out a sigh. "A visit home?"

"Yes, to see my father." Noor tracked his gaze, half expecting to see the girlfriend.

"You always said it's a shame Lily hasn't met him."

Then, with a small shrug, he said, "Yes, maybe it will be a good distraction for her. You'll be careful, won't you?"

"Of course," Noor replied, fixing him with an assertive look. He wouldn't stop her from taking Lily to visit her grandfather.

To Nassim, the trip seemed a desperate flight for Noor to mend her broken heart. "You're going back to the city of your imagination, not the real Tehran. Do you understand? That place exists only in your mind. You're a foreigner with a beautiful daughter who doesn't speak a word of Persian. Face it, Noor, you're running away!"

*Oh no*, Noor thought, *I'm running to.*

Still, she couldn't find the words to break the news of their trip to Lily. When she called Lily to her bedroom, her throat tightened, paralyzing her. As a child Lily had considered every outing an adventure, dutifully scrambling into her car seat—a happy spectator of her parents' lives, sweet as custard between them. But at fifteen it took days of pleading to persuade her to accompany Noor anywhere.

Lily saw the open suitcase on her mother's bed and asked, "Why are you packing?"

"Well," Noor answered in a small voice. "I had a letter from your grandpa and I'd like to go see him."

"So, I'm going to Dad's?" Noor moved back to the closet with empty hangers, avoiding her daughter's gaze.

"No, sweetie . . . you're coming with me. He'd like to meet you."

Lily stared at her. "When will we be back?"

"Two, maybe three weeks."

"What about camp? What about my friends?" Her eyes were already welling up.

Noor shook her head. "Don't worry! You can go to camp when we come back. This is your chance to learn a little Persian and see where your other half is from."

Lily sat down. "But I don't want to go. I'm from *here*. I don't want to learn Persian." She was trying to blink back the tears but they just kept rolling down her face.

"Oh, Lily," Noor leaned her forehead against Lily's and wiped at her daughter's face with cool thumbs. "I need to see my father. I want to take you to the place where I grew up. I promise it will be an adventure." It was too much—this false promise, saying it as if it would make everything okay.

Lily stormed out of the room before Noor had a chance to tell her that they were leaving in a week. She sat wearily next to her suitcase and felt an immediate mix of relief and regret. Could she have handled it better? Probably. Noor felt incapable, though, of conveying the range of emotions, the dismay, the humiliation and sorrow that choked her. Only the vivid picture of her father waiting, his voice asking, *How are you?* kept her on steady footing.

# Four

───◆◆◆───

The night the girls were expected to arrive, Zod and Soli had gone to the airport early, but now the plane was late and people were restless. A monitor read DELAYED but they didn't know for how long. At one o'clock in the morning, the Tehran airport still hummed with anticipation of landings, the coffee shop stayed open serving Nescafé and sponge cakes, and a cluster of men stood smoking and browsing the newsstand.

In the waiting area, rows of vinyl chairs were occupied by families and excited children squirming away from their mothers' arms to twirl and chase one another while their fathers nodded off. There lingered a pungent smell of socks and lilies from bouquets that lay waiting on the ground next to discarded shoes. Two boys kicked a sneaker back and forth, scoring easy goals between shopping bags. Not finding a seat, Zod, bird-boned and frail, switched his cane from one hand to the other and leaned against Soli's broad frame as they paced the corridors, maneuvering around weary-eyed night porters and the lone janitor pushing a dank mop.

Then a barely audible announcement, and the monitor flashed ARRIVED. People stopped talking and gathered their belongings, pressing towards the gate where passengers would be coming through. Zod held onto Soli's arm as they nudged forward, his heart beating loudly in his chest. He remembered a time when Pari, his late wife, was flying home from a concert in Vienna and he went to meet her at the airport carrying six-year-old Noor on his shoulders. To pass the time, he galloped through the terminal while Noor shrieked and tugged on his mane, forbidding him to slow down. He blinked away the picture of her ribbed white tights wrinkled at her ankles and the patent leather Mary Janes knocking against his chest.

Two weeks ago Soli had come upstairs to give him a message. "Your daughter telephoned while you were sleeping. She said, 'Tell Baba I'm coming home.'" Zod thought about how if his mother were alive, she would know what to cook for a daughter turning home after thirty years with a granddaughter she had never met. Of course, Zod remembered Noor's favorite dishes, the marble-size meatballs, the pomegranate soup, the sour cherry rice, but what about the little one? Raised in America, what does she know of his food? He must remember to tell Naneh Goli not to burn the incense. She will do it anyway to banish the evil eye, but it might scare the child and she'll surely think Naneh is a witch.

One by one the passengers stumbled through the gate wearing the same forlorn look of travelers after a long flight, pushing carts with oversized luggage, searching the crowd for familiar faces before being swallowed by large welcoming parties. Zod craned his neck and stood on tiptoe to catch a first glimpse of the granddaughter he'd never met. It was unbearable, the waiting. What if they weren't on this plane? What if he had the wrong day? He was so forgetful these days.

Then, instantly, the crowd parted as if they knew and a woman fell into his arms and cried, "Here, Baba! Baba, I'm here!" Zod's ribs felt like kindling beneath her palms. Some people watching them wiped away their tears. Lily stood by, wisps of brown hair escaping from a loose headscarf, anxious eyes moving from her mother to her grandfather until she was pulled into their embrace. When they finally separated, Noor stood between them, each of her hands holding one of theirs—her father's papery and trembling with the thrill of their arrival, and Lily's twitching like a sparrow. Zod looked over at Lily, her face so familiar to him. They were Pari's eyes that looked back at him reproachfully. *Poor chicken*, he thought, *plucked from your coop.*

NOOR WAS TALKING ABOUT the cost of housing in San Francisco. Zod sat a few feet away from her. Lily was asleep upstairs in Noor's childhood bedroom that Naneh Goli had prepared for her with an electric fan and a feather bed.

Illuminated only by a lamp on the side table, this dazzling girl with almond eyes was sitting here at last, in the room that was filled with thoughts and prayers for her. She gave Zod a present wrapped in pink tissue paper.

"Look, Baba, I found this for you in Japantown."

He unwrapped a navy blue kimono embroidered with white butterflies and pulled the silk sash against his cheek. Though worn from the emotional homecoming, he couldn't tear himself away from Noor—could not believe that she was standing in front of him. He gave in to the wail that was lodged in his throat and buried his face in the new robe. Noor dropped to her knees, laying a cheek on Zod's lap as he stroked the gray roots of her temple. Wasn't she the girl who used to jump into his lap and thrust her hands into his thick, black hair to count the stray white wisps?

"Tell me about yourself." He was asking about her marriage, the ruin of it. Zod met Nelson once, when he went to America for their wedding, carrying an old-fashioned leather valise that held little more than his suit, polished shoes, and a cargo of seeds culled from the pomegranate trees Yanik had planted years ago. All he knew of the groom was that he was a heart surgeon with a nice car, and that his parents were Spanish and spoke rapid Catalan and he had not understood one word of their conversation. His daughter seemed happy, radiant, and Zod was never one to dismiss happiness. But the life he dreamed of for his child had unraveled. Noor did not know where to begin. She still felt the betrayal was her fault, that she had mistaken warmth and ease for desire. The decomposition of her life with Nelson and her tenuous hold on Lily were not topics she was expecting to discuss with her father on this first night home, but he persisted and she could at last be her true self. The rush of sentiment that her girlhood home aroused in her was reassuring and soft. He wanted to know, and she wanted so much to tell him, to shout, to sob, to let her anger out of the cage where she had kept it and let it tear this way and that until she could breathe again.

Yet what did Behzod Yadegar know of women? Pain and death and sorrow, he understood. Now seventy-five, his stamina diminishing, Zod had been housebound more or less since his twenties. When his father had summoned him back to Iran from Paris to manage the café, he didn't know his brother's fiancée would become his wife and he would never leave.

His brother, Davoud, three years senior, was expected to run the family business and build a hotel adjacent to the café. When he died in a car crash on a treacherous mountain road, he was engaged to Parvaneh Parsa, an eighteen-year-old soprano studying opera at the conservatory of music. Already promised to the family, Pari—fine-boned, with round red cheeks, hazel eyes, and a slightly lopsided walk due to a hip wound—had no other prospects, and Zod was told to step in for his brother.

Neither of them could have known of the keen love that would grow from this inconvenient code of honor. He came to love her tenderly, gratefully. He expanded the garden, installing birdbaths and a raised gazebo to accommodate an orchestra that accompanied Pari on summer nights. When she was invited to sing in Paris and Vienna, Zod packed her suitcase and tucked love letters in the folds of her silk half-slips. He sent her off, then waited for her. She came back to tell him stories about everything she'd seen and it was as if he had gone, too. She brought him souvenirs and chocolates, elegant ties and soft leather shoes, detective novels, architecture books, menus from Café de la Paix and La Coupole, and once even a linzer torte. His Pari had bought one from the famous Demel *konditorei* in Vienna and carried it home in her handbag. It came in a beautiful tin box, which Pari kept for her buttons. They tasted the hazelnut torte together with the children at teatime, and it was so delicious that he was inspired to recreate it for the café confectionary, using sour cherry preserves instead of raspberry. *What a pity we don't make pastries anymore*, he thought, *what with the price of butter and sugar.*

Denied courtship and hurled into marriage, Zod and Pari remained their best selves. Thirty-two years since she died, and still his brittle-boned hands burned when he thought of her skin, still they reached out across the mattress to find her in the valley where she used to lay. He knew only one woman but called her by dozens of tender names: Parvaneh, Parichehr, Parinaz, Pariroo, Parisa, Parinoor, Parastoo, Parishan, Golpari, and she answered to all. A witness to their everyday love, Noor could hardly be blamed for being bound by that measure of fidelity. Who could ever match it?

# Five

———— ∞∞∞ ————

L ily was startled awake by a rooster and the simultaneous call
to prayer that echoed from a nearby minaret—a rich, mournful wail, nothing like the early-morning moan of the foghorn
from the bay. This was the worst part for Lily, those first few minutes when
she wasn't sure where she was and then remembering that she was so far
from home.

She got up to open a narrow wooden window that overlooked a small
terrace facing the garden. Still in her flannel nightgown, she peered out and
quickly retreated upon seeing a large man in his undershirt—hairy and
grunting like a bear—lifting barbells right below her window. *This place
is insane*, she thought. There was an armoire in the room where Noor had
hung their clothes, which mingled with the musty, dark green school uniforms of her mother's youth and party dresses with puffy sleeves, vestiges of

the left-behind self her mother came to retrieve. Finding them objectionable, Lily pushed them to the farthest corner of the closet and stuck her head inside to sniff her sweatshirts and jeans that still smelled of the laundry soap from home. She didn't want them to go through the wash, so she'd been wearing the same hoodie and pair of jeans for the past three days and that's what she pulled on again today, lifting her long hair up and letting it hang down her back uncombed. It didn't matter because she wasn't going anywhere.

She had not left her bedroom since their arrival four days ago, nor spoken a word to her grandfather. Noor didn't insist—not yet—instead bringing her meals on a tray and sitting quietly in the armchair. Sounds of heaving continued through the half open window and then came her grandfather's voice. Lily had no idea what he was saying but the tone was apologetic and when she peeked again, Hedi was gone. Then came Naneh Goli mumbling under her breath and twirling what looked like Aladdin's lamp, with smoke, pungent and peculiar, curling through its spout. Lily had met Naneh Goli the first night, the old woman small and folded over as if rooting the earth. She had pulled Lily down into a bony embrace, her claim on Lily, the beloved grandchild of the boy she had raised, had seen suckle and drool, was swift. Now Lily heard the *tak tak* of Zod's cane on the stone path. He was calling urgently to Naneh Goli and soon she, too, was gone.

The next time Lily looked out the window, her grandfather stood gazing up, a pipe smoldering at the corner of his mouth. He lifted his cane up in the air to wave, scaring the finches in the birdbath. From where she stood he looked tiny and vulnerable, but his eyes danced beneath bushy eyebrows and he smiled big and made a motion for her to come down. She turned away.

Lily heard feet padding along the landing outside her room and then her mother pushed open the door without knocking, carrying a breakfast tray: bread and jam, a glass of pomegranate juice, and a pot of tea. Yesterday, Lily couldn't drink the milk. It was warm, tasted too much like cow, and the egg yolks were bright orange, so she just ate the naan. She had never before eaten flatbread like this—baked on hot stones, dimpled and crusty, it tasted sour and earthy and so delicious, she could eat an entire slab. Her mother told her that Soli stood in a long line at dawn to buy their morning bread and would go back just before noon for another fresh loaf. Lily eyed the breakfast tray and a growl surged from her stomach, but she would wait to eat until her mother left the room. Noor, who was in no hurry, pulled a chair closer and put her teacup on the bedside table.

"I have good news," she said, the corners of her mouth curling up hopefully.

"You're sending me home?" said Lily, raising her eyebrows sarcastically.

"No, but the Wi-Fi is working. It's slow, though, so you have to go downstairs for it to work. You can write to your father now. I already told him that we've arrived safely, but I'm sure he's waiting to hear from you."

"I'm not leaving this room unless it's to go to the airport," Lily snarled.

"Suit yourself," Noor said, then turned away from her daughter with a sigh.

As soon as Noor closed the door, Lily reached for a piece of bread, spread a thick layer of jam on it, and shoved it in her mouth. Maybe she could run away . . . that was her chief recurring thought. There was an eight-foot wall enclosing the yard that would have to be scaled. Beyond that, she had only seen a narrow alley in the dark when they arrived. Even if she were to lower herself into this unfamiliar street, she lacked the language to even call a cab. And where could she go without money or a passport? Noor had warned that unaccompanied young women on the street were bait for the morality police, that the most mundane social activities were forbidden and you never knew when they might stop you on the street to tell you to fix your headscarf.

She remembered how on the plane when the announcement was made, "Ladies and gentlemen, welcome to Tehran," all the women pulled scarves from their handbags to cover their hair. *No way I'm wearing a turban*, she thought, rejecting this sudden, phony show of piety. That it was done out of respect or necessity was unfathomable.

When her mother had reached over to show Lily how to wrap the head-scarf, Lily ignored her. She persisted, still trying to tie it for her, and Lily screamed at Noor right there in front of the whole plane, "Leave me alone! I hate you!"

"Lily, please," Noor said, gently enough, then looked around apologeti-cally at nearby passengers whose eyes filled with pity as they busied them-selves arranging their belongings. At that Lily had twisted in her seat and pressed against the plane window. She imagined flinging herself out onto the lights below. How sorry her mother would be. That made her feel better—envisioning her mother's remorse and sorrow when she was gone.

Lily looked out the bedroom window again and sighed. Once, she had overheard a teacher say, "Kids these days, they wouldn't make it through a single day in the wilderness." At the time, she'd wondered what that meant. What wilderness? But now she had a pretty good idea. Beyond the walls of Café Leila lay an unruly landscape she could never navigate on her own. She would either have to make nice with the company downstairs and secure a liaison to assist her escape, or kill herself.

NOOR HAD UNDERESTIMATED HER daughter's will. For the first time in months she wished she could talk to Nelson. He was pragmatic, would never sidestep or shy away from a confrontation. Noor needed to decamp Lily from her bedroom, but how to go about it eluded her. She walked past her own bedroom, glanced at the unmade bed and her clothes on the floor—how quickly she had reverted to her girlhood. Downstairs, Naneh Goli waited to inspect the breakfast tray Noor had cleared. To spare her feelings, Noor lied and said Lily wasn't feeling well, but the excuse no longer held up.

Finally she dialed Nelson's number and left a message. "Please call me. I need your help." Within minutes, her phone rang. Unlike her, he never antic-ipated the worst. If Noor heard that message, she would have automatically assumed an injury or death. But Nelson's voice was calm, as if he was being called upon to mix a pitcher of sangria.

"*Qué te pasa*, Noor?" She winced at his slightly condescending tone and tried to be brief, but the standoff with Lily, once she began explaining, proved difficult.

"Will you please talk to her? She's so much better with you."

She bounded up the stairs to Lily's room. "Your father is on the phone," she said. Lily glared at her. "*Don't*. Don't call him 'your father' like you have nothing to do with him. He's Dad!" She grabbed the phone and Noor turned to go, but her daughter had dissolved into tears and wailed to her father, "Daddy! Oh, Daddy, how could you let her bring me here?"

Seeing Lily come undone, she sank at the foot of the bed and clasped her hands in prayer. Lily was right, of course, to admonish her for removing herself from the equation that was their broken family. As long as a child walked between them, she would never be separate from Nelson, even across continents and oceans. It was hard to hear what Nelson was saying but slowly the sobs subsided to a soft whimper. Lily hung her head, one tight fist to her nose, but didn't resist when Noor reached timidly for her feet and caressed them like baby birds, each toenail a glossy blue. Between hiccups she said good-bye to Nelson. Noor fetched a glass of water and sat on the rumpled bed. "What did Dad say, sweetheart?"

When Noor looked into Lily's eyes, it seemed like the rain clouds had parted—at least for now. She wasn't that naive to believe one phone call had made everything all right, but reaching out to Nelson, recognizing she couldn't sway Lily without him, was a big step for her. Her pride would ruin them all if she wasn't careful.

Noor switched on a lamp and studied her daughter. They were both looking gaunt but Lily's skin shimmered and the roundness had tapered off, emphasizing the high planes of her cheeks. Lily got up to wash her face and even allowed Noor to plait her hair into a thick braid—a simple pleasure of combing and parting that was nearly forgotten. With her scrubbed face and her hair tied back, a small, splendid girl emerged, and gone quickly was the sullen teenager of the last year and a half.

Noor took a chance and said quietly, as if not to scare off a timid animal, "Baba would love to have a cup of tea with you." She paused. "Come on down if you're up to it," and with that she left the door open and went to look for her father.

ZOD STILL MADE HIS way around the kitchen. He often cooked up a batch of pomegranate soup and ate what he could, but not much agreed with him. His chest caved in and his clothes had grown roomy, his belt tightened to its last hole. A clever eye could see behind his gallantry, the efforts to dress and greet and ask after your health. Noor, preoccupied with Lily and the marvel of finding Café Leila unchanged, had failed to notice until now, in this hour when the light poured into the living room, how frail her father had become.

Now she watched as he gripped furniture to traverse the room, a withdrawn look in his eyes. Maybe their arrival had worn him out. Maybe he was feverish. She poured him some water from a silver pitcher always kept full on a side table and sat down next to him on the sofa. She reached out and felt his forehead, suddenly overcome with concern.

"Hi, Baba. Would you like to lie down?" She spoke more loudly than usual.

Zod tilted his head as if he'd just now seen her. "No, no, no, I want to sit here with you. And Lily."

"Baba, are you feeling all right? When was the last time you had a checkup?" Zod looked up amused, unaccustomed to her stern, nursely voice.

For months he had been losing weight, his appetite diminishing, wretched back pain keeping him awake at night. He had asked Dr. Nasseri, one of his Friday regulars, to prescribe some pain medication, but the doctor insisted on an exam and blood tests. Not long after, Dr. Nasseri and his colleague,

Dr. Mehran, came to see Zod at the café to deliver the diagnosis, but Zod did not want to hear it until he had fed them. Only then did he sit across from his glum old friends to receive the news of pancreatic cancer. The two physicians wept openly into their cloth napkins and their patient consoled them. All he wanted to know was how long. How long did he have?

He swore the household to secrecy. He did not want to worry his children halfway across the world. They would feel obliged, he thought, to come, to leave their families, their jobs, their lives. And for what? To see him unable to manage simple tasks? To urge treatment he had already refused, or worse, force him to leave Iran for better care abroad? Never. This was his home, every inch, every crooked wall, and this is where he would die. Yet here sat his wounded girl, unaware of his disease, and by the time she understood, it would be too late to retrace her steps back to his bedside.

"My doctor says I am the picture of health."

"Hmm. I'd like to talk to him."

Lily appeared at the edge of the doorway, standing stiffly with her head bowed. Particles of dust, visible in the afternoon light, floated midair over a sitting room that slowly revealed its features—the faded Persian rug with pink and blue paisleys, a radiator, an upright piano cluttered with photographs, a credenza stacked with newspapers, crystal candy dishes placed over lace doilies on a tea-stained coffee table, and in the corner, Zod seated next to Noor with a blanket on his lap, merged into the patterned couch and the carpet beneath his feet. He stood up with some effort, rested a hand on Noor's head, tilted his chin, and reached for Lily.

She took two wobbly steps forward, like an unsteady toddler, then two more, then managing a weak smile, she rested a hand trustingly in her grandfather's palm. He led her to the piano and gestured to the dozens of framed pictures. "Our family," he said in a shaky voice.

Noor, feeling light-headed with relief, made her way to the kitchen for tea and bumped into Karim racing out the door.

"Where are you going in such a hurry?" she asked.

Karim hopped from one foot to another in the new Nike sneakers Noor had brought him and flashed a gap-toothed smile.

"T-t-t-to b-b-b-buy i-i-i-ice cream," he stuttered and Noor felt ashamed for making him speak, but his wide grin seemed to forgive everything.

At thirteen, Karim shouldered responsibilities Noor couldn't fathom for her daughter. His after-school activities were helping in the kitchen, running for provisions, tending the fire, ferrying a mop bucket that slapped against his skinny legs from room to room, and the occasional ironing.

News of Lily's descent had caused a stir in the household. After all, people who lived and worked close together in a house were naturally roused with the lightest footstep on the stairs, the slightest creak of the banister. She found Naneh Goli chirping around the samovar, preparing the tea tray. "My prayers have been answered," and her eyes gleamed with the pleasure of knowing, no, *believing*, that incense and her hushed pleas to God had brought Lily into the fold. "My beloved daughter of my beloved son, take the tray and I'll bring you each a dish of ice cream as soon as Karim comes back." *How wonderful to be on the receiving end of such kindness*, Noor thought. Naneh Goli sat at the table where leeks waited to be trimmed for the evening meal and wiped her eyes on her sleeve. Then, a little yawn, for she was tired. For days before Noor and Lily's arrival, she had lorded it over the household to dust, polish, and scrub, to scour the upstairs bathrooms, to sweep and freshen the bedrooms, to wipe the windows with vinegar until Hedi nicknamed her "Colonel." They understood Naneh's absorption with these tasks, just as they accepted her inspections. *Let Noor find everything just as she'd left it.* Naneh had earned the right to savor this homecoming. The waiting was over. At last she could kiss their cheeks and hear the voices of children in the house.

There were other things Zod could have said. He could have questioned Lily about her absence, or wondered about her attitude, but he seemed to be taking it for granted that his girl's girl had drifted into this room like the pleasant breeze that came late in the day. Maybe if you've lived as long as he had, you knew all too well that looking for blame was futile, that you need not go back and ask for explanations.

The afternoon had brightened and Zod asked for little but to invite Lily into a room he had lived in all his life. Dozens of family pictures, bleached from the sun, nudged for space on the upright piano: a tall, bespectacled father and a young mother holding a bundle with two small boys on each side, standing in front of a fountain; a woman seated at this same piano looking over her shoulder; three boys—one slightly older—with their hair licked back; Noor and Nassim in their college sweatshirts on the Golden Gate Bridge; a young man in a cap and gown; a wedding portrait that matched the one Lily still carried of her parents.

But the oval frame Zod blew dust off of and handed to her was of Pari in a cloche hat with an open smile for the photographer she was clearly fond of. Peering at that face was like looking in a mirror after a haircut—the girl who looked back was so alike, yet different. That this woman was her grandmother unsettled Lily—how could she be related to all these people? It scared her to think that this could not be undone, that she could not go back to who she was just a week ago. She was glad to sit down, grateful for the tea being handed to her.

THAT NIGHT, ZOD, NOOR, and Lily ate dinner at a corner table in the café. Noor provided headscarves and they sat with their backs to the diners. Of course Noor and her father had been eating their meals together here most nights, but the addition of Lily sent a ripple through the room and folks were having a hard time averting their eyes.

Zod made his way slowly to the regulars, exchanging customary greetings, accepting their affection, asking after their families and thus diffusing the solicitude. Quickly the general clatter of things resumed and the men ate greedily, chewing big mouthfuls of food. Ala set a vase of silk flowers from his late wife's dresser on their table and lit a candle from the drawer where they kept such things for blackouts. Soli made a leek and potato *kuku* that Hedi carried to the table in his meaty hands, sizzling hot straight from the skillet, and served with homemade yogurt and fresh tarragon.

Lily was startled to see the bear up close, too afraid to look at him, having seen him half undressed and grunting in the yard. The restaurant was hardly as grand as her mother had made it out to be, but it was cheerful with conversation, people coming and going.

Back at the head of the table, Zod sipped broth from a teacup and looked down the length of the room, at customers, at a daughter and a granddaughter, and his only thought was, *Please, just a little while longer.*

WHEN LILY HAD RETURNED to her room after dinner, she noticed her clothes—the ones she'd been wearing since her arrival and finally changed earlier that afternoon—were washed and folded neatly. Her jeans, and even her nightgown, were ironed. The bed was made with fresh sheets, and pulling the cool covers to her chin, she brought them to her nose and inhaled deeply—Naneh Goli used a rosewater spritzer for ironing, she even kept a bottle by the sink to dab behind her ears like a new bride.

It took awhile for the house to settle down after the lights were turned off, only the tapping of Zod's cane on the stone path and the faint cherry wood scent of tobacco from his pipe drifting into Lily's bedroom. She had trouble falling asleep, so she silently repeated a rhyme her father had taught her:

| | |
|---|---|
| Había una vez un barquito chiquitito, | Once upon a time there was a tiny little boat, |
| Había una vez un barquito chiquitito, | Once upon a time there was a tiny little boat, |
| Que no podía, que no podía, | That could not, that could not, |
| Que no podía navegar. | That could not sail. |
| Pasaron una, dos, tres, cuatro, cinco, seis semanas; | One, two three, four, five, six weeks passed; |

| Pasaron una, dos, tres, cuatro, | One, two, three, four, five, six |
| cinco, seis semanas; | weeks passed; |
| Y aquel barquito, y aquel barquito, | And that tiny boat, and that tiny boat, |
| Y aquel barquito navegó. | And that tiny boat sailed. |

On the telephone with her father earlier that day, she had cried so hard she couldn't bring in enough air. "Lily," he cooed, *"mi hija, no llores* (don't cry, my daughter). I promise, if you meet Mom halfway, you will gain her trust and show that you've made an effort." From the time she was little, Nelson knew how to soothe his daughter. He was good that way, never sparing comfort, addressing problems straight on. The few words he offered softened her and Lily resolved to take his advice. She would make an effort.

Feeling a chill, she reached for her sweatshirt and pressed her face into it. Just touching it made her want to cry. It smelled sweet and good but it wasn't hers anymore. Deeply tired but restless, she kicked off her sheets and went to listen at the door. All was silent. It was late, past midnight.

Stepping barefoot down the creaky stairs, past the coatrack in the hallway, she followed pinpricks of light to the kitchen, where she found her grandfather with a mug of tea in one hand, gazing into the distance. His face lit up when he saw her, as if he'd been waiting, and he didn't seem at all surprised to find her standing in the doorway. Behind him the kettle gurgled over a blue flame. The table was laid for breakfast with white plates, silver butter knives, sugar cubes and jam in glass bowls, teaspoons, and folded napkins. It wasn't formal, but homey and effortless, in anticipation of their next meal.

"Come," said Zod softly, motioning to a chair.

She sat down and joined him, tucking her bare legs beneath her nightgown. Zod poured them tea. His hands were trembling but he managed to keep the spout over her cup without spilling. He offered sugar, holding a finger up.

*"Yek?* (One?)" Then two fingers, *"Do?"* Their first lesson in numbers.

"*Yek*," she replied shyly, dropping a sugar cube into her tea and stirring it with a doll-size spoon.

Lily sat tilted towards her grandfather at the far end of the kitchen where they could hear the steady chorus of cicadas through the back door, and that voice inside of her intent on running, leaping into the dark streets and away, grew quiet and sleepy.

# Six

———⚬⚬⚬———

Everything in this house was so familiar to Noor that she easily made her way through it without a light. Except for the trees, which were now overgrown with heavy branches clinging to one another in a dense web. She knew where to look for a spoon, a box of matches, or a washcloth, things she hadn't sought out for thirty years.

Everyone would be up before long to resume the business of the household—Zod and Naneh Goli competing to light the stove, Soli rushing to the baker to stand in a long line—but she pulled on an old cardigan against the morning chill and ventured downstairs into the tangled garden. The birds were just beginning to stir in the trees, before the faint light of dawn. Noor was glad for this half hour to rouse her nerve, since each day felt newly hatched and she was the fledgling, pausing on the moss-covered swing set that supported one end of the clothesline.

Today she was taking her father to the doctor, although he had refused with a thousand excuses. But after dinner with Zod and Lily last week, she had heard Zod dry heaving in the bathroom, and when she knocked on the door he told her to go away. He had eaten almost nothing, and Noor noticed the stiff way he sat at the table, as if in pain, and the waxy color of his face and hands. So the next morning she made an appointment with Dr. Mehran, who seemed relieved to hear from her but was unwilling to say much on the telephone. "It's best if you come in, miss," he said.

In the first bit of morning light, she tripped over her rusty old childhood tricycle trapped beneath the leafy vines that tumbled into the yard. Why did Zod keep this? He had even planted azaleas in an ancient bassinet. This garden contained their history, everything important had happened here.

Growing up it had been her entire world, an oasis where on hot summer afternoons they drank iced mint sherbets under a canopy of trees, and when the sun went down they ate juicy kebabs on three-feet-long skewers. As the evening wore on, they lit lanterns and the yard acquired depth like a stage. The waiters wheeled out a three-tiered chariot of fruit compotes, rum babas, crème caramel, and charlotte russe, with bottles of liqueurs and digestifs glowing on the lower shelf. Soon after, the music would start. Noor sat on her grandmother's lap, spooning pistachio ice cream into her mouth with vanilla wafers, while Pari serenaded them. Her brother Mehrdad scrambled up a mulberry tree to take his seat, legs dangling to and fro, capturing moths that fluttered under lanterns and mocking the grown men moved to tears by Pari's song—his mother's voice, the first music he ever knew and thought he owned.

Noor took her first steps here, holding Zod's hands as he walked backwards. She played hide-and-seek, ducking behind recently washed bedsheets and towels drying shoulder to shoulder on the line. The red tricycle was Mehrdad's, then hers, and not wanting to give it up, she didn't learn to ride a bicycle until nearly eight years old. Round and round she pedaled, knees to her chest, pulling odds and ends tied with string to the axle and making such a racket that a bare-chested Yanik would rouse from his afternoon siesta to holler from the bedroom window, "*SHOOSH!*"

They were all supposed to take the obligatory nap after the noon meal, but you couldn't get Noor to stay in her room longer than fifteen minutes. The moment Pari and Zod drifted off, she strapped on a pair of smelly jelly sandals and bolted outside. With her doll, Niloufar, secured to the back, she would make the rounds in the busy world of her imagination. Once she ran over a frog, slicing it in half with the front wheel and letting out a squeal of horror so shrill the entire household came running. The men in boxers, the women in cotton housedresses buttoned haphazardly, raced to the court-yard, thinking that Noor had smashed her skull, only to find two halves of a twitching frog. Yanik scooped it up and threw it into the bushes like he was casting a fruit pit, yelling at Zod, "Get your yardling back inside!" Then he stomped back to his bed with everyone but Pari trailing behind. Pari dropped to one knee to comfort her daughter with birdsong—mimicking their chirps and embellishing their notes so convincingly that the birds, silent for a moment, trilled, *Who are you? Where's your branch?* She washed Noor's face with cold water from a stone basin then took her inside to change into their afternoon dresses.

Even if they weren't doing anything but fixing afternoon tea, Pari insisted on a fresh dress after naptime. These were shapely cotton frocks, in shades of custard and pastels, sewn on a Singer from yards of fabric purchased during her travels. One often heard the hum of her sewing machine like a beehive in the bedroom, with the occasional curse when she pricked her thumb. Soon after marrying Zod, Pari learned to sew from her mother-in-law. Nina tied a small red bow around the needle on the sewing machine and patted the seat beside her. For weeks they poured over patterns and made everything from gowns to handkerchiefs in hues of violet and rose. Although Nina was still mourning her lost son, she refused to wear black after the wedding.

"We have lost enough, my pearl. We will not lose our color," she declared—consenting only to black armbands for the men. Always generous with Pari, she cried, "You light up my eyes! You deserve to be at the center of our big, noisy household," each time her daughter-in-law paused to question a gift, another bolt of creamy silk, a gold thimble, a red velvet pincushion.

Appreciating Pari's quiet company, Nina stitched her journey with Yanik from Samara to Iran in measured swaths. "We left in the night with one suitcase and Niki's coat on my back. We wore all our clothes, used our wool socks as mittens, and stuffed our boots with newspaper to keep our feet dry. I ripped the lining in his coat and filled it with his mother's recipes but I didn't tell him until we got here, otherwise he would've yelled at me for being foolish. Of course, now he thanks me. I still make her *kulich* and *nazuki*."

"Where are the recipes now?" asked Pari.

"For a long time they stayed inside the overcoat. Then he bought this café. He wanted me to help out, but I didn't know how to cook. So I ripped open the lining and showed him the pages from his mother's notebook—everything written in her tiny, stingy print. He wept for a long time, so much left behind. My eyes stayed dry. I was glad to be away from his family. His mother's hand in the kitchen was delicious, but her tongue was a sword. She was a coarse woman, thick and lumpy, but she could spin gold out of a turnip, I tell you. From a dusty root in her cellar, she made soups and pickles and casseroles. Everyone was starving, but Lena could stretch a wormy apple fifty ways."

"Did you use her recipes?" Pari tried to follow the story.

"Bah! Her instructions were harsh, like she was standing behind me at the stove with a stick yelling, *No! No! Not like that! Too much pepper! What a mess!* I was only eighteen. Your age, for goodness sake! At first I read and memorized each one. Then I locked them in a drawer and went in the kitchen to make something. But still I could hear her shrill. Whatever I touched tasted sour. *Too much vinegar. Your mother raised you in a pickle barrel!* Then one day I bought fabric to upholster seat cushions for the chairs

Yanik bought for the café—a beautiful red brocade. I took Lena's recipes and sewed them inside the seat cushions."

"You mean there are recipes inside the chairs?" Pari gasped.

"Pearl, there's a recipe under every ass!"

They fell into stitches and Yanik, walking by, listened bewildered and breathed in their delight from the crack under the door. This is how, in the long stretch of those gray afternoons, Nina grieved for her firstborn by turning her attention to this good-natured girl Davoud had chosen and left for his little brother. The hollows beneath her cheekbones deepened and her brow furrowed, but inside Nina never hardened. "You are my melon," Yanik would whisper at night when he clung to her back, "Tough on the outside, soft and sweet inside."

Although Pari frequently invited Noor to look at dress patterns, Noor was not interested in sewing, preferring to help her father in the café. She felt her work there was important, refilling saltshakers and folding napkins, setting a table for her dolls with a clutch of tiny silver ashtrays as plates. Still, she adored the matching dresses Pari made for her and Niloufar.

For weeks after the frog incident, Noor wandered sheepishly through the yard, searching for the remains of the dismembered creature to give him a proper burial. Little did she know that her status with Mehrdad was elevated for having performed this mucky dissection and he took great pleasure in sharing with her his collection of matchboxes, where trapped beetles, grass-hoppers, horseflies, and roaches with clipped wings resided. Her attempts to mend them with glue and set them free infuriated Mehrdad, who would then sneak them into her shoe or leave them disabled on her pillow like turndown chocolates. He teased that he had swallowed the frog bits and she imagined slimy webbed feet caught in his throat and ran screaming to Pari. Two years apart, at times a perfect big brother if a neighborhood bully tormented her, he was mostly aloof to his sister's willfulness. When Noor called to tell him about their trip to Iran, it wasn't to ask for his opinion and he knew to hold his tongue.

AS MORNING BROKE, SOLI wandered outside to get his motorbike when he saw Noor on the swing looking up into the trees, lost in the latticework of the branches. He asked if she'd like him to accompany them to the doctor and Noor said no, better he stay to prepare for lunch. She rose reluctantly to go inside, where she found Zod at the kitchen table silently drinking tea by the light of a table lamp while Naneh Goli, in her flowered chador, hovered over him as if he would be late for school.

Relieved that her presence didn't interrupt the rhythm of their days, Noor stood behind her father's chair and scanned the bleak but orderly kitchen: its crockery and blackened frying pans on freestanding shelves, a hulking refrigerator humming in a corner where a smaller one had once stood, the chipped porcelain sink above a curtained dark space underneath, an oval mirror with a small shelf that held Naneh Goli's comb and a pot of cracked rouge, the square enamel stove pressing its shoulders against a wall that was splashed red and brown, like graffiti left by all the cooks who had fed this family. This kitchen was turned inside out, its contents hung from hooks and nails, ladles and sieves within easy reach—an openness in stark contrast to the discreet cabinetry of her American kitchen with its quiet drawers and hidden trash bins.

Zod patted the hand Noor put on his shoulder and smiled up at her. His skin was yellow, but how distinguished was his white-haired head and the scent of his cologne. Dressed to go into town in dark gray pants and a black sweater vest, he pushed his chair back and said, "Let the day begin," displaying an outward calm she knew was for her benefit. "Noore cheshmam, come have your breakfast, and then we will call a taxi."

It was remarkable how quickly she switched back to tea when for so long it had been a strong cup of coffee that made it possible to face the day. For sixteen years Nelson carried a thick café con leche to her bedside, and she had mistaken his affection for ardor. Naneh Goli motioned for Noor to sit down, then lifted a soft-boiled egg from the pot bubbling on the stove. What consolation this morning ritual here, the warm bread, this sunny yolk, the gurgling samovar, the souvenir saltshaker from a long-ago voyage. Everything in its place, the furnishings just as they were when she left, the front hall already filling with odors of onions browning for stew.

*How did Naneh Goli manage to keep the cold out, tend the chickens, grow vegetables?* she wondered. How did they maintain this household day after day when she wasn't even sure how to live the next hour, how to wake her daughter, how to dress to go outside of their compound, how to talk to ordinary people on the street?

Lily was awake, winding herself up to approach the klatch downstairs. Like the person lurking in the corner of a theater just behind the very last row, near the exit, everyone was aware of her but went on about their business. They listened for movements upstairs—it didn't help that the toilet rolled like thunder when she yanked the pull chain—while she bathed in the tub with the handheld showerhead, which had been a nuisance until she learned to kneel and adjust the spray at just the right angle to wash her hair.

Reluctantly a new sweatshirt and jeans were pulled from the armoire, still smelling of American detergent. Watermelon lip gloss was applied, black Converse high-tops laced. Downstairs, all heads looked up when her bedroom door groaned. She carried an iPod in her pocket with earphones looped around her neck—a precaution in case Noor tried to engage her in a conversation about her feelings, launching into speeches about how it was okay to be sad or angry, or how much it meant to her that Lily was giving their "adventure" a chance.

The sight of her at the kitchen door was too much for Naneh Goli—she simply could not hold back from gushing a string of endearments that spun around a stunned Lily. To Lily, this ancient person, all bumps and barnacles, was possessed, and she was slightly afraid of her. The others stood gazing, elated as if the curtain had finally fallen and she was joining them backstage for a celebration.

Zod gave a gentle command to break the spell and suddenly there was a great commotion as Soli cut bread, Naneh Goli poured her tea, Karim pulled a chair forward, and Noor peeled oranges. Lily, in the center of this attention, was compelled to say the only Persian word she knew. Before their departure, in a lame attempt to teach her a few words, Noor had made a chart with words and pictures and attached it to the refrigerator door with magnets. "*Merci.*" That was an easy one. They were impressed.

Karim could not keep from staring at her—so exotic was this creature before him, with honey eyes and glossy lips like a candy he could lick off her face. It was as if a door had opened and he had walked through it. Everything behind him had fallen into a deep abyss and never again could he retrace his steps to that boy, the one with unruly hair and scraped kneecaps, the kid with fine fuzz above his lips who kicked everything in his path, who caught roaches and mice with bare hands, who sometimes smelled like a wet sheep. What solitude he had lived in. His world expanded with Lily in the kitchen and it was all very new looking. Then, realizing his dirty nails and ugly pants, he was deeply embarrassed and hid behind Soli, his heart beating in big thumps.

Karim would go to school that day windswept and airborne like a dandelion in the wind. How fortunate that these were the last days before the summer break. His teacher would rap his knuckles with a ruler and he would be grateful for the sharp voice that tethered him to his desk. Friends would admire his shoes, beg for cigarettes stolen from Ala, but Karim would be lost in the task of cleaning his nails with a toothpick. A boy from Mazandaran, raised near the Caspian Sea, delivered to his uncle just days after his village had turned to rubble and swallowed a mother, a father, a baby brother; a boy who had survived the earthquake because he'd gone fishing. Until this moment he had never understood why he'd been spared that morning three years ago when the sound of his baby brother's cooing in the early morning hours had woken him and sent him racing to the stream.

The clock said eight fifteen. He desperately wanted to hear Lily say *merci* again, but Naneh Goli folded a piece of naan around a boiled egg, placed it in his knapsack, and pushed him out the door with a long list of instructions he didn't hear. All he could think was, *I fell in love at eight fifteen on the morning of June 9.*

Later that afternoon he scurried around the kitchen underfoot until Naneh Goli sent him to the storeroom for jam. The cellar, illuminated by a bulb on a string, was like a pharmacy, with shelves of rosewater, orange blossom water, quince syrup, lime syrup, vinegars, and jars of pickled vegetables, all painstakingly labeled in *Agha* (Mr.) Zod's shaky script. Karim paused to read the labels but found nothing to ease the knocking in his chest, so he took the last jar of fig preserves for Lily. His Lily *jan* (dear), Lily rose, Lily *shirin* (sweet), Lily morning, Lily moon, Lily merci.

# Seven

———— ⚬⚬⚬ ————

Everyone knows the rules. Never yield the right of way. Never stay in your own lane. Never slow down at a yellow light. If you missed your exit, simply put your car in reverse. You may change the direction of a one-way street. Blow your horn angrily and with abandon.

Noor cowered in the backseat holding a thermos of strong black tea and clenched her teeth as their taxi driver slammed on the brakes and jerked the car through traffic. Lily had her earphones in and glanced curiously at the relic Zod held in his lap, a Sony Walkman. They both seemed unmoved even though an accident seemed certain.

To Lily it resembled a video game, and indeed their driver seemed to be enjoying himself, fluid through the frantic rise and fall of horns as the world expanded beyond the compound. They were on a wide boulevard, which, like many streets, had been renamed post-revolution after imams and martyrs. But like childhood friends insisting on a nickname, motorists used the old street names in cheeky contempt of the clerics, and not unlike cabbies the world over, their driver sized up his three passengers and knew what he could get away with.

Without speaking a word, Noor's foreignness was manifold in her bewildered gaze, the awkward knot of her headscarf, her sheepish smile—years in America had taught her to smile at everyone and apologize often. The driver slipped a cassette into the stereo and Noor softened with the first chords of Cat Stevens' "Moonshadow." Their eyes locked in the rearview mirror and she saw the driver was about her age, late forties. She looked around the cab's interior, at the worn trim of the seat cushions, and it occurred to her that this song was played for her—a reassurance that within the confines of this beat-up metal box, they were safe. A bootleg library of cassettes under the front seat, ranging from the Bee Gees to Madonna to sermons, assured a good tip. Nevertheless, he attempted to refuse payment when they arrived at the hospital—an ingratiating and obligatory ritual common among tradesmen. Zod pressed a bill into his palm and asked if he could return to pick them up in an hour.

Dr. Mehran, a compact man with a thick head of salt-and-pepper curls, met them in the lobby and rushed them past a waiting room choked with patients. They were soon inside a small office, simply furnished with a desk and mismatched chairs.

"Miss, you didn't have to bring your own tea. We may not have much left in this country, but we can still provide tea for our guests." Noor blushed and quickly shoved the thermos into her cavernous handbag. *Idiot*, she thought. To have forgotten the ancient rules of hospitality in her homeland was proof of how far she had traveled from the essential ingredients of her culture. This wasn't Kaiser Hospital, with its coin-operated dispenser of dishwater coffee and fake cream in Styrofoam cups. Within minutes an orderly rapped on the door and came in with a tray, serving them each a glass of tea and leaving a plate of butter cookies and a bowl of sugar cubes on the desk.

Zod looked comfortable seated between Noor and Lily, as if they were here for a social visit. And indeed, the doctor's eyes, though weary, shone with warmth. He and Zod had only known each other within the walls of Café Leila, but their friendship ran deep. Year after year he sat in the company of other men like himself, who had their own problems yet came to share a meal at Zod's table. They all had burdens in their lives, but they always cheered up as though seeing one another after a long absence, when in fact it had been only days and they were just glad to get away for an hour or two to chat over a bowl of stew. In Persian, the word *del* refers to both the heart and the belly. Considering that Zod lived in people's stomachs, he may not have been as beloved if he were a mechanic or an accountant.

They spent fifteen minutes chatting before Noor felt the urge to interrupt. She had so many questions and worried they were running out of their allotted time—surely this doctor had other patients to see—but *Doktor* was in no hurry to put his friend through any discomfort.

"Each generation has less patience than the one before," he said, reaching for a cookie and reciting a line of poetry alluding to youth. He came from a generation of Iranians who quoted verses as if they floated in the air above them and simply needed to be plucked like apples to clarify their opinions. Noor took a polite sip of her tea while Lily bit daintily into her third cookie. Nassim's words echoed in her ear—what was she doing at this tea party when they could've been at Stanford Hospital?

In the days prior to their appointment Noor had pleaded again with Dr. Mehran on the phone to tell her what he knew, and although the doctor had finally broken his promise, Zod had no intention of undergoing chemotherapy. He only agreed to come to the appointment to please his daughter. Having suffered bouts of food poisoning as a child, he dreaded relentless nausea more than the plague itself. He did not want to lie in a hospital bed with tubes in every pore. He wanted to live his life, what little was left of it, and face death in the privacy of his home.

"Don't you think, Doktor, that my father should have the treatment?" Noor blurted out, trying to steer the conversation to Zod's health.

"*Should* he?" Dr. Mehran queried, raising his eyebrows.

"Yes, shouldn't he at least try? There must be a way to slow this down. Do you think he'll have a better chance if we go to America? You can't just give up!" Noor urged. Abruptly, Dr. Mehran stood up.

"Give up? *Give. Up?*" His voice cracked. Veins bulged from his temples, threatening to erupt, and he cleared his throat before launching into a litany of statistics and offering to show Noor the CT scans that showed the metastasized cancer. Zod and Lily drained their tea and frowned into their empty cups while Noor gazed at the cross-sectional images of her father's organs, at the pancreas protruding below the stomach like a conch shell—gravelly with tumors. She covered her mouth to stifle a sob. Dr. Mehran turned to face her, a gentleness returned to his wide-set eyes.

"My dear, you are a nurse, so I don't have to tell you that the best thing we can do for your father at this stage is to offer palliative care and make him comfortable so he can at least enjoy your company. If we had caught it sooner, yes, you could have taken him abroad for care. I concede that he may not have had access to the drugs here that we can't get for our patients, due to *sanctions*, not knowledge."

Sufficiently chastised, Noor looked back at Zod's shrunken frame, his long bony fingers folded on his lap, a painful realization, no longer private, occupying the space between them. Dr. Mehran slumped in a chair, his skills exhausted, wounded in much the same way as his patient. A doctor relies on clinical intuition and he blamed himself for failing to see the symptoms earlier.

Lily, spared by the language barrier but sensing the gloom, searched Noor's face for clues. It had been so long since Lily looked at her without cold contempt that Noor felt unnerved. If only she could run outside, if only she had never left, if only she had come back sooner. *I'm always too late*, she thought, feeling as if she was a migratory bird separated from her flock.

Dr. Mehran stood to embrace his friend and kissed him on the cheeks, first the left, then the right, then retreated behind his desk, bowing to Noor and Lily. They filed out into the lobby, past tired mothers and colicky babies, past sullen husbands, through messy wards crowded and noisy with mobile phone conversations augmented by the delivery of lunch trays, banter between medical personnel, visitors bearing bags of fresh fruit, and a lone security guard lighting a cigarette then flicking the match into an open trash bin. Outside the main entrance the air was dry and hot. A cluster of men stood around smoking and parted to let them through, throwing sidelong glances in Lily's direction.

Their taxi was waiting for them at the curb and Noor caught the driver's eye again as they climbed in, knowing that without Zod's presence, he would feel at liberty to chat. She wished for someone to talk to, someone who didn't know her and wouldn't judge her. How often in movies did a troubled person pour her heart out in the backseat of a cab while they drove aimlessly through dark streets? Zod, sitting between them, leaned forward and spoke softly, instructing the cabbie to take them uptown to Darband. Noor, about to object, was silenced by the hand placed on her lap.

"Shush, we are going to lunch. I want to take my granddaughter to the hills for some fresh air and a nice kebab before she goes back to America." Then he sank back, offering a jaundiced palm to each of them.

What he really wanted was the plain pleasure of sitting across from them, to look into Lily's eyes and to hold his daughter's hand. There were so many things they ought to know and he had so little time left to tell Noor to start living up to her name, for God's sake. Blinded by her troubles, unable to raise her head, to exert herself, clinging to the exaggerated memories of her youth. When had this girl, who defied them in childhood, who never got her way fast enough, grown timid and undemanding, so frustratingly

passive in the face of humiliation? Why did she think herself so undeserving
of love, merely enduring life like a pebble in her shoe and sidestepping people's shortcomings, talking as though *she* had caused Nelson's infidelity—a
watchfulness grown inward, doubtful and wary of her own child even. Lily
seemed a loose tendril, unattached and spiraling, with no direction from
either parent. She may have looked eighteen, but there was still a small,
uncertain girl underneath that vengeful silence. What lesson did Noor aim
to teach by bringing her here?

In the old days, when they went to the restaurant in Darband where they
celebrated special occasions, Pari would dress the children in party clothes,
choose a silk tie for Zod, and come downstairs in one of her pretty gowns,
the scent of Diorissimo filling the front hall, reminiscent of lily of the valley.
They would pile into the Peugeot to drive the narrow roads towards the
mountains that hugged Tehran.

Zod especially had loved these outings that opened a world beyond
Café Leila, that offered the taste of another's hand. He often grew weary
of his own cooking—the predictableness of it—and his stomach rumbled
joyously at the thought of spooning someone else's rice into his mouth.
How rare to be just the four of them, a family all his own. Even now, in
spite of the writhing in his stomach, he tingled at the thought of taking
his girls there.

The road curved as they climbed the mountainside, the driver not once
signaling or slowing down at the sharp bends, winding upward, round and
round. Noor grew queasy and cracked the window to let the wind blow into
her face. A part of her was curious to see again the pretty village deep in the
mountains. Darband was their special place when she was growing up—it
was where the water in the streams sparkled and on weekend hikes she could
cool her feet in the icy water while sitting under the shade of trees, but so far
there wasn't a tree or a bush in sight. Tall buildings towered on both sides
of the narrow road, their stark gray facades rippling as they raced past and
Noor searched for intervals in between where she might catch a clear view

of bare ridges, but it made her dizzy. Much longer and they would have to pull over.

At last they swung round and stopped at the foothills. Zod tapped the driver's shoulder and asked him to wait for them as Noor and Lily slid out the backseat. Noor paused to breathe in the cool air, looking up at café terraces fanning the hillside, dotted with colored lights. They set out to walk the steep trail following the scent of hot bread and the clattering of pots and pans.

Lily dropped behind, taking in the modern apartment buildings straddling the rugged hills, the train of mules bearing panniers of pomegranates and eggplants, and the noon call to prayer. So this is what it's like outside the walls of their compound: concrete, cars, open ditches, men gaping at her, and this in-between landscape, not rural, not urban, Tehran pushing against it, arm wrestling the mountain.

They sat under a walnut tree on wooden benches draped with kilims and soon the table was covered with small dishes of yogurt, olives cured with angelica, eggplant and whey cooked to a silky paste, piles of basil, cilantro, and tarragon, and a pitcher of *doogh*, the tangy yogurt drink spiked with mint that a jolly waiter in a snug tailcoat poured into stem glasses, all the while exchanging pleasantries with Zod.

"You must not miss us as much as we miss you," he teased, bowing at Zod's request to have lunch delivered to their taxi driver waiting at the bottom of the hill. Lily watched as a waiter traversed the narrow stairs to the parking lot, holding aloft a plate of kebab with rice and a Coke.

Noor wondered how her father could stand to look at all this food, to smell it, to remember the taste of it, and not eat it. But Zod had eaten his fill of olives, orchards of them, eggplants dressed one thousand and one ways, bushels of mint and tarragon, towers of naan and barrels of doogh—he saw it all before him like a mural, layers upon layers of shapes he had sampled and savored. How much does a man need to eat in a lifetime? What he longed for was to watch Noor wrap warm bread around sheep's milk cheese with walnuts and basil to make parcels for Lily, to feed her child by hand the way he and Pari had done. Did he really have to show her how it's done? Perhaps, because Noor sat before him like a stone with an impenetrable gaze while his granddaughter stared at the dishes before her with mild curiosity.

Exasperated, Zod showed Lily how to assemble a tasty wrap and fed her. "She can do it herself, Baba," Noor murmured. "No. She can't," he replied, irritated. "You must make it for her." So when the oval platters piled with rice and skewers of saffron chicken arrived, he kicked Noor under the table, urging her to serve Lily first, to fold an egg yolk into the steaming rice and sprinkle it with sumac.

Zod had not been back to Darband since his sister-in-law's brief visit last year. Here he felt like a country boy, saw it as an island that rose from the foothills all the way to its snowcapped peaks. He had hiked these trails with his brothers and later with Pari, starting out early and stopping for breakfast at one of the many teahouses tucked in among the ridges, mopping comb honey with slabs of just-baked bread and washing it down with hot black tea.

There were more houses on its slopes than he remembered and garbage strewn in the murky brown streams, a garish reminder of a city hand encroaching, but it remained earnest as a place you could still walk under a gray sky and accept a glass of tea while sitting on a cold rock. He would like to take Lily along the footpaths, to prolong their outing—that they would walk in silence didn't matter because it had become unspokenly clear that she was glad Zod deflected her mother's attention from her.

Having Noor with him for the past week had been a trial and a comfort; she was present but absent, attentive but distracted, circling him from dawn until sundown. If he rested his eyes for a moment, she asked if he wanted to lie down. If he went to lie down, she urged him to walk in the garden for fresh air. If he took a stroll, she followed a few paces behind. If he sped up to prove his endurance, she tugged on his sleeve to slow down. If Naneh Goli fried him an egg, she swabbed obsessively at the delicious grease with a napkin until it cooled and he didn't want it anymore. She searched for a blender to puree dandelions and carrots to make healthy shakes and watched him politely sip the brackish contents of a riverbed, which he promptly vomited back up. If he did his crossword puzzle for too long in the bathroom, she stood vigil, compulsively knocking at the door—"Baba? Baba? Baba?"—until he replied, "A river in northern France?" She mumbled something and slouched away. *What had they taught her in nursing school?* he wondered.

AFTER LUNCH THE TAXI driver safely returned them home and Zod, exhausted from the outing, dozed on the couch, snoring away beneath an old quilt. Noor watched him sleep. She understood that her father wished to write his own ending. Noor had seen people suffer. She helped keep them alive. You know how it ends yet you continue as though you don't. Her father seemed to have rebounded after their visit to Dr. Mehran, appearing happy even, as if having the cancer spelled out for his daughter relieved the burden of fighting the disease.

Noor thought about how the years had passed her by, like the ripped pages of old calendars, then this single bittersweet week that stretched with remarkable detail. The excitement of homecoming, the first day back, sleeping in her brother's tiny room on the top floor, across from her old room with the shared bath, where her daughter now sleeps, the familiar scents of a house she grew up in, Lily coming downstairs to sit quietly with Zod, and, finally, the darkest hour in the doctor's office—Noor remembered every moment.

Naneh Goli took her hand and sat Noor down at the kitchen table, then resumed stirring the Turkish coffee in a long-handled copper pot on the stove. She placed two demitasses between them and they sipped in silence. Later Noor would carefully flip her cup over the saucer and Naneh Goli would twirl it in her calloused hands, interpreting the patterns and symbols left on the walls of the cup by the coffee grounds.

"Do you see this tree, Parinoor? See, it is late autumn and it's lost all but one leaf—one stubborn leaf swinging from a branch, not letting the tree sleep. Look here, look at this person sitting on a rock facing the horizon. She thinks she's alone, but there to her right, see the figure standing on the bow of a ship?"

Noor listened to her soothing voice and remembered the days she had come home from school to find five or six women, including her mother, leaning into Naneh Goli while she read their fortunes. There was always, always, a figure sitting on a dock waiting for her ship to come in, a ship carrying a prince or a sack of gold coins, or a way out. This was Naneh Goli's way of saying, *Noor, I see farther than you. Don't stay too long to see your father weakening. Go back to your real life.*

Noor had a different take on Naneh Goli's clairvoyance. Never mind the boat, the suitor, or the gold—there were no loopholes. She would cling to her father like a leaf to a tree and stay to look after him.

# PART TWO

# Eight

The night Zod packed all his belongings into a single suitcase, Madame Chabloz rang the dinner bell early. She was going to see the new Truffaut with her daughter and was anxious to feed her boarders. A year and a half ago, when he arrived in Paris at age twenty-one to enroll at the École des Beaux-Arts, Zod had rented this damp room—no bigger than a cupboard with a metal cot, a desk, and a chair—at a small pensione on the Rue Mouffetard. This was 1961. It was his first time away from his family and if it weren't for the tall, narrow window overlooking the busy street, loneliness would've swallowed him up.

Those first few weeks, leaning his forehead against the cool glass, he observed a new world below: a man sweeping the sidewalk, small dogs on leashes, women hurrying to an open-air market that spread from one end of the street to another like a colorful patchwork quilt, waiters in long black aprons sliding swiftly through café tables, and sometimes a reflection of his own pale face with a newly grown mustache he barely recognized. *Who am I now? What am I doing here?*

Finally finding the courage to leave his room, he wandered the streets for hours, unable to find the way back, stumbling in long past dinner to find a note from Madame slipped under his door: *This is not a restaurant, something-something* (he could not make out all of her grievances), *you must let me know if you will be absent for meals.* He had apologized the next morning, told her he'd lost his way, and Monsieur Simon, a history teacher at the Lycée Henri-IV, drew him a map on the back of his sketchbook—a beautiful grid divided by the curve of the Seine and a cheeky castle with turrets where their little pensione stood.

"*Voici* (here is) Château Chabloz." He winked at Zod, his hands flying like doves across the page to rest on monuments. "Notre-Dame, La Tour Eiffel, L'Arc de Triomphe, La Bastille, L'Opéra, *regard* (look)!"

It was Monsieur Simon, red-cheeked and full of enthusiasm, who took Zod under his wing. One night Zod walked in from a cold rain to find Simon waiting for him in the drafty foyer wearing his narrow black coat and clutching a tweed cap, with an umbrella tucked under one arm.

"*Cher petit prince*! *Allons-y à l'opéra*! (Dear little prince! Let's go to the opera!)"

Before Zod could protest or make excuses, he was nudged outside into the downpour and hurried along to the Métro. A few stops later Zod emerged from the subterranean tunnels to find the Palais Garnier opera house looming above them, a building so magnificent that Zod gasped and stepped back, colliding into irate commuters. For a moment he stood there staring; it was almost eight o'clock and behind him the city grew darker and darker as he hurried with Simon towards the lights ablaze before him.

Once inside, the air in the standing room section was damp and clouded, as if the white brume of burning cigarettes was the only thing keeping them aloft above the small luminous stage where big notes soared from tiny instruments as the musicians warmed up. And then came the roar of the orchestra. Zod didn't know how long the performance lasted, but upright against a wall, he forgot about his soggy trousers, the jostling and the bobbing heads. Someone passed him a flask and cognac pooled into his stomach and he was warm and swaying happily.

Afterwards they ducked into a candlelit bistro and it felt like they were still in the theater, elbow to elbow with actors and musicians in the dark wood-paneled room with its red velvet banquettes and gilt-framed mirrors. Zod felt the weight of the leather-bound menu, which he held open like a briefcase. Laid out before him were dishes detailed in gold inscription: *Tourte de Faisan aux Truffes, Blanquette de Veau, Barbue aux Huîtres, Tripes à la mode de Caen.* Simon explained the preparation of each dish so lovingly that it would have suited Zod to not eat at all and simply listen to this man as he translated the truffled pheasant in pastry, the creamy veal stew with pearl onions and mushrooms, the poached brill with oysters in brown butter, the baked tripe with calvados, and the wine they must order to accompany it, as he considered whether they should choose this dish or that dish and the sequence of how they ought to proceed.

"*Mais êtes-vous tout à fait certain, cher Simon, que nous avons assez d'argent?* (But are you certain, dear Simon, that we have enough money?)" Zod inquired anxiously, to which his friend let out a belly laugh and reassured him that he had enough money to pay for their dinner. Better to see *Tosca* from the rafters and save our francs for supper, "*N'est ce pas, mon fils?* (Is it not, son?)"

By the time they finished their meal, the table was covered with glasses, bottles, and plates of bones picked clean. Simon had worn himself out. There was so much he wanted to teach Zod that he sometimes ran out of breath. Laying a hand on Zod's shoulder, he gasped, "We will see it all, all that Paris has to offer, from the Jeu de Paume and *The Gates of Hell* in the Rodin garden, to racing our boats in the Luxembourg fountains and betting on horses at the Bois de Boulogne. And yes, we will come here again in the winter and order the mutton and the kidney casserole. "*Je te ferais voir, mon fils.* (I will show you, son.)"

Walking out into the night, the rain had stopped and the wet cobblestones glistened in the light of the street lamps as they made their way back to the pensione without speaking, their hands deep in their coat pockets and the wind from the river against the skin of their faces.

ZOD LEFT A RAZOR, his shaving mug and brush, and a shard of soap by the small basin and grabbed his jacket from a peg behind the door. This meal was included in his rent and he felt obliged to eat it since Madame Chabloz had no intention of returning one centime of the sum paid dutifully on the first of each month. He had no appetite but took his seat in the dining room across from Pierre and Claude, two fellow students from Brittany, and Monsieur Simon, who stood to shake his hand. He enjoyed their company, learned useful phrases and accepted their friendly corrections.

On Sundays, when Madame took the morning off, Zod cooked lunch for the four of them in the galley kitchen, recreating Nina's creamed chicken with tarragon and leeks, poaching figs for compote, and frying duck livers to serve with thick slices of brioche. They ate together companionably, passing platters of beef tongue and parsley potatoes, refilling one another's glasses with cheap Beaujolais, and wondering where this skinny boy from Iran had learned to cook.

"*Chez ma mère,*" he explained.

Afterwards they would go to the café for a coffee or play backgammon in the chilly sitting room wearing their hats and scarves, rolling dice with gloved hands, and on those afternoons Zod's homesickness was a little less persistent. He missed his family terribly, but he was young and living in Paris, learning to draw and wandering into buildings that men had conceived on paper and then breathed life into every brick. He was deliriously happy, with a hunger inside him so fierce he could barely walk to his classes and had to sprint the last few avenues.

His letters home carried sketches of a reimagined Café Leila with a courtyard and blue tiled fountains, alcoves beneath hanging wisteria, rooms with wrought iron balconies facing the garden . . . the hotel his father dreamed of. He requested recipes from his mother and combed the markets for ingredients, shaping his nostalgia for her cooking into Sunday meals—pickled beets with crème fraîche, crabapple and cabbage dumplings, plum turnovers— and filling envelopes with fantasy menus addressed to Nina. *Maman, we must add crepe soufflé to our desserts. You simply fold meringue into your vanilla custard, spoon it into the pancakes, fold them in half, sprinkle with sugar, and bake them. They puff into golden pillows!*

Three thousand miles away, drawn with exhaustion, his mother smiled at his exuberance, couldn't keep the happiness to herself, and Yanik would touch her nose and ask, "What? What did he write, Ninotchka?" When she read the letters out loud, Yanik griped, "Is he training to be an architect or a cook? Why did I spend all this money to send him abroad when he can learn to cook downstairs?"

The one letter Zod did not have the heart or the words to compose, Claude wrote for him, explaining to his professors why he had to abandon his studies midterm. Days earlier Madame Chabloz had carried a telegram from Yanik to Zod's room and waited at the door while he read it. She watched his face collapse and continued to hover, expecting him to share the news. *Davoud terrible accident. Come home.* Five words.

"*Mon frère. Mauvais accident.* (My brother. Terrible accident.)" was all he managed to mumble before he shut the door on her pinched face.

After putting down the telegram on the desk, he sat motionless in his chair for a long time, listening to the clock tick. He thought about his parents, how they could not bring themselves to write the outcome of the accident because, of course, they would have if Davoud had survived it.

Zod remembered Davoud's hands. When they were boys, his big hands scooped Zod up like a kitten and he was glad to be one of his older brother's pets—Davoud kept so many small animals in cardboard boxes, he even fed the birds that flew regularly to his windowsill. They were three years apart and slept in the same room across from their parents, above the café. When Zod had nightmares, Davoud let him crawl beside him and sleep against his strong back. When Zod was two, their mother put a night vase under his bed (he was too afraid to walk to the bathroom alone at night). One morning he woke up and shit in the pot. He was so proud. Finally he had something to offer. He ran down to the kitchen, fetched a bowl and a spoon, and woke his big brother to serve him. Davoud just yelled "Maman!" then turned to the wall and covered his head with a pillow.

If Zod cried, Davoud would dry his cheeks with his sleeve, give him a teaspoon of jam, and spin his younger brother by the legs to shake the sadness out. If Davoud had a bag of green plums, he gave Zod half. Zod remained his baby brother even after Morad was born.

Morad tumbled into their lives like a big, juicy watermelon one August afternoon. Their mother carried him through that long, dry summer, her bird legs wobbly under his weight. At one, Zod's pajamas were already too small for Morad, riding above his potbelly, and by age two, Zod trailed behind both his brothers. They played war, building forts and making slingshots to fire rocks at enemy pigeons, and Davoud, too generous to leave Zod out, lifted him up under the armpits to hide with them in their bunker where they crouched together in a warm pile until their mother called their names.

A week after receiving his father's telegram, shaved and dressed, Zod carried a suitcase downstairs where his three friends waited in the living room to say good-bye. Madame Chabloz served coffee and patted his back with uncharacteristic tenderness, and when he walked out into a bright Paris morning one last time to catch the bus, they stood on the steps outside the front door to see him off. Taking a seat by the window, Zod stared at the buildings and bridges along the way, not thinking of anything in particular, not knowing he was on his way to a funeral and a wedding, that the rest of his life was about to begin.

ZOD REMEMBERED HIS CHILDHOOD like a story, with happy and sad parts. Pari teased that he remembered only the happy, but he kept the sad stored in an attic and rummaged there occasionally. Yanik and Nina's story had begun when they left Russia and Zod had not considered their lives before he came into it. Everything that followed their migration had been about hard work and the possibilities they imagined for themselves. Their children fell into these choices like worker bees in a hive, industrious even in play, instinctively knowing what was expected of them.

Zod was only three when Nina brought him into the kitchen and set him down on the gunnysacks of rice in the corner, handing him a spoon and a skillet to bang around. Already the print apron was taut on her belly, with Morad growing inside as she went about her chores, stopping to pat his crown absentmindedly while Zod stirred imaginary ingredients in his pan. It had not occurred to him to drum when all he'd ever seen his mother do with a wooden spoon was paddle through the things she peeled and trimmed and threw into the pot. His eyes followed her deliberate movements between the stove and the pantry, the furrow of her brow when she lifted a lid on something simmering on the burner and raised a spoon to her mouth to taste, the way she rested one of her small feet against her calf when kneading dough, the scent of vanilla cake on her cheek when she bent to kiss him, the tomato wedge salted and slipped into his mouth.

Zod had not deliberately learned to read or count, but after staring so long at the sides of oil drums and vegetable crates, the letters became words, and somehow weights and numbers, telling time, and chemistry were understood involuntarily. Slowly the world became comprehensible in this space. Yanik coming in at nine, Yanik going out noon, Yanik patting Nina's bottom, Yanik wielding a cleaver in hot pursuit of the knife sharpener who was ogling Nina, Yanik delivering a swift kick to a lollygagging iceman (huge blocks of ice were delivered from the mountains via doroshke long before they had a refrigerator). Davoud darting in after school, Davoud darting out with three apples, one in his mouth, two in his pockets, Davoud stopping to bite off a piece of fruit to share, *Are you hungry, little brother? Huh?* Davoud chasing Toofan the cat, which caught a mouse scent and took flight. Zod staying.

A steady silhouette against the kitchen wall, they could have measured Zod's growth through those early years by the marks he left on the wall-paper from the variety of things he picked up to inspect, to put into his mouth, and to fling over his head, wearing grooves into the wood at three, at four, then five. Is it possible that he would remember all this and recognize it as part of his early apprenticeship?

Goli came to them at sixteen, newly wed to a bricklayer from her village. She arrived at dawn to help Nina with her morning chores, and once the children were off to school she washed and ironed and swept the house from top to bottom until Nina summoned her to the kitchen for cooking lessons.

Before going home at night, Goli filled the tub with scalding water and scrubbed each of the boys until they emerged pink and clean, and while Yanik and Nina worked downstairs, she told once-upon-a-time stories and sang to them until they collapsed into her soft lap. She was more like a big sister than their nanny but they called her Naneh, which made her laugh because she was just a girl who chewed her nails and loved frilly things.

When Goli's husband tumbled off scaffolding and died, a boy was dispatched to deliver the news to Yanik, who whispered it to Nina, who cradled Goli for hours and stopped her from pulling tufts of hair from her scalp. The boys came home from school the next day to find that Nina had cleared her sewing room and furnished it with a bed and a dresser, and to their delight, Naneh Goli came to live with them.

For weeks afterwards Zod heard Naneh Goli crying at night and he'd brave the dark stairwell to crawl into her room, kneeling by the mattress to sing songs and retell the stories he'd learned from her until she fell asleep.

Once upon a time, there was a prince who lived with his two little brothers in a castle. One day the brothers rode their horses into the woods and the prince galloped so fast, he fell off his horse and broke his arms. An owl saw him lying on the forest floor and swooped down to pick him up. She took him to her house in the trunk of an oak tree. When the boy woke up, his owl mother had stitched wings where his arms used to be. "Can I fly now?" asked the prince. "Of course," said the owl, "but remember, you must never fly during the day or humans will capture you and put you in a cage." Under the bright moon, the boy learned to fly and he became a stealthy hunter. When the sun came up he crouched in their den and looked through the trees, and he was sad because he missed his family.

One day, when his owl mother tucked her feathers and went to sleep, he heard the sound of horses' hooves and saw his brothers riding below. He soared above them until they reached a clearing and there he perched on a tree stump to call to them. "Is that you? Is that really you?" they cried, and the prince gathered them under his enormous wings and told them what had happened. "We will take you to see the king and he will know what to do." But when they reached the castle the king was ashamed to have an owl son and ordered the guards to lock him up. *Whooo, whooo,* called the owl prince every night. *Whooo, whooo.* Deep in the forest, mother owl heard him and wept.

Up in their rooms, his brothers listened, biding their time. One night, while the guards were asleep, they went prowling and stole the key to the cage and set him free. The owl prince thanked them and promised never to forget them. When he flew into the darkness, owl mother's eyes shone from their tree house like a lit window, welcoming him home where they lived happily ever after. From then on, the boys were forever looking up, searching the sky, and whenever they heard the flapping of wings, they made a wish to fly someday with their owl brother.

Zod wept with every version of this story. No matter how often Naneh Goli cupped his face and kissed his brow—*it's only a story, buttercup*—he shuddered when the moon came in the window. He prayed for a new ending, the unforeseen tame conclusion of "The Old Woman Who Lived in the Woods," but his brothers loved "The Owl Prince" and begged for it every night, lying with their eyes heavenward, listening again and again as though they didn't know the ending, imagining a game of chase, the horses galloping in the woods, the owl's talons stretching to stun an unsuspecting rodent, the freedom of flight with a swooping view of the world beneath them. Zod would shift his weight to lean against Naneh's side and she'd whisper, "*Shhh*, don't cry." But tears pooled and trickled down his cheeks and he covered his ears to skip the end. On cold nights she slid a hot water bottle under the covers in a bed across from his squirming brothers—a small comfort to his shivering fear that he clutched to his chest like a shield before he fell off to sleep.

FOR HOURS ABOVE THE clouds, flying home from Paris, Zod recalled the old stories until they blended together. He was moved by his brothers' fearlessness, their awe of the world, their faith in it beyond the safety of their street, their yard, the people who looked like them and spoke like them—how patiently they had waited for the ending.

Yet it was Zod, the child who had mourned the owl boy's estrangement from his family, who had been the first to fly away from home. *He* had changed the ending. Whenever fear or sadness had stopped him, Davoud had cupped his hands to drink from the fountain in the yard and ordered

Zod to do the same, convincing him of the water's magic powers to make men brave. For years to follow he would stop at the fountain for a dose of courage. He was parched imagining a world without his brother.

They said that Davoud had died instantly, that he didn't feel any pain, but Zod didn't believe it. He couldn't imagine that being hurled through a windshield and splattered on the pavement with limbs torn from your body could be quick or painless, and what he couldn't bear most was that his brother suffered, that he lay there alone, his blood staining the asphalt, while Zod sat in Luxembourg Garden sketching a wretched fountain. It was beyond him to understand how grief can fill you so with the feeling of your own flaws and frailty.

# Nine

‒⦘⦙⦗‒

When the waiters took a break after lunch to smoke and huddle under the eaves, Yanik said, "This is not the time to tell jokes." One by one they put their cigarettes out against the wall, sending sparks into the air, and slumped away. The birds wouldn't shut up. It was so strange to see them there, in the trees, unmoved by grief. *Where is that slingshot so I can crack their beaks?* thought Zod, squinting into the bright light coming through the branches. And his mother. His mother. Not a sound when he placed his ear against her door, and when he looked in, not a light shone in the room, only Nina's face shimmered like a white moon against the black drapes.

Naneh Goli knocked and knocked on Zod's bedroom door. Eventually she burst in, pulling him downstairs to the kitchen where a cheery light pushed through the back door. Together they toasted the flour to bake tray after tray of halvah, taking turns stirring rosewater and saffron syrup with the flour, rocking the dense pudding, anger, sorrow, anger, sorrow, rippling the surface with the back of a spoon.

It was a house full of people, but quiet save for the clocks Yanik wound every morning, wandering forlorn through its rooms until he reached the kitchen. There, in the darkness before dawn, a single yellow light shone. Naneh Goli shuffled from sink to stove. She made breakfast. She made lunch. She stripped the beds. She made the beds. Then, one day, Naneh Goli ran water in the tub and carried Nina into the bathroom. She peeled off the nightgown and washed away the gray film of grief from her skin, leaving a thick ring of soap scum behind. Scrubbed clean and dabbed with rosewater, Nina sat at her mirror and let Goli's gentle hands comb her hair and tie it back with a blue ribbon—her first color in months.

At the table, everyone sat without saying a word until Naneh Goli brought them a clear, salty chicken soup with tiny dumplings. Earlier, she had poached kilos of bird wings and necks with leeks and carrots, saved the broth and spilled the wings and tidbits on a tray to cool. Zod had sat with her at the kitchen table to pull the warm meat off the bones, which her slick fingers quickly folded into dumplings.

Nina broke the silence, very softly at first, complimenting the broth that slowly warmed her vocal chords. Then Yanik, undone by gratitude for the sight of her, for the sound of her, sang in Russian, his voice high and cracking like an adolescent boy. Zod and Morad shared a glance and followed, hoarse at first, then urgent, before the moment vanished.

> Once upon a time there was a tavern
> Where we used to raise a glass or two
> Remember how we laughed away the hours
> And dreamed of all the great things we would do
>
> Those were the days, my friend
> We thought they'd never end

We'd sing and dance forever and a day
We'd live the life we choose
We'd fight and never lose
For we were young and sure to have our way

That very evening they went to Pari's house. She was playing the piano in her parents' sitting room when they knocked. Zod didn't know the music, didn't know the girl, but felt the full blow of the decision his parents had spelled out for him—to ask for Pari's hand. *What do you think?* What did he think? It was a gratuitous touch, asking for his opinion when the prologue and the epilogue of the engagement were already written. Until now the proposal had seemed abstract, but planted on this girl's doorstep, staring up at the lit window where he could see her silhouette, he staggered under the weight of it, wishing for a drink from the magic fountain.

Nina reached out a hand to squeeze his arm and they moved together through the courtyard, up the steps, into a parlor with a thick Persian carpet and ornate chairs, where Pari, in a black skirt fanned out on the piano bench, sat with her hands perched on the keys. She turned to look over her shoulder, greeting them with a shy "Salaam." There were dimples in her cheeks. His heart, unaccustomed to such a jolt, pounded in his chest.

Long ago, Yanik had told him that once he'd seen Nina's mother, he had asked for Nina's hand. "Before you marry a girl," he'd advised, "look first at her mother." Mrs. Parsa came in carrying a bowl of green melon and set it down to greet her guests. Zod couldn't bring himself to look at her, instead staring at the brightly framed oil paintings on the wall.

Outside, traffic hummed, dependable street noises calling to Zod who considered running downstairs to hail a taxi. Desperately, he turned towards the door, but then Mrs. Parsa was holding his hand, her palm still cool from the chilled melon bowl, and his eyes swept across her pretty face and saw an expression of sympathy he had never seen before. Her eyes filled with tears she blinked away. He lowered himself to a chair and watched his father take

Pari's face in both hands and kiss her forehead. Davoud's death had opened something inside them, and except for Zod, who thought he would pass out, they all moved towards each other with tender familiarity, putting their faith in one another to get them through life without a son.

And then what happened, what really erased the last trace of formalities, was that Pari played the piano for them and sang in her sweet voice. It felt like an offering, a folk song about spring coming late and waiting for the first bloom. When it was over, she stood up to smooth her skirt and for an instant Zod expected her to bow, but Pari lifted her chin to look Zod in the eye. Did he even know how to speak? Let the grown-ups do the talking. Just let him stand in the heat of that gaze. Architecture be damned! He tried hard not to be jealous of all the things she had ever looked at before, of people, of flowers and trees and piano keys and sheets of music. Pari's eyes were mirrors reflecting his future and there he caught a glimpse of a life beside her.

Eager to begin that life, he urged his parents to forgo the elaborate wedding they had initially planned for Davoud. It would be perverse to insert him so obviously into his lost brother's place. He insisted on meeting privately with Pari to explain his devotion to her as entirely new and under no obligation. It was unheard of, a boy and a girl meeting unsupervised. "You'll be married soon enough," Nina said, but Zod prevailed.

Fierce now, with newfound courage, he invited Pari to hike the footpaths of Darband with him. Her father had agreed, as long as Pari's brother could follow a few yards behind. Wearing a peacoat over slim navy trousers, she was fetching with her seesaw gait and her slick black ponytail in a barrette like a schoolgirl. Zod longed to take her small hand but kept a chaste distance, his arm ablaze with each incidental brush. There was nothing between them but air, nothing keeping him from reaching for her, nothing, that is, but Davoud's eyes. He felt his brother everywhere, sure that the lanky figure following them was Davoud, not Pari's little brother, and with aching hope he wanted it to be true, wished for Davoud to pummel him, to pellet his skull with the pebbles from the trail.

Out of breath with love he could hardly bear, he finally said, "Pari, I am not my brother. I will never replace him. I come to you as a man carrying my heart in my face, and a blank notebook to write our story." He exhaled, having spoken the most words he'd ever uttered to a woman, and she turned to hide a smile. From her coat pocket she pulled a small paper bag and reached inside for a fistful of sunflower seeds and her eyes flicked from Zod to the birds darting on the gravel between their feet and held the bag out to him. They fed the birds and walked without a word as if they had always walked this way. In one hand Zod held his fearful, restrained, and predictable self, and in the other, seeds—the latter, light as gold dust.

THEIR PARENTS CONSENTED TO a quiet wedding in July, just six months after Davoud's death, aware now that these two regarded each passing day as a lifetime spent apart. Energized by grief, Yanik finished a second floor apartment, Nina sewed curtains, pillow shams, and a satin quilt embroidered with butterflies, and with every stitch, every beam, every coat of paint, they worked to seal the crack in their hearts, trusting again in the brightness of another child's future.

It left them breathless, the care with which they crafted this nest, going so far as installing a dumbwaiter so the newlyweds could take their meals upstairs if they wished. Naneh Goli's face filled with glee when she imagined breakfast rising to wake them from their dreams, how she would fill that black hole with pink roses and jasmine, bowls of purple figs and peach jam, loaves of warm bread, jugs of milk, crocks of sweet butter, goblets of pomegranate juice, and song. Yes, she would sing and let her voice rise, too.

Zod and Pari honeymooned on the shores of the Caspian Sea, where their toes, wiggling in the cold sand, were exposed to each other for the first time. Pari's were like miniature ivory dolls with iridescent faces. Still bashful, she buried them, but the tide rushed to unveil them again and again. Even a kiss, full on the lips, wasn't as intimate as this introduction to her skin. Words still caught in their throats, so Zod and Pari were happy to let the waves chaperone the silence between them, always close at hand. Their shyness coming and going, they took their time telling each other everything about their pasts, but even that seemed unnecessary because Zod felt like Pari already knew him, and he her. Soon he would feel like her voice was his home.

So began their habit each morning of walking down to the sea, where Zod would spread his jacket close to the hem of the water and they would sit and eat their breakfast of bread and cheese and Pari would peel them an orange. Even this tidy nesting of the rinds inside one another in her palm told Zod of the orderly home they would make together. With their life in her hands, Zod felt he would never again feel afraid.

By the third day Zod and Pari had shed their clothing and went in the water, stroking sideways so they could look at each other. Pari was the stronger swimmer, her delicate arms gliding through the water effortlessly. Zod flailed and kicked hard to keep up with her and had no breath for talking.

"Behzod!" she shouted. "Behzod, you mustn't slap the water! Sweep and stroke. See?"

"*Shoma* are a wonderful swimmer," Zod gasped and spluttered.

They still addressed each other as *shoma*, the plural of the second person like the French *vous* (as if the singular was too slight), but not in the stiff manner reserved for teachers and elders, and not as Zod's mother would do when she was cross, but with a kindness between a man and woman in splendid love. Even afterwards when they went to their room and Zod tasted salt on Pari's breasts, even when he was inside her, even when they lay bare, facing each other under the whirring ceiling fan, he said "Parvaneh, shoma have the most beautiful face I've ever known." She blushed like an apricot. Zod thought he could just eat her.

BACK AT CAFÉ LEILA on a hot August afternoon, an upright piano stood under a blanket in the courtyard, its bench still out on the street. Yanik was instructing the two burly porters leaning against his recent purchase to carry it to the parlor, or *salon*, as he preferred to call it. Zod and Pari would be home soon and Nina wanted everything in its place before their arrival. She was happy, and her happiness spread through the rest of the household. The piano was very much a part of this cheer, a prelude to the new life that was to unfold. She slipped her hands under the coarse blanket to feel the lacquered wood, lifting the wing to tap the keys, though she didn't play. The temperature was ninety-eight degrees and the men's shirts were soaked with sweat, but Nina brought them glasses of iced cherry sherbets and that got them moving again.

Earlier they had been to the Saturday market with a trolley to do their weekly shopping, but with greater purpose this time. In preparation for a feast to welcome the newlyweds, crates of melons, eggplants, tomatoes, basil, apricots, and figs were stacked in the shade. Naneh Goli sat at a table set outside the kitchen, stringing green beans to cook with minced beef in a bright tomato sauce for *lubia polo*—a favorite dish of Zod's boyhood. Forty game hens already lay in their saffron yogurt marinade, and tomorrow they would roast them over an open fire to serve with mounds of jeweled rice.

All morning Yanik shaped lamb *koofteh* (meatballs) mixed with allspice and thyme, browning them in small batches and infringing on Nina's burners, which she needed to simmer mulberry preserves for parfait.

"My God!" he exclaimed in an effort to discourage Nina from making jam. "These berries are far too tart to soil the pan."

Not an inch of stove space remained, the multitude of dishes filling the house with steam and forcing Naneh Goli to pull a table outside to do her work. A heady perfume hung in the air just outside the kitchen and through the open front gate Naneh Goli could see passersby pause for a moment to inhale the colliding scents. Some stopped to talk, some swerved around the piano and wandered in to ask, "What in heavens is cooking?"

That night, exhausted from preparations and the lingering heat, they lined up their mattresses on the roof and slept soundly under mosquito nets. Yanik rose before dawn to wash the sidewalk with a hose. He would've washed the entire city if there had been time, but the garden tables needed to be set and garlands of roses to be strung and coals to be lit and dolmas to be wrapped, and piles of cress and scallions to be chopped for kuku.

Already Nina was lighting the samovar and Naneh Goli was scurrying to the baker.

"Do you want the tables set like we did for the banquet last summer?" Yanik asked Nina.

"No, Niki," she chirruped, "I have prettier tablecloths and embroidered napkins. This will be better."

They had discussed the celebration for days, walking through the garden, imagining and reimagining the festivities, feverish from anticipation.

Only Morad remained on the periphery of this spell, disgusted with his parents for muting the memory of his brother so conveniently. Bad-tempered and vicious, his threats to contaminate the meal fell on deaf ears.

They had never been close, Zod and Morad. To Morad, the middle brother Zod was an obstacle between him and Davoud, always getting in the way, stumbling and crouching in terror like a girl. The closest, most sacred friendship of his life was gone, his face cut out of a marriage portrait and replaced by a witless ass. It was an unforgivable betrayal. Gnashing his teeth with rage, Morad paced the streets with clenched fists and spat at the thought of Zod with Pari, scraping his chair away from the dinner table when talk inevitably turned to the homecoming. He could not understand how battered his parents were, that the preparations lightened their grief, and that all this work was done in the name of their firstborn.

Counting the hours to his departure for America, where he would soon be going to university, he looked forward to putting an immense distance between himself and a family he'd already forsworn. At nineteen, Morad wrote himself out of the family equation and no amount of coaxing would bring him back to them, so Yanik and Nina lost two sons in one year. It was a sinister beginning for any marriage but love holds promise, and those who stayed found themselves huddled under its umbrella grasping one another against the overwhelming tide of sorrow.

IT HAD BEEN A dream, walking into the garden that night. Snowy tables covered with damask shimmered beneath dozens of gas lanterns suspended from branches, pink rosebuds floated in the fountain, barberries, pistachios, and slivered orange peel glistened on pyramids of saffron rice.

Yanik, in a white tuxedo, led the waiters like an admiral and they followed his orders, polishing and buffing silver and glass. Even the gold buttons on their lapels sparkled when they stood shoulder to shoulder to escort guests through a maze of candlelit paths and as they circulated trays of liqueurs. Nina had finally untied her apron to wear green chiffon and seemed to float a few inches above the ground. Even Naneh Goli unpacked her wedding gold to wear for the occasion.

Pari, already seated with her parents, searched the crowd for Zod and saw him walking away to the far corner of the yard to where his younger brother lurked. She couldn't see and would never know what happened as the men receded into the dark. Morad, in funereal black, accepted Zod's outstretched hand and held it in a vice-like grip, fixing him with a stern gaze.

"You don't deserve any of this, you hypocrite."

No one but Zod heard his index finger snap like a wishbone in Morad's hefty hand. A teetering back, a grimace, before he thanked Morad, for he knew he had not sufficiently loved, nor grieved his lost brother—so quickly he'd been wrapped in his parents' care and shepherded to Pari, that a broken digit was a paper cut.

"Break my arm, brother," he begged.

How often in their youth had he seen Morad grab a kid in a headlock and threaten to crack his neck, spoon an eyeball from its socket, or arch his fingers back until the kid wailed his apologies for a misdemeanor. Instead of feeling reassured by his brother's brute strength, he had wet his pants more than once just bearing witness, knowing it was practice for when it would be his turn to fall prey to his brother's torture. Morad smelled Zod's fear, never missing an opportunity to push him into a muddy ditch or trip him up when they were alone, then stepping back to wipe the foam of pleasure from the corners of his mouth.

Now, with his ample torso hovering over Zod's wiry frame, he sneered "Hah! Your *arm*? You mean your chicken wing, you shit? I'd break every bone in your body, one by one, if my mother wasn't enjoying herself so much." Then he let go, like flicking a cigarette butt, and stalked away, leaving Zod stricken and yet relieved, for underneath the anguish was peace and something like a laugh racked him when he sniffed a hint of Morad's aftershave on his clammy palm—that his brother had remembered cologne for the reckoning, that they would never again be as intimate as they had just been.

He returned to the table with a deep hunger and ate enormously after such a long vigil, loosening his belt to dance with Pari, anesthetized with a dose of joy that would tide him over the next hours. It wasn't until the last guests staggered home just before dawn and the house creaked and settled into sleep, that he crept to the kitchen and fashioned a splint from a wooden spoon. Thereafter, a crooked finger reminding him that it hadn't been a dream.

# Ten

***

Morad flew off with Pan Am. They watched him go. Zod did not intend on living a life of reparations. Morad's intention had been to shame him, to punish him for life, but he turned away too quickly to know that a savage handshake had only released Zod from a compulsory allegiance to a boorish brother who did not love him.

Every morning by seven, Zod was at Nina's elbow, no longer cross-legged on gunnysacks stirring an empty pot on the floor. Over the years he had memorized his mother's every move like a chess game, so when she reached for a sieve, swept a pastry brush, folded a piroshki, he didn't follow because he was already there, her muscle memory traveling through him so that if you stood watching them at the kitchen window, their arms moving in billowy sleeves, it would have looked like a well rehearsed ballet, choreographed until the moment when Nina lifted a cutlet from hot oil with bare hands and Zod yelped from the burn that singed the first two layers of his skin. Nina's calloused hands, numbed long ago from pushing pots from fire to fire with bare hands, made a dismissive wave towards the icebox where he plunged his purple flesh into its frozen depths.

Back at her side, they rolled yeast dough into transparent sheets to fill with cabbage, ground beef, and onions. She was mostly silent, thinner than ever, her broad behind shrunken now beneath one of the dozens of print smocks sewn with two deep pockets in the front where she kept pencils and tissues and lists. Ancient scars speckled her rough hands but her upper arms remained a creamy white and jiggled with the to and fro of the rolling pin.

Zod, watching from the corner of his eye, afraid of falling behind, grew delirious with hunger but he knew better than to pinch a bite into his mouth, lest his mother smack his hand away. Every time she left a pan of poached birds on the counter, he wanted desperately to steal a wing, to pick at the warm carcass after they'd carved away the meat. The truth is, cooks starve to feed others. Nina never nibbled as she went along, "We set the table. Then we eat. Not now. Now, we work."

In the thirty years since Yanik had tied an apron around her belly and shown Nina how to separate eggs, she had explored countless recipes, decoded the subtleties of Persian food, its ancient alchemy of sweet and sour, hot and cold, its deference to plants and herbs, soliciting Naneh Goli's palate to measure and fine-tune. What triumph to turn out a pot of rice with a golden potato *tadig*—that magical crust beneath the steamed rice. Trial and error taught her which rules to observe and which to rebuff.

"Me, I like lemon, but the recipe always calls for too much or too little," she explained. "Think of the people you're cooking for. Learn their passions and adjust without straying too far from the basic rules. Your father eats with one hand on the saltshaker. Goli eats whole preserved lemons like gumdrops. Squeeze a lemon on the salad, add a little salt, but don't be so keen to kill the lettuce."

Zod didn't realize he was training to trust his eyes, ears, and nose to tell him when to lift the lid off a simmering pigeon-and-pomegranate stew and add more molasses, to imagine flavors like layers of colors and know how they interact before squeezing them onto his palette.

Everything in the kitchen of Café Leila had purpose and meaning. It was a room filled with knowledge that Nina, in her grueling devotion, acquired and carved into its walls. From the hooks above the stove to the stone for sharpening knives to the spice cupboard arranged according to heat and subtlety, emerged an efficient pattern, never whimsical or decorative.

Over the years, she allowed herself a small Zenith radio that sat on the windowsill and aired soap operas, and a framed mirror mounted on the wall along with her comb and lipstick in case she had to go into the café. To walk among its pots and casseroles was no different than a stroll through a laboratory. Clean and narrow, with a door leading to the courtyard on one end and another entry on the other providing natural light and a pleasant cross draft.

"You might mean well, son," Nina would say, shuffling behind Zod like a crab. "Now do it over, please." She confided in him her share of disasters that outweighed the happy accidents, all the while prodding him to keep his workspace tidy. "No one wants to eat something that came from a mess."

It was no longer unharried little Sunday lunches prepared in Madame Chabloz's kitchen for three or four bachelors who forgave his errors, his over-cooked lamb gigot, the curdled custard and convivial chaos. There, he had been an earnest boy toiling in a workshop, turning out a delightful hodge-podge of flavors to unconditional enthusiasm. Here, they fed far too many people to indulge in exotic experiments, yet Zod's eagerness didn't wither. He became stove-bound, rooted to the tile, good mannered but a little crazy. Like all young cooks, he had a pathological urge to change and revise—ego and curiosity compelled him to alter recipes with mixed results.

Only on Thursday mornings would Zod leave Nina's side to accompany Naneh Goli to the market. Zod liked dressing for the occasion, shedding his standard uniform of gray flannel trousers with shirtsleeves rolled up for a double-breasted suit, necktie, polished shoes, and fedora, regardless of the weather. Coming downstairs, clean-shaven and dapper, Nina teased that he was on his way to a ball. Yanik had already taken him to the bazaar and introduced him to all the vendors, and Zod felt his attire showed respect.

Nevertheless, the instant the gate closed behind them, a boyish enthusiasm surfaced in Naneh Goli's presence, and they would stop to sample street food from the little stands that dotted their path. Steam rose from giant roasted sugar beets, wrapped in newspaper and piping hot. A young boy sat on a wooden crate behind his makeshift juice stand, slicing pomegranates with a meat cleaver and squeezing their juice into small plastic cups, his flushed cheeks matching the color of his fruit. Men sat behind charcoal braziers turning ears of corn and fanning skewered liver kebabs they slipped sizzling into pockets of lavash bread with a tangle of cilantro and mint. Ribbons of fruit leather, apricot, plum, tamarind, and cherry, draped like laundry from wires strung between awnings. The two shoppers zigzagged from one stall to the next, with Naneh Goli trotting to keep up with Zod who whirled between the stands, eating as he went, in a frenzy she described as the mad dervish.

At the market it was Naneh Goli who led the way, picking up a quick banter with Mostafa the fruit vendor, who followed her longingly with his sunken eyes, ignoring the clamor of other women. Here, you pointed at what you wanted and Mostafa presumably selected the best for you. Only Goli was allowed to fondle the fruit and he hollered at anyone else who dared touch his peaches. He filled their bags with fat yellow pears and clusters of ruby grapes, all the while maneuvering to brush against Goli's hand, to catch one glimpse of a small earlobe when her veil slid back.

But Naneh Goli sensed his hunger and was hard with him, taunted him, surveyed the pyramids of oranges with mock disgust and discouraged shoppers behind her from buying them. Her cruelty surprised Mostafa and his mustache drooped, but all he could do was nod gravely to Zod, as if he would understand, before Goli turned away demurely and walked to the butcher.

Zod could not imagine his Naneh in a romance, for she seemed old and obstinate, though she was still in her thirties and quite pretty. Mostafa had been to see Yanik more than once to beg for her hand, and there had been a string of suitors before him: Hamid, the tailor, Kaveh, the barber, Najib, an electrician, all dispatching their mothers to Café Leila where they settled themselves in the salon, making small talk until tea was served and then coming straight to the point, breathlessly embellishing their son's intelligence and entrepreneurship, the family's wealth and stature. Naneh Goli overheard these exchanges and whispered to Nina in disbelieving huffs, "Why? Why would I ever marry that old codger?"

Once, a few years after her young husband's sudden death, she consented to marry a shopkeeper eighteen years her senior with a good income and two housekeepers. It was arranged with formality and without affection. Nina sewed her a gown, a reception was held at the café, and a driver took Goli, a dresser, and two carpets to her new home. Zod shivered when he peeped inside her former room that first night and saw it empty, stripped of everything but the drapes and her rosewater scent. They did not furnish the room for weeks even though Yanik offered more than once to move Nina's sewing machine back in there.

At first Naneh Goli came to visit one or two afternoons a week, staying longer each time, until the visits became more frequent and her husband sent word that he required some attention from her. But Goli felt lonely in his big house, lonely for Nina and the boys, jealous that another girl would take her place. She was unaccustomed to a cook and a servant who didn't need her interference, and a husband who expected her to share his bed. Upon her defiant refusal, they quarreled bitterly and she escaped to Nina, who held out hope that he would eventually earn Goli's affection, that they would start a family.

Nina spent long afternoons stirring nougat and sugared almonds to cajole her young protégé to go back to her home with newlywed treats to sweeten the match. But the breach between the couple widened when he took to beating Goli with a cane, and he eventually threw her out. Naneh Goli happily moved back, forgoing her *mehrieh* (a dowry pledged by the husband at the time of marriage) but returning with the dresser and two rugs. She concluded that marriage was without benefits.

THE WEEKLY TRIPS TO the market energized Zod and he pulled the loaded trolleys into the courtyard, handing out parcels like trophies to the waiters who came to help him unload. "The first figs!" he hollered, as if the arrival of every fruit, every leafy green, every root, was something to celebrate. There were seasons for produce then and you couldn't find tomatoes in December.

His mother was tired, and he took advantage of her fatigue and occasional absentmindedness to rework a recipe when she retreated upstairs to her sewing. In the afternoons, after sweeping the floor, in the hour before Pari came home from the conservatory, he would make an elaborate minaret of cold sandwiches, or rhubarb preserves spooned over yogurt, or a persimmon pudding layered with coarsely ground almond brittle.

With his eyes trained on the front gate, waiting for Pari to walk through with music books clutched to her chest, he set a garden table with a white cloth, silver, and china. She became his lab mouse, sniffing happily at the poached pears with peppercorns and cardamom before running through a labyrinth of delicately assembled snacks, while Zod ran like a colt from kitchen to table, fetching more and more accoutrements for his dishes. This favorite time of day, between lunch and dinner, when time stood still for them, could have been a period of courtship, the wooing of the belly below the heart, except they were already married.

Pari always volunteered to wash up but Zod wouldn't hear of it, shooing her to Nina's room, listening to their soft voices rising and falling through the open bedroom window. Alone, he circled the table to see what she had scraped clean and what was discarded, trusting her palate above all others. Just crumbs, stems from the halved pears, a radish, or half a spinach pie remained.

But how to translate this love over and over again, to make each dish appear fresh, like a first crush? True, he looked forward to serving this food to customers who had been raised at Yanik and Nina's table, introducing them to these flavors slowly, like the rock 'n' roll records he played for Pari. But he had to temper his desire to show off. He remained mindful of Nina's resourcefulness, her no-nonsense soups and batters that were the spine of his repertoire. Without them he would have remained a clumsy amateur powered by ego. Zod's mother said there was hope for him because he knew his limitations. He knew to follow her rules before breaking them, to remember what she had already discovered because, unlike her, he wasn't born with inherent knowledge.

But Zod could still delight in foraging for the herbs and flowers and roots to flavor his soups and vinegars, to tuck bouquets of seasonings inside the cavities of whole whitefish and pigeons, and to save tree trimmings and apple blossoms for roasting lamb, even making piroshki dough from a sourdough starter that he would combine with well water. All these began as experiments, but he did not stray from the basic rules.

By five o'clock most afternoons Yanik, waking from his nap and looking for a cup of tea, would find Zod alone at the kitchen sink washing dishes. He stood at the entryway watching him, wondering how this had happened. How did Zod close the gap between what he wanted and what he had? He had not simply acquiesced to a plan his parents had proposed, but seemed to slip into it like a good shoe, comfortably. Yanik allowed himself to conjure grandchildren—four or five tiny versions of Zod and Pari running through the yard, climbing trees, scraping knees, and Nina doting on them—then waved a hand to dispel the image. After his loss, he succumbed to superstition the way his parents and grandparents had in response to tragedy. It was best not to forecast; prophecy was a clergyman's business. The ingredients were there for a good life if Zod and Pari wanted to live it, as long as Yanik didn't tempt fate, as if his thoughts alone could bring down the house.

Zod carried a tray outside and they drank tea through a sugar cube held delicately between their two front teeth. Yanik often repeated what had already been said in so many ways: "It takes courage, son, to make this your life."

"Yes, I know, Baba jan," Zod would reply. "There is nowhere else I would rather be." And after that the only sound was the clatter of dice against the backgammon board, until the sun dropped lower down the sky, urging them back to work.

# Eleven

———⚬⚬⚬———

Guests who said the finest feature of Hotel Leila was the Juliet balconies often booked a room for one or two weeks during the summer, when the orchestra played in the garden every night. After dinner they would retire to their rooms with a drink and un-latch the shutters, spreading them out noisily. Looking up, Zod would see men in shirtsleeves rolled above the elbows leaning over the wrought iron railings behind a fog of cigarette smoke. The women, too, with cardigans draped over bare shoulders against the chill, leaned into the night to hear Pari, their lips moving to the lyrics they knew. No one slept much, but no one complained.

It had taken Yanik and Zod six years to build the hotel, Yanik having agreed at last to stop at twelve rooms, four on each floor. He wanted a grand hotel, a Ritz, with a marble lobby and an elevator boy. They had quarreled and shouted, each having envisioned an establishment of different proportions—Zod in favor of the quaint and his father persisting on a stately mansion where international stars and heads of state would stay.

"They will need just twelve rooms for their entourage," he'd argued, and Nina had come to her son's defense. "Truly important people will value a place where they will be taken care of and left in peace."

She was right, of course. Room eight became the pied-à-terre of a certain diplomat and room eleven was frequented by a celebrated actor when working in Tehran. Nina even kept their slippers and bathrobes in storage until their next visit, always filling the rooms with flowers and fruit baskets before their arrival.

But what really kept guests coming back was the scent. By 1968 Café Leila ranked among the city's best restaurants and Zod was beloved for his imaginative cooking. A genuine bonhomie filled the air with the chime of cutlery and chatter as the waiters swayed through the high-ceilinged dining room like arabesque dancers. The café was so popular that by midday people would begin lining up outside the bakery, where cream-and-yellow-striped boxes were filled with Zod's specialty piroshkies. This simple *pirog*, a yeast bun really, brought men, women, and children to the south side of Tehran, "threatening to tip over the ship" as Yanik liked to joke.

It wasn't that Nina didn't make equally tasty buns, but Zod, her rogue apprentice, had refined the dough to a featherlight brioche with a subtle tang. He filled the pockets not just with beef and onions, but peach jam, saffron rice pudding, smoked sturgeon, potatoes and dill, cabbage and caraway apples, duck confit and chopped orange peel, and, once, even a pearl that fell into the lemon custard when Nina's necklace snapped, beads hitting the counter like hailstones. By chance the boy who bit into it didn't swallow it, but dislodged a baby tooth hanging by a thread and his parents found the incident quite fortuitous. It wasn't every day one found a precious stone in a roll and a rumor circulated around town that Café Leila's piroshkies carried good omens, and thereafter their orders multiplied for holidays and happy occasions.

Nina was happy to have her pearls restrung, and Zod spent sleepless nights shaping and proofing and brushing row after row of fat little pillows with his paintbrush dipped in egg wash until Pari pitter-pattered down in her nightgown to take him to bed. But he'd be up before dawn to slide them into the ovens and within minutes a marvelous aroma would creep through the seams of the kitchen door, up the stairs and into the garden, rising above the tall birches that lined the alley to hover over rooftop sleepers escaping the summer heat, and wafting into the rooms where guests unfurled and woke one by one to that baked goodness. Only then did Zod feel entitled to some respite, sitting down for a quiet tea in the kitchen, with the back door open to a shaft of first light, before waking Pari and the children for school.

Downstairs, in the lobby at dawn, Aladdin's quick footsteps returned from the newsstands with the daily papers. Upon his return he lit a pot-bellied samovar and lined slim tea glasses, saucers, and teaspoons on the credenza. He was bellhop, concierge, and butler, aproned at seven to sweep outside the revolving hotel door (a feature Yanik had insisted upon), waiting to receive the first tray of hot piroshkies from the bakery. Breakfast was served on the veranda, and Aladdin changed into his tuxedo to carry the tea caddy and platters of warm buns to the guests seated around Persian brass tray tables. It was all-you-can-eat and guests took advantage, tucking a few rolls into their pockets for later.

By eight o'clock Nezam the barber arrived. Yanik, denied a palace hotel, nevertheless found ways to offer the services of one. The lobby barber was the epitome of luxury, and to reassure his guests, he had installed the chair in a discreet corner facing a gilded mirror and initially sat in it himself to attract customers. By and by, Nezam, a taciturn Turk, became a fixture and guests tipped back to relax into a wet shave, as he took his time to sweep his blade while demanding more hot towels from Aladdin, stroking a cheek where he had just run the blade to admire his work, and deftly singeing wayward ear and nose hairs with a lit match—an alarming sight to Noor and Mehrdad, who snuck in to fill their pockets with sugar-coated almonds from silver candy dishes on the front desk before rushing to school.

Noor remembered the night her father brought a man home from the hospital. Shoja Yazdan was one of his good customers, a widower recovering from an operation that had left him blind in his right eye. Noor saw him leaning against her father with an arm around Zod's shoulder, the man's gait unsteady as they walked up the steps to the hotel. Her grandfather followed behind with a small suitcase and they marched the sick man along the polished marble floors to a room on the second floor. There were pink geraniums in the window box and after three weeks in a grim hospital room, the sight of them with his good eye cheered him up. They brought him a dinner tray and he sat up in bed to share supper with Zod, who slept that night on a fold-out cot next to the man, should his friend need anything.

"What a man I married," Pari said. "Cook, husband, father, now doctor!"

There was a strain in her voice that Noor had never heard before. Her parents were always short on time with each other, what with running a hotel and a café, Pari's concerts, and caring for Noor and Mehrdad, but Zod and Pari's love throbbed from one heart to the other without pause. She loved him for the care he took of his friends and family, and even strangers, but that night Noor thought she envied Mr. Yazdan, "Hotel, restaurant, sanatorium!"

However, Pari truly loved the hotel. She returned from one of her trips abroad with an antique Victorian birdhouse for Zod, with the idea of keeping it in the lobby. Handcrafted and painted canary yellow with a light blue trim, it sat across from the front desk. Inside, two white-eared bulbuls serenaded guests and these songbirds, too, added to the hotel's charm.

Noor would bring her friends after school to see what she called her dollhouse—with its ample size, tiny windows, and arched doorways, it resembled just that—and Pari encouraged her to name the birds and talk to them. Peeking inside, Noor longed to furnish the cage with miniature chairs and teacups, to tuck Sonbol and Bolbol into wee beds and sit them down at their desks to do their arithmetic. It seemed this diorama was lacking, and so it was that she pried open the door one day to make some improvements when Sonbol flew past her and out the window. If Pari had not intervened, Yanik would have spanked Noor, and he stormed out murmuring Russian expletives. Nonetheless, just three days later Zod found Bolbol lying still and cold on the floor of the birdhouse.

"Missing his partner," he explained to a tearful Pari, but they told the children that Bolbol flew away to find his wife. Aladdin was most relieved, for the chirping had always made him feel anxious and tardy, *wake up wake up wake up, you're late you're late you're late!* Nina was pleased, too—caged birds made her sad. *What's more*, she thought, *who needs birds in the house when they have Pari?*

Years later, those guests who had leaned out their windows to hear Pari sing would sometimes confuse the old days with the new, would sometimes mutter about the Shah and Queen Farah, or the Danish Bakery near Vanak Square, as if they still existed, as if they could order a birthday cake and pick it up tomorrow, but if you mentioned Hotel Leila, their eyes would glisten, the tears earnest, and with a wistful sigh cry, "Ah, but that was the golden age."

# Twelve

——— ⌘ ———

What Pari first noticed about Tehran after she had been away for a few weeks was the smell. She caught it almost as soon as she walked off the plane: an odor of diesel and wet asphalt that sharpened her nostalgia. If you were in it day after day, you didn't notice it so much, but Pari noticed it—this smell of home and its familiar settling on her clothes.

Zod usually met her at the gate with a bouquet, offsetting the scent of engines with lilies and aftershave, although he wouldn't be there tonight. Arriving a day earlier than expected, Pari was planning to take a taxi to Café Leila. She felt a happiness in her chest imagining Zod's surprise, his urgent steps towards her nearly a run he kept in check anytime they had been apart. She could taste the sweet homecoming. In London, a bad flu had led to two cancelled concerts and she longed to be nursed by her husband. She also craved Naneh Goli's hot chicken soup.

Wisps of hair escaped from her headscarf but Pari didn't mind the scarf too much, it kept her hair clean. Still, she wasn't used to this version of her country, the watchful eyes of bearded guards, the black-clad women and multiple checkpoints. It was two years after the revolution and yet the changes still unsettled her. On previous trips the contents of her bags were dumped on the floor and poked through, her copies of *Elle* magazine and tubes of lipstick confiscated, her body searched roughly by dour female guards.

Bitterly cold, her breath rose in the night air as she tugged on the belt of her wool coat. Anxious now to be home, she pushed a luggage cart to the curb and climbed into the first orange taxi. They started out into the black night and the driver glanced through his rearview mirror at Pari, who leaned her feverish forehead against the frosted window. He pushed a button on his cassette player and a mournful sermon rose from the speakers to press against her, a monotone the driver was compelled to interrupt with a frequent hollering of "Allahu Akbar!" Before long, the rippling tones of Arabic grew louder, filling her ears with a liquid that pounded against her eardrums and though the heater blasted hot air into the cab, she shivered and held her throbbing head in both hands. He mistook her convulsion for rapture and turned the volume up, at which Pari yelled, "Shut up! Oh please, *shut him up!*" She was just so tired.

PARI WAS A HAPPY traveler and took great pleasure in packing. She would lay out each item on the bed—shoes, stockings, handbag, jewelry—to consider its visual effect and comfort level before assembling complete outfits. Then she would fold them into her case, finally allowing Zod to carry her bag downstairs to where Naneh Goli and the children waited for their good-bye kisses, each holding a bucket of water to throw at the departing car—a send-off to assure smooth travels. She especially enjoyed packing for the return home. Every souvenir she selected for her family was first fondled, then wrapped in leaves of tissue paper, and then unwrapped once more for a final approval. These weren't trivial little gifts borne from guilt—there simply was no other way for her to convey how much she missed them, how she wished they were there. These were pieces of a place carried home so as to see their delight in opening boxes with exotic patterns and lettering and a promise of something meant entirely for them. To return empty-handed was unthinkable, a statement that in her time away, they had ceased to exist. During this trip, she had braved a freezing rain to do her shopping and caught a terrible cold.

On the morning of her departure, Pari woke early to have a pot of strong black tea. As she pulled on the clothing laid out for the journey, she indulged in one last look at her *soghatis* (a traveler's gifts) before fastening the lock on the tan leather suitcase that would lay in the trunk of the taxi. For Noor, a pair of white mittens from Selfridges to brighten the obligatory drab school uniform. For Mehrdad, the risky purchase of a Talking Heads album. Western pop music was forbidden under the new regime, and she had carefully slipped the record into a *Beethoven Piano Sonata No. 15* sleeve. Also for her children, Mars bars and Cadbury Flakes. She bought a barrette with rhinestones for Naneh Goli, who coveted shiny things like a crow. For her mother she had purchased six white Marks and Spencer wool camisoles— her mother was always cold—and McVitie's Digestive biscuits. There was a sky blue umbrella for Nina, along with some Yardley English Lavender soap. And finally, for Zod, a double-decker bus made of chocolate with marzipan headlamps and a blue silk tie from Bond Street (even though ties, too, were a symbol of Western dress and discouraged under the new order). She had strung it through the belt loops of her dress to make a pretty sash.

THE TIRES SHRIEKED WHEN the taxi swerved to the curb, jerking Pari and her suitcase roughly. The driver tossed his cigarette out the window and got out to yank the door open, grabbing Pari's hair to throw her onto the street, hurling her to the concrete, and when she raised a hand to steady herself, he kicked her in the stomach. She dropped to the cold stone.

It was hard to tell who was screaming louder, and within minutes a column of bodies gathered, pushing for a look at her but not to stop him, because with two words—"whore" and "infidel"—he had already sanctioned their support. Their voices rose in a dark hum, closing in on her. They encouraged him to break every bone in her body, to rip out her hair, and one by one they peeled off their shoes and flung them—all but one woman who interfered, kneeling to shield Pari, but they dragged her away by her feet. *Sister.* That's what they called her. "Back off, sister."

Pari's teeth spilled out to bob in the blood gushing from her mouth, an arm was twisted awkwardly, where bone had torn through flesh. Someone was slapping her head with a shoe, and she lay stretched out with her face smashed to the pavement, hair matted with blood, eyes looking at nothing at all, her legs splayed immodestly, like a corpse hemorrhaging on the sidewalk, powdered with fresh snow while dozens of wet black tracks circled her making an awful noise.

Before the first stone was cast, revolutionary guards patrolling the streets arrived to shove Pari into the back of their van and drive to the station where she was arrested as a counterrevolutionary and accused of enmity against God.

She lay unconscious through the proceedings and was eventually seen by a prison doctor who stitched her multiple wounds and cast her broken arm. Her bags were "lost" so she remained nameless through that night and the next, waking up in a cold cell, stiff and aching. Two times twenty-four is forty-eight, but how long had she been here, how many hours since she left London? Some sort of struggle had taken place but there was a blot of black ink in her memory beyond which she could not remember what had happened and did not know why she lay on this narrow cot under this coarse blanket in a dingy cell. Hurt everywhere.

UNTIL THAT NIGHT, PARI and Zod had lived sequestered from mass politics. She had had no interest whatsoever in revolution nor a longing for an alternative order. Of course they were attuned to the injustices, the corruption, the surveillance of the secret service, but Yanik and Nina's escape from brutal Bolshevik oppression made them wary of any change that would disrupt the hum of everyday life. It wasn't so much passivity as it was a lack of ideological fervor. On the other hand, the goal to overthrow the Shah glued their customers together and Zod found himself on the periphery of a movement that unfolded as much in his dining room as in classrooms, homes, and the bazaar.

In the early days of the revolution, secular men and women, communists, socialists, intellectuals, and political dissidents had marched side by side with the religious zealots. They poured into Café Leila, hoarse from shouting slogans, to slurp soup and speak openly for the first time in their lives before linking arms to go back out into the streets. The rapidity with which that fraternity crumbled and their purpose degenerated into fear and violence was breathtaking—had they really imagined that they would have a say in the future of their nation? Ah, but revolutions have a way of disappointing us and with each slain body, each dreadful disappearance, mistrust bloomed into profound betrayal.

Under the guise of tearing down tyranny, the new order ushered in a totalitarian theocracy, stripping people of hope, forcing them back into their foxholes or into exile, *if* they managed to escape execution. The fury of the Islamic regime did not blow over—it only gathered steam and effaced all those writers and thinkers who had never thought about life after the fall. They had assumed with glimmering hope that when a tyranny collapses, whatever comes next must be better. What began as grassroots rallies became government-staged theater—a dark sea of angry men and women shouting well rehearsed slogans, then offered a hot meal for their performance.

Café Leila remained open through the turmoil, even on the darkest days, even when revolutionary guards stormed in for impromptu inspections. Zod, nervous and acquiescent, offered them lunch. When an ayatollah and his entourage showed up, Zod lit the coals. The dumbwaiter had proven useful after all—what Naneh Goli had once labeled the "honeymoon ex-tension," camouflaged by wallpaper, became a liqueur cabinet, and later a hiding place for an eclectic library of books by revered poets and writ-ers forbidden under Islamic rule, such as Forough Farrokhzad and Sadeq Hedayat, as well as Zola, Tolstoy, Nabokov, and Solzhenitsyn, among doz-ens of French and Russian novels in translation (other than a few songs, the three brothers had never learned to speak Russian, so fierce was Yanik's determination to assimilate). There were also several leather-bound editions of novels by Balzac and Flaubert inscribed to Zod by his old friend Ge-rard Simon, who continued correspondence until his letters began to arrive opened and read, to ensure that he and Zod were not planning a coup. Hidden among the books were other incriminating evidence of debauch-ery—playing cards, records, cassettes, and old issues of *Towfigh* (a political satire magazine), all suspended in a time capsule between two floors.

After the guards had filled their stomachs with kebabs, gnawed on raw onions, and scraped the filth from under their nails with the forks, they upended the café. Marauding the kitchen, the bedrooms, they dumped out the contents of endless drawers on the floor, and when they found nothing incriminating, they ripped the upholstery with dull knives and found Elena's recipes, written in Cyrillic, which to these ignorant men looked like spy material.

A terrified Zod stood openmouthed (Nina had told only Pari of their existence), until Pari emerged, trembling under a black chador she kept for these intrusions, to explain that these were just instructions to make dump-lings and salad Olivier (a chicken and potato salad bound with eggs and excessive mayonnaise), not manuals for overthrowing the regime.

"My husband is an *ashpaz* (cook). He stirs *abgoosht* (a hearty beef and chickpea soup), not trouble."

What she couldn't explain was why they were sewn into seat cushions, so the men, gloating over their discovery, yelled obscenities, shredded the recipes, threatened arrest, slammed Zod against the wall, and having sufficiently intimidated them, left as suddenly as they had come.

In the wake of this violence, husband and wife collapsed against each other and fell to the floor in a heap. Naneh Goli, returning home lugging shopping bags and clutching twelve-year-old Noor's hand, wailed at the sight of them amid the rubble. She knew only that she loved these two like her own children, that this home was as sacred to her as any place of worship, and that it was up to her to put things back together. And though the intrusion made her blood boil, she took solace in the tasks of sweeping, scrubbing, and mending. Chores became lifeboats in the storm that lapped at the edges of their lives and threatened to drown them.

Nina had retreated to an oblivion that saved her from witnessing the slow and deliberate destruction of her adopted country. Yanik, too, was spared, having died of an aneurysm at seventy-one, leaving Nina so bereft that Pari wondered if she had willed dementia just to bear her sorrow. What use for memory when it fills you with remorse: *I should have loved him more, I should not have let Davoud get in that car, why didn't I take better care of him?* Better to fold it all away and outsmart loss.

Nevertheless, she still woke up every morning and went down to the kitchen where every day for the last fifty years her first task had been to peel two dozen hard-boiled eggs for the salad Olivier they served at lunch. Knowing the urgent impulse within her to follow a need to be somewhere, to complete a task, Zod would leave a few eggs on the kitchen table next to his mother's chair before going to bed each night. He would wake to find her sitting still with an egg clutched in her hand and a knowing grin that he presumed meant, *Aren't you clever?*

After the siege, Zod leafed through the torn recipes. The script, as cryptic to him as to his assailants, seemed embroidered on the thin sheets of yellowed paper. He did not doubt that something precious lay beneath this hard alphabet and wondered if archaeologists felt similarly when they came upon a shard of pottery and were compelled to dig for the remainder. He scooped all the scraps into a shoebox, carried the box and a cup of tea to his mother's room, and emptied the contents on her bed. A twinkle returned to Nina's eyes, the look she sometimes got when the boys had been mischievous.

"Davoud, look what you've done to Elena's recipes," she scolded him (for she now interchanged her sons' names randomly, just as she had when they were small and she had yelled "Morad!" for Zod and "Zod!" for Davoud, like all parents do). "Wait till your father finds out."

"Yes, Maman, it's horrible of me," Zod agreed. "Can you please help me glue these back together?"

Who can explain how a mind, so untethered that she could not remember the loss of a spouse or a son, could recall the arcane alphabet of her birthplace? Out of a field of no-memory came sheets of ancient instructions. Peeping in through the bedroom door, Zod saw her figure bent over the task like a child assembling a puzzle—a tranquil face with the tip of her tongue sticking out. Often they would find her dozing behind stooped shoulders, but Nina always went back to her intricate work while Naneh Goli stood by to hand her strips of tape. The eternal tracing and patching took weeks: walnut and caraway strudel, apricots in syrup, chicken necks with turnips and prunes, *ponchik* (fried dough balls filled with custard), rice porridge, *vatrushki* (savory tarts), beef *pelmeni*, kulich, each one translated by a family friend in exchange for meals. His mother had salvaged these formulas from the hands of Bolshevik barbarians, learned what she could from them, and stowed them away until fate brought another round of fanatics to their door.

Zod convinced himself that these notebook pages held a key to his ancestry, and he meant to decode the mysteries of his grandmother's kitchen. For she was a marvelously gifted and disciplined but oppressive and authoritarian cook, whose kitchen mirrored the dictatorship his parents had fled.

AFTER HER ARREST, PARI was blindfolded and taken to a pit where she was asked many questions. Every day the same questions were repeated over and over again, but Pari had no right answers for these faceless men. For two months she was lashed, raped, and threatened with execution. They did not contact her family. By day she was forced to make false confessions about her ties to Western powers and involvement with dissident groups and when she told them what they wanted to hear, the beatings subsided and she was left in solitary confinement with pen and paper to write bogus confessions and letters to her family explaining her absence and atoning for her sins.

Time becomes vague in isolation. Without the shifting light of day into night, without sun, with no moon or stars, a person vanishes. Stay alive. Stay alive. Pari knew she had to stay alive for Zod, for Mehrdad and Noor, and to do so she had to obey and abide by a schedule, to make everything she did matter, to listen for sounds. It helped that meals were served at a set time to mark the hour. Every morning she hobbled the length of her cell one hundred times, an exercise she repeated in the evening. She thanked the female guard who brought her breakfast of watered-down tea with bread to dunk and practiced effusive expressions of gratitude. After breakfast she asked permission to wash and she scrubbed her bra and underwear in a plastic washtub. It was important to put on clean underwear every day and to keep her remaining teeth clean. During the thirty minutes of *hava khori*, when they were shepherded outdoors, she recited silent lyrics to arias and folk songs, the Beatles and ABBA, Googoosh and Hayedeh, going through genres in an obsessive chronological order.

The guards grew fond of her and brought her milk like she was a stray cat, or extra helpings of yogurt, knowing most of her teeth had been knocked out, but she ate very little and asked instead for more soap, a comb, and paper to write letters.

For three months Zod did not know where she was. Insane with worry, he spent day after day at police stations and hospitals begging for information but, other than confirming her return from England, they had no record of a Parvaneh Yadegar. Then one night, when he was warming rice and chicken for Mehrdad and Noor, he heard Naneh Goli yelp and shoo the children upstairs. A familiar voice came from the salon and he ran towards it with a mad, joyful flutter in his chest. Pari was on television admitting to being a liaison between political dissidents and Western contacts. Extremely thin and pale, her black hair streaked with gray, she sat with a dull look in her eyes, which frequently slid away from the camera, lisping through a list of alleged crimes. She was one of many who had been coerced into these taped confessions that the government staged as a warning to would-be activists.

Blinded with tears of rage and relief, Zod didn't know how he drove to Evin Prison that night. He leaped into the darkness and howled, howled like a wounded dog, hurled himself against its concrete walls, but he wasn't a lone wolf. The guards were used to mothers and fathers, husbands and wives scratching their fingernails raw at the gates. At dawn they found Zod on his knees with his forehead to the pavement, thought he was praying and took pity. He was given a number and allowed to make a phone call.

"Did you get my letters?" Pari cried upon hearing his voice, raspy from hollering all night.

"No, what letters, *janam* (my life)?" he croaked, "For three months I haven't had any idea where you were."

"Those bastards," she screamed. "Those filthy bastards!" shrieking louder and louder. Then, both were crying so hard they couldn't speak and the phone was yanked away. Her confinement may have ended after the confession if only she had kept her mouth shut.

Noor never wore her new white mittens and Mehrdad never heard a song from *Remain in Light*. Naneh Goli tore out her hair and Mrs. Parsa shivered through that winter and the next until she died of pneumonia. Nina couldn't remember what an umbrella was for. And Zod, he would've noosed himself with that tie. The taxi driver, now a local hero, was invited to kick the chair from under Pari's feet at her hanging.

# Thirteen

How to live after this? Zod spent most of his time wondering why Pari didn't call to tell him she was arriving a day earlier. How was it that she had changed her flight? What words were exchanged in the taxi? He wished he could claw his way back to the early hours of that February morning before his wife had left London. Or even before, to when the idea to surprise her family first crossed Pari's mind, and he'd scratch it away. Days, weeks, years later, when he opened their closet to take a shirt off a hanger and saw her small pumps on the shoe tree, or walked past the gazebo where she had sung or the piano his father had bought for their wedding—always silent now—he still wondered what it was that had changed her mind.

Mehrdad had stopped speaking altogether, but fifteen-year-old Noor kept asking about her mother. Zod would tell her about the time Pari decided to teach him how to swim. How they couldn't stop laughing and he swallowed half the water in the sea. How Pari liked to eat oranges sprinkled with salt. How carefully she gathered grains of rice on her fork. How she loved white carnations. Zod told it all like a folktale, like Noor was six years old. But Noor still tugged at his sleeve impatiently, insisting that he tell her why her mother vanished.

"Did you try to find her?"

"Yes."

"Is she really dead?"

"Yes."

"Did you see her dead with your own eyes?"

"No."

"Then how can you be sure?"

For months Zod went to Evin every day and stood outside, crazed, begging, flailing, afraid of going home to face his children. The guards threatened to lock him up but he went back and he went back until one day they took him inside and showed him her picture, and the worst thing was that she looked so afraid. They told him she died instantly, painlessly, her small neck snapped, they told him she'd hanged herself. But Zod knew his Pari would never do that, his Pari wouldn't leave them, she would try to stay alive. He also knew it wasn't painless. He would always know how much she had suffered. *Parijoon, Parisa, Parinaz, Pariroo, Parishan, where was I when they did this to you?*

Zod looked for exhaustion in the kitchen. Nina sat at one end in a chair that was too big for her, so he eased a cushion behind her back while she went on with the impeccable organization of buttons. Their roles had reversed—now she was the one who sat in a corner while he chopped ingredients and filled enormous tubs with cubed vegetables and marinated meats to keep himself from going insane. Suddenly Nina would look up misty-eyed and Zod knew she had drifted back in time, sinking into the first, or fifth, or third decade of her life, burying Davoud again, buttons forgotten in the cake tin, weeping and muttering softly—"Whywhywhy?"—probing through the remains of her memory.

Zod would make a second cup of tea and sit across from her to feed her small bites of cake until an awareness leapt into those blue eyes and she called his name in a happy shout, holding out her arms to fold him inside.

THE CAFÉ WAS CLOSED for weeks, with a black shroud draped over the door, the gate locked, but people kept coming. They left rows and rows of wreaths and letters and crates of oranges and pears and toys for the children, as if they were still toddlers. Naneh Goli instructed Hedi to bring everything inside, then wash the sidewalk and sweep the dead flowers away. What fresh flowers remained, she put in half a dozen galvanized buckets and pinned moist white carnations on the waiters' lapels. Then she opened the door just a fraction and started frying onions for pomegranate soup—bitter, sweet, sour, this is how it would be. Thereafter, Café Leila stayed open. Zod couldn't call it living—but at least it was an existence.

Noise. Laughter. Blue sky. These things are what surprised Zod every time he borrowed Hedi's bicycle to fetch Noor from school. Not that she needed to be picked up, she had been walking home from school with her friends for two years now, but Zod waited outside the schoolyard to follow them home to safety. Rumors were rampant of random arrests and lashings by chastity squads targeting women for improper observance of the hejab, such as loose headscarves, makeup, nail polish, and sandals. Terrifying stories circulated of irrational rage on the streets, of vigilantes attacking young women for alleged provocative behavior.

*Anything can happen*, Zod thought, *so I best be there to collect her.* He was never empty-handed—stopping to buy cream puffs or fruit   and Noor would act peeved at first and complain that he was being overprotective, but brightened once the snacks were dispensed. As a concession, he pedaled a good distance behind to let the girls giggle freely as they walked. He looked at the girls' heavy black cloaks, a red thermos or the tip of a white sneaker, the only color in their habit, and wished he could run and get them each a bouquet of pink and yellow tulips. Who would want to be a child in this country? It was too hard. Funereal.

Home at last, her curly hair loose, Noor's youthful preoccupations were a happy distraction for everyone. She stayed close to her grandmother, coaxing and caressing Nina when she grew agitated. The old woman would hold a tight fist to her chest and whimper, "Remind me again of your name, dear?" When sunlight poured in, she wheeled Nina into a square of light to French braid her snowy hair and the years fell away, giving this grandmother the unexpected look of a young girl with flowers tucked behind her ears. To-gether they spooned jam straight from the jar into their mouths, hiding from Naneh Goli's disapproving glare.

Mehrdad lost his puppy fat and grew tall, seventeen years old, broad-shouldered and good-looking, with chestnut hair and eyes that changed from hazel to emerald green when he wore light-colored shirts. He mostly ignored Noor, simply lost interest, and when he did acknowledge her it was to mock her jungle hair or new wire-rimmed eyeglasses, calling her *koor* (blind) if she bumped into him in the hallway, or *bisavad* (illiterate) if she went to him for help with homework. The worst offense was her inadvertent humming of Pari's songs—he threatened to yank her tongue right out of her mouth. He swerved from hostility to tears without warning, his face cloud-ing over each time he carried his grief outside the walls and into the streets, trying hard to compose himself, so that from a distance he would not seem anguished but for the Adam's apple bobbing up and down as he struggled to swallow a sob at the mere sight of a mangy alley cat. He withdrew from his friends and people got used to his crossing to the other side of the street to avoid greeting them.

No one could understand the care with which he preserved a handker-chief, a small white square with his initials *M.Y.* embroidered in the corner. This scrap of cotton kept alive the memory of a birthday long ago when he woke up and heard Pari humming a tune while the smell of cardamom, warm and sweet, wafted upstairs to his bedroom. He had felt so happy and looked forward to breakfast. He got up and washed his face, combed his hair, put on a clean shirt and trousers, then went downstairs in house slippers. There was a vase of pink and white carnations on the breakfast table and a brown paper package wrapped with a red satin ribbon at his place. His family sat waiting for him. Pari buttered a slice of bread, slathered it with sour cherry jam, and put it on his plate. They wished him happy birthday and he circled the table to kiss each of them on both cheeks, then sat down to open Pari's handmade gift of six white cotton handkerchiefs with a light blue border, monogrammed and starched. Just a year ago he was playing war with swords and slingshots and now he was carrying a handkerchief. Few knew of his dreams or longings, but on that morning long ago, Pari was aware of the man behind the boy. "You never know when it might be useful," she said. He didn't know then how often he would need it to wipe his eyes.

By the time he turned eighteen, Mehrdad was ill at ease among his peers and resented the indignity of accepting pocket money from Zod. Mandatory military service loomed and the upside was the pain from physical exertion, the garrison training, the hours of misery, the marching, endless marching under the hot sun. *The army will make my hands rough and brown*, he thought. *The army will make me a man.* Up and down he paced, impatiently scowling at his reflection in the mirror above the dresser. *Do something with yourself, you pansy! All you do is drink tea and wander aimlessly around here getting kissed and petted and washed by your nanny and your senile grandmother who cries over you and thinks you're her dead son.*

With the ongoing war between Iran and Iraq, Zod would die before letting Mehrdad fulfill his military service, but he was also aware of the rage stirring just beneath his son's hard exterior—a desperate warning and he was quietly making arrangements to send both his children abroad, deciding without telling them. Just because *he* had always been here didn't mean *they* had to stay. No longer would they face the mother-shaped hole of Pari's absence.

Like thousands of other disenchanted citizens, Zod resorted to bribery, pleading for visas, asking favors of faithful customers with connections, growing a bushy beard, peppering his speech with Muslim piety to acquire passports, soliciting Morad in Los Angeles to help with college enrollment in America.

At first Morad tried to discourage him with absurd warnings: *In America they will lose their manners*, and so on. Zod, returning briefly to the elements of childhood, listened earnestly, just as he had when Morad had fabricated stories of the glutton lurking in the cellar eating pickled penis, or broken glass traveling through the blood stream to puncture your heart, or cockroaches swimming in Coca-Cola bottles.

Oblivious to Morad's vexed tone, he persisted. "Manners be damned! Don't do this for me, brother. My children are traumatized. Do this for your niece and nephew." Only then was he able to breathe.

He broke the news first to Mehrdad in a solemn man-to-man voice and watched him grow red with anger. Zod was too familiar with this misguided fury. Though nobody had told Mehrdad of the exact circumstances, he silently blamed his mother's senseless death on Zod for appearing blind to injustice. If he left, who would avenge her? It made him wild to think about it. He formed fists with his hands and cracked his finger joints, for he had no other means to express the torment of watching his father run the café, greet people, conduct business as usual, and make plans to evacuate him.

"I *won't* run away!" he shouted. But it could not be undone.

"One day this life will be quite distant and you will have no use for it, son."

Zod knew that his children thought he was a coward. He remembered the day the police came and told him he was no longer allowed to serve meals in the garden and music was prohibited under Islamic rule. Pari had started to question which page of the Koran forbade people from eating outside when Zod quickly bowed his head and promised to shut the patio and silence the musicians, then offered the police refreshments. Afterwards the couple argued loudly and he knew the children could hear. Until that day they had never heard Zod raise his voice, and now he had made their mother cry.

"I can't stand it," Pari said, "I can't stand it, it's unbearable, how you're afraid of them."

"Pari, dear, now be sensible, there are some things one simply cannot do, things that are not worth haggling over with idiots. It's useless."

"You bowed to them. You offered them tea. You are the idiot."

Pari stared out the window into the garden. Were these brutes offended by the sensuality of the garden itself, the spicy-sweet scent of its daphne shrubs, its lush flowers and strings of colored lanterns? She went to her bedroom and shut the door. Zod buttoned up his coat and went out. Not a word was spoken. Not a sound was made. That night the whole family went to bed hungry.

After that day, Zod and Pari's peaceful marriage was muted, as if they had to find a new way to talk, waiting their turn to speak in low, careful tones, the clink of their teacups filling the silence as if they had forgotten how to laugh or joke or sing like they used to. The light, crisp sound of Pari's high heels, once beautiful with the promise of her arrival, now signaled her leaving. *One, two, three, four*, the children counted her steps going away.

Then, a week before Noor's thirteenth birthday, she was doing homework when her mother came through the door carrying a bundle wrapped in brown paper, neatly tied with white string. She sat on Noor's bed and unwrapped the paper, revealing a bolt of smooth, turquoise fabric.

"I'm going to make you a lovely birthday dress," she said. "You've always been so fond of blue."

Zod came in and sat beside her. For a split second, from behind Noor's desk, it felt like her parents were the children, they were so little and lonely and she wished she could protect them. Her father's stone face melted, open and anxious again. "Your tea's getting cold," he said, and they went to the garden where he'd set the table with sandwiches and currant cake. Pari sat back in her chair, talking animatedly and fanning herself with a magazine, and the flush in her cheeks told Noor that warmth was restored, that they really could plan a birthday party. Quarrels and silences were new to their house— infrequent arguments had always ended in sudden forgiveness. They had never before been fretful of their mother's outbursts, and many nights after that argument, Noor lay in her narrow bed interpreting noises, listening for the cadence of her parents' voices drifting through the crack in her door, waiting for her mother's merry laughter and her father banging pots and pans—announcing the return of peace by cooking something delicious.

In telling Noor about her forced exile to America, Zod was sick with apprehension, in agony of losing his bright, shining daughter. For the next few days there was a great deal of arguing, stammering accusations, tears, and slamming doors, but Zod stood behind the closed bedroom doors to knock softly, to remind his children of the dinner trays that remained un- touched and were carried away and replaced with the next meal. He had never spoken sharply to them and he wouldn't now, when they needed him more than ever.

It pained him to spend these last few weeks with them like a sentry, in- stead of holding them, memorizing their features, imprinting accurate pic- tures of their beautiful eyebrows and mouths and the shape of their ears to memory, recording their voices on cassette tapes and cooking their favorite meals. When they were small he nicknamed them for their preferred dishes and from time to time he still called Noor, "*Nokhodchi*" (chickpea cookies) and Mehrdad, "*Koofteh Berenji*" (rice meatballs).

He wanted to tell them everything he knew about California, even if it was piecemeal and gathered from dubbed cop shows. Back and forth he paced the narrow hallway between their rooms, aware of every minute slipping away and so many precautions left unsaid. And what about all the things they would learn that he never knew, like ice-skating and bowling, as if these were skills that could only be acquired in America. He would soon go mad if their bedroom doors remained closed.

It felt like Mehrdad's quietness would last forever, but the day eventually came when he left his room and ventured downstairs with his unshaven shut-away face and found his father alone in the garden. He came from behind and put a hand on Zod's shoulder. "Baba," he said, startling Zod, who pulled his big boy to his chest, and they shook from the savage sobs that erupted between them.

Naneh Goli, too, was jolted awake early one morning when Noor pushed the door against the mattress wedged on the landing and stared reproachfully at the lump camped outside her bedroom. For a week Naneh Goli had stationed herself just outside like a sheep dog—*Golabcheh* (a nickname she had given Noor at birth, a hybrid of the Russian *golubchik*, meaning "dear one," acquired from Yanik, and her favorite scent *golab*, "rosewater"), *I shall remain here all night, so let's keep each other company*—buttering her up, telling stories through the keyhole about places she'd never been to, as if she were a world traveler.

Together Zod and Naneh Goli joined hands to shove Mehrdad and Noor from the nest, insisted that they fly, and stood at the threshold frantically waving good-bye, because to prolong it would have been unbearable. *Go now, before I lose my courage*, thought Zod. *Please go.*

# PART THREE

# Fourteen

Noor ruffled through her English-Persian dictionary. "Flimsy" was what Professor McCann had scribbled in the margin of her paper. She loved learning new words—ornaments to her rudimentary English—but wasn't sure if flimsy was a compliment. Did he mean delicate, or feeble? What were all those little red robins darting between the ruled lines? Last week, on a beautiful fall day, he had ushered his students outside to a grassy hill where they assembled in a loose circle. He wanted them to imagine one week alone in a place they knew nothing about and to write their first impressions. Noor hardly needed to make anything up. She was so green in terms of what she knew about California that it was a relief to have an assignment she could grasp. How bizarre, seeing her English professor cross-legged on the ground, his head tilted back to the sun. Here was Prof. McCann in a polo shirt and tousled hair, looking more like an errant schoolboy than a teacher. What made him different from her classmates, who were similarly dressed, sockless and equally at ease stretching their long legs, some even discarding sneakers to wiggle their toes? This casual open-air classroom was as much a part of her initiation to a culture unencumbered by decorum as any ice cream social in the dorm.

McCann had informed his students that when he was in his twenties he had been a teacher in the Peace Corps and taught children outdoors under thatched roofs in Cameroon. Noor was amazed that this was voluntary, not mandatory service. She had imagined Americans as being insular but instead found them to be restless dreamers, earnest and intent on shaping and changing an imperfect world, while she, at seventeen, didn't expect much, didn't think she had it in her to ever take on anything so ambitious.

After that day, she hung around the quad pretending to read, but really studying her peers, gathering bits of knowledge the other students let fall while gossiping, arguing, and flirting. She told herself not to gawk, but the novelty of it all, their clothes, the way they moved, their talk—well, she didn't want to miss something in the way of a useful lesson. Adorable in rumpled T-shirts and shorts, some girls chased Frisbees while others with perfect hair and wearing snug stonewashed jeans observed from the sidelines, a sexually charged playfulness between them that at times made Noor feel like a voyeur, but she remained unnoticed until the afternoon darkened and she doubled back to her dorm.

Noor shared a narrow room with Sue Sullivan. In the fall of 1984 they had arrived on campus within minutes of one another, Sue with her parents and two little brothers, each carrying a box labeled SULLIVAN/SHEETS, SULLIVAN/TOWELS, SULLIVAN/ALBUMS, and so on, while Noor heaved a lone hefty brown suitcase to the third floor. Smiling warmly, her roommate introduced herself as Sue-Sullivan-from-San-Diego and Noor thought it an exceptionally long name. At six feet and two inches, Sue dwarfed Noor. Later, cupping one of Noor's sneakers in her hands like it was a small wounded bird, she'd cried, "Look at your tiny feet, Nora! Gosh, only five and a half," showing genuine dismay at not being able to swap clothes.

Pointing to the bunk bed, Sue offered to sleep on the bottom and Noor watched as Mrs. Sullivan unpacked a box to unfurl a twin fitted sheet with rainbow stripes and a matching comforter. Immediately their drab room became cheerful and Noor was glad her plain white sheets would remain in the weak light of the top bunk. There was a three-drawer dresser for each girl and Sue quickly filled hers with balled-up socks and pastel underwear while Noor fit the entire contents of her suitcase into one drawer and hung her parka in their shared closet. She answered "Yes!" to every question until Sue's parents shrugged and gave up to resume the task of furnishing their daughter's room with bright pillows, posters, lamps, mugs, a stereo, and a small refrigerator. Delaying their departure as long as possible, the actual good-bye was swift—the brothers already outside throwing a football while Sue's father collected empty boxes and her mother pecked her daughter's cheek just once.

Noor missed her parents most at just that moment—how Pari would fuss with zippers and buttons on her daughter's coat, how she kissed her eyelids and "the little raisin" (a mole on her left cheek), how they used to stand every morning at the gate and wave good-bye until she disappeared around the corner only to run back to them for another farewell. And how she had returned to them in the afternoon to be embraced again and again. Oh, how they loved her.

Zod called her frequently, at a designated time, so she waited by the pay phone in the hallway, and each time she said, "Baba, I want to come home. Please let me come home!" He wished he could tear his liver out and feed it to the stray dogs. Powerless, what could he do but repeat every word of false comfort that had been said a thousand times already? White knuckles curled around the receiver, his nails bored into his palm. *Oh, what have I done?* he wondered.

Noor was not enamored with her independence. It was too vast, wide like the ocean. She preferred the safety of her room and especially her bed. The area just beneath the ceiling where she lay, warm, covered in the childhood quilt that Naneh Goli had folded around a little framed picture of her family, was home. She rolled onto her stomach and hugged the pillow to her face, fondled the stash of cookies and crackers saved from the cafeteria. Sleeplessly she counted the days since she left Iran, then the hours, then the minutes, reading Zod's letters and tracing the lines to take herself to that place of comfort between her mother and father, one holding her left hand, one her right, swinging Noor along the middle of the garden path—*one, two, three, up!*—and the thrill of kicking her heels in the air and landing softly before being lifted again. How old had she been? Three? Four? Six?

Nighttime was the worst of the worst. How she wished for a story. *Here, Noor, tonight I have one just for you.* Zod had modified Naneh Goli's fairy tales for his children and many nights they had fallen asleep to the sound of his voice narrating "The Emperor and the Mouse," "The Cobbler and the Elves," "Porcupine in a Pickle"—tame stories, told and retold, of underdogs in unfamiliar places that ended in friendly hospitality, reassuring Noor of a compassionate world. She grew up within these predictable stories just as she had grown up in a comfortable house where every corner was familiar. In writing her essay for Prof. McCann, she struggled with the pronouns—the *he*'s and *she*'s a tangled mess—but she tried to follow the arc of those bedtime tales.

> I was seventeen years old when I arrived in United States. I did not know much about America, except for what we see sometimes on television. My English tutor was British and he told me some things. He say now I will be free but she never go there before so how does she know? First week I spend with my uncle and aunt in Los Angeles. I never saw ocean before and so many gas stations. Unfortunately they taught I would miss the Persian

food so instead of taking me to the famous Mac Donald's, my aunt cook a lot of Iranian food and one time we went to the kebab house. I was surprised because everyone look like us and speak Farsi there and dress very nice, especially the ladies wear a lot of jewelry. My cousin was angry and made sour face and said to my uncle "Why these people wear so much perfume?" My uncle was mad and also he say "These people? Who do you think you are?" Marjan was very quiet. She bring also a book and no speak to nobody. I taught everyone smelled good, looked good also, but leetle bit sad. When lunch finished my aunt order some tea and baklava but Marjan walk to front door and take some red and white candy from a dish and put in her mouth. Maybe candy make her feel better because he looked back and made half smile. Then he come back and my aunt said "Why you always make a face?" Marjan said "Because I am sick of this place." I taught the kebab was a little dry but not so bad. I wish Marjan would teach me some English but always her room is closed. She is painful. I count five television in my uncle's house! In the kitchen my aunt watch while he cook her favorite show Donahue. She said I will learn a lot of English if I watch television. Already my first week in America I like to smell things here. I like the bed sheet and some soap my aunt put in my bathroom and very many delicious corn flakes and chips and all advertisement on television but already I miss my father very much.

One night Sue crept in long after Noor had turned out the light, bringing with her the scent of cigarettes and pizza. She grabbed her toiletries and tiptoed out to the bathroom in her fluffy slippers, leaving the door open to the music and conversation in the hallway. Eventually she shuffled back in to crawl under the rainbow comforter, quiet at last.

Aloft, Noor whispered, "Good night, Sue."

"Nora, you're awake?" Noor loved Sue's peppermint scent and the soft *a* she tagged onto her name.

"Yes. You smell very good, Sue."

"Oh thanks! It's this lotion my mom buys from Avon. You can totally use it any time."

Such close talk at the end of each day, brief as it was, made Noor happy. She frequently surveyed the items on Sue's dresser: her collection of scrunchies and hair ornaments, the scented creams and array of makeup, the bottle of Charlie perfume. The variety! It made her curious, sniffing tubes and bottles, wondering aloud whatever is to be done with this, trying not to disrupt Sue's arrangement. Sue was so kind, filling their room with warmth. Just before Noor fell off to sleep, she blurted, "Thank you very much, Sue," and at that moment she felt tied to Sue and pulled along into the next day and the day after that.

On Saturday mornings they served brunch at the cafeteria. This in-between meal was a revelation to Noor. It gave her even more opportunities to linger at the table and eavesdrop on conversations. Plus she discovered bacon—could not believe that she had lived this long without it—and piled the crisp porky strips next to her pancakes, another fresh discovery of syrupy spongy goodness.

"What is this?" she had asked Sue that first weekend as they snaked their way through a slow-moving line of drowsy students in pajama bottoms.

"Oh, Nora, blueberry pancakes!"

They slept in on weekends and woke up famished. Noor brushed her teeth and pulled on jeans (unthinkable to go outside in sleepwear) before racing into the cool morning air heavy with the scent of griddle smoke. Through the tall windows the sun cast a soft glow onto the long tables dotted with salt and pepper shakers. What promise! Coffee. Yes! With cream and sugar. Fork. Knife. Napkin. Good morning, Miss Eleanor. Five pancakes, please. Bacon? Yes! Two butter balls. Warm maple syrup. Yes! Yes to everything. Yes to brunch. Yes to class outside. Yes to being alone in a crowd. If only that breezy morning feeling, which made it seem possible that she could do this after all, would last. But in the harsh light of noon the caffeine-induced courage would fade and she lost her grip on the flimsy reins.

WHEN HER FATHER TOLD her that she would be going to Oakland, Noor had no idea where Oakland was, so he opened the atlas. Still, what did Noor know of this Mills College or the people who lived there? Did they look like Mrs. Wells, the English tutor her father had hired last year? Noor spent most of the hours on the flight to America staring out into the clouds, wondering about this faraway place and saving the roll from her dinner tray in case she didn't like the food there.

Uncle Morad met Noor and Mehrdad at the Los Angeles airport. He held out a stiff arm to shake hands with Mehrdad and patted Noor on the head. Their relatives normally smothered them in their embrace, so they were confused by his lack of affection. Mehrdad and Noor slid across the soft leather seat of their uncle's Mercedes-Benz as they sped down a boulevard lined with palm trees. Noor could not take her eyes off the blue band of the Pacific to their left.

Uncle Morad lived in Beverly Hills, an affluent area where many Persians resided. His home was a white villa with pink bougainvillea creeping up to a terrace that overlooked the city. He said at night it looked like a carpet of lights below. They had met his wife, Aunt Farah, years ago when she came to Iran to visit her parents. She had brought Noor a Malibu Barbie in a red swimsuit with matching sunglasses and a small terry towel. Noor would take it out of the box, play with it for a few minutes, and return it to its package. It was still displayed on a bookcase in her room. Aunt Farah smelled of lilacs when she kissed their cheeks. Her daughter Marjan came out of her room to say hello, then went back to her room and closed the door.

Aunt Farah moved about Noor and Mehrdad protectively, lightly pushing Morad aside if he started to lecture about Zod's unwillingness to sell the café and leave Iran for good. Mehrdad stammered under his uncle's close scrutiny and Noor cringed when he glared at them through his narrow eyes. Later, they heard their aunt and uncle arguing in their bedroom.

"You will never understand what it is to lose your mother when you are young, to know that never again will she hold you in her arms. It is not right to talk about their father, it is not right for you to question his ways."

"Ach!" said Uncle Morad in disgust. "Did my brother send me his children to nurse?"

"Of course not!" Aunt Farah protested gently. "But please, for once put aside whatever grudges you hold. That's all over now. They are your family for God's sake!"

"Humph."

After breakfast the next morning, Aunt Farah insisted on taking a photo of Noor and Mehrdad with their uncle. So they stood next to him on the patio with Los Angeles framed in bougainvillea, and Aunt Farah brought a chair for Morad and asked Noor and Mehrdad to stand a little closer.

"Yes, now I can see all of you." She said she was going to print an extra copy for their father, "So he can carry a picture of you three together like that."

It was her way of letting Zod know they were okay, reassuring him that his brother would take care of his children. Uncle Morad rolled his massive shoulders up and down the way wrestlers do to loosen up and cracked his knuckles before stiffening in his chair for the portrait. Weeks later, Zod wrote in a letter how surprised he was by his little brother's gray hair. "I always imagine Morad as a boy crouching behind a bush, waiting to ambush me. Who is this distinguished old man sitting in a chair?"

# Fifteen

———✺———

I n the days before his niece and nephew's arrival, Dr. Morad
Yadegar had a bitter taste in his mouth he could not get rid of.
He always paid close attention to dental hygiene, having his teeth
cleaned every three months instead of the usual six, and took pleasure in
hearing the hygienist's praise of his immaculate mouth. He gargled powerful
mouthwash and inspected his tongue frequently in the bathroom mirror.

A big, fastidious man, Morad the bruiser was a surprisingly gentle doctor,
performing with cool precision the delicate task of anesthesiology. He was
not a particularly kind nor considerate husband (his needs and comfort
came first, since he was the provider and felt that sharing a bed and bath
was sufficient sacrifice). Sleeping in dove gray silk pajamas from Neiman
Marcus, of which there were a dozen in the dresser, he laced his fingers
across his abdomen and did not wish to be touched when falling asleep. His

toothbrush and toothpaste were kept in a separate medicine chest, as were all his toiletries.

"I do not wish to smell like a woman," he explained, insisting that Farah take a hot shower before sex on Friday nights. If she reached for him on a Monday or Tuesday, he would turn to the wall.

Farah countered this lack of warmth with tenderness. If they had a few friends, if they were invited to an occasional party or hosted a dinner, it was because of her efforts. On the rare occasion that they had company, Morad insisted that Farah address him as "Doktor," thus encouraging the guests to do the same. He did not allow her to serve salted pistachios or any noise-making hors d'oeuvres, unable to bear the human conveyor splitting the shells, the kernels traveling to munching molars while another nut was already being cracked between the right and left thumb.

He endured these meals grudgingly, questioning her motives, the purchase of filet mignon or champagne for "people who don't know a filet from a donkey's rump" and wrinkling his nose at her beautiful roast, with a sneer that called to mind his grandmother, Elena. How well Morad carried these ancestral features—the narrowing of his eyes as though he needed glasses and the dismissive smirk were family heirlooms that couldn't be hidden in the back of a closet like furs but were imprinted on his face and passed along to his young daughter.

When she was a girl in Iran, the youngest and plainest of four daughters, Farah allowed herself to dream of marrying a strong, handsome man like Omar Sharif and living in a home very similar to the one where she was growing up. In these dreams her husband came through the door every evening and swept her into a passionate embrace. And there were children, too. Four or five of them, well-mannered and scrubbed clean. Morad had fit that picture, more or less, but after Marjan was born he announced that he would have a vasectomy and did not want any more children. "You have a nice healthy girl. Why should we take a chance of having an imperfect child?" When she touched his sleeve to plea, he withdrew. Brokenhearted,

Farah went along to get along. It was as if she truly believed that underneath this hard shell of a man, there was a bruised little boy who missed his big brother and needed her unconditional love.

Conversation being a task for Morad, he had given Farah an abbreviated version of the family history and she had mostly believed it, until a trip to Iran unveiled a mild-mannered brother-in-law and a gentle Pari who welcomed her like a sister. Only in movies had she seen a man gaze so lovingly at a woman. Zod's attention to Pari, his *vigil*, really, was tireless. He anticipated his wife's thirst, chill, hunger, fatigue, without fawning, but that was just his way, he did the same for his customers as if he was there solely to serve. Pari would say he was a mind reader because Zod knew before *you* knew that you had to lie down, that you preferred your peach peeled and cucumbers salted. It crippled him sometimes, carrying all this information, and Pari would stir warm milk with honey, pluck the wrinkly skin off its surface, and carry it to the easy chair where Zod waited for her to rub his temples. To their sister-in-law they seemed more like friends than husband and wife when they exchanged inside jokes and comic imitations of customers. Their lightheartedness filled her with longing.

Farah learned just from watching daytime talk shows that people went to psychiatrists for wounds far less severe than her husband's, but it was unthinkable to suggest as much to Morad, who took great pride in his sanity versus his family's madness. During twenty years of marriage, their worst argument had been over Morad's refusal to attend his father's funeral in Iran. In response to Farah's pleas, he refused to speak to her for months—an interpersonal cold war dear to Iranians called *ghaar*, wherein the sole strategy is to break communication for an indefinite period of time over a minor offense or simply to avoid confrontation. It is at once a verb, an adjective, and a noun: Zod and Pari rarely *ghaared* with each other; North Korea is *ghaar* with America; the dentist's *ghaar* with her hygienist meant she had to do the cleanings herself. Farah's own aunt had been *ghaar* with her mother over a borrowed tablecloth returned with a tea stain, which lasted six years until Farah's mother died and the person who shed the loudest tears was the pigheaded auntie.

Years ago Morad severed himself from his family and hurtled himself across the world without fanfare and, unlike many in exile, never dreamed of a grand homecoming or harbored fantasies of a return. It sickened him that Iranians cherished their past and their intangible properties. Whenever fellow countrymen pined for home—*Ah, but give me anything that resembles the majestic peak of Mount Damavand! Oh, such happy summers on the Caspian shore!*—a blue vein rippled across his wide forehead and he'd recall the repelling sight of his brother going down on hands and knees to kiss the earth when he came back from France as if the dusty courtyard of Café Leila was Shangri-la and he had escaped a labor camp.

Morad had no patience for these pampered men in pastel polo necks who left Iran for good after the revolution and had since grown richer but refused to shut up, reminiscing and driveling on like they had lost a toy. With utter revulsion, he scolded them. "I suppose the Sierras and the Pacific coast are not good enough for the Persian Polo Club, hmm?" Pleased with the facetious label he coined—*polo* shirts and *polo* (rice) eaters—"You prefer your beaches piled with trash?"

Chastened, they learned to curb their nostalgia in his presence. In his brutal boyhood Morad would have beaten some sense into them, but fortunately he found an outlet in American football. If it weren't for the NFL warriors acting out his violent impulses, he may have unleashed the quick fury of a boxer on these hapless immigrants. Morad devoted entire Sunday afternoons to watching the games alone in the den. He lived for the flagrant violence, the satisfying slow-motion replay of it, because it wasn't a movie with stuntmen, but real men manifesting his notions of manhood. Farah tiptoed in only to bring a meal tray he barely acknowledged, and left just as quietly.

For Marjan's sake, a faithful Farah settled for this imperfect version of her childhood dream and never complained, reasoning that people settled for far less all the time; nevertheless, her eyes brimmed with sorrow.

While a cold anger swelled in Morad's belly and a taste of metal lingered in his mouth, Farah awaited Mehrdad and Noor's arrival with open delight. She aired the guest rooms and refreshed the bathrooms with scented soaps and green apple shampoos. Multiple trips to the grocery store had filled the refrigerator with gallons of whole milk (otherwise never permitted), fruit yogurts, sugared cereals, cookies, potato chips, and candy (also forbidden), the likes of which had never been seen in this pantry. Doktor imposed a nonfat diet on the household—his breakfast had been the same for as long as they had been married: two pieces of dry wheat toast cut into tidy little squares and half a grapefruit sectioned with great precision and eaten in silence, but he still expected a staple of Persian rice and stew every night.

Even Marjan emerged from her room to inspect the cabinets and sighed a weary "Finally, some real food," then shuffled back to her den with a bag of Doritos. Farah followed with a bowl of sour cream and onion dip but her daughter took a sniff and curled her lip. It didn't matter, for even this familiar rebuff was endearing. At last her home would feel less barren. At last she could draw from the deep, dammed reservoir of love inside her to coddle these motherless children, because to Farah, even at eighteen or nineteen, they were babies, and for a whole week (the maximum time Morad allowed for their stay) she would pamper them with Iranian affection and American snacks.

Marjan showed little curiosity about her cousins. Adolescence had been cruel—coating her legs and forearms with thick black hair, knitting her eyebrows into a trellis, shadowing her upper lip with dark fur. In the bathroom adjacent to her bedroom, she pinched the pimples that peppered her forehead, repulsed and pleased by the sudden gush of puss that no amount of cleansing creams could diminish. Who, she wondered, had invaded her body? Who was this hairy, pockmarked creature in the mirror greeting her every morning with a fresh new blemish? If only she was someone else, like Tracy Banks or Ashley Avery with pale skin and fine golden hair on their arms. If only she could strip the jungle from her armpits. If only her parents were normal.

Farah, anxious for Marjan to fit in with the freshman class, had forced her to try out for the swim team. *Of all things*, Marjan thought. She could barely swim a lap without gasping and to be partially naked in front of the entire school was a deranged idea. Marjan had loved soccer in elementary school. Like her father, she was a strong, fearless player, scoring goal after goal for her AYSO team and reveling in their victories. Farah and Morad went to the games with folding chairs and a thermos of tea and sectioned oranges. It was the only time she'd seen her father happy, showing her genuine affection with the nickname *Tank*. "Mow them down, Tank!" he'd shout from the sidelines, more than once inviting the referee to admonish him, oblivious to the long looks from other parents.

Then in the fall of seventh grade, Marjan announced she would no longer play soccer and Morad stormed out in a huff like it was a personal offense against him, and the only good thing that came of it was that he no longer called her by that unfortunate nickname. That ghaar lasted over a month.

"Swimming is the best exercise," chirped Farah, walking into her room with bright Speedo suits.

"Not if you're a gorilla," cried Marjan.

"Who is gorilla? You are beautiful and this will look so pretty on you, dear heart." Farah finally furnished her with pink disposable razors, warning, "You are soft as sheep now. If you shave the arms, you *will* see a real gorilla . . . and don't you dare touch your virginia!"

Sheared as best she could, Marjan went to the first practice—it was also the last, for she spent the rest of the season hiding out in the library and running to wet her hair and suit a few minutes before Farah picked her up. It wasn't so much the swimming, but the showering and the locker room exhibition that stunned her. Nude in full view, teammates gossiped and shampooed leisurely and no doubt she would've eventually gotten used to that, but it was the sight of Sheila Schaefer shaving her vagina that had distressed her. Why on earth would anyone do that, she wondered, and would it grow back, like her mother said, not like a lamb, but in coarse black bristles like her father's five o'clock shadow? It was appalling to leave that delicate seam bare.

Of course, the scene was too alarming to discuss with her mother, and for all she knew, her handful of friends did the same, so Marjan spent most of her adolescence alone, rejecting Farah's pleas to have slumber parties. Even the arrival of cousins did not alter her sense of alienation—she was just relieved for the distraction they provided her mother.

In the weeks prior to Noor and Mehrdad's arrival, Farah maintained an exhausting cheerfulness in front of Marjan and Morad, as if to convey a sense of hospitality she knew they lacked. It was hard for them to pass through doors in the house without being startled by her sudden gleeful appearance. Morad staged a frozen smile and made awkward lurching motions to get past her, while Marjan resisted the impulse to scream. The only benefit of these newcomers was the appearance of Pop-Tarts (a coveted snack she'd seen kids munching on the school bus).

They only stayed for a week but it felt like an occupation, forcing Marjan to retreat even further. Given the grace of it—the sudden appearance of two cousins in her life, it was a missed opportunity for kindness, for rescue and camaraderie. If she had invited Noor to her room, Marjan would have discovered a girl equally estranged and riven by doubt, but she quickly decided that Noor was weird like her parents, and that they had nothing in common but a last name. And Mehrdad being shockingly handsome made Marjan ever more fretful about her appearance.

Farah gave it her best—a wholehearted welcome she hoped was contagious. *Oh, if you only knew how much you need one another*, she thought, knocking softly on the closed bedroom doors to invite the children down to breakfast.

THE FIRST CARE PACKAGE to arrive for Noor at Mills College was from Farah. She found a slip in her mailbox and collected a large box from the mailroom filled with a careful selection of things Farah guessed her niece may be homesick for: fruit leather and dried plums from the Persian market, homemade sour cherry jam, but also, instant coffee, Pop-Tarts, M&M's, tampons, Juicy Fruit gum, soap, shampoo, and deodorant tucked in between.

What a scent filled the room when she ripped off the lid—at once familiar and exotic. She had never used tampons before, but had noticed the pink applicators in the bathroom bin and wondered what they were for. Even after reading the instructions carefully, it took multiple tries and hot tears before she succeeded, overcome with an urgent need to call Pari with news of this wonderful invention. Ah, to wear underwear without that nasty thick wad between her legs, wondering, always wondering, if it would saturate when she was sitting on the bus or in a classroom, blood seeping through, leaving an unmistakable stain when she stood up, waiting for everyone to leave before making a lateral exit. At last she felt, oh, what was the word she was looking for? Clean? No . . . fresh.

There was a fragrance to everything here and Noor could not help but sniff her way to belonging. It all started with the morning shower—a ritual so sacred in her dorm that it seemed the obvious place to start. After all, these were the cleanest human beings she had ever seen. At home, a luxurious evening bath every other day or so had been sufficient, but to emerge smelling *fresh*, she must lather daily and apply lotion liberally. She must also drink coffee, chew gum, and carry flavored lip balm. Gone were the organic scents of home, the rosewater, the wood-burning stove, the pile of rotting leaves in the yard, jasmine, hyacinth, incense, ripe melons, Zod's tobacco. America was the boy who wears too much cologne and Noor had a mad crush on him.

Thanks to Aunt Farah, a clear path appeared and Noor marched its scented trail. Throughout her college years the packages arrived at regular intervals, providing the essential ingredients to naturalization.

NOOR AND MEHRDAD SPENT most of their school holidays at their uncle's house. They watched their classmates transform in anticipation of these breaks, tingling with the excitement of slipping home as soon as the last final exam was taken, while Noor and Mehrdad did not know what to expect or what to do in the long idle days that stretched before them.

Dispatched by Farah to fetch Noor for Thanksgiving dinner, Mehrdad was driving down Highway 1 in his brand-new Firebird, annoyed with Noor's frequent wails of "Aaaagh!" Nauseated, his sister lay on the backseat of the car, resting her head on his denim jacket.

Mehrdad's square shoulders rose above the seat and Noor observed his profile when he fiddled with the radio dial. He had arrived in Oakland two days earlier with Reza, a friend from school, and Noor hardly recognized him with his long hair and mustache. But when he took his sunglasses off, she knew those autumn brown eyes and he looked happy to see her. Noor had invited Nassim and the four of them went to the movies and suddenly Mehrdad wasn't so serious . . . her brother was funny! When did this happen? He was cracking jokes, imitating Uncle Morad's menacing voice until Noor almost choked on her popcorn and begged him to stop.

"Let me know if I have to pull over," Mehrdad said. "Please don't throw up in my car!"

Neither of them was in a hurry to get to Uncle Morad's, so Noor asked him to stop the car and they climbed out to stand on a crest of a grass-covered cliff overlooking the sparkling blue Pacific. A cold wind was pushing them back, but it felt good and Noor took a few deep breaths. It was nice standing so close to her brother and following his gaze below to where tiny black dots floated on the waves. Surfers. They so easily fit into this California landscape that was open and wild and that was slowly becoming hers.

*And my brother, too*, she thought, *though he can be cruel, poke fun at me, know just what to say to hurt my feelings, he will always be mine.*

"Feeling better?"

"No."

"Wanna stop at McDonald's?"

For some reason this was the funniest thing Noor had ever heard and they both burst out laughing.

# Sixteen

The snow had stopped by the time Zod woke up. He eased down the stairs, avoiding the creaky second and fourth step so as not to wake Naneh Goli, and walked outside into the unmarked snow in his house slippers. Tehran is never prettier than when she's draped in snow and he just had to see it, to look back at his tracks and the tulip prints of a small bird, to know its depth.

He picked up a handful of powdery snow and washed his face. Ah, the close freshness of it! Soft and white everywhere, it glittered against the dark tree trunks, charging his little yard with such brightness it was hard to believe anything could sleep in the winter. His thoughts turned to his children then. How they would hoot and hop to see this, as if he had forgotten that they no longer slept upstairs in the bedrooms that faced the snowy rooftops. But there was not a soul and not a cry.

He began to wipe the front window with his bare hands to have a clear view of the garden from the kitchen table, and when he brushed the flakes away there was Naneh Goli looking out at him with a big grin, a thick knitted cap pulled over her head and two or three scarves wound around her neck. She was wriggling into an old coat to join him. Zod smiled back and motioned her to stay put. He was growing cold but he did not want company interrupting the stillness just yet.

Increasingly, Naneh Goli kept a close eye on him for any signs of gloom. A few months before, he had taken Nina her breakfast tray and found her dead. She had fallen out of bed and hit her head on the nightstand. So Naneh Goli was relieved now to see him smile, just as she was when he brushed his teeth and changed his underwear, though he no longer shaved as often—bearing his grief with dignity. It was order that held them so. They continued to cook and clean as if their lives depended on it. Morning and night, they built a fire, they set the tables and polished the silver—all to close the gaps that might let sorrow creep in.

Back inside at the kitchen table, they allowed themselves a long interval to sip tea and gaze out the window while two eggs bubbled in a pot on the stove. They sat like a tableau inside a snow globe, enclosed in their quiet world until lunch preparations shook them up. After breakfast Zod swept the ashes from the grill and spread them near the entrance so customers wouldn't slip on the ice. He soaked prunes and took out meaty shanks to roast with onions for plum soup. He shaped chickpea patties, strained yogurt, and stirred quince custard.

The snow cheered Zod and brought a renewed friendliness as he sat down with the mustache-and-Marlboro regulars to play a few rounds of backgammon. All but one lived alone. Each had sent his family abroad and lived a solitary life except for these moments of fraternity when they leaned over the board to slide the cream and black discs across the inlaid wood. They wore their loneliness with characteristic Persian humor and self-deprecation, referring to the sorry state of bachelorhood and bald-headedness, cracking jokes about habitually unfaithful Rashti women (a standing shtick among Iranians), and the prohibitive nature of an Islamic Republic that made sex taboo. This subject alone provided good pantomime—the rapid raising and lowering of their thick eyebrows or two hands crossed over the groin.

"Every night my wife says she is closed for business," complained Abbas, whose family was intact. "She feels the ayatollah's eyes looking down on her!"

Zod listened but wouldn't partake in their saucy banter, now or ever; he didn't like obscenity, but knew they had suffered and this dice game is all that remained. In a better world they would have talked about their children, graduations and weddings, wives who waited to eat supper with them, in-laws who visited too often, grandparents, brothers and sisters, aunts and uncles. But instead all they had were splintered limbs scattered across the globe; an exodus so vast and irreparable that each man was unmoored and every letter brought news of a relative adrift.

When Zod received a letter from Noor, his heart welled and it was all he could do to walk, not run, to the sitting room, tear it open, and gulp it down. Then he would tuck it in his breast pocket and carry it around the rest of the day with a private smile until he found a moment to reply. His letters to her opened with vivid descriptions of the place where he sat with pen and paper, to give himself and Noor the illusion that they were there together—at the kitchen table, on a stone bench under the almond tree, in the café during the lull between lunch and dinner.

He could not remember when Noor first requested a recipe, but he stuffed each envelope with loose instructions for making the dishes of her youth, trusting her to improvise for ingredients that were difficult to find, and Noor would respond, eagerly reporting each time she came across fruits or spices—blood oranges, dates, persimmons, saffron, sumac—like long-lost relatives she had never expected to see again. This was before pomegranates became the darling of consumers, and chefs squirted yellow spirals of saffron on every plate.

Whenever there was some break in correspondence, due to the mess of the Iran–Iraq war, Zod moped. Twice a week he would walk his letters to the post office, calling to Naneh Goli, "I'm going to the post office!" as if he had somewhere else to go, then return to wait impatiently for the mail. Drafting one letter after another kept him busy—never in his life had he been such a devoted correspondent.

Zod reckoned daughters wrote letters, sons didn't, and that was all right because Noor's letters, lush with details, included news of her brother. Zod learned that his son was a spendthrift and his daughter was frugal, that Mehrdad had a sports car and Noor didn't have her license, that one worked in a record store and the other in the college cafeteria (*so you don't have to pay for the meal plan, Baba*). *Bless you, my dear*, he wrote, *but please resign from this job immediately and concentrate on your studies!* He had not sent her across the planet to become a sandwich maker.

Zod tried to forget about the snapshot taken by Farah of his children on the white terrace with their uncle seated smugly between them. Their anxious gaze had not reassured him. A rapid inventory of the setting—the ornate patio chair, the pink backdrop of bougainvillea, Morad's sledgehammer hands crossed on his lap—was unsettling. Age had not softened his brother's features, if anything he looked more petulant, like he had a sour plum lodged in his cheek. Twice he took a razor blade to carve out Morad's face from the photo, something that furious devil had so often done to deface family pictures. Finally the picture was shoved in a drawer.

It eluded Zod how Farah endured his brother, though he was overcome with gratitude for her kindness towards his children. Noor wrote of how Farah invited Mehrdad, who also lived in Los Angeles, for Sunday night dinners and frequently sent Noor special parcels of chocolates and toiletries. Recalling his own brief stay away from home, he understood the comfort of food and a good smelling bar of soap. It pleased Zod that Noor could write of this heretofore unknown side of his family. Yet how did Mehrdad sit across from the furrowed face of his cantankerous uncle every Sunday?

If he could only see how his son came through the doors of that household like a song, that he brought bouquets of narcissus for Farah and mixed
tapes of Dire Straits and Tears for Fears for Marjan, that he'd lured Morad
to backgammon by claiming that he wasn't a good player, thus leaving the
door open for Morad to counsel him, drop by stingy drop, then crushing
him in swift victory. Not surprisingly, Doktor declared that he'd been easy
on his nephew, so as not to discourage him. Nevertheless, they played five
rounds every Sunday after dinner and if Zod had walked in, he would've
found them almost cordial, with plates of melon balanced daintily on their
knees. Patiently, Mehrdad thwarted his uncle's malevolence with mirth and
even developed a curious liking for him, going so far as calling Morad *"Amoo
jan,"* a familiar and endearing term for uncle that Farah could hardly believe
was permitted. *Poor brother*, thought Zod, *that you can't see what a gift I've
sent you.*

# Seventeen

In the fall of 1988 Noor and her best friend, Nassim, rented an apartment in San Francisco facing a café where the scent of roasting coffee and baking bread drifted into their bedrooms every morning. Their building was a ruin of a place—the over-painted window frames wouldn't close, a threadbare tawny carpet and stained linoleum covered the floors, and on sunny days, termites swarmed the windowsills—but nothing could have diminished the wonder of their first apartment and being on their own.

They loved the quaint Cow Hollow neighborhood, they loved furnishing their space with mismatched chairs and a round table, a television and lamps and an antique ironing board that doubled as a bookshelf. At Macy's they bought bright flannel sheets and thick towels, a shower curtain with a pattern of yellow ducks, pretty mugs and cereal bowls. Just eating Raisin

Bran from those blue-and-white bowls, sinking into her bed, ironing blouses in her underwear and bra brought Noor enormous joy.

In the evenings the girls would return from work, uncork a bottle, and pour themselves big goblets of red wine. They feasted on buttered toast and fried eggs with tomatoes and danced to Persian disco in bare feet on the carpet—their hand motions and mock flirtatious expressions improvised and hilarious. Noor had passed the nursing board exams, finally acquired her driver's license, and was working at Kaiser in South San Francisco. Nassim studied journalism and worked part-time at the Macy's cosmetic counter where she faked a French accent and seduced women into handing over their credit cards. Soon she was named Employee of the Month, given a seventy-five-cent raise and a coffee mug, and her picture was mounted on the wall in the staff lounge where she sat with her legs crossed, eating dainty spoonfuls of yogurt on her break.

On Saturday nights they wore high heels and little black dresses purchased with Nassim's employee discount, and went to pubs on Union Street or to comedy clubs, perching on little stools sipping margaritas. Neither of them really understood the jokes, but they laughed when everyone else laughed and before too long the mannerisms and intonations seeped into them until they were speaking English with each other, sticking hybrid words between their phrases like mortar. Noor wasn't entirely at ease with this wild new independence, not always keen on leaving the apartment, but once she linked arms with Nassim, her anxiety lifted.

Soon Nassim was meeting her other friends after work, often leaving Noor behind. If Nassim invited guests over, Noor served cheese and crackers, lingered in the kitchen, took their empty plates away like an innkeeper, then faked a headache and went to bed early. She lay awake and listened to strangers flushing her toilet and hoped she wouldn't have to use the bathroom and smell the aftermath of their visit. Sleep came when the front door was finally latched. And then, there was a man.

Nassim kept him a secret but the sudden change in her eyes, her skin, her hair and clothes, the exceedingly soft tone of her voice when she answered the phone, lit the small rooms they shared like embers. When she wasn't there, which was more and more often, the only light came from a spotted window in the kitchen where Noor warmed canned soup on the electric burner and ate in the dark. They no longer sat at the round table together or divided the Sunday paper or walked to their café for cappuccinos and blueberry muffins.

Noor tried to remember her last sight of Nassim, as if they had boarded different buses and she'd lost her pupil. How quickly Nassim adopted the ways of the women they saw on television and in clubs, with their glossy hair and bare legs. With what sensual ease she spoke to men, enchanting them with the sweep of her black lashes, writing her phone number in the palm of their hands. Where did she learn to do that? Every day, Noor went to work and came back to an empty apartment. Some days there was mail and she would sort through the envelopes by the mailboxes, hoping to walk upstairs with a letter for Nassim from her parents—believing that news from home would bring her back.

One day Noor sat across the street slouched over a coffee at Café Moka when she saw a boy carrying a huge vase of red roses. He paused in front of her building, checked a piece of paper, then rang the bell. When there was no answer, he turned to leave. Noor intercepted him just as he was about to open his van.

"Are those for apartment 4A?"

"Yes, ma'am! Is that you?"

"Yes!"

"Well I'm glad you caught me."

The small card stapled to the cellophane read: *I miss you all the time, P.*

Noor carried the flowers to the dumpster behind the building, lifted the heavy lid, and threw the roses headlong into the garbage below, shattering the globe vase on the metal wall. Rage cleared her head and, back at the café, she sat at a sidewalk table and lifted her face to the sun.

The following evening the telephone rang while Nassim was in the shower. A man named Paul asked to speak to her. Relieved that she had picked up the receiver before he could leave a message, Noor told him that Nassim wasn't home.

"Gone away for the weekend."

"Where?"

"Napa," she said, because it was the first thing that came to mind. She then quickly hung up before he asked more questions.

Nassim came out in her bathrobe with her hair wrapped in a towel, carrying a manicure caddy filled with an assortment of polish. Nassim diligently maintained her long, tapered nails and tonight's appearance of the caddy made Noor smile, because it meant her roommate wasn't going out for the evening. Noor offered to run to the video store to pick up a movie. "Sure," came an indifferent reply. It had been ages since they had curled up on the couch with ice cream to watch a film, so Noor bolted out the door and ran down the street, returning less than fifteen minutes later with *Moonstruck*.

Noor carried in a plate of vanilla wafers and a pint of chocolate chip ice cream. Nassim looked up from the couch and shifted to make room for her.

"*Moonstruck* again? How many times have you seen this film?" She said it as if Noor had watched the film alone, as if only Noor had memorized the dialogue and knew the songs.

"But this is our favorite! We love Cher!"

Nassim shrugged and leaned back. How many times had they seen it? How many times had she yelled, "Bring me the big knife!" when they were making dinner? How often had Nassim compared Ronny to her crazy cousin Vali? Noor had always related to the dutiful Loretta, but tonight she recognized herself in Rose, Loretta's mother, in a lilac housecoat making breakfast, dining alone in their neighborhood Italian restaurant, especially when Rose cries, "Ya gotta love bite on your neck, your life's goin' down the toilet!"

As the silence between the roommates opened and bloomed, Noor half laughed, half cried after many of her favorite lines. A nail biter in her youth, she raised a hand to her mouth to chew a raggedy nail. Nassim seemed to endure the movie, studying her opaque enameled nails, crossing and re-crossing her arms, glancing sideways at the telephone like she wanted to call for help.

A week later, on Sunday morning, Noor allowed herself to sleep until nine. Assuming Nassim was still asleep, she tiptoed to the kitchen, but Nassim was already at the table with a mug of cold coffee. Even red-rimmed, her eyes were beautiful, and for a split second there shimmered a trace of an earlier compassion that she blinked away. A small duffel bag rested at her feet. Noor pulled out a chair and sat next to her, resisting the impulse to pull open the pink section of the *San Francisco Chronicle* for movie listings, to brew fresh coffee and make toast. Whatever Nassim was about to tell her was not good, but it would help if she had a hot beverage.

"Did you think we could play house forever?" Nassim's sarcasm was sharp. She told Noor everything then, about the man she'd been seeing, the missed calls and missing flowers. That Paul was married was irrelevant, she said.

"You had no right to interfere!" Nassim fumed. "And don't you dare tell my father."

"I don't even know your parents!" Noor shot back. Did Nassim think she would cross the ocean to carry them this news?

Paul, the professor, eleven years Nassim's senior, had been a devoted husband until Nassim spurred his appetite. Each day brought an endless parade of lovely young women into his classroom who could've donned burkas for all the attention he paid them, but Nassim blew into his office one day like a soft breeze—indeed that was the definition of her name—in a floral print dress cinched at the waist and peep toe sandals that showed just the tips of her pretty red toenails, and by the time she sat on the edge of the chair across from him, he felt a new hunger for this girl who observed him with her dark eyes as if she understood that there was so much more to him than his pasty complexion and marshmallow physique.

Within an hour, a long-suffering wife, who had put up with his stale breath and wet palms for twenty-three years, was dismissed for hardly glancing at him anymore, always rushing about, always reminding him to do this and that, getting exasperated when he forgot errands and chores, barking *"I'll just do it myself!"* Why, just that morning she had berated him in front of their two daughters, ages eleven and fifteen, because he misplaced his keys—quickly bemoaning, "It's like having three children in the house!" The best part of his day was spent alone in his car, removed from that sense of duty, of never getting it right. Yet here was this girl who wanted nothing from him and he would pursue her for pure pleasure. Nassim had never received the devoted attention of a grown man who gazed upon her with such passion.

Upon finding out that this was an affair, Noor erased any of her misgivings over the discarded bouquet or the few white lies pertaining to Nassim's whereabouts, pleased that her instincts about this charlatan were warranted and that every action had been taken to protect her friend.

"Nassi, did you think about his wife? What about his kids?" Noor inquired with unmistakable judgment in her voice.

Nassim lashed out. "What? Yes! Well, not really. How should I know about them?"

Nassim's fury confused Noor. "But isn't that what we're supposed to do . . . to look after each other?"

"No! You see, I don't want you to look after me, to babysit me, to cook my eggs and iron my clothes like you're my nanny!"

Poor Noor. Since leaving home, she had unwittingly assumed the role of Naneh Goli. However, Nassim's secret affair was not nearly as devastating as the heartbreak that followed.

"I'm going to stay with my aunt in Phoenix for a few days," Nassim said. "She'll help me find a job. I'll come back for my things. I just have to get away from San Francisco."

"What about our apartment?" cried Noor. "Doesn't it mean anything to you? This place is our home." She flung open her arms to the four walls of their shabby apartment.

Nassim gazed straight ahead, a haughty chin in the air. "I want my space, Noor. Space for big love, a big job, a big house." She stood up to pry open the window. Street noises cut through the silence that had settled in the kitchen.

When Nassim finally spoke again, she shook her head and said, "I mean, look at this," scoffing at the rusty hinges that held the window frame. "It's so sad."

By June Nassim had packed her clothes and books, loading them into a friend's Honda Accord for the road trip to Arizona. She was so eager to go that she skipped graduation and left Noor all the housewares they had purchased together. Noor flinched at the clap of the car trunk closing on the brief happiness of those few months. The former roommates exchanged a wooden embrace on the curb and then only a hand waved good-bye from the open car window before Nassim was gone.

In the years to follow, Noor often thought that she was never as happy as when she lived in that apartment. She remembered coming home from work, feeling the reassuring weight of her keys in her pocket. She would open the lobby door to the soft sound of the evening news from the ground floor unit and the scent of someone's laundry soap suspended in the stairwell. No matter how much her feet ached, how dire the prognosis of a patient, how ill-tempered the doctors, the light in the window would shine in a place of her own and there would be supper to share with her best friend. There was so little space between her and Nassim and they crossed over it again and again. Beyond the doors of 4A, there was nothing but space between people. No one could get enough of it—everyone crying for more ("Give me some space!") and flapping their wings like caged birds fighting for their lonely lives. *Flap flap flap.*

# Eighteen

_____

Noor remained single among her married colleagues and they could not help pecking at her, trying to set her up at every opportunity. There were friends and relatives who wished to settle her life for her, perhaps in order to feel settled themselves. Yet Noor never bothered to correct their poor choices, nor their assumptions about her desires. To do so seemed impolite, and she wanted to remain hopeful that, given the chance, one of these men would appreciate her, that she would marry, and life could begin.

"Good luck meeting a man in San Francisco," a resident at the hospital once said, upon hearing where Noor lived. "What, why?" Noor asked.

Less than fifteen minutes from the city and people were suddenly homophobic. AIDS was the plague that frightened even the president, and Noor wept for the young men she nursed and watched waste away. Jerry was a waiter at a little Italian restaurant who had served Noor her first bowl of risotto Milanese, annoyed that she ordered the same boring spaghetti each time. The idea of a creamy bowl of rice did not appeal to a Persian palate and she shuddered at the thought of porridge for dinner, but she eventually relented and after that she rarely ordered pasta again—ultimately finding the short grains infused with broth and saffron heavenly. When she tried to describe it in her letters to Zod, he assumed it was a Persian saffron rice pudding that Italians had hijacked and skipped the rosewater.

*Persian food is the mother cuisine*, he wrote. *Remember, Noor, everything you eat originated in Iran.*

In fact, Zod traced everything back to the ingenuity of Cyrus the Great's empire. His allegiance was disarming but not uncommon among immigrant communities who found refuge and prospered in Iran before the revolution. Noor shared Zod's observations with Jerry, who laughed and dared her to go tell this to Umberto, the chef.

Jerry didn't stay long at Kaiser, but while he was there his boyfriend Liam slept in the chair next to his bed. When Jerry's mother came from Indiana, she and Liam fought over who would stay overnight, who would shave or bathe Jerry or wipe his chin, and Noor had to be the arbiter. Sweet Jerry, a skeleton now but for his belly, bloated grotesquely from the medication that could not save him, still teased her while she fed him teaspoons of take-out risotto from Enrico's—the only thing he managed to keep down.

"Look at all these handsome doctors, Noor. Don't tell me you haven't gone out with any of them," Jerry nudged every time she wheeled him to the sunny terrace.

"I don't want to date a doctor like in those hospital soap operas, Jerry!"

"Well aren't we Miss Picky-Picky. Hmm?"

"I'm not picky. It's not as if they've asked me, you know."

"Noor, what century are you from? You do know it's 1991 and women ask men out, or do you suffer from some Persian hang-ups?"

"Ha, too many to count. But I'd rather die a virgin than ask a man on a date."

There was a pause and Jerry slapped his knee, shaking with sudden, brief laughter.

"Oh, oh, dear lord! Don't tell me! Please don't tell me you're a virgin! Can I please change your name to Prudence? Because a sexy name like Noor just doesn't suit you with your turtlenecks and white Wallabees."

"*Shhh.* That's enough about me," Noor objected. "Let's talk about you."

"Oh no, sweetheart, we're not done here." And he counted off his fingers compiling a list. "First, shopping. Liam will go with you to pick out some clothes that don't make you look like a warden. A haircut—at that new salon on Sutter, and your eyebrows could use some thinning, too. Oh, and your nails! Would you please quit gnawing on them like little Bobby Burmeister from down the street who used to wet his pants in third grade?"

He wasn't finished. "So get a decent manicure and, while you're at it, a pedicure . . . *then*, I'll give you a crash course on how to pick up guys." He smiled and nodded knowingly at her.

There was a moment of quiet assent.

"Should we warm up your risotto for lunch?"

"Yes," he said with new vigor.

It was nice to give Jerry a project, something he could command from his hospital bed, and he moaned anytime she wore brown or corduroy, "Oh, I think I might just die today, Prudence."

Although Noor tried to make adjustments to her wardrobe to look the part of a foxy nurse, if only to please Jerry, it made her uneasy to try, as she was no kitten, and even he realized that Noor's makeover would not happen in his lifetime.

Jerry was gone before another blind date was arranged, this time with a radiologist. He asked Noor to lunch and maybe it was just as well that Jerry wouldn't know, because he would not have approved of this reticent, sluggish man who dressed like an eight-year-old in Bermuda shorts and ball caps. They went to a handful of movies where popcorn filled their mouths and the dress code was lenient, until Noor found herself longing for her sofa and flannel pajamas. She had moved into the second floor of a Victorian house, her apartment uncluttered except for a dusty, dry flower arrangement she was too lazy to discard and thought might give the space a sense of domesticity.

Noor and Liam were close friends now—they had comforted each other after Jerry died, crying for days to Whitney Houston records. They went to dinner once or twice a week and sometimes shopped together in boutiques, where Liam patiently selected dresses for her to try that she would have never chosen on her own.

Noor had not inherited Pari's sense of style. Her mother had a sensual relationship with fabric, she appreciated soft leather shoes and well-made handbags, polishing and caressing her accessories like house pets. Her closet wasn't stuffed with impulsive purchases of ready-made, hastily stitched ensembles, but rather an exquisite, handcrafted collection. A cobbler on Jamshid Avenue still had a pair of Pari's custom-made cream-and-white slingbacks in his shop, for he never had the heart to tell Zod to pick them up. Every so often he took them out of the shoebox to admire his craftsmanship, the clever left heel he had designed to accommodate the little hitch in her step—a memento of a discerning woman from another era.

Maybe Noor should have spent more time on the sewing bench instead of filling saltshakers and enjoying the attention of the customers who always stopped to pinch her cheeks whether she was doing homework or entertaining dolls at a tea party. Mehrdad, on the other hand, or "Mr. Armani," as Liam had nicknamed him when they'd met on one of his visits, was the stylish one, and Noor never felt as dowdy as when she was out with her brother and Liam, but they made her laugh and their companionship felt good.

Friendly and cheerful, Mehrdad came to see her often, never without chickpea cookies from the Persian mini-marts in Westwood, and sometimes with a girl on his arm. They happily crashed on the sleeper sofa and Noor tried to act casual each time a pretty, long-legged woman in her brother's oversized T-shirt perched on a kitchen stool, eating the scrambled eggs he had cooked for her. Noor would observe the flirtation between them, the longing look in the eyes of a girl with a fantasy already taking shape in her mind, of a big life with this beautiful man who was steaming milk for their coffee. Mehrdad fawned over his girlfriends, but he did not love them. Noor's own solitary existence provided the luxury of imagining committed couples living in domestic bliss—all the things she thought she wanted in life, too.

One night late in the fall, Noor was covering a shift for a colleague. Everything was slightly wet from the rain, making her hair frizz and look uncombed. She ducked into the bathroom to tie her hair back, wishing that it was 1952 and she could just pin a cap to her foolish hair. Ever since she agreed to the most expensive haircut of her life, she had a miserable time coaxing the layers of indeterminate length into a rubber band.

Back at her station, she studied the charts and two names popped out: one, a Dr. Olivero, new to Kaiser and rumored to be gallant, though she had not met him yet, and his patient, Mr. Ali Nejad, an Iranian man in room 220. Mr. Nejad had undergone surgery earlier that week and been moved out of intensive care to her floor. When Noor looked in, she found him awake. His head had vanished into the pillow and dull eyes were glued to a blank television screen.

"*Agha* (Mr.) Nejad, how are you feeling?" She greeted him in Persian and he took so long to respond that she thought he hadn't heard. Nearing the bed, a small, bald head lifted to look towards the sound of these familiar words, showing Noor a pair of bewildered eyes that were instantly wet with tears.

"Sweet girl," he said, considering her closely. "How old are you, sweet girl?"

"Twenty-seven, sir," Noor replied.

"The same age as my son! He lives in Seattle. Are you married? He's coming tomorrow. He couldn't get off work. Are you here tomorrow?"

No sooner had she checked his blood pressure than he was matchmaking, asking for his wallet to show Noor photos of his son—a prodigy, a wizard, a virtuoso. Noor tried to change the subject, asked if he'd like some tea, suggested he watch some TV or try to get some sleep. He couldn't find the remote, he said, and didn't want to bother the nurses. She brewed some of her own Darjeeling in a water glass (knowing Iranians preferred their tea in a clear glass to see the amber liquid) and served it on a saucer with some Lorna Doones, then flipped the channels until settling on *Murder, She Wrote*.

Before taking a sip, he lifted the glass to admire its color as she knew he would, moaning a Persian "*Akh, akh, akh*," of pleasure and pain. Returning later with his medicine, she helped him to the bathroom and turned his pillow to the cooler side. Just before falling asleep, he took her hand and whispered, "Merci, my sweet girl."

The next morning, on her day off, Noor went to see Mr. Nejad, stopping to buy him a potted blue hydrangea and some fruit. At the nurses' station she exchanged greetings with colleagues who didn't know a Mr. Nejad when she asked about him. "Oh, you mean Ali!" they'd exclaimed. "What a sweetheart!" It was disconcerting, the ease with which first names were thrown about in America. There were people she'd known for years—supervisors, grocers, landladies, building supers—whom she never called anything but "Mrs. Campbell" or "Dr. Starr," yet who called her "Noor," though not without a reminder for her to drop the "Mr." She would not dream of calling Mr. Nejad "Ali." And then there he was, in the corridor outside his room, wearing the striped hospital robe, leaning on a walker, a smile of recognition growing on his face.

Noor put her arm around his shoulders and encouraged him to walk, but he said, "My leg hurts, and besides, I don't want to miss my son."

Noor thought of when she was small, waiting for her mother to pick her up from school and how fretful she would get if Pari was late, how rooted to the spot by the front steps of the nursery school lest Pari come and go home without her. She found herself praying, as she did back then, that Mr. Nejad's son would arrive soon, but instead a man in pale blue scrubs approached—a free and easy walk like a promenade by the water.

Dr. Nelson Olivero smelled of soap and pine, and beneath a globe of thick, black hair was a pair of chocolate eyes searching Noor's face, as if maybe they had met before and he couldn't place her.

"How are ju today, Signor Nejab?"

"It's Nejad," Noor corrected him. Did he think Mr. Nejad was Hispanic?

"Ethcuthe me?" Those eyes again traveling from her forehead down to her feet and back.

"His name. Your patient's name is 'Ne*jad*,'" said Noor.

"Ah, *bueno*. And who are ju, Signorina?"

Noor wasn't sure where the accent was from, but it was as if the man spoke through a pocket of saliva. She explained that she was a nurse, that she'd come back today to check on Mr. Nejad since he didn't seem to have family here yet. The doctor took all this in, appraising her again with that slow, appreciative gaze. Poor Mr. Nejad, now a spectator to this exchange, interrupted them.

"Doktor, please, when I get for there, it hurt my lamb shank." They both turned now to look at their patient.

"Did ju say *lamb*, Signor?"

"Yes, Doktor." Mr. Nejad motioned to his right shin.

"Do you mean your leg?" Noor tried to clarify.

"No, no, no! My lamb shank creak when I go for there," and he pointed to the end of the polished linoleum where he must have ventured before Noor's arrival. She understood then that he meant his tibia and translated for him.

Dr. Olivero ushered him back to his room. "Then I can ethamine your lamb shank, Signor," and turned to wink at Noor who trailed behind.

They lifted this fragile, featherweight man onto the bed, their faces so close she could count the orderly row of his perfect teeth, and when her hand brushed against the doctor's, Noor would say later that there was a sizzle—so hot she wanted to run it under cold water.

She stayed to help Mr. Nejad out of his robe, to be his interpreter and surrogate daughter through the exam and in the days that followed. By then Dr. Olivero had invited Noor to coffee, then lunch, then to Café Jacqueline for chocolate soufflés, to La Traviata, to his favorite sushi bar, and one clear morning in November, to a picnic on Angel Island.

They saw each other every day, sometimes just a quick glance across a patient's bed, but she lived for this. The secret smiles, the light touches. He strolled past her in the corridors with a flock of interns on his heels, then turned around quickly to look, to see if Noor had turned (of course she had), and the rest of the day was all about the next time she might see him in the places he was expected to appear, and there he would be as if waiting for her.

Everything was as it had always been, going to work, walking past the lobby gift shop displaying buckets of premade bouquets by the entrance, sampling a piece of coffee cake in the nurses' lounge, but oh, the Golden Gate Bridge was so beautiful, and the flowers gave off the sweetest scent, and every cake she had tasted before paled in comparison to *this* cake. She loved him and didn't think of anything else but the flame in her belly.

Sex at twenty-seven with Nelson—not that fumbling clumsy endeavor with the radiologist she slept with just to get it over with for heaven's sake—was to break free, like tumbling on summer grass.

"Would ju like to see my home?" he asked her after the soufflé, and they walked hand in hand to his little garden apartment on Russian Hill with its subdued lighting and emerald sheets, and she overlooked the haphazard housekeeping, the ring in the tub, the pee-stained toilet bowl, even the hideous painting of a fat naked woman above his couch. Lush, with all her shyness gone, Noor's thinking on this evening was *anything can happen*. And it did, only it was nothing like the scenes of urgent, breathless arousal she'd seen on film, but a murmur, a slow and quiet awakening of a fantastic feeling she didn't know existed; his body moving around her, an explorer's voice in the dark, responding to her smallest breath.

It wasn't about the parts of her body that had been in the shadows, but the all of it that was now lit. And because he loved Van Morrison, he played "Sweet Thing" for her and she put her arms above her head and gave in to the lyrics, too. In the morning she woke up to the smell of coffee and chocolate toast, raised her eyes to the ceiling and asked Jerry, "Who's Prudence now, huh?"

It seemed that Noor spent the first year of their relationship in one of Nelson's white undershirts. *Yes!* Noor thought, *Finally I can walk around braless in my boyfriend's T-shirt.* He was her *boyfriend.* "My boyfriend, Nelson," she would say out loud to no one and a ripple ran through her. When she stayed overnight at his place she brought flowers and bags of groceries to cook elaborate meals.

Before long, she filled his small kitchen with cutlery and ceramics, replaced curtains, towels, and bath mats, arranging them with such vitality that when she wiped the bathroom mirror, a prettier woman with fuller breasts and flushed cheeks gazed back at her. She would go to the hospital and a boy would come out of the elevator carrying two dozen red roses through the ward. The nurses always gathered to see who the flowers were for and seemed genuinely surprised when they were for Noor from Dr. Olivero, finding it hard to imagine an erotic charge between those two. Noor sensed their doubt and saw how easily Nelson flirted with them, as he did with the cafeteria ladies who wore their hair in paper bonnets and scooped extra servings of mashed potatoes for him. He called them all *"mi amor"* and brought chocolates for each one on Valentine's Day. But Noor was *"mi vida,"* and that's what set her apart.

Who can explain the spark between two people? It wasn't that Nelson tired of the glamorous rumors about his affairs—some of which had turned messy and one that required a move from Boston to San Francisco—but he appreciated nuance and found Noor's well-shaped, desirable little body, her unruly dark hair and honey-hued eyes that changed color like fall leaves, captivating. She was beautiful and didn't know it until he'd come along and plucked this rosebud and put it in a vase. She never quite believed it, which may be why Nelson held an upper hand that never quite gave way, skewing their relationship from the start.

Noor, the person least likely to be interested in nature, now accompanied Nelson on long hikes through the woods and camping trips to Point Reyes and Yosemite. The camping frightened her, especially when she had to go to the bathroom at night, even with Nelson's headlamp strapped to her forehead. Mehrdad suppressed a chortle when he visited and found outdoor gear piled in her apartment, but it was nice to see his sister happy. He was baffled by their attraction but kept this to himself. After all, Nelson was charming and easy to get along with. In Los Angeles, Mehrdad, too, had recently met Chrissy Kaufman, and he was starting to cultivate emotions that were new and warm, making him evasive if Noor asked him about the absence of girlfriends.

Letters home diminished and Zod, though melancholy, suspected that romance had finally distracted his children and he was glad, recognizing that it was long overdue. Aunt Farah was curious, feeling it was her responsibility to check on this heart doctor Mehrdad casually mentioned to them. Over the years she had grown increasingly protective of Noor, assuming a motherly watch over her. Though Morad accused her of being meddlesome, she accompanied Mehrdad on one of his visits to Northern California and they brought Marjan along. Marjan, now a senior at UC Irvine, had outgrown her petulance but was prone to a gloominess in her mother's presence that only Mehrdad, with his good humor, could diffuse.

Noor put fresh sheets on her bed and clean towels in the bathroom and surprised her aunt by staying at Nelson's house during their visit, inviting them to dinner as if she were married—shocking information that Farah kept to herself. Quickly enamored with Nelson, Farah was glad for the blood, not ice water, that ran through his veins, yet she privately hoped

Noor wouldn't marry him. Chagrin over the course of her own marriage made her wish they would stay lovers. Nassim, too, came for a weekend visit with her fiancé, Charlie. Absence healed old wounds and the two friends had reconciled after a temporary freeze. They huddled on the couch while Nelson cooked mussels and Charlie mixed margaritas. Men and women alike fell under the spell of Nelson's lisp—everyone except for Liam, who regarded the doctor with cautious optimism.

That summer, in Napa for her thirtieth birthday, after tasting too much champagne under a hot sun, Noor fell off a rented bike and Nelson carried her back to their B&B on his shoulders like King Kong. She sat on the edge of the bathtub and as he kneeled before her to clean and bandage her scraped knees, Nelson looked into her flushed face and said, "Noor, would ju like to be my wife?" In retrospect it sounded condescending, like asking a clerk "How would you like to be assistant manager someday?" but befuddled as Noor was, she wanted then to wrap her shanks around him and never let go.

It would be hard to say which of them, Noor or Nelson, was the poorer judge of character; probably Noor, but for reasons of age, and significant advantage in the realm of romance, Nelson, who seemed to have become quite unexpectedly domesticated in the light of Noor's radiance, should have remained a boyfriend and nothing more.

Noor eventually came to learn that we see what we want to see. She used to ask Nelson, "When did you fall in love with me?" Sometimes he would say it was when he saw her that morning in the hospital with Mr. Nejad, or the first time they kissed, or sometimes he would say it was in the mangy yard of his garden apartment when he saw her planting bulbs. In due course Noor would learn that the moment had been specific only for her and gradual for him. Jerry would've said, "Loosen up! *When* doesn't matter, he loved you and the applause was wild in the background."

What a wedding they had. Noor kept the bride-and-groom cake decoration made of sugar that topped the cake in a box on her dresser. Aboard a boat out on the bay with a live band and a seven-tiered *sacripantina* from

Stella's, Zod held her hands aloft like when she was small and danced with her under the stars. Mr. Nejad came (thankfully, so Zod had someone to talk to). Nelson's parents, Anna and Teodor, and his little sister, Clara, flew in from Barcelona. Mehrdad and Chrissy, Nassim and Charlie, Aunt Farah, Uncle Morad, and Marjan, gorgeous in a glittery sleeveless dress. Sue Sullivan was there, of course, and her entire family—three kids and her husband, even taller than her. And sweet Liam, always elegant, kept an eye on Zod and witnessed two brothers who had not seen each other in three decades exchange perfunctory greetings and retreat—"Without even a handshake," he recounted.

Loving Nelson meant that Noor would never be lonely again. He made her feel good. She would swear she was even in love with the sound of the telephone when he rang. She put aside all doubt and forgave his flirtations, to keep the idea of him safe. When Lily arrived, it was for her and the little backyard and the skinny pomegranate saplings already twice her height, for the swing set, and the sunlit breakfast nook. We see what we want to see.

# PART FOUR

# Nineteen

The fourth of July in Tehran came and went without a spark. At home it was the highlight of summer. Families opened their backyards for neighborhood barbeques or headed to the beach. Car after car, packed with coolers, blankets, and boogie boards, snaked across the Golden Gate Bridge towards Marin County, where the celebration would climax with fireworks after dark. Lily had not outgrown the festivities, nor the food or the games. Nelson would place cones in the sand and invite a group of children to play soccer. Lily loved being on his team, chasing the ball and watching her dad huffing and puffing to keep up with the kids. She felt bitter now, a little past two o'clock on this July afternoon, nearly two months since their arrival in Iran. Being so far away, she realized anew how colorless her life was without her father and friends, but did anyone at home feel her absence?

The day stretched out before her and Lily stood at the bathroom mirror, brushing her hair and braiding it, then taking it out and doing it again. Again and again, she twisted the plait, over and under, reversing the loop from time to time. She glanced at her watch and counted back the hours, wondering what her friends might be doing right then, composing in her mind a happy tableau of classmates huddled at a Starbucks—a futile pre-occupation with their whereabouts that only strengthened her melancholy.

Time passed indifferently here, each day hotter than the last, with no breeze and too much sunlight coming into her room. School would be starting in a few weeks and Lily wondered how much longer her mother intended on staying. Had Noor lied to her? Had she planned all along to stay through the summer? It was no use asking. Noor would launch into another tale of duty and devotion that Lily couldn't bear.

The thought struck Lily then that her friends had forgotten her. Emma and Zoe, her best friends since kindergarten, busy with their own summer lives and family vacations, didn't answer her emails anymore, and if she couldn't text, she didn't exist. And then there was Jeremy Ross. He wouldn't care if she returned because he had never noticed her anyway. On the last day of school, she slipped a note to him, thinking there was nothing to lose now that she was leaving.

*Jeremy, I don't think I can ever tell you this in person. I love you. L*

On ruled binder paper she wrote it, crumpled it up, and started over. Just before sixth period, she ran to his locker and pushed it through the slot. She would never know what he had done with it. *Most likely*, she thought, *he showed it to his friends and everyone had a good laugh*. But now it didn't even matter.

Lily would not admit it, but a part of her was beginning to appreciate the freedom that came with captivity. Freedom from peers. After two months of isolation, not worrying about what to wear or what anyone thought of her, not having a public profile or being surrounded by people who had known you all your life and were full of expectation, she was discovering what it was like to have an independent thought. Freedom even from family, because she remained unconvinced of her relation to this tribe. It would take more than a faded photograph of a grandmother she had never met to bring her into their company.

Lily tried to imagine her mother standing at this wobbly sink, collecting her wayward curls into a rubber band, wearing the school uniform that still hung in the closet. She squinted into the mirror, wondering if Noor would have known what to do with a boy who didn't notice her. Would she try a touch of rouge or glance in the mirror and think, *Why bother?*

Her bedroom was bright due to a window facing the garden and the wallpaper, though faded, was a trellis of sweet peas on a sky blue background. On the dresser, in a jewelry box made of inlaid wood, were tucked Noor's first gold chain, a charm bracelet, and a green velvet pouch with all her baby teeth. That was a creepy discovery. Lily had peered into the ornate dollhouse that once housed birds, amused by the cardboard people in matchbox beds lined with calico sheets. She had inspected the contents of the drawers and the bookshelf, which held a Barbie doll still in its original box and worn copies of *Jane Eyre* and *The Secret Garden*—books her grandmother Pari had brought home from her trips to England.

Lily rummaged through the closet and held her mother's old clothes up to her own body—drab uniforms with pleated skirts and an interesting turquoise dress that was too long, with a lovely scoop neck. Still, she couldn't quite conjure an image of teenage Noor, who had slept in this same room, with the same pipes rattling, waking up to the same yard birds, and doing her homework in the clamor of the busy café.

But in fact both her mother and uncle grew up here and opened their textbooks every afternoon on a table in the dining room, facing the nook where their grandfather greeted his customers. They ate Nina's jam on sweet rolls, listened to the echo of their mother's voice running up and down the scales and the pleasant ting of the cash register, which swayed the large brass balance used for weighing candied nuts and Turkish delight.

The cluster of men who sat at the same table day after day offered them coins and chewing gum, while elegant women draped their coats on the backs of chairs and filled the room with perfume as they leaned forward for a kiss when Noor served iced coffee, leaving lipstick marks on her cheeks. There was work for everyone here. Even the children swept, refilled teapots, ran to the store for more eggs, and pitted crates of cherries. Age did not exempt them from doing what needed to be done, and they were no less cherished. Maybe if Mehrdad and Noor had not been sent away, they would be here now, polishing the glass shelves behind the bar. It wouldn't be glamorous or even interesting work, but they would be grounded, not strangers in their own home.

It was hard to picture her mother living in Iran. Throughout her childhood, Noor had tried to impress Lily with stories about Iran, about its rich culture and history, its poetry, music, and food, even the cats. Her father would tease Noor and say things like "It's too bad they can't play soccer," and her mother would get angry and defend the players like they were her sons. Yet as certain as Noor was about Iran's glorious past, she was evermore ambivalent about her country's future.

What Lily never understood was Noor's parallel pride and dismissal of her origin. If Iran was so great, why did her mother warn her every day *not* to tell her friends that she was half Iranian? She was always so afraid of being found out. During heritage week in third grade, Lily took churros to school and everyone said, "Are you Mexican?" Lily answered that she was half Spanish. So they asked, "What's your other half?" and she told them Italian. Then they demanded she bring spaghetti next time.

Nelson said that Noor was paranoid, and after September 11 it got worse. Lily was only a year old on 9/11, so kids her age were all used to the cycle of bad news. It just didn't make sense to Lily how her mother would brag about her country one minute and then lie about it to strangers the next. Nelson would roll his eyes and remind Noor that September 11 had nothing to do with Iran, but her response was "You don't get it. These people lump everyone from the Middle East together."

A colleague once asked her what it was like watching the television series *Homeland* when "some of those characters look like they could be your relatives."

"You mean Claire Danes?" Noor replied, laughing it off, seething inside. There were many days she related to the neurotic Carrie Mathison.

So for Lily, Iran was a colorful fairy tale full of kings and princesses at night and quickly forgotten by daylight.

A sound drew Lily to the window, where a bulky air conditioner was installed, whirring noisily day and night. Even with the dial on high, the heat was unbearable at midday. A pebble hit the windowpane again and Lily opened the shutter to peer outside. Karim stood below in a white T-shirt, his arms tanned brown, holding something against his chest. When he raised a hand to wave, she saw what it was. With a finger on his lips to be quiet, he motioned for her to come down.

No one saw Lily go outside. Naneh Goli and Zod were napping and Noor had gone to the fabric store. Soli and the waiters were in the café. She met Karim in the garden.

Since her arrival in June, she had spoken to him only once, when she went to the kitchen looking for ice and found him scrubbing the stove. His face had broken into the widest grin and once Lily gestured to the freezer, he'd scrambled from stove to sink to wash the grime that reached his elbows and then filled a tumbler with ice, holding it out with both hands and turning bright red when she said "merci." Then she asked how to say *ice* and he could hardly breathe to speak, but every day since then there would be a short knock on her door, and when she opened it there was a small tray with a bowl of ice. Every day.

And now here he was, with that generous grin that stretched from one floppy ear to the other. She took the kitten from him and held it against her neck. It squirmed and tickled and made her laugh. Karim stood watching her. He'd never heard her laugh and really it sounded exactly like the gurgling stream within earshot of the house where he grew up, an arrangement of water and pebbles that had accompanied his youth.

Together, Karim and Lily sat in the shade on the gravel path and played with the kitten and an old tennis ball for over an hour, during which a saucer of milk and two cold Cokes were pilfered from the kitchen.

The cat was snowy white, so Karim asked Lily how to say *milk* by pointing to the saucer. He repeated after her, "Mil-kuh," making her laugh. Then, preferring the word in Persian, they settled on naming her "Sheer." And it made no difference at all that Karim imagined staying here next to Lily and Sheer forever, while Lily believed that she had finally found an ally who would help her escape. In the stillness of a late summer afternoon, it made no difference at all.

# Twenty

———⊗⊗⊗———

Tehran was like the blank page in a coloring book, gray but for the two landmarks Noor discovered. One was the fabric store where her mother and grandmother used to bring her to choose fabric for a new dress in the weeks before the Persian New Year. It was hard to believe it was still there, smaller than she remembered, but stacked from floor to ceiling with bolts of silk, satin, velvet, in every hue. The saleswomen had fawned over her mother, but Noor did not expect to be recognized. And she wasn't, but they sensed her foreignness and treated her kindly, draping cloth over her shoulders and letting her see it in natural light on the sidewalk, where she was struck with a fantasy of running through the streets and unraveling reams of color behind her.

Noor had lied to Zod and Naneh Goli about taking a taxi. She knew they worried that she would get lost, but she couldn't stand another ride in one of

Tehran's bumper cars, with the cabbie's manic swerves and abrupt stops to pick up multiple passengers. Afraid at first to walk alone, she soon realized that no one cared about a frumpy forty-nine-year-old woman as long as she covered her head and appeared busy. Walking the two miles became routine and returning with swatches or a few yards of violet and blue made her happy, thinking that she would eventually gather her courage to ask Naneh Goli for a tutorial on Pari's sewing machine.

In a search for color, the flower shop on Amir Parviz Street became Noor's second destination. It was where Zod used to buy flowers for Pari on his way to fetch her from the airport, and Noor had often tagged along. Now she came here once, sometimes twice a week. Ever since she moved Zod's bed to the salon where the light was more cheerful, she filled the room with flowers. Mr. Azizi, the owner, kept his shop cool and was always kind, offering Noor tea and almond brittle. His family had a nursery outside the city where his brothers tended the greenhouses, and he drove into town at dawn every morning to open the shop. Noor imagined him behind the wheel of a truck carrying a bed of flowers to a city where every effort was made to defeat plant life. Mr. Azizi made exquisite arrangements, taking his time cutting the wet stems, selecting ferns and ribbons to embellish the bouquets.

Noor enjoyed walking out into the hazy, concrete city, carrying an enormous cellophane bundle wrapped with a huge bow. Every single head turned to look at this glorious spray of color and scent. Noor felt the mood around her lightening, softening the set jaws of the men and women who shouldered past her. Inevitably, drivers rolled down their windows to shout, "But you, miss, *you* are a flower yourself!" or "Oh, a flower carrying a flower!" or some such corny compliments. It was good to see the verve of her people, to learn that it still existed, and she was still a part of it.

Noor wished she could convince Lily to come on these excursions with her; they were Noor's only distraction from the feeling of gloom and helplessness that had pervaded the house since she learned the seriousness of her father's illness. But little had changed between them since their arrival—

Lily, reticent and friendless, stayed in her room and Noor made futile attempts at reaching her. She would emerge only for meals or an occasional cup of tea, sullen and ill-tempered, responding to Noor's queries with an equal measure of self-pity and contempt that unnerved Noor, ending their conversation with a resigned sigh.

One morning Noor found herself walking behind a group of young girls in jeans, gray knee-length coats, and elaborate headscarves. She was curious about these girls her daughter's age. Where were they going? What did teenagers do in Tehran?

They led her to an unmarked building with a mysterious entrance covered by a black tarp. The girls slipped behind the tarp and through two or more curtains before coming to a door that led to a front office. Noor caught the strong scent of chlorine and realized it was a swimming pool. Ladies' hours were nine to noon every Monday and Wednesday morning and the attendant (in shorts) let her peek inside in exchange for her cellphone, lest she take any photos. Noor was elated to see women shed their cloaks and emerge from the locker room in bright bathing suits, running with madcap joy to the pool with its blue perpendicular lines and nothing to get in their way. The atmosphere was relaxed, with women lounging, chatting, and splashing—unburdened for a few hours before they had to cover and compose themselves once again. There was even a small café with soft drinks and sandwiches, and beautiful turquoise tiled showers where they bathed, naked.

Rushing home to tell Lily, feeling certain that in this heat, she would not resist, Noor rehearsed her pitch: *You should see these girls, Lily! They're your age. We'll invite them to lunch! There's even a nice café!* This seemed like a promising premise to ease Lily's resistance, for Noor had little time left to wait it out. In a few weeks Lily was registered to start school in Tehran but Noor didn't have the courage to tell her.

When the bell rang to start the day in the neighborhood kindergarten, Noor stopped across the street to watch a few latecomers kiss their mothers and skedaddle inside. *It's the same everywhere*, she thought, *they're small and they live with you and you're in love with them and they move away and a slightly bigger version of them moves in.* Then you fall in love again, only to watch that little person leave, and yet a slightly taller, more agile version, who still fits in the toddler bed, but just barely, arrives and there you go again, head over heels. Another birthday will come and this one, too, will go, pigtails and all, and so on, until your heart could burst. You see them turn two, then three and four and you miss that tiny newborn who smelled like milk, the one-year-old who teeter-tottered, and how sweet was that two-year-old who would not let go of your hand, and do you remember running alongside her bicycle at five? Where did she go? Noor had never given Lily's clothes away, had kept every pajama and party dress neatly folded in storage boxes labeled zero through thirteen. It wasn't at all like she had an only child—there were fifteen so far. Lily, her first and last of one, enough to make her heart break.

When she got home she headed upstairs, but Lily's door was closed. She knocked. Silence. Lily was not downstairs or in the yard, and no one had seen her. Beads of sweat trickled down Noor's back. It was unlikely that Lily would go outside—she despised the scarves and layers of cover. Zod was in the salon, awake with his eyes closed, when Noor rushed in.

"I can't find her," she cried.

"Who?" Zod answered as if in a dream.

"Lily. She's gone!" Her voice caught and she tried to breathe.

"Excuse me?"

For a brief moment Zod wasn't sure who Noor was or what she was talking about—he was becoming worryingly forgetful—then he caught himself and nodded.

"Have you checked the Vieux Hotel?" Karim shared a room with his Uncle Soli in the old hotel, or as Zod preferred to call it, *Le Vieux Hotel.*

Years ago, during the war, the hotel had been badly damaged after an air raid. By then it was already cheerless, just a shadow of its previous elegance.

The rooms were rarely occupied and the few guests were fortunately evacuated. But after the destruction, Zod no longer had the desire to reopen it. Instead, it was rebuilt simply, without its pretty balconies, antique rugs, and pink tiles, to serve as housing for the staff and occasional guests. What used to be the lobby now served as a common room with a television set and couches. It was there that Noor found Lily and Karim, sitting cross-legged on the beige linoleum with a kitten pouncing on the tennis ball between them.

Noor was so relieved that she burst into tears and ran to Lily, who held the terrified kitten like a shield.

"God, Mom! You scared her. What's wrong with you?" The others turned away. Soli, eyes ablaze beneath the thick knot of his eyebrows, yanked on Karim's arm and dragged him back to work, leaving the mother and daughter to contend with one another.

"I'm sorry," said Noor. "I panicked when I couldn't find you."

Lily's response was furious. "You drag me here to your crappy country and I'm basically in prison and all my friends have already forgotten about me and there's nothing but crazy old people here and finally *one* person here wants to be my friend, a person you guys treat like a child slave by the way, and you barge in here like the police and ruin *everything*!" she screamed.

"I'm sorry, Lily. I'm so sorry," whispered Noor.

"You're always sorry," hissed Lily. "Why don't you try leaving people alone so you don't have to be so sorry all the time?" She stormed out, pushing past Naneh Goli who hovered outside, and ran to her room.

It had been a long time since Zod had heard a door slam in his house. Noor appeared in the sitting room moments later and, without a word, sat next to Zod on the couch and covered her eyes with her hands.

"Why are you sitting there?" he asked Noor. "What is the matter with you?"

The second time she was asked that in less than fifteen minutes.

"Why aren't you there now? Upstairs? Are you her mother or are you playing a part in a play?" His voice was shaking. *"Is this child your house pet?"* he shouted, losing patience with her.

Noor winced. How it hurt, his rough tone. Whatever harm she may have done, she had come to him to repair it. Was he dismissing her? She searched the floor for what to say. If only she could speak, but she was choking on her own tears.

"I cannot, I cannot," she cried fitfully. How to reach the dark landing of the stairs? Her legs stiffened at the thought.

"Parinoor," he said evenly, his eyes reproachful. "Is it because you lost your mother at a time when a girl needs her mother most that you don't know how to talk to your daughter?"

She began fiddling with the tassels on the upholstery. The tears falling freely now down her face. Zod softened, leaned close, and reached out to touch her cheek.

"Baba, I'm sorry about this afternoon . . . I was so afraid. Everything is all right now."

He watched her wearily. Her answers were unsatisfactory.

"Baba, I can run the café with Naneh Goli and Soli's help. We will live here. Lily will go to school and she'll get used to things." The words tumbled now, one after another.

He inhaled and exhaled a light whistle. "You think I'm worried about Café Leila?"

"We-ell . . . yes," Noor fidgeted. "It's meant so much to you."

"Long ago, before the revolution, before the war, when the café was open and we built the hotel from the ground up, and my mother and father were alive, when you were a little girl and your brother, a bigger boy, long ago, when there were no hard feelings between people, and families came to hear your mother sing, this was our place, a miniature, sovereign world we built to contain us. Even when everything changed outside, we kept working. There was always so much to do. We had our own family and our big family of customers. I never had to leave because the world came to me. But these days we're like your old dollhouse, still standing, but just a curiosity. What's more, the families are gone. See? Everything interesting and exciting has already happened. I haven't wasted the time I've been here and I've fulfilled my promise to my father but you, you—" he faltered, seeing his daughter's brow furrowed with confusion.

"Do you remember when you let Sonbol out of the birdhouse and Bolbol followed? That is nature, Noor," he sighed, flapping his hand. "It was a lonely business after your mother died. The habit of hard work kept me here. *Habit*, not nature."

He threw her a brief glance and took a sip from the water glass on his nightstand. "I dream of my wife. I like to think that if there is a place we cross over to, that Pari will be the first person to greet me and I've kept her waiting long enough, don't you think?"

Noor didn't answer. She didn't feel like reminiscing, she wanted to understand. At last he was giving her permission to ask her unanswered questions.

"Baba, do you know that I still have no idea how my mother died? I mean, what happened to her? You kept it hidden from us. One day she disappeared and no one could tell me where or why or when she'd be back. We were just supposed to carry on like we had amnesia."

"My only choice was to exclude you and Mehrdad from the events of her death." Zod stared ahead, jaws clenched. "I thought it was hopeless to speak of it, to explain it to you, to put that fear in your thoughts. Perhaps you can be too careful with children, but I think I may have been more afraid than I realized. Afraid of damaging you, of exposing you to unspeakable violence." A white handkerchief shook wildly in his grip like a flag of surrender.

"You see, Noor, once they put someone in prison, it is like that person isn't known as a human being who is alive, who has relatives, a mother, or a husband, or children. Nothing. No one." Zod looked at her as if he wasn't sure she'd heard.

"I've been saying things I should have told you years ago. I always thought there was no comfort to be found from knowing what they did to your mother. I'm sorry, Noor. Forgive me." He heaved a sigh and sank back on the sofa.

Noor took a deep breath. *What is this?* she thought. She had not expected to talk about Pari, but it felt like an opportunity and she needed to say this now that her presence, her return, had prompted him to speak to her not as a child, but as a grown woman.

"For years, Baba, when I'd come home from school, I'd know even before coming inside whether Maman was home or not because I could smell her and it never changed, her perfume. Then she was gone, yet her aroma was still there. I could still smell Maman. I couldn't understand it then, but I do now. I wasn't imagining it, Baba. She left her scent to stay alive in me."

"Of course, precious, the world of children is above and outside the confines of adult minds. It was beyond my ability to explain the wretchedness of it, but you found a way to keep Pari alive in you, which makes the circumstances of her death inconsequential."

Zod wiped his eyes with his handkerchief and before Noor could protest, he went on. "Pari used to say that I talk in my sleep, mostly nonsense, but sometimes it made her uneasy when I thrashed about and she would gently shake my shoulder to wake me up. Probably I still talk, but I'm a widower and sleep alone. My dreams are more vivid now, places and things and people are restored with startling clarity like in a museum.

"You've seen the postcard of the Italian painter Giorgio Morandi's studio on my dresser. Pari sent it from a tour in Italy when she visited the museum in Bologna. The photograph has faded but I've kept it all these years because I was so intrigued that the interior of a man's workspace had remained untouched for fifty years, save for the velvet rope that kept voyeurs at a respectable distance. Was there a scent of the man's work? Of canvas and paint, turpentine and tobacco? I have looked again and again at the careful placement of his jacket draped on the back of a chair, his hat on the seat, his cigarettes and matchboxes, the cot where he slept and the pocket watch that hangs from a nail above it, and I worry that he may not have wished to be exposed this way. I enjoy his deliberate paintings, too, but not as much as this diorama of ghostly objects and their relationship to the painter. I suspect his thin shadow lurks somewhere between those carafes and pitchers that he collected and drew.

"I have been dreaming that I'm outside the yellow brick building, looking into Café Leila. Pari sits in the garden sewing the hem of a dress for you, as you lay in a bassinet at her feet while Mehrdad digs in the dirt with a stick. She looks up but doesn't see me standing at the gate. 'But they told me you died,' I cry. I try to tell her that I miss her so much, every single day, everywhere, all the time. I yell louder, 'I love you so much, Pari,' and I'm so happy because I realize I've died before her and that's why she can't hear me. Two crows watch from a branch above her, one dangles a large worm in his beak, but when I look again I see it's not a worm. It's my finger. Then I wake up and look at my hand and my wretched finger and everything is still here: my pipe, a clock, my slippers, her shapely bottles of perfume, her dresses, her comb, but when I reach for Pari, the sheets are cool and I'm alone with all our things."

Zod was crying now, as was Noor, but he was sobbing like she had never seen before. He opened his palms in a pleading gesture.

Noor took his hands in hers. "Don't cry, Baba *joon* (dear). Don't cry," she soothed.

"Noore cheshmam, you cannot stay here. Do you know why? Because staying here makes you a child."

He stopped to gaze at her. "I'm one foot closer to Pari, but I won't go while you girls are here. I want to die with dignity and every day that you stay, you prolong my suffering. You brought Lily into danger and discomfort for what, to watch me die? Everybody else has left because this is no place to live, Noor. People who've gone to seek their fortunes, even those who failed, chose freedom over roots—flight over captivity. You are a part of everything I have made here, but everything your mother and I have taught you is portable. Take it all with you, the hard work, the will, the appetite!

I've lost mine, but oh, to be hungry again, Noor!" He put a hand on the hollow of his stomach.

It felt urgent, the force with which he pleaded. "You *must* leave this place, Noor. Take Naneh Goli with you if you like—she will probably outlive you. Go back to nursing or open a ponchik shop in San Francisco, if that's what you want, *but take this child home!*"

There, he said it, but it left him exhausted, so that his thin neck became a burden on his skinny frame and he cocked his head for some kind of affirmation that Noor had understood. They listened quietly to Soli's footsteps on the gravel path taking the trash bags out. Noor gently lifted Zod onto the bed, straightened his sheet and blanket, and smoothed his silver hair away from his face in a soft caress that put him to sleep. She knew her father wasn't through with her—she carried his caution, the image of the woman he wanted her to be, his way of looking at the world, inside her, and though he had named her Noor to illuminate the narrow path, he couldn't help her find her way because she needed new names for the places she would go.

HAVING SETTLED HER FATHER and drawn the shade, Noor came into the kitchen and found Karim. He had been punished with the task of peeling an enormous bag of onions, which he did soundlessly under Naneh Goli's supervision. He lifted his head when Noor walked in and quickly looked back down. The kitten lay asleep in a box at his feet, nestled in an old pillowcase.

Noor took a bib apron off a hook on the wall and asked Naneh's permission to talk to Karim. Naneh Goli obliged, getting up and giving Noor her seat. Noor picked up Goli's knife and continued the work of peeling the onions beside Karim.

"Karim jan," she said, "you are my daughter's only friend in Iran."

Noor watched the boy, saw his skin deepen a shade, but he said nothing.

"I want you to keep her company, teach her some Persian and she can teach you English. Would you like that, Karim? Can you be Lily's friend?"

Karim looked up warily. Just an hour ago his uncle Soli had warned him that if he were to go anywhere near Lily again, he would castrate him, and now here was Noor asking if he would keep Lily company.

"Bu-bu-but, my uncle—" he stammered.

Noor cut him off, "I'll talk to your uncle, don't worry. Can you come closer, please?" She reached over and wiped away Karim's onion tears with a handkerchief from her apron pocket. Then she gently lifted Sheer and put the kitten into the boy's hands.

"There now," she said. "You three need one another." Karim understood.

NOOR PACED BACK AND forth across the wooden floors. It wasn't that long ago that she had carried Lily in her arms when her baby cried. After the warm milk, after a lullaby and bundling her in the blanket with the satin edge, together they had walked up and down the hallway. What solace in the rocking, how easy then to soothe her baby. *Go on*, she said to herself now, *speak to her. GO*. And she said it as she went up the stairs, step by step, into her daughter's room.

Lily raised her head from the pillow and looked at her, annoyed. Noor sat at the foot of the bed. Lily turned to the wall, so Noor spoke to her back.

"I panicked when I couldn't find you because I'm so scared, Lily. Scared of losing you. Scared of losing my father. We've stayed this long so I could take care of him, but I can't make him better. And what's worse, *I* end up being the one he has to comfort. I feel like a stranger in this house—my childhood home! I thought if I came back to the place where I used to dream, I would remember what it was like when everything seemed possible, that I could pull myself back together. Instead I've walked in on exhaustion. There is less of my father every day and he sleeps through whatever time he has left. Without him, I have no home and there is no Café Leila. Do you understand, Lily?"

As if from a voyage, Noor had brought in so much that it spilled out of her. At last, Lily sat up and gave her mother a long look.

"But why'd you have to bring me?" she asked.

"Because you are my daughter," Noor replied. She wanted to reach over and touch Lily's sleeve. She looked older in the bright light. "Leaving you behind would have been like leaving part of myself behind."

"But I'm *not* part of you! I'm me. I have my own life. And I just don't understand: if this place mattered so much, why did you always make me lie to everyone about where you're from? Why didn't you ever teach me any of the language? I miss Daddy, Mom. My life, my friends are not here."

"But you could have friends here," Noor began.

"How? How could I have friends? I don't even speak the language! And what about you? What happened to all your friends? I mean, like your high school friends? Didn't you stay in touch with them?"

"Well," Noor paused, "Uncle Mehrdad and I left without much notice. I hardly had time to say good-bye to anyone. Everybody was looking for a way out then. It was a crazy time." She was flustered knowing how inadequate her explanation was.

"Like you just vanished? Didn't you try writing to them? Find out what happened to them?" Lily was genuinely baffled that her mother couldn't look up an old friend now, try to reunite. If her life was falling apart, didn't it make sense to turn to people who would presumably understand her better than anyone, because they had known one another for so long?

How could Noor explain to her daughter that she was too broken, unrecognizable now to girlfriends long out of touch, who were once inseparable—their names stored in muted memory: Farnaz, Roya, Soheila, effervescent with gossip, jokes, heartaches, gripes, and disappointments, nothing ever left unsaid between them. Could Lily go to school here and make such fast friends? Could Noor persuade her to try? It wasn't impossible, but perhaps she expected too much from one afternoon.

"History broke us apart," Noor replied, "You don't know what it's like to be young and insecure and sent away from home to fend for yourself." At that, she rose to her feet.

"Don't I?" There was a long silence, intimate, with no trace of sarcasm.

"You have to feed your cat," said Noor and she went downstairs, feeling transparent. For once Lily saw through her. She couldn't plot or hide her motives, like from a child. The truth was, Noor wished it wasn't so rapid, this change in her daughter becoming a young woman. She had hoped to keep the imperfect world at bay, to gloss over her own flaws and foibles, but there was no turning back, no quiet shushing, no rocking, no crooning to her chickadee. Their walks together would be in the open now, into the wide world.

THE RULES WERE CLEAR. Karim was allowed to complete his chores in the morning so that he could spend the afternoons with Lily. They were not to leave the premises. Sometimes he was given money to buy ice cream and he raced to the shop alone, so as not to be away any longer than necessary. They were allowed to watch television in the old hotel. Soon Karim would be going back to school and there would be no time for such activities. Zod dismissed Soli's objections. "For a few weeks in the summer they can be children, no?"

Noor discovered a box of videos that turned out to be old home movies that Zod had transferred from film to videotape. Lily and Karim sat cross-legged in front of the screen and watched women and children at a long-ago birthday party, seated around a large table in a corner of the garden, their glasses of tea in silver holders. Crystal candlesticks with pink pendants glowed over pyramids of fruit and there was a burst of applause at the sudden appearance of a huge domed cake lit with dozens of candles. The film had no sound, but you could almost hear the noise and bustle of the singing and clapping and gesturing to the camera with exaggerated waves. A cranky-looking man in a three-piece suit smoked on the veranda while half a dozen boys and girls in party clothes played a chaotic game of hide-and-seek.

Where were they now, these rosy-cheeked children and their elegant parents? Lily was particularly drawn to one frizzy-haired little girl riding a tricycle and the slender woman reaching for her, but try as she might, Lily still felt little connection to these people on the screen, even though they were her family.

Karim would look back on the sweetness of those August afternoons as the happiest in his life. Since leaving his village, he never had free time, loss having forced him into a man's life at an early age. But Lily taught him to play. They found a deck of cards and an old Monopoly set, gradually teaching one another the words for colors and numbers in each other's languages. When a match was broadcast, they watched the World Cup. Karim delighted in Lily's squeals of enthusiasm whenever players knocked in goals from inconceivable angles.

She was astonished when he told her that women were not allowed in the stadium, that girls had been arrested for going to the matches disguised as boys. Lily thought he was making it up. She loved going to soccer games with her father. It was wonderful to sit on the bleachers under a blue sky, to smell the freshly cut grass, to cheer wildly. How could girls be denied the immense pleasure of rooting for their team, of watching the players run around in the heat and plow their hands through their sweat-soaked hair when they missed a shot? Oh, and what about the pure joy of a win in the slipping seconds before they charged the field to get their hands on one another? What was the harm in being a spectator?

To hasten his chores Lily would often help Karim. Donning one of her great-grandmother's aprons, she joined him washing dishes, scraping tidbits off plates into a bowl Naneh reserved for Sheer. Lily stacked the crockery and silverware in a soapy bath and together she and Karim fished out forks and spoons, rinsed and wiped each, one by one, gathering them into bouquets and placing them in metal pitchers. For Karim, it was glorious standing so close to Lily, smelling her fruity shampoo, and he nearly swooned when their fingertips brushed against each other under the foam.

Once, when a knife slipped from Lily's towel, cracking a glass bowl in the sink, Karim cut his thumb on its jagged edge. Lily gently washed and bandaged his wound, smiling bashfully at him from under her dark brows, murmuring soothingly "*Pobrecito niño.* (You poor thing.)" When everything was clean and dry and put away, they sat at the kitchen table and listened to music on Lily's iPod, sharing the earbuds, Karim trying to follow the movements of Lily's head since he'd never heard these songs.

Sometimes, if Karim's chores took him outside, Lily would spread a blanket in the shade of the mulberry tree and wait with Sheer in the crook of her arm while he swept the ashes from the grill or cleaned the chicken coop. Playfully, he'd scramble up the tree to shake a branch, pelting Lily with ripe berries, loving the ripple of her laugh as she let Sheer slip away. The cat was always with them, exploring every corner of the house, wandering into the salon to roll on her back and stare at Zod as if challenging him to do the same. It surprised Zod how old he was yet still, when faced with a kitten twitching its whiskers, he felt like a child, patted his knee and reached for the curious creature. The children would come calling and find her asleep on the old man's lap.

MEANWHILE, NOOR HATCHED A plan. There had to be a way to draw Lily to the lives of teenagers like herself before she could broach the subject of school. The idea of going swimming excited her. She thought that if she could get Lily to the pool, then she would see all the girls her age, relatively free, having fun, giggling and splashing one another like girls everywhere. Noor summoned her courage by playing this scenario over and over in her head: if Noor could catch the mood of this environment, then in the days to come she could tell her daughter about going to high school in Tehran for the fall semester.

Anyone seeing them might have thought they were friends, strolling past the kindergarten and the little grocery, carrying their towels in Lily's backpack, the sun already fierce on their backs. Under baggy coats they wore swimsuits beneath T-shirts and jeans and covered their hair in matching headscarves. Lily had grown taller and took longer strides past the men hosing the sidewalks in front of their shops, forcing Noor to trot behind her.

At the entry to the pool, through the confusing panels of cloth hung during ladies hour for "safety," they paid the attendant, who demanded they turn in their phones and handed them a locker key. The fifteen-minute walk in the intense heat had made them irritable so Noor suggested they take a quick cold shower.

"Okay, Mom."

Normally, Lily would have ignored Noor's ideas, a pattern so consistent that Noor thought this sudden willingness was a sign that it was going to be all right, that her daughter would take the news well.

They undressed and hung their towels on the line of hooks above a row of wooden benches. Whooping in the cold shower drew curious looks from the handful of women who had arrived at nine o'clock sharp to take advantage of the allocated three hours. *When had they last done anything fun together?* thought Noor, as she watched her daughter clearly enjoy herself, laughing while dousing herself with the cold water.

They came out of the changing room still laughing and stepped out into the bright sunshine. Out by the deck, Noor watched Lily hold her nose for a cannonball, and she remembered a holiday long ago in Mallorca, where they stayed with Nelson's grandparents in a pink-and-white villa. They went for long swims in the Mediterranean and sat for late night meals in fish shacks along the beach, eating fried sardines, with Lily between them smacking her little palms together—a memory so vivid, it made her stomach hurt to think Lily would never be nestled between her parents again.

Lily surfaced and swam the length of the pool to where Noor and a few other women sat watching her. She performed frisky and playful hand-stands, somersaults, and held her breath underwater, enjoying the attention. *Who is this new girl?* they all wondered.

"She's my daughter. She's fifteen," Noor offered. Bold now, she asked if their daughters were joining them. A woman with dyed reddish hair in a loose bun and wearing big designer sunglasses shook her head *no*.

"My girls are in America. They have swimming pools in their backyards!"

Her friend stretched her legs and nodded in agreement, "My son and his wife are also in Los Angeles."

"You must miss them so much," said Noor.

"Yes, they have two enchanting little girls I haven't seen in three years," she replied.

"Do you have more children?" the redhead wanted to know.

"No, just one."

They searched Noor's face to guess her age.

"You should have more," they chanted in unison.

"Oh, I'm afraid it's not up to me," and Noor excused herself to swim some laps, not wanting to continue a dead-end topic. People felt obliged to offer their opinions. She'd had a few miscarriages after Lily, then given up. One day she had asked Nelson to put Lily's crib and high chair on the sidewalk and watched from the kitchen window as a young father wheeled the crib to his pickup truck. Later an elderly couple, too polite to haul away the high chair without asking, rang the doorbell and gave her an earful about the grandchild who would be visiting soon. She walked to the curb to show them how to snap the tray on and off and helped them load it into their trunk.

Noor pushed off a wall and swam energetically from end to end—the water icy at first and then just right. Lily, balancing on a noodle, paddled towards her, gleefully shaking her thick hair and lifting it like a curtain to twist in a knot. Her vessel tipped and she dropped back smoothly below the surface, exposing darling pink toenails like periscopes. Horizontal now, they floated on their backs for a little while longer with the sun in their eyes and nothing but water between them. As they climbed out, Noor could see the girls she had followed a few days ago coming out from behind the screen that separated the changing cabins. Two were already lounging on their deck chairs and waving to the newcomers. Noor grabbed their towels and unrolled them near enough to greet them and Lily sat beside her hugging her knees.

"Excuse me, ma'am, are you a swim instructor?" asked the oldest in the group.

Noor laughed, "Me? Oh, no, sweetie."

"It's just that you swim so well and my little sister, Bahar, could use some lessons," she explained.

"Oh, well, I'd be happy to teach her but my daughter here is really the better swimmer."

She turned to Lily, "Don't you think you could teach swimming?"

Bahar looked Lily right in the eye, probably contemplating the benefits of a lesson from a peer rather than an instructor. Lily worried about how they would communicate, but there was hardly a need for words in swimming. She nodded and gave Bahar a pleasant smile, "Okay, I will," she said, sensing that Bahar liked her.

Noor felt that her hunch had turned out to be right—the company of these cheerful, curious girls, provided just the setting she had hoped for.

They nearly had the pool to themselves, as most women were sunbathing. Bahar, only a year younger than Lily, was reluctant at first. But urged along by Noor and the other girls, they walked together to the edge of the pool and Lily gently torqued her student's back, tucking her chin for a dive.

But Bahar solemnly shook her head, "No dive."

So Lily jumped in and held her arms out to her as Nelson had done when she was a toddler.

"One. Two. Three. Jump!" she cried and Bahar flew into her arms submerging them both and they rose to the surface laughing hysterically.

*How easily they transcend barriers*, thought Noor as she watched their pantomime—*how do you say kick, how do you say elbow, how do you say high, how do you say low, breathe out,* forgetting most and remembering some of these maiden words. Noor wondered if this was real, if her daughter could be happy here, or would this playfulness dry up once they toweled off.

Just before the café closed for the morning session, Noor ducked in to treat the older girls to cold sodas, which they accepted graciously. They asked Noor if she and her daughter would be back and Bahar kissed them shyly before they gathered their belongings and left.

Walking home, their hair still damp beneath their scarves, Noor reached for Lily's hand and Lily didn't pull away, slowing down her youthful gait to walk beside her mother.

"You had a nice time?" Noor asked.

"Yeah! Bahar is so funny."

"In a half hour you taught her to swim!"

"Can we go again, Mom? Do you think she'll be there?"

"Sure."

"Can Karim come, too?"

"Sweetie, didn't you see there were only women there? They don't let boys and girls swim together."

"That's insane. I don't get this country, mom. Like, why is everyone so afraid of women?"

"I agree, it's crazy, but just pretend you're in an all-girls school."

"*That's* your solution?" The edge in Lily's voice was back. Why was her mother so passive? How could she dismiss this blatant discrimination that was all around them?

"Lily, speaking of school," she began, but the words caught in her throat.

"I'd never go to an all-girls school, mom. It's not natural. Besides, girls can be so mean."

"Oh honey, you saw how nice Bahar and her friends were." She hurried along, emboldened by the turn in their conversation. "You'd like school here, they will love having a friend from America. Come September, you'll be quite the celebrity."

"Wait, what are you talking about?" said Lily. She stopped walking, all the color drained from her sun-kissed cheeks. She pulled her hand away and held it over her mouth, a storm gathering behind her pale face.

"You better be joking, Mom, or I swear I will tear this rag from my head right here and scream for help."

"*Shhh*, now calm down, Lily."

"Does this backwards country even have child services? Oh no, of course not, otherwise poor Karim wouldn't be slaving it in that dump."

"Watch your mouth! If it wasn't for your grandfather, Karim would be in an orphanage!"

"I'd rather be in an orphanage and so would he!"

"Please listen, Lily," Noor pleaded as Lily tried to talk over her.

"So this is your plan, for us to stay here? Does Dad know? Have you even spoken to him?"

"Just come with me to see the school. All right? And if you really don't like it, we'll find another one. It's probably only for a few months until Baba—"

"Answer me! *DOES HE KNOW*?" People stopped to look back at them.

"Let's go home and I'll explain everything." Noor tried to keep her voice even but she was shaking—petrified that Lily would do something that would alert the police patrolling the streets. "Please don't draw attention, Lily."

"I'm not going anywhere until you answer me because if Dad doesn't know, your little experiment is *over*." Suddenly she pulled the scarf loose and threw it at Noor who just stood there paralyzed by the fury in her daughter's twisted face.

"How many times has your precious father called you, huh? If I didn't leave him a message to call you—" Noor caught herself. She didn't know if they were the morality police, but two men in uniform were weaving through the cars towards them. They absolutely needed to get off this street and she grabbed Lily's arm, pulling her home.

KARIM WAS PRETENDING TO sweep the courtyard and water the plants so his uncle wouldn't find him idle while he waited for Lily to return. He felt ashamed each time he imagined her swimming. Two hours went by like two years and then, when they finally came through the front gate, Lily jan was crying and her mother was calling to Karim to close the gate behind them and fetch a glass of water.

But Lily ran past him and up the stairs to her room. *Khanoom* (ma'am) looked so angry, he didn't dare ask what happened. Noor was kind to Karim and he felt bad that she and Lily were always arguing. Karim thought his mother would have hit him with a stick if he ever talked back, but khanoom, she was always apologizing to her daughter.

# Twenty-One

O ne afternoon, waiting for Karim to return from the shops, Lily was writing in her journal in the courtyard when she noticed the motorbike leaning against the gardening shed. She had ridden on just such a bike one summer in Mallorca, clasping her father's thick torso, her eyes closed to the rise and fall of the road. Queasy when they stopped at last for ice cream, she rested her head against his chest, warm from the sun, and listened to the steady pulse of his heart until the feeling passed.

The memory struck her deeply, and as if retracing that moment, she went to the bike, dropped her notebook on the lawn, and grabbed the handlebars to clamber on top. It was heavier than she had anticipated. She turned and twisted the front wheel, toyed with the key in the little drum, half expecting the engine to roar. She looked back at the house. Not a sound. Everyone was taking their afternoon naps. She stared through the gap in the trees at the gate and a quiver ran through her.

Lily climbed off the bike, wiped her palms on her jeans, and stood for awhile wondering what to do next. She picked up the diary, filled until today with angry one-line entries. The motorbike would be her escape vehicle. It was so perfect she could not believe it had not occurred to her sooner. The rage that consumed her since the last battle with Noor turned to frantic euphoria, popping and crackling inside her as she tried to articulate the thought on paper as the idea began to form. She knew Karim would help.

THAT AFTERNOON, COMING HOME from the market, Karim paused under the mulberry tree and squinted through the branches to see Lily absorbed in her notebook. Lily, hearing his footfalls, turned and smiled. Feeling the familiar flare that rose from his chest when she called, pronouncing Karim as "Cream," he resisted the urge to run to her, and put the shopping bags down to wipe his brow.

He walked over to sit beside her on the dried-up patch of August grass. The household rarely stirred between two and four. Everything was still except for the wheezing chorus of the air conditioner grilles clinging to the windowsills. Everyone retreated to a cool corner of the house to sleep. Even Noor, who once resisted the obligatory afternoon siesta, was fast asleep in the middle of the day, waking up startled each time as if napping was something extraordinary.

Lily held out her notebook to show Karim her plan, which she had illustrated in a series of cartoons. A comic book, plotting out the scheme—and the part Karim would play in it. It took him some time to make sense of her drawings, to understand what she was asking him to do. Each panel had a clock face in the bottom right hand corner that indicated the time of day action was taking place. The first page was filled with pictures of supplies, a gas can with a spout, money, passport, scissors, backpack, watch, food, hat, and sunglasses. An arrow pointing away from Café Leila (with bars drawn on the facade, to imply a jail) arched over the ocean and a continent, to a house on the west coast of America, where a man waited on the front lawn.

On the second page, she had drawn herself with short hair, wearing mannish clothing, riding behind Karim on the motorbike. The clock read two thirty. The drawing took them through the streets of Tehran to the single geographic center Lily knew, the swimming pool. At a quarter past three, Karim and Lily enter the building during the afternoon men's session. The figure drawings were rough but clear enough for Karim to gasp at the images of him bare-chested in swimming trunks and Lily in an oversized T-shirt and shorts jumping into the pool. *No, no, no.* Pointing at her, then at himself, miming breaststroke, he shook his head emphatically, *no.*

It was, to Karim, as if Lily had presented him with pornography and color flooded his cheeks. She chatted in mixed sentences, plucking Persian words from her limited vocabulary, bubbling over, like an excited child. Karim tried to protest—Lily must understand how outrageous this was—that no one would buy her disguise, that they would be found out, mobbed, arrested, beaten, jailed. So many people were arbitrarily detained. But Lily wasn't interested in consequences. Laughing at the terror in his eyes she cried, "C'mon, Cream, don't be such a scaredy-*gorbeh* (cat)! We're going swimming together." She rotated her long slender arms in a mad windmill and he caught a whiff of her sweat, tangy and pleasant.

"But why?" he managed to ask in English, pointing to the picture of the pool. Lily eyed him.

"Because I want us to do something special together before I go." She smiled. He shook his head, trying to fathom the meaning of her words.

"Cream, didn't you tell me you grew up by the sea? Don't you remember feeling free in the open water? I want us to do that together, to swim in this little blue sea." What she didn't say was that, for her, going to the pool as a boy, however rash, was her own small act of civil disobedience, a rebuke to the regime's absurd restrictions.

Karim swallowed and didn't say anything more.

The next page of the notebook took them to the airport, with crudely drawn jets and a control tower. This is where he would leave her—there he was pulling away from the curb while Lily waved good-bye. On the runway, her face peers out from one of the tiny windows of an airplane.

Lily reached into her pocket and pulled out a fistful of dollars and the passport she had already stolen from her mother's dresser, to show him she was serious.

"I have enough money for a one-way ticket right here. I need you to drop me off and I'll get on the first flight out of here." She had close to two thousand dollars and a rough itinerary that could take her to Frankfurt or Amsterdam, and from there she would call her father. "I can't let my dad know until I'm almost there," she said.

"Am-ester-dam?" Karim repeated slowly and shot her a dubious look. Was she really going to go all the way there? It was so simple, she explained, but it could not be done without Karim driving the motorbike.

Karim thought no one but a fool would attempt this, then again, why not? What did he have to lose? It gave him a very special feeling to be chosen and pulled into her world, a world where thoughts became actions. He figured he wouldn't have many chances to get this close to Holland. In the heat and hum of bees in the late afternoon, he felt his chest dilate, diffusing the anguish within into something delightful and sweet, like honey, like courage.

Ironically, the task that filled him most with dread wasn't the escape or theft or even being caught—it was chopping off Lily's silky hair. He wondered if she would let him keep it. Then he could run his fingers through it when she was gone, because *gone* she would be—of that he was certain. *How can I help her run away?* he thought. *But how can I not?* Grief over losing her was already gripping him, twisting him apart. Karim shifted to his feet but nearly sank to the ground again.

"Until tomorrow then," he said without looking at her, and strode off with the shopping bags before he lost his nerve.

THAT NIGHT, KARIM LAY wide awake beneath a sheet, parallel to his uncle Soli who snored noisily in the bed beside him. He had always drifted off to the reassuring sounds of his uncle's rhythmic inhaling and exhaling, but this night, each breath was immense, drawing air and crumpling his lungs until he gasped. To quiet his thoughts, he played a game in his mind, invented long ago, in which he skipped stones on the shore, and each stone leaped farther away, troubling the flat surface of the water, on and on into the infinite sea, until at last he fell asleep.

Just before daybreak, he woke up to the smoke from Soli's morning cigarette and opened one eye. Yesterday's buoyancy plunged, but he had made a promise and knew that today he must be his most obedient and effusive. Before Soli had a chance to shout any orders, he rose and scuttled about, dressing swiftly and offering to fetch the bread.

Once outside, Karim drew deep breaths into his lungs. *I mustn't appear too eager*, he thought, taking long strides along the dry dusty road, counting coins from a zippered pouch, the sun already piercing his neck. Even in the freshness of dawn, the city breathed in the heat.

He returned with bread, first stopping in the yard to hide the can of gas and bottles of water he had procured behind the shed. Coming into the kitchen, the fragrance of tea welcomed him and he thanked Naneh Goli for the honey and cheese she put before him, cramming it all into his mouth at once and she smiled approvingly at his appetite.

Being sly was not his nature—the trust he had earned here would be tested today. Looking at Naneh Goli, hunched over, frail and forgiving, made him feel shame for his forthcoming deception and he looked away, avoiding her eyes. He was older now than when he'd come with the open wounds of an orphan boy.

He remembered arriving one chilly winter night without even a bag. The yellow lights all along the café windows were lit and the clink of utensils and scent of grilled meat had aroused a savage hunger. Zod had greeted him warmly and Naneh Goli had bathed him because he had forgotten how and he must have smelled primitive. They fed him and gave him clean clothes, then they sent him to school. Zod treated him like a son. *I have been absolutely loyal until now*, he thought. Then, before this sense of mixed allegiances overpowered him, he bolted out of the kitchen to finish his chores.

"Don't you run off, now," Naneh Goli called after him, but his life led only to this moment and to the afternoon hours when he would deliver his promise to Lily.

IN THE LAST HOUR of lunch Karim, seized with apprehension, nearly tripped while carrying a tray of clean glasses to the dining room and Soli yelled, "There's no need to hurry!" But a little later, rushing back, it happened again, and this time Soli blocked his path. Tall and muscular, he held Karim's shoulder in a tight grip.

"Sorry, uncle," he gulped. His heart wouldn't settle down for fear of his uncle's intuition. He breathed in deeply, and finally Soli let him go with a small shove.

Usually a confrontation with Uncle Soli shook him up, but just then, his guilt gave way to longing and Karim didn't care what his uncle would make of his haste. He wanted only to see Lily happy.

By the time he'd washed all the dishes and put everything away, it was after two o'clock. The plan was to meet at two thirty by the garden shed where Karim had hidden their supplies. At last, when the household turned in and everyone retired to their afternoon slumber, Karim crept outside with a bag of fruit.

He found Lily hastily pulling on his favorite shirt. Seeing her in his clothes made him gape, overcome with the special intimacy of the moment. There was no way he could let her go. Never.

"Na," he murmured, but knew there was absolutely no chance that he could change her mind.

Then, as if she read his thoughts, Lily narrowed her eyes and held out the scissors. "What's in the bag?" she asked.

"*Gojeh*," he offered. He knew Lily loved the sour green plums and she took them in exchange for the scissors. Then, kneeling with her back to Karim, she let her hair out of the ponytail and bent forward with her hands on her knees.

"Are you afraid, Cream?"

But he didn't answer. He stood behind her and ran his hand just once over her hair, about to enter a zone, as he often did in her presence, where everything outside it faded.

"Hurry up, then," she said, irritation creeping into her voice.

Karim lifted a handful of hair, made the first cut, and then gathered another, even and steady, until the pale skin of her beloved neck shone.

Karim looked down at his hands, as if he couldn't believe what they had done. He shut his eyes to the exposed back of her head lolling on her shoulders. It seemed to matter more than ever to protect her. Lily touched her bare neck and sat up.

"Good enough," she said. "Now, let's go."

She slipped the backpack over her shoulders and ran to open the gate. His face glistening with sweat, Karim idled the bike through the gate, closing the latch softly behind him. He planned to follow a route he knew that would take them through a quiet stretch, not running the risk of being seen by too many people. The swimming pool. The airport. Two places that had been separate were suddenly connected, the distance between them more than eighty kilometers, but it appeared much shorter in his youthful estimation.

Dressed like a boy, a ball cap pulled down over her cropped hair, Lily heeded Karim's warning to keep her eyes downcast all the while. They rehearsed once again their entry to the pool, but what worried Karim most was keeping her quiet because she blurted out English and laughed when he shushed her. To minimize speech, he insisted on a few hand signals and crossed his forearms now to stop her clowning around with a small sigh of irritation.

With one hand on her heart, Lily promised, "I'll be quiet, Cream."

Shyly, he patted her arm and hung the bag of plums from the handlebars. Lily straddled the bike and wrapped her arms around his waist. Then Karim started the engine and they went into the road.

GONE WERE THE DARK curtains that had been hung for ladies' hour and the men lingering outside didn't look twice at the two young boys making their way through the archway. Karim was glad for the relatively dark interior of the front office where a bald attendant with a pockmarked complexion was welcoming an elderly man ahead of them. Karim handed over the entrance fee using the monthly pocket money Soli gave him, instead of the dollar bills Lily had forced into his palm yesterday.

Pretending to look for something in her backpack, Lily pulled out a bath towel to drape over her shoulders in an attempt to look casual. The attendant carried on an animated conversation with the old man, taking the money from Karim absentmindedly and the two slinked away exchanging a quick victory sign.

"Hey!" he called after them.

They froze. Karim turned slowly, his legs wobbly, "What?"

"Put up your playthings," he hollered.

"Excuse me?"

"Hand me your phones, please."

"Oh, sorry, we don't have phones," said Karim, his heart pumping. Turning around and walking out the door was the obvious option. *Go. Now.*

"Listen kid, you take me for an idiot? Come here and empty your pockets or leave." The loud rap of his knuckles on the counter rattling Karim's nerves.

Lily didn't understand one word of this exchange, but she knew it wasn't going well. Karim took one short step then stopped and turned to Lily and made the telephone sign—thumb to ear, pinky to mouth.

"What's the matter with your brother, is he deaf or something?"

"My brother?" Something inside Karim opened. "Uh, yes, sir."

"Okay, okay, never mind. Go on in." He dismissed them and turned back to his friend.

Karim hurried them into the locker room, fear trickling through his pores. Panic liquefied his insides and even though he didn't want to leave Lily by herself for a minute, diarrhea raged through him and he rushed to the bathroom where he sat with his head in his hands and almost gagged at his own stench. This was a mistake. A grave mistake he'd made agreeing to this scheme, believing that the real divide between them was just a matter of coverings.

When he returned to the locker room Lily was sitting on a bench next to a locker, absorbed in a brochure she had found on the floor, easily ignored if you didn't know her. Disguised in an old soccer jersey and long baggy shorts, the blue cap pulled low, she wore a pair of Mehrdad's rubber sandals found in his closet and had wiped the polish from her toenails. Raucous shouts came from the pool, from the men horsing around. She looked up and smiled, gave him a thumbs-up even though he had explained a thousand times that it meant something entirely different in Iran—was in fact an insulting gesture. But he returned the signal. He loved her and it didn't matter that the signal meant "up yours," because everything in his head was upside-down and anything seemed possible.

That was how he had to think, that they could really do this, but the instant they were by the pool, doubt sneaked its way through brainwaves of courage. Again, arms crossed against his chest, he pointed to the diving board, *No jumping*, he warned, and walked towards the stack of kickboards and inner tubes. It was 102 degrees and the pool was swarming with men and boys, but they would be all right as long they just floated and she kept the hat on.

Lily, however, had other plans. She turned on her heel and marched straight to the diving board. Karim ran after her, urgently whispering in

Persian, "Don't you dare, don't you dare." She may or may not have understood, but his tone was clear. She tried to protest and lapsed hurriedly into English.

"It's so crowded, no one will notice me. Cream, please."

A deep frown, so unfamiliar to his face, and for the first time a spark of real anger flashed in his eyes.

She shrugged, "Fine, fine." and he pulled the invisible zipper across his lips to silence her.

They slid gingerly into the water, feet scarping the abrasive shallow end, and waded forth in their tubes, cooling their nape with wet hands. They couldn't stay mad at each other for long. Karim cupped his hands and splashed Lily to make peace, she quickly followed suit, and they played like this for a few minutes, sending off ripples on either side. How she longed to dunk him.

"Hey, Cream," she said softly, her voice drowned out by the noise, "How do you say brother?"

"Baradar," he said, repeating more slowly, "Ba-ra-dar."

"Oh, that's so easy," she said, pointing to him, "My bra-dar."

Karim swallowed, it wasn't exactly right, but he nodded soberly and gazed at the droplets of water on her pale forearms.

Lily looked on bitterly as the other swimmers plunged and surfaced, romping about poolside as though they were at the beach, while she and Karim were stuck puttering around in their inflatables. She inadvertently locked eyes with a hairy chested young man on the deck, who returned her gaze steadily, forcing her to look away quickly. But he continued to contemplate her.

His approach was gravely serene, the way one would approach a bird, the slight tilt of his head, the measured stride across the deck. Even with eyes cast downward, Lily, like a creature in the wild, sensed movement. What freedom she imagined when immersed in water drained in that moment.

Karim, preoccupied with smacking horseflies foolish enough to land on his arm, thought Lily was trying to engage him in another water fight, kicking him underwater. Then he saw her frightened expression, eyes wide and shifting side to side. A dark figure stood above them.

"Hey, you," he called to Lily who kept her head down and vanished into her shirt.

Play deaf, play deaf, play deaf.

"Hey, I'm talking to you!"

Karim looked up.

"Not you, him," pointing to Lily.

Karim shielded his eyes from the sun, "Oh, him? He can't hear you. He's deaf."

"Oh?"

"Yeah, why?"

"Where'd he get that Bagheri shirt?"

It was a knockoff number six jersey worn by Iran's retired star midfielder from the nineties, Karim Bagheri. It had been Soli's and handed down to Karim, who adored his namesake. He'd felt a ripple of pleasure seeing it on Lily that morning, not thinking that it would bring trouble. But sports fans are the same everywhere—soccer, football, basketball—they covet jerseys.

"Tell him I'll give him thirty thousand tomans for it."

Karim glanced at the spasm in the thin slope of Lily's shoulders beneath the nylon shirt, glad that she couldn't understand what was being said.

"Okay, I'll ask," he said, trying to sound friendly and signing to Lily who stared panic-stricken at his improvised gesticulation. Wisely, she shook her head, no.

"It's not for sale. Sorry, bud."

"Okay, make it thirty-five," the man persisted.

"No way, he sleeps in it, man. Hey, so you like Bagheri, huh? No one has that right leg." Karim kept his voice steady. As much as he needed to get rid of this man and get out of the pool, he had to keep his alarm in check.

"Bagheri's a legend, man. You follow Persepolis (the Iranian soccer club)?"

"Oh yeah! Damn shame they lost last week."

Someone shouted to the young man from the café.

"Later," he nodded to Karim and left.

Karim looked at Lily, the color drained from her face. It was time to go. He took her trembling hand underwater and paddled quickly to the shallow end. They waded out, warily stepping from the pool onto the hot stones, water dripping down their legs. Calmly they picked up their towels, clutching them for cover, slipped into their rubber shoes, and crossed the space between the pool and the changing room in slow, deliberate movement.

Karim felt that everyone was watching them, that everyone knew what they were up to. Terrified, they somehow retained the presence of mind to change into dry pants in adjacent stalls, where Lily knelt at the brink of the toilet to vomit and it was a horrible sound that wrenched his guts. They wrung out their trunks in the sink and kept their shirts on to dry in the heat. Walking past the dim office, the bald man drank tea and barely looked up to acknowledge Karim as they left.

They found the motorbike where they had tied it to a post, Karim silently sending up a prayer of gratitude that it was still there. Bikes were regularly stolen and he saw it as a good omen, or maybe his mother was watching over them, maybe Lily herself was a lucky charm.

Lily was still shaken, her mouth twisted with worry. This was only the first phase of her plan and it had curdled. After the absurd sequence of events, which Karim had yet to explain to her, especially about the magic jersey, relief washed over him—a thought popped in his mind that Bagheri, too, was smiling at them, keeping an eye out for them. And, with that realization, he burst with a gust of giddy laughter and took Lily by the shoulders, "Lily jan, we did it, you see? We go swimming! Boy with girl. Bra-der and seester!" he exclaimed in his broken English.

For an instant tears pooled in her eyes, but seeing his happy face, she just laughed. For there it was, they had done it—they had really done it!

The sun was still burning down through a cloudless sky when they mounted the old bike, which sputtered, then roared with the sweet sound of the engine. Lily's arms coiled around Karim's waist, her hair damp through the cloth cap pressed to his back, her breath still sour from throwing up blew warm on his neck—it all made him delirious. He swung past the parked cars and surged forward up the road, flying over hills that came afterwards where he was certain of another miracle.

# Twenty-Two

———⊗∞⊗———

Summers were hard in Tehran. The boil of asphalt roiling at midday left drivers evermore impatient and most people stayed inside with the shutters closed. Noor had stopped her afternoon forays to the flower shop, having given herself over to the custom of midday napping. She came downstairs in the rumpled T-shirt dress she'd slept in and cleared her throat, "Let me make the tea, Naneh."

But Naneh Goli just clucked at Noor's cough, or maybe it was her dress. Naneh Goli could not understand why Noor slept in her clothes when there were crisply ironed, clean nightgowns in her dresser. She had a tray already prepared with milk biscuits and stewed red plums for Zod.

Noor was about to object to the cookies when Naneh Goli cut her off, "Nothing is bad for him anymore, Golabcheh."

Noor nodded and accepted the tray, carrying it to the sitting room where a rotating fan blew warm air, every other turn lifting the white sheet over her father, who lay shriveled beneath like a pile of crooked twigs. He accepted a single spoonful of compote, shaking his head to a second serving.

Lily didn't show up for tea and Karim was not sitting on his footstool by the kitchen door, where he usually kept vigil waiting for Lily. However, she was accustomed to the disappearance of the children in the afternoons and hoped they were playing in the air-conditioned hotel lobby and not in the yard, where Lily would surely suffer a heatstroke. After the last episode on the street, Noor had given up suggesting the pool, but soon she would find them, bring them some cold drinks. She offered to read the newspaper to Zod, but he looked away. Weary, was he, of the news, or annoyed that she was still here? She didn't press him and he closed his eyes. Nobody knew what he was thinking about these days.

Noor went to the kitchen to fill a pitcher with ice water and cherry syrup. She found Sheer snoozing on the cool marble ledge. "Aren't you lonesome here all by yourself?"

Sheer just flicked the tip of her tail and closed her eyes. The cat was never far from the kids—or Zod. It seemed odd. The house was quiet, but then again, they were inclined to whisper so as not to disturb Zod when he dozed.

"Where is everybody?" she asked Naneh Goli, but Naneh Goli had the water running and didn't hear her. She set off to the hotel to find the kids, the pitcher of cherry juice forgotten.

After nearly an hour of searching the compound for the children, Noor began to panic. When she stepped into the café, having hastily wrapped a scarf over her head, Soli shook his head vehemently when asked about their whereabouts. How should he know where they were? He had never approved of this arrangement between his nephew and Zod's granddaughter. Their romping about, chasing that cat, and the infernal crack of the Ping-Pong ball, interfered with Karim's duties. *This will all end badly,* he thought each time he heard their shrieks of laughter, shaking a finger and pointing to the heavens as he did now.

"Alley cats," he spat, his throat cording, beads of sweat on his forehead from manning the grill.

"Excuse me?" Noor asked coolly, then seeing his worried look, she let it go.

"They're probably in the garden, khanoom, or the hotel" he said, embarrassed now.

"I looked. They're gone."

He gaped at her, mystified. Karim came and went as he pleased, but the girl wasn't allowed to leave the premises without her mother.

Noor never did know quite how, but together they ran rhythmically, without another word, back to the house for keys to the Peugeot. In America Noor would have called the police. She wanted to call the police now, but Soli and Naneh Goli convinced her to wait, to drive around before dark to see if they could find Lily and Karim themselves, though neither of them could possibly guess where the two may have gone. They thought it best to search separately, so Noor, despite being wary of facing Tehran's traffic, took the car and Soli went for his motorbike—only to discover it was missing.

ONCE AGAIN, DESPERATE AND desperately out of place, Noor found herself navigating the city streets, shocked at how inept she was— *what did the signs even mean?* She choked back a sob. Suddenly darting into a thoroughfare, she drove haltingly, a white-knuckled seize of the wheel pressed to her bosom, her foot on the brake, raising the ire of other drivers who converged upon her from left and right, screaming obscenities, blinking their lights and leaning on their horns, drawing so near they could reach through the driver's window and slap her, a deafening shriek of a siren, and people, so many pedestrians everywhere, weaving through the cars. Every assumption about lights, lanes, right of way, crosswalks, was obsolete. A camel in the Wild West, she was frothing now, her harness bell clamoring but drowned in the torrent of sound, of wheels and wheels and wheels spinning. Noor steered the car towards the curb and cut off the engine.

The rap on the window came so suddenly she jumped. A woman peering

212 | DONIA BIJAN

through the glass was asking Noor if she was all right. Hemmed in between the curb and a pickup truck, she was sitting with her forehead against the wheel, resigned after just a few kilometers. The traffic had not subsided, the children had not been found, and with no idea what street she was on or how far she had driven, Noor rolled down the window to see a police-woman. Young, no more than thirty, she eyed Noor quizzically.

"Do you need a doctor, khanoom?" she asked.

"No, officer." What she really wanted to do was to burrow her head in this woman's neck and cry. "I'm lost. I came looking for my—"

Mentioning Lily meant mentioning Karim. Unaccompanied, unrelated boy and girl meant trouble. Yet strangely, she felt a lack of fear in the presence of this woman who had cut through the throng to reach Noor.

"I came to buy medicine for my father. He's very sick, he's dying. But I can't find the pharmacy and it's getting late and I'm afraid to drive in this traffic. I don't know how to get back home." She was panting the words.

"All right, all right, calm down. Which pharmacy? We'll escort you."

The thing was that she didn't know because Dr. Mehran made daily house calls, administering medication to Zod himself, and she had only been to the pharmacy for cough syrup and maxi pads.

"First, let's see your license."

Noor turned and reached for her purse just as one would, but the Cali-fornia driver's license she retrieved from her wallet was not what the officer expected.

"What's this," she snapped. "This is no good here. You can't drive with this." Narrowing her eyes at Noor, "I have to take you to the station. Please get out of the car."

"What? You can't be serious! You said you'd help me find the pharmacy!"

"I can't let you drive with this," she said, inspecting the plastic card with bemused curiosity.

"But why not?" Noor demanded, raising her voice.

"*Because*, khanoom, we are *not* in America." A sharpness surfaced in her voice and she drummed her fingers on the hood.

"Oh, *really*?" Noor mocked, "I see, I need a special license to drive in your circus," her voice was rising dangerously. "Shouldn't you be taking these lunatics—" she cried, gesturing to the traffic, "these maniacs to the station, instead of harassing *me*?"

Then she mumbled *bitch* in English under her breath.

"I'm losing my patience, khanoom. Get out of the car. Now!"

"Oh, oh! Wait! I get it. Hold on a minute." Noor reached again for her purse and pulled out her wallet. "Sorry officer, it's been awhile. What's the going rate?"

The only sensible thing that Noor did was not mentioning that her daughter was missing. When the phone rang in the kitchen Naneh Goli snatched the receiver. Noor was detained for driving with an invalid license, insulting and attempting to bribe an officer of the Islamic Republic.

THEY WERE IN THE maze of the city for about an hour. Karim had little experience driving a scooter, but he managed to maneuver the narrow spaces between the cars and avoid the ditches on the side of the road. He would not have minded getting lost, going west instead of east, prolonging the journey and their freedom. Splendid was the clamor of angry car horns and shrill police whistles, the gnarled trunks of lifeless trees, the gritty sadness of the city.

"Look, how pretty," said Lily, pointing to a flock of geese flying above them in *V* formation. "I wonder where they're going."

The brightness of her voice, even when he didn't understand what she said, released him from the confines of his small life. They could not have predicted the sweetness of their escape, how it amplified all the sounds and sharpened their perception. How time stretched before them, the way it does in childhood when an hour feels like an eternity.

The airport was still far away and Karim had avoided the short cut, continuing straight instead of turning left onto the freeway ramp. There were more cars along this flat stretch. Buses thundered by, taxis blared their horns cutting him off, and he turned into a side street to avoid the congestion.

At a red light he adjusted the mirror and his eyes were drawn towards some young men lurking on the sidewalk near a newsstand. Two wore dark sunglasses and cupped lit cigarettes in their palms. The other two in loose Adidas pants and black warm-up jackets hovered with their hands in their pockets in front of a corner grocery, peering into the glass window.

The heat made Karim weary, the insides of his pants' legs were hot and sweaty, and with the change left in his pocket he thought of dashing into the store for a cold soda.

"Lily, Coca-Cola?" She nodded *yes* but he continued to stare dubiously at the men and then at the clear sky, hesitating then pulling forward a few yards from the curb, ignoring the wave of uneasiness. Weren't there always men on street corners? Out of the hot sun, he parked in the shade of an awning.

"Stay here. I'll be right back," he said in Persian and walked quickly to the market.

The four men glanced at him, their faces masklike, then quickly looked away when the door was pushed open and a man walked out with two large plastic jugs, letting the screen slam behind him.

Reaching the front door, Karim stood aside, catching his own thin reflection in the glass, to let two women carrying shopping bags come out. As soon as he was away from Lily, he wanted to return to her as quickly as possible, but the men nudged ahead and stood in his way blocking the women's path, not bothering to look at him. Karim noticed the younger of the two was only a girl, with a grave, watchful expression on her face as she studied the four guys, then brushed past them, pulling her companion along.

One of the men, squat and beefy, catcalled but she quickened her steps and he straightened up, gesturing to his friends to follow in the direction where Karim had parked the scooter. Sensing that these were a band of street thugs, he turned back towards Lily to see the women drop the bags and break into a run, the flying hem of their veils billowing like sails and sliding down from their heads to their shoulders to resemble capes of superheroes. Yet they failed to outrun the hooligans.

There was some sort of brawl at the far end of the street where the men ambushed them, jeering and taunting in crude language, and now the stocky one held the girl in a chokehold while she screeched and struggled and another prodded and poked her. The older woman clawed at their backs until one of them broke away to have the space to kick her in the gut before returning to combat, leaving her to collapse on the sidewalk.

Suddenly, a sound pierced the brawl. Foreign. English. Female. "*STOP! Leave her alone!*" Lily screamed.

*Shit*, thought Karim. *Shit. Shit. SHIT.*

Until then they were totally unaware of the slight figure behind the motorbike. Now she stood squarely in the middle of the street, squinting into the sun, one arm held up against the light and Karim looked past her at the men. Men big enough to tackle a truck stared back, astonished. They understood *stop*, but that it came from a kid in a ball cap with a feminine voice was unbelievable and in the few seconds it took them to register the witness to their brutality, one got to his feet.

Whatever happened next hinged on Karim's instincts—he watched Lily, she watched them, and his mind was full of words but not a single one came to him, nothing but a howl like from a mute, a stammering mute "*LEEE-EEEEL-EEEEL*," and he lunged, grabbing her arm and running in a breathless gallop away from the hulking brute who came after them.

It was all he could do to shove Lily inside the small grocery ignoring her protests. "No you! You here!" he warned desperately in the language he had learned playing games, but this was no longer a game.

When he stepped back out onto the sidewalk the man pounced on him, forcing him down to the pavement, pressing an immense chest against

Karim's back, hollering obscenities into his ear, and holding him down spread-eagled with hands that were so much larger than Karim's that he was trapped inside them. A shriek made the man turn sideways. Then came a strange, animal cry, so wild and intense, that it drowned him out, and the minute he loosened his grip to swivel towards the sound, Karim wrestled free and stood very still. The mob at the end of the street was calling to his assailant who rose furious, aiming a fist once more, shouting right into Karim's face. He was the spitting image, literally, of a bulldog with a big, open, square jaw and dreadful breath, and Karim squeezed his eyebrows to avoid the spray of spit into his eyes.

"Who are you, you ignorant son of a bitch, huh? A spy? We're just doing our job, you know. I should knock your baby teeth out of your skull, or better to kill you, you little shit—"

"We weren't here, I swear. We *weren't* here. We didn't see anything!" Karim begged.

"*SHUT UP! SHUT YOUR MOUTH, FOOL!* You think you can hide your foreign girlfriend in there? Huh?" he yelled, tilting his fat head towards the store. "We'll wait right here as long as it takes and I'll service her, too. Then I'll drag both of you to the police for a good lashing and you can spend your honeymoon in jail, sleeping in your own piss with your pants down . . . " all the while jabbing Karim's chest with his index finger as he spewed vulgar threats.

"*COME ON! LET'S GO!*" shouted his cohorts. "He's just a stupid kid, let's get out of here!"

"I'm not finished with you, boy," he vowed, punching Karim hard in the stomach. "I'm coming back to break your neck."

"*HEY! Let's go!*" came another urgent call.

Then he turned and ran to his friends, leaving Karim doubled over and drenched with sweat, his mind reeling feverishly. How? How did they embark on this misadventure? They were so young. He was so young. With the back of his hand he wiped the blood and spit off his face. His knee hurt and he pulled up his trouser leg to see the flap of raw skin and blood seeping through the fabric, swollen and stiff. He knew what he had to do. Anything that could be explained to Lily about what just happened would be incomprehensible. *I have to get her to the airport, away from here*—his scattered thoughts flattening into a clear picture like one of Lily's drawings.

Trudging to the entrance, he pushed the door and hobbled inside the store to fetch her, but she wasn't there. All the blood drained from his face. He could not fathom where she could be. Searching the aisles deliriously, a sneaker came untied and he nearly tripped and fell onto the tiles before giving up and going back into the heat. How? How did he ever think he could do this when he couldn't even keep his shoelaces tied? The street was deserted and the bike leaned idly in the shade as if all hell had not just broken loose.

THERE CAME A CRY from a stack of bricks on the curb, so jagged and hoarse that Karim thought at first it was a crow. Then it came again, sharp and unmistakably human. Nosing the scooter warily towards the sound, Karim slowed down and came upon three women nestled behind piles of rubble next to an unfinished construction site. Intent on shielding the women, Lily released her hold on a warped metal pipe and twisted around to wave frantically, urging Karim to stop, her color ashen against the masonry. How was she over here? Relief washed over him and then spoiled quickly, giving in to unspeakable rage. *What the hell is she doing here?* he thought.

"*GET OUT OF THERE!*" he yelled in Farsi, losing control. "*GET OUT, GET OUT!*"

"*Shhh!*" she said, fixing her eyes on him.

"Lily, what do you think you're doing? We have to go! *NOW!*" Expressing fury in English eluded him.

"*Shhh! Shhh!* Cream, come here! *Quickly.*" She gestured madly.

Karim got off the bike and stepped forward awkwardly, lowering himself to see. A girl, fourteen at the most, lay in a woman's arms. Her lowered face wasn't a face at all. The side of her head was burnt flesh, her eyes a sticky blood pudding beneath scorched brows, she lolled back and forth beneath a strip of plastic sheeting, making that same raspy groan. He kneeled beside Lily.

"Ask them what happened," Lily said.

The woman bent her leg and tried to raise herself without hurting the girl, "I beg of you. Please, help my daughter," she pleaded. "Some men attacked us and threw acid at her face." She had dragged her daughter behind the rubble to hide from the perpetrators.

"Can you get me some more water? This bottle is empty. I need water. Please."

How could he explain acid attacks to Lily? Neither Lily nor Karim could be expected to understand a world where such things were possible, that an innocent girl would be burned alive for refusing a ludicrous marriage proposal. Karim had last seen her unharmed—a wary lowered brow, fresh pink cheeks, the pressed line of her mouth, all gone now, melted into a black tarmac.

Karim translated for Lily the best he could, but she had already understood "please," "help," and "water" and given the water bottle from her backpack to the woman who poured it on her daughter's face.

"Cream, hospital. Right now!"

"How Lily?"

Karim would have preferred to call an ambulance or even the police and leave before their arrival, but the girl's mother begged him not to. The assailants would come back if authorities were informed, she explained, and they would ask too many questions at the hospital. She said if they would just take her home, she'd call a doctor.

And then, everything happened at once. Lily motioned for Karim to fetch the bike. Extending a hand she lifted the ragdoll body and with the mother's help they brought her to her feet. With tender authority she hiked up the girl's veil, hooked her shoes into the footholds, clasped her arms around Karim's waist, then straddled the bike herself to sit behind the girl, cushioning her between them.

"Tell her we're taking her back to our house," she commanded in half English, half Persian, squeezing the mother's hand reassuringly.

Wide-eyed, Karim stared at her, "Go back? To Café Leila?"

"*Begoo* (say) my mother's a nurse. Begoo, we won't tell anyone. Give her the address . . . *Zood* (hurry), Cream!"

Color disappeared in the waning light, the noise of Tehran falling in the dark. Three children clutched one another as the scooter wheezed past dark rows of residential blocks and shops closing up for the night, the small headlight shining a path before them to the sanctuary of Café Leila.

Karim saw the bleakness around him, all the splendor gone now. The parched streets, the dirty shop windows, leafless trees, a lead sky, the weight of ruin against his back, and Lily, like a wildflower, pushing through the crack in the sidewalk, stubborn like spring itself, insisting on coming back and coming back. Impetuous, invincible, unstoppable, Lily jan.

WHEN THE SCOOTER PULLED into the yard, its wheels crunching on the gravel, all the lights in the house were on. Karim quickly disembarked, running to peer furtively into the kitchen window. There was an eerie silence before the dark square of Soli's head snapped up to leer back at him through the glass. Did Karim really think their absence went unnoticed? There were one or two afternoons when no one had called or checked on them until after dark and he desperately hoped that tonight, too, they were preoccupied enough to forget about him. Soli thundered towards the door and, once outside, he grabbed Karim by the collar, lifting him up to throw him against the wall. Naneh Goli came screaming on his heels, batting one shoe in her hand, "Where is she? Show me your face you shameless son of a dog. Where have you taken the girl? Where were you?" Karim remained composed, a calm born from repeated blows. He knew the ax would fall and here it was, mild compared to what he had been through.

Then Lily's voice again, "Stop!" And still another, more savage cry, pierced the night, startling Naneh Goli, and she froze with one arm raised in the air.

The girl with the charred face, propped up against Lily's strong frame, whimpered under two watchful pairs of eyes. Karim pushed himself off the ground and rushed to her other side. Together, they strode up the path, arms draped around necks, their heads turned towards the injured girl between them, Lily muttering, "There there, you're safe now, we'll look after you," while Karim attempted an explanation to Naneh and Soli, who stood solemnly aside to let the threesome by, following them in, having acknowledged that the two children in their charge were safe, and the third, in desperate need of help.

Naneh Goli had never felt as frightened as she did that night. Her entire history, apart from her brief marriages, had taken place in this house. She had remained deliberately behind these walls, housebound in her shrunken world, and not only did Lily and Karim break free, but they brought the outside in, and Naneh felt menaced by this damaged stranger in their home. Standing back to survey in silence the three figures moving inside, she knew then that nothing would ever be the same.

They brought the girl into the kitchen. Lily and Karim lowered her into a chair and she tilted her head back to show them again the horror under the glare of the overhead lights. Soli dialed Dr. Mehran who had only just left after paying Zod a nightly visit. No one had yet mentioned Noor's or the children's absence to Zod and if it weren't for Naneh Goli's screaming and the telephone, he would have slept peacefully through the whole thing. When they heard his call, Naneh sent Soli to reassure him, knowing that even in his groggy state, Zod would discern something amiss in his home. She instructed Karim to push the girl's chair closer to the sink, put her head in his hands and dipped it back to show Lily how to flush the burns under the spout while she diluted baking soda and water—a home remedy that may have come too late, but she wasn't one to stand idly.

# Twenty-Three

———❧———

When the overzealous cop hustled Noor into the back of a patrol car and took her to the station house, Noor was strangely relieved to not be behind the wheel, realizing that she hadn't ventured too far from Café Leila. Traffic hadn't eased up at all and she relaxed into the backseat, looking out the window like a tourist, seemingly oblivious to the trouble she was in. There were two other women in the detention area. Already, they were making their dissent clear, protesting loudly "We've done nothing wrong!" Flustered, Noor made a frantic call home.

"Are the children back?" she asked six times before Naneh Goli replied.

"Yes, but it's a mess, you need to get back here!"

"What mess? What are you talking about? Are they all right?"

"They went to the swimming pool! But there is more—I cannot tell you now."

"What? How can that be?" cried Noor, as if what mattered was the how. "Listen, I'm at the police station. But don't worry, I'm okay."

Then Naneh came to a boil and shouted over her, "What are you doing at the gendarmerie? Did you wreck the car?"

"No! I—" she faltered.

"Do they know who you are?" Naneh could not control her voice.

"What does that matter? Don't say anything to my father. I'll try to clear this up and come as soon as I can."

"Should Soli come for you?"

"No! Stay with the kids. Don't let Lily out of your sight. I'll take care of them when I get back."

The male officer in charge, in short sleeves and open collar, crossed his massive hairy arms and leaned back into his chair to hear Noor's story: her reasons for driving without a license in light of her father's illness, her inability to find the pharmacy and so on. Then suddenly, as if the ringing in her ears finally ceased, Noor felt the awakening of a long forgotten skill.

"Officer Husseini was so kind to come to my rescue. Otherwise I would still be sitting on the side of the road in despair," Noor offered, ingratiating herself. "I sincerely apologize for my behavior. Please commend her, she was right to admonish me but honestly, I ran out of the house without even thinking about my license. I've been so worried about my father, I haven't had a chance to apply for my license, but I promise to take care of it, sir. I promise I'll go first thing tomorrow."

"Tell me something, khanoom, would you offer money to a police officer in America?" he asked with a raised eyebrow. He came around his desk to observe Noor more closely. She held her breath.

"Sir, it was stupid of me and I'm very sorry," Noor replied sheepishly. Bribery had not worked, but she thought she might have a chance with flattery and remorse.

"I would very much like to apologize to her in person. But please, I beg you, don't tell my father. He would be so ashamed if he knew what I had—"

The sergeant turned wearily to glance at the address on the report.

"*You* are Mr. Yadegar's daughter?" he asked, surprised. "I know he's not well . . . and yes, a good man like him would not approve of this." Dismayed on behalf of Zod perhaps, he walked to the door and called out to another officer.

Fifteen minutes later, Noor was given a juice box and driven home in a police car, where once again she sat in the backseat watching the street lights come on, as complacent as a runaway child who never got very far. *So, the children had gone to the pool on a lark*, she thought—*it could be worse*. Then, feeling expansive after her close run-in with the law and a desire to foster her father's goodwill, Noor leaned forward between her uniformed escorts to extend an invitation to dinner at Café Leila.

HALFWAY TO THE KITCHEN door, Noor was surprised that no one heard the gate or their footsteps on the stone path. The two police officers came behind, maintaining a polite distance. As she approached, she saw a strange tableau through the kitchen windows. It reminded her of a Dutch painting she had once seen in a book—dark figures surrounding a supine body lit from above with his listless arms hanging down.

Unobserved, she stood for what seemed to her a long time, noticing Lily's cropped hair and her hands intent on a task that from Noor's angle looked like she was shampooing a girl's hair. Is this what Naneh meant by a mess—that Lily cut her hair, that the children had somehow gone to the pool? If that's all it was and her daughter had found a friend to play hair-dresser with, then all of the night's anxiety, the arrest and detention, were worth it, and the thought made her smile as she entered and they all looked up to meet her eyes.

"Lily, who cut your hair?"

"My hair? Who cares about my hair! Jesus, Mom, where've you been? Look at this poor girl!"

Noor raised her eyebrows quizzically, stepped closer, and her hands flew up to her face. Dumbfounded, she opened and closed her mouth and tried again to say something, but nothing came.

*"MOM!"* Lily shouted, *"HELP!"*

Mobilized, Noor was barking instructions, some made sense; others didn't. She shoved everyone aside to lift the girl's head from the sink pooled with water and black tissue.

"Who sent her here?"

"We found her on the side of the road. We brought her," Lily said calmly.

"But this is not a hospital! Don't you see? She needs to go to the hospital!"

*"Aren't you a nurse?"*

"What am I supposed to do?" Noor was petrified, separating herself from them.

Lily wiped her hands on her thighs. Eyes beckoning, she reached over and took her mother's hand.

"It's okay, mom," she said, *"Shhh*, it's all right. The doctor is on the way."

A faint voice called from the other room "I'm not sleeping . . . I can hear you."

Just outside the door, the policemen were sizing up the situation and the senior officer gave his colleague a knowing look, cleared his throat, and went inside ahead of him.

Karim felt a hand on his shoulder and a deep voice ask him from behind, "Where did you find this girl, son?" He jumped and turned, taking a step back in astonishment, and gasped, releasing the terrible fear that had been pressing his lungs for hours. He was simply too tired to dodge this one.

They were courteous, in a way one would expect from dinner guests, but certain forms of politeness on the part of the police could be chilling. Flustered and jabbering, Noor ushered them to the dining room where they stood stiffly and did not sit down.

"She is your daughter?" Noor did not know who they meant and thought it would be simpler to say *yes.*

"Please understand, Mrs. Yadegar," said the younger officer with a shrug, "we have a duty to report this incident and we need to question the two youths." They continued to look towards the door, behind which a girl whimpered.

"We'll call the station for an ambulance," said the other officer, "and for backup."

"*NO!* Please don't! A doctor is already on the way. We can explain every-thing," Noor's voice was becoming shrill. She felt sick with the thought of Lily coming before these men when Soli walked in with a tray and nodded benevolently at the two men. Orange sodas, bread, and two bowls of cold cucumber soup.

"Please sit down in the café," he said. "I've just lit the charcoal."

Ever since Pari's disappearance, Naneh Goli had an irrational fear of the police, and seeing them in her kitchen sent her running to protect Zod who was sitting up in bed with a searching look. It was an appalling mess and she couldn't hide it from him. Zod heard all he needed to know—that Noor had been arrested and two gendarmes were in his house. He got up, pushed Naneh aside, and reached for his cane hanging on the back of a chair. In a heroic effort to dress, he pulled on a knitted cardigan with one button too many in the wrong buttonholes, shoved his feet into flannel slippers and shuffled out to meet these unwanted guests.

Even before he reached the café, smoke filled his clean-smelling rooms and he made a noise in his throat that wasn't a cough but a growl. The younger cop stood up as soon as he saw Zod step through the door, leaving Naneh lurking behind. The other had taken his jacket off and sat in his yellow-stained shirtsleeves smoking a third cigarette.

"Have you come for me at last?" asked Zod.

"I'm sorry, sir?" replied the young officer.

"Hello, Mr. Yadegar! I'm Officer Sadeghi, this is my colleague . . . " He rose abruptly to shake Zod's hand.

Zod kept his trembling arms at his side. "What are you doing here? The café is closed. Please get out. Now."

They gawked at him—at this old, wasted man with pillow hair in bedroom slippers swinging his cane. Sadeghi eased back into the chair, took a sip of his soda, lit another cigarette and blew the smoke towards the ceiling.

"We have to do our job, Mr. Yadegar. Your daughter here offered . . . "

"Your *job*? You mean murder and abduction? Then do it! Don't come in here and eat my food and stink up my house."

Noor rushed to put an arm around his quivering shoulders but he shook her off. A foamy wrath collected at the corners of his mouth and he spat *"OUT! YOU SONS OF WHORES!"* None of them had ever heard an obscenity from him. Never.

The young policeman flinched and glanced around as if looking for an escape from a bad party. Sit? Or stand? Where to stand? Sadeghi blinked twice to clear his vision. They heard the distant sound of a siren.

"What have I done? Huh? *WHAT. HAVE. I. DONE?*" Zod roared. "What have I done to deserve such disrespect? Didn't I feed your father and your grandfather and your ayatollahs? Didn't I feed the citizens?" He seemed to hover above them now with his cane aloft.

"There. There. And *there*," he pointed with his stick to tables in the dining room. "Your father sat *there* and ate beef stroganoff. *There* he ate pomegranate stew. And *there* he ate my baklava! Everyone knows you are the devils who took my wife . . . *EVERYONE*! You left my children motherless! And *STILL*! I stayed and I fed you and kept the place open by the sweat of my brow. And now, *now* you dare come for my daughter? Take me! I am the almost dead—less work for you."

He took a handkerchief from his pocket and wiped his mouth. The last flickerings of fury still shone, but bit by bit the fight was going out of him.

They all stood very still. At last, Zod had spoken the truth and set free the awful cry, trapped for so long in the blackness of his throat. Noor was stunned. Everything her father had never the heart to tell her was unleashed here tonight. The air in the dining room was stale and thick with smoke. Sadeghi was no longer sitting.

"Why don't you calm down, Mr. Yadegar? Please go back into the house. We will sort this out. It's getting very late. You're wearing pajamas, you obviously need to lie down . . . the captain told me you're very ill." The shivers took over his body then and Zod lurched forward to steady himself against a chair.

"Listen, you bastard," he hissed, "are you saying I'm not *presentable* in my own café?" The sparks and flame returned to his eyes. "*GET THE HELL OUT. NOW!*"

Dr. Mehran walked in then, having just arrived at the house after being urgently summoned back. He wondered why the house shone like a lighthouse when his patient was supposed to be resting. On his way in he shouldered past two police officers who hurried past him, and he looked up to see the family on the landing watching them until they crossed the threshold, waiting to hear the car start. He indicated with his head the gate through which the men had left.

"Never mind, Doktor," said Zod. "They are never coming back."

His face red from exertion, Zod rested a hand on Soli's arm. "Brew us some tea, please, Soli. And put two sugars and some whiskey in mine." He went inside towards the bathroom. "I may be some time—Noor, call me when it's ready." At last there was a lightness in his chest, as the weight of years, days, the hour, came to rest.

# Twenty-Four

———&⁂&———

They learned that the girl's name was Fereshteh. Dr. Mehran had taken the girl to the hospital where she was treated for her burns. She needed reconstructive surgery that her family could not afford, she had lost vision in her right eye and the left eye was blurry. Despite Dr. Mehran's urging, her family refused to press charges against the spurned young man, who had sought Fereshteh's hand in marriage. He was the son of a contractor and nephew to a prominent judge. An impoverished family with small children, they feared retaliation.

Fereshteh's father was a day laborer who did occasional construction work for the contractor and when Noor went to plead with the girl's mother to seek justice, she found them huddled in a ramshackle one-room apartment that stood empty except for a tattered rug. Exasperated after hearing the woman's repeated, "I trust in God," Noor went to see Dr. Mehran.

"She wants me to pray," said Noor, "as if prayer will put an end to brutality! They're so afraid, they can't imagine standing up for their rights. They're willing to sacrifice their own daughter! Can you imagine?"

Dr. Mehran listened patiently.

"Your expectations are too high, khanoom," he said. "Your assumptions about legality are a Western notion that have no grounds here. These are ordinary people, fragile people, frightened by the ever-present threat of violence. They have surrendered to corruption and indifference because the alternative may be worse."

"Yes, but tell me, Doktor, how am I to explain this to my own daughter?"

Lily asked her every day if they had found "the jerk who did this to Ferry."

He gave her a pitying smile.

"Go home," Dr. Mehran paused, "and pack your bags. This is a bad place for tourists."


NANEH GOLI CONTINUED TO fret about the sordid intrusion into their private lives and worried her beads—a string of evil eyes. Yet there was also a sudden elation, for Noor and Lily had latched onto each other in a light-headed, post-trauma truce.

Every morning Soli dropped off Noor, Lily, and Karim at the hospital and they spent the day with Fereshteh while her mother went home to mind the younger children. They brought cold watermelon and currant cake, they fed her grapes and filled the room with fresh flowers from Mr. Azizi's shop. Twice they even snuck in Sheer in a large canvas bag.

Noor wondered why Mrs. Taslimi came alone to see her daughter. She arrived breathless in the afternoon, a pervading scent of fenugreek clinging to her headscarf when leaning in to kiss them, and leaving at sundown to return again to the hospital in the early morning before her husband went to work. Her unabashed affection for Karim and Lily embarrassed them and they stood in awkward silence when she praised Lily and called her *fereshteh*, which translates to "angel." "May God watch over you and bless you. Such good children you are," she said, grasping their hands.

"Even my husband and the children are afraid to see Ferry," she whispered to Noor, "but your daughter, she flew in like an angel. She wasn't afraid."

Just days after Ferry's discharge, Mrs. Taslimi, utterly bereft and distraught, came to see Noor and asked if her daughter could stay with them because the twins were terrified and her husband could not bear looking at his daughter without flying into a rage. Ferry was afraid to sleep alone and mewed all night. Meddling neighbors stopped by under the guise of paying a visit to gape at her.

"What sort of future awaits Ferry?" she wailed. "The neighborhood kids are calling her a monster."

"But you cannot banish your own child! It's unconscionable! It's bad enough that you won't report the man, but this . . . this is unforgivable. Do you realize that Ferry already blames herself for this?" Noor was incensed. "Flesh wounds are superficial, but have you thought about her psychic wounds? You know this is wrong—how can you abandon her?"

Mrs. Taslimi bristled at Noor's judgment and regarded her levelly.

"It is easy for you to talk this way because you have not lived in this country. We don't know each morning if there will be work, if we'll have food. What good will come from going to the police, going into the streets to protest? It means going to jail. Tell me, who will look after my babies when I'm in jail? My daughter was given a chance. She did not take it, fine. But did she have to insult the man?"

"So you not only forsake your daughter, you accuse her of bringing misfortune onto your family?" Noor's face had darkened at the wretchedness of it.

She asked about school and whether Mrs. Taslimi had spoken to the principal to see if there was a possibility for Ferry to attend later in the fall.

"School? What school?" replied Mrs. Taslimi. "Fereshteh cannot go back to school."

"What do you mean she can't? The doctors say her left eye will gradually heal." Noor half expected this but had hoped for better.

"Look, I know you mean well but going back to school is out of the question," she said, sinking back in her chair. "Maybe someday . . . if she has the surgery."

Noor stared at her with raised eyebrows.

"Please, khanoom. Don't look at me like that. This is for her own good; she's already been through enough pain, I can't subject her to the public eye." Mrs. Taslimi said, looking away from Noor.

"I think you mean you can't subject the public to *her*."

*God! What is wrong with these people?* thought Noor. *These people.* Her people. Powerless people. Where did this matter-of-fact acceptance of injustice, this catastrophic surrender, come from and when would it end? But her opinions didn't matter here and in countering Mrs. Taslimi, she risked Ferry's slim chances of ever resuming a normal life.

Noor understood then what she would have to do.

"I'm sorry if I've offended you, Mrs. Taslimi. I have a daughter, too, and it's thoughtless of me to suggest that you can send Ferry back into the world. Lily is so fond of her, please bring Ferry to us tonight. We'd be very happy to have her and I promise to take good care of her. I'll prepare a bedroom for her where she'll be comfortable."

Fidgeting with her veil, Mrs. Taslimi thanked her and left quickly.

IN SOCIAL STUDIES, LILY had learned about the untouchables, but like every chapter in the textbook, it was mostly forgotten by the time their teacher moved on to the next continent. That Ferry was cast out was medieval, yet despite being baffled by Noor's explanation, Lily was thrilled to have a roommate. Even with all the bedrooms in the house and the Vieux Hotel virtually empty, Soli and Hedi hauled an extra twin bed into Lily's room and she covered the mattress with tissue-thin sheets softened from years of wash. Beside the bed she positioned a small electric fan and cleared the night table of her scattered pens and notebooks to make room for a vase of pink freesias from the garden.

Karim, too, was pleased to hear the news and didn't seem nearly as surprised that Ferry would convalesce away from home. "No one can hurt her here," he told Noor, "Besides, the doctor comes every day and you're a nurse."

Noor had asked Zod's permission to house Ferry, mostly as a courtesy, knowing that he wouldn't deny hospitality, but the part of Naneh Goli that believed in ghosts and incense tried to talk her out of it—she warned them not to let a stranger in.

"We let strangers in every day," said Noor.

"But they go home afterwards. I tell you, this girl is a bad omen," cried Naneh.

And although Zod was too weary to argue, he reminded her of the story she once told him of the king who threw his owl boy into the dungeons so he wouldn't be seen and of the brothers who set him free to live in the forest where he would not be condemned. It was not the first time he had offered refuge to the dispossessed.

Lily's new ritual was to help Ferry dress in the mornings, laying out jeans and one of several long-sleeved cotton blouses with childish animal and flower prints that Mrs. Taslimi had packed to avoid anything that needed to be slipped over her head.

Noor brought a change of dressings on a tray with ointments and sterile gauze to clean the burns and soothe the flare while Lily watched the careful swaddling that Ferry endured in silence. The risk of infection was high and throughout the day, Noor changed the bandages with infinite care and cleaned the yellow discharge that oozed from Ferry's eyes.

Lily had never seen her mother work—Noor only nursed her through the occasional cold and rarely spoke of her patients unless it was a case that involved Nelson. Watching her mother tend to Ferry with such a sure hand, all the while talking softly about how nicely she was healing, was like seeing her for the first time and she felt a peculiar pride, uncertain of what it was because it was so new. How could her mother be so capable, and yet so helpless? It was odd seeing Noor so self-possessed, standing in her childhood bedroom with the small bed and the yellow birdhouse and her dolls on the shelf, clasping surgical scissors and leaning over a mangled girl.

Ferry didn't talk much at first and Lily would ask in English, "What are you thinking about?" and stroke her hair until she spoke. Ferry's composure, the gravity in her slow movements to the bathroom, the way she groped her way like a creature in the woods, sometimes frightened Lily, but she never winced at the garish wound plastered to the girl's face.

Before long a peculiar bond had developed between the three children, who spent hours together in the air-conditioned hotel lobby with the drapes drawn against the afternoon sun, which bothered Ferry's tender skin. Karim reluctantly detached himself to get his chores done and once away, his thoughts would return to them, and he hurried back to their den as if they were in a play he had interrupted. Their familiarity allowed them to tell one another things they may have kept to themselves, secrets too tedious to keep, all in a new language they cobbled together.

"What would you say to the man who hurt you?"

"I would say 'I hope you die in a fire.'"

"Why didn't you tell the police?"

"Because they would hurt my family."

"Are you sorry you didn't marry that thug?"

"God, no!"

"What did he look like?"

"A monster."

Often they devised a scheme for revenge, interrupting one another and making Ferry laugh with the outrageousness of it, much of it involving arson. Little did they know that the law in Iran permitted an eye for an eye. But blinding the perpetrator wouldn't strike them as punishment—no, that would be too generous a respite from the ugliness they wished to inflict upon him. Karim's eyes cast about, always on the lookout for his uncle, who was ever more vigilant since their mad escapade. Whenever a door opened, whenever he heard footsteps, he turned uneasily towards the sound because he knew one error, one forgotten task, and Soli would berate him and separate him from his friends. Yet Karim did not bear grudges against his uncle—he did what he had to do and that was all.

Lily told them stories of her life in America. She talked about her father, how much she missed him, of how he had chased women and hurt her mother. But she also felt a need to defend him, to make clear that he was not a bad person. She told them that she did not want to go to the all-girls' school, nor to her old school, where every hour and every move was spelled out for her—all those bells telling her where to go next.

"I feel different now, I like not having homework, not caring about grades." It wasn't that Lily found school exceptionally difficult. "Before, I was really good at every subject. I was so sure of what I wanted, but lately, I don't know—" And now she wasn't as eager to go home.

With school back in session, Karim could only join them in the late afternoons, bringing home candy or a pack of gum to share. He multitasked, scooting across the empty room with a mop, stopping to recapture a story mid-sentence. His voice was changing and he couldn't understand why one moment his words screeched like a girl, so it was best to keep mum and take his place in their circle as a listener.

He knew next to nothing about what sort of life Lily had led before coming to Iran, but the more she talked, the more her words confused him—teasing his poor lovelorn heart. *How can both be true?* he thought. Did she want to go back to her father or would she stay here? A small flame of hope flickered and he would fan it with all his might, until his arm fell off. These moments of promise were so bright, they warmed his chest and left him reeling with happiness even when he was in the classroom, even when

Soli grabbed his arm and pulled him away. Without that kind of hope, his heart would freeze into a hard, solid lump.

NELSON HAD ASSUMED THAT Lily would return for the beginning of the school year and that Noor would stay until her father died. He wrote encouraging emails to Lily, but knew she would see through them. Her acquiescent sighs to the broken words he repeated through the static of telephone lines were never reproachful, yet it worried him because what he knew and loved about his daughter was that she could not be depended upon to comply with form. Her bold, brutal honesty was what he admired.

Conversations with Noor were circuitous and she was evasive, making Nelson wonder if it was because the phones were tapped or just more of her Persian punishment strategy where grudge was perennial. What Noor lacked in wiles, she made up for with virtue, mystifying him with alternating pride, fury, and vulnerability, like a wounded soldier.

The problem was that he had never stopped loving her and would have begged forgiveness, foresworn women forever had he been willing to live an unatonable life with a woman he loved more tenderly than ever. When she had asked him plainly, "Have I not been a good wife to you?" he'd gasped as if seeing her naked, luminous skin for the first time. In all his outings with other women, he never met anyone like Noor. She had comforted him with the simple rewards of everyday life, a life he loved so much—their first cup of coffee in bed, the perfect square fold of his underwear in the top dresser drawer, and yet he'd shown a deliberate indifference to the future like an unmanned engine, never once asking himself, *What am I doing here? Suppose Noor found out?* Worse, *Suppose Lily found out?* Nelson enjoyed women the way a gardener delights in roses: their unique scent, the few small prickles in the hollow of their shaved armpits, their fleshy strawberry hips and sickle-shaped nails that dug into his back, and he had to sniff each one—it would be negligent otherwise.

Still, it wasn't remorse so much as misery that troubled him now, because Nelson did not want to be apart from his wife and daughter who were supposed to be the evergreens he could not imagine losing. Yet he had. And with every thought of Lily on the far side of the globe, Nelson loosened his tie to make room for the lump that would rise to his throat.

ABOUT A WEEK AFTER Ferry moved in, Lily's dad phoned her. She was glad to hear his voice. Had he ever gone this long without knowing what was going on in her life? Where could she begin? He sounded tired, like he'd been up half the night in surgery and could use a hot shower. Lily remembered how she used to hear the front door and the clomping upstairs in his clogs when he'd come home late and peek into her room to chat if she was awake, to kiss her good night, still wearing his scrubs, in a cloud of hospital smells—alcohol, blood, and sweat intermingling, as if he'd come from a battlefield. It was so different from his morning scent of pinecones and peppermint breath.

He laughed into the phone when she told him about going to the pool dressed up as a boy. Then she told him about Ferry. She knew if she told him about her other plan, to go to the airport and fly home, he would worry and tell her mother, and Lily didn't want them to suspect anything in case she decided to try again, or accuse Karim of being her accomplice. Although, now she was afraid to go outside, or to leave Ferry alone. She felt responsible for her new friend. And if Ferry's family didn't want her, Lily supposed that made Ferry part of her family now.

When she finished talking to her dad, Lily handed the phone over to Noor. Then she lingered, just outside the doorway, listening to their conversation. Her mother was trying to explain what had happened and at first she was talking in that icy voice that Lily hated—that *we're-fine-thank-you-very-much* tone she used frequently with Nelson.

But eventually she softened, exhaled deeply, and said "I'm just exhausted,

Nelson. I don't know what to tell Lily and I ask myself how this could be possible, that I've exposed her to such cruelty, that a girl can be disfigured, then shunned by her own family. And to top it off, my father is slipping away fast and he doesn't even want me here."

Then Lily heard nothing again, until her mother said, "No, Nelson. I don't want you to come. What would you come for?"

# Twenty-Five

———∞∞∞———

In mid-September, Lily convinced Noor to have a birthday party for Ferry and to invite her entire family. They decorated Café Leila with spools of red and green crepe paper, stringing the ribbons across the beams and pushing a few tables together to make one long rectangle. Lily and Karim's complete lack of discretion was one of the true signs of childhood; they had no need for it, so filled with eagerness were they to please their friend.

Compared to Lily's own birthdays that had stretched into extravagant weeklong events from pony rides to beauty parlor visits, this party was sedate. Ferry took a bath and borrowed a dress from Noor's closet and Lily painted her nails blue. These three friends, an orphan boy, an American sojourner, and a wounded girl, knew little of one another's past but already they had a history of their own. And this little celebration was as much for Ferry as for all three of them, for having found one another.

Lily ignored Soli and Naneh Goli's cool looks when she brought Ferry into the kitchen to help her bake a cake. Their youth and proportionate hunger would've made Naneh Goli laugh in happier days, but worry dampened the pleasures of watching two girls bake. Soli marched formally between the kitchen and pantry providing them with stingy portions of flour and sugar—he could not bring himself to part with more than six eggs.

The girls were oblivious to all this austerity. The wholesome feeding of large numbers of people had been this café's business for decades, so why this sudden begrudging of a birthday party? Because there was a cultural divide that mandated sobriety in a house where a man lay dying and a damaged girl brought tragedy upon tragedy. Every day, anguish welled up and held, but children can't be expected to hold their breath so long.

Ever since Zod had fallen ill, the tension in Soli's stomach would not let go. If Soli had experienced joy in his youth, he hardly dared to remember it. He was not the cherished child of doting parents, but one of six, and mostly left on his own until he was the extra pair of hands in his father's orchards and he would've spent a quiet, uneventful life outdoors by the sea, if at seventeen he had not been sent to fight Saddam, where good fortune meant coming back with your limbs intact. War hardened Soli—he could not understand why they were sent to the minefields, why he was spared, and the unspeakable horrors he witnessed haunted his dreams. Even the camaraderie he once felt with fellow soldiers waned and he was alone.

Zod was the only person who had ever paid attention to him in a meaningful way and taught him to turn out such things as a good lamb stew and the satisfaction that comes from serving food that people would share over confidences and conversation. Yet those same people who came every day to eat a bowl of warm stew would taste the sorrow in Soli's food and miss the fragrance and bright flavors that had nourished them for so long, but they didn't complain and they didn't reach for the saltshaker, as though performing a simple penance for Zod's demise.

Naneh Goli, too, came from a rural life to live with the Yadegars under a roof where every day her heart grew bigger and she fell in love with each of them. She was the ox that had pulled this family through despair so often, yet she now felt desperate watching Zod's fire diminish no matter how hard she blew on the ashes. She couldn't find the strength anymore to protect her little family and vulnerability stiffened her towards Ferry for bringing the world's woes to the confines of their home. That habitual ease of hospitality, so fixed in their day-to-day lives, turned to a dull necessity. The love feasts, the anniversaries and birthdays, the excitement and the whetting, belonged to yesterday and what she really wanted was to take a sword to the balloons and streamers and shut off the lights.

Cake baking is a bittersweet thing. There are so many reasons to be in the kitchen with a sieve and a cup of flour, and what one baker does, another cannot because it reminds him of something or someone. Baking is always with good intentions and good cake can never be anything but that, a special treat, whether the eggs came from a backyard coop or a supermarket shelf, or perhaps there wasn't quite a cup of sugar but just enough. There's no best way to make a birthday cake, but tenacity helps, as does optimism. How else to lift the gloom in this house? Nina would have liked to see her great-granddaughter cream together butter and sugar with her old wooden spoon and turn out a vanilla cake into a fluted copper mold once used for charlotte russe.

Even Noor, caught off guard by this youthful enthusiasm, bounded down the stairs and into the living room to find Zod lying so still that her immediate thought was *Oh, Baba, don't go dying on me now.* She bent over him just as she had done when Lily was a baby sound asleep in her crib, holding a finger beneath his nose to feel the warm breath and just then Zod flared his nostrils, blinked, and opened his eyes. The sparks shooting from those eyes belied age or disease, and if you looked into them and nothing else, not the yellowish complexion or shrunken frame, you may just believe that everything you were told was a lie, that this scrawny man, alert and bright, would live a hundred years or more.

Before he could protest, Noor lifted him, pulled his arms through the wide sleeves of the butterfly kimono, slipped his socked feet into bedroom slippers and, gripping his elbows at shoulder height, legs apart, stood him up to waltz backwards away from his sickbed.

"Haven't we done this before?" he asked.

"Done what?"

"This dance. Only I was the lead and you were a toddler learning to walk. If I let go, you tumbled forward."

"I'm not letting go, Baba jan."

"I know."

She settled Zod into the big chair propped with cushions against the kitchen wall, poured him a glass of tea with two sugar cubes, and demanded step-by-step instructions for making the yeast dough for piroshkies.

While the dough rose beneath a large linen towel on top of the refrigerator, he told her to take a black frying pan from the hook above the stove and heat some oil to brown the meat in small batches. He instructed her to scrape the bottom of the skillet to gather all the dark bits and pieces, to dice onions and fry them slowly in butter with turmeric and cinnamon until golden sweet, to sliver apricots and orange peel and simmer them with a tablespoon or two of vinegar and honey, cooling them and then seasoning with the salt that was always kept on the hood of the stove in a small silver bowl with a little spoon. Then she must fold them with the meat and onions, but he wouldn't tell her how much or how long. Instead he raised his tea to his lips, sipping slowly, allowing for her memory of these familiar scents and colors to reawaken.

Noor wanted two fillings, so Zod told her to wash spinach, and to wash it again, and once more still to remove all the soil before steaming. She filled a large saucepan with water and placed it on the rear burner, then strained fresh cheese through cheesecloth and crumbled it between her fingers before pounding allspice in the mortar and chopping scallions unevenly and squeezing out the excess water from the cooked spinach.

"Didn't you used to put cream in the spinach filling?"

"Mm. And sometimes hard-boiled eggs," he replied. "My mother used to say 'Make each bun like it's your first.'"

"Maybe that's why you never got tired of making them all these years."

Noor looked at him, there at the table watching her with his lively eyes. She went over and bent down to him. Why couldn't they stay like this?

Naneh Goli shuffled in, arched an eyebrow, and Zod answered her with a wink. He sat quite still watching Noor's movements, jittery and uncertain, her hands smooth and unscarred unlike his own battered claws with gnarled blue veins that ran across the back—he often examined his hands as though they weren't his, but objects from a toolbox. Every urge to push Noor aside, to do it himself more quickly, was let go. He was enjoying himself, but why now? Why not forty years ago when his shoulders filled his shirts and he lifted her on the counter to watch him bone a bird?

She had been a stubborn, single-minded girl, that's why. She had complained about the pervasive smell of fried onions in the house and cringed at the sight of raw meat, pink and fatty. She would gag at a whiff of hard-boiled eggs, held her nose and breathed through her mouth when he brought home trout, slicing open the stomach and pulling out the slimy intestines with his fingers. His little Noor had vowed never to cook, yet ate everything he prepared and asked for second helpings. How heartening to see defiance creeping in through the half open back door.

"It would be good to die after this," he said softly, but she heard.

"You don't get to choose when you die, Baba."

"Sometimes you do."

Lily helped Noor with the delicate folding of the piroshkies, which are traditionally made in large batches in order to justify the effort it takes to knead the dough, make the fillings, and wrap by hand a bun that stays fresh for only a few hours. Together they scooped and folded and sealed the half moons late into the night. Never had they worked side by side in such good spirits and never once, not even after they had filled six dozen, did Lily complain.

FERRY'S PARTY WAS A small but cheerful gathering: Mrs. Taslimi with her six-year-old twins who clung to her legs, Lily and Karim, Noor and Zod, and Dr. Mehran. Naneh Goli's attempt to stay busy elsewhere in the house was thwarted by Zod. "You're not going to become a bitter old nanny now, are you?" Offended, she joined the party.

Lily entertained the twins, making paper hats and blowing balloons, while Karim grilled kebabs of tomatoes and chicken and passed around tumblers of orange soda. Dr. Mehran sat with Zod, resuming where they left off the day before—the doctor's house calls long ago became an excuse to keep Zod company, spooning broth into his mouth and wiping his chin while picking at the dinner Soli served him at Zod's bedside. It pleased them to reminisce about a time when they were young and untroubled and nothing hurt for long.

"Do you remember being fifteen, Doktor?"

"Ah yes! My father was very harsh with my sisters, but I was the golden boy and spoiled rotten," Dr. Mehran said, slightly embarrassed. "My mother always served me the marrow bone from the soup, the rooster crown, the chicken hearts, and the biggest slab of tadig."

"Ha ha! A prince! That explains your vitality. They fed you the nuts and bolts!" said Zod.

*It's good to laugh like this*, thought Zod, *to defy expectations about how a dying man should behave.* Ever since the blessed girl's arrival, Noor was too preoccupied to hover awkwardly at the edge of the room and Lily came to him regularly and unreserved, even sharing her earbuds and propping up her iPod on the nightstand.

"Listen to this, Grandpa," she'd say, and play him the soundtrack to *The*

*Sound of Music*, a movie she had watched obsessively through kindergarten and first grade. Zod jiggled his foot to the familiar tunes. Pari, too, had loved that film and bought the record to sing along with it. It was still there, buried within the stack of records in the dumbwaiter. *If only they could play it now*, he thought, *and let these kids dance in the gazebo, to take turns twirling in the middle as they themselves had done years ago, before music was taboo and dancing became vulgar.* Persians are festive, it has long been their custom to look to the sky and break into song without reason, and no amount of curbing or curfew will crush that primal desire for revelry. They cannot, need not, *will not* live without song. Nowadays, people did everything they used to do: drink, dance, rap, and frolic—only underground.

Ferry, nestled between her mother and Noor, was virtually hidden from the early evening customers. When Lily came to fetch her to cut the cake, leaving the mothers alone, Noor didn't ask why Ferry's father hadn't come. The two women sat side by side in somber silence watching the twins chase Sheer around a table.

"Do you know they call their sister 'Fig Face'?" blurted Mrs. Taslimi.

Noor looked at her quizzically. "Excuse me?"

"They overheard some children at school say Ferry's face was like the inside of a ripe fig."

"And what do you say to them?" Noor tried to control her fury from surfacing.

"What *can* I say?" she shrugged.

Ferry blew out the candles on her cake and they sang "Happy Birthday" in Persian, Lily spiraling into giggles at the unfamiliar lyrics. Even Soli untangled his brow, nailed a smile to his face, and uncrossed his arms to serve tea. Lily cupped her hand over Ferry's, like a groom, to guide the knife and served the twins first before bringing plates to Noor and Mrs. Taslimi.

*Where did Lily learn this baking and serving?* thought Noor. And here their thoughts converged because Ferry's mother was equally baffled by the easy comfort and absence of anguish in the girls. It seemed they had jumped the glass walls of the fish bowl to roam the room, while their mothers circled inside.

Afterwards, in the hazy summer dusk, when the crickets began their courting calls and the guests grew tired, Noor wheeled Zod away, slipped off his worn leather moccasins, and tucked him in. Ferry walked her family to the gate to prolong the good-bye and held her mother, forbidding herself to cry when the twins hid behind the trees, too afraid to come near. When it became clear that there was no longer the least hope of returning home, Lily and Karim escorted Ferry back on the gravel path to the kitchen, where she was given a dishcloth to dry the dishes while they swept and mopped.

Noor pulled off the blue cleaning gloves to stack the plates in the cupboard, and Naneh Goli snoozed in the big chair. Later, weary and famished, Karim plated leftover chicken and they ate in the kitchen with the back door open to a full moon, and Noor remembered suddenly the afterglow of soirees in the garden when her parents would sit in this kitchen, with Pari's feet propped on Zod's lap, sharing a late-night snack and trading stories about who came, who danced, who was gay and who was dreary, and oh, what a night.

All Noor ever wanted was to give her daughter a childhood like her own, happy and festive. There was a time in her life, when she was eleven or so, that she'd sit in the back of the classroom with her best friend, Roya, and suddenly dissolve into a fit of giggles over some tiny slip, reignited at the slightest arch of the teacher's eyebrows, helpless to stifle their laughter. If there's one thing she remembered, it was that sidesplitting laughter, especially when Mehrdad would pin her down and tickle her fiercely until she screamed, begging him to stop but all the time laughing wildly, uncontrollably, until their father turned the hose on them.

Lily and her father had that—the teasing smiles and wink-wink jokes, an effervescence between them that flattened when Noor stepped in. Noor remembered this well, the expression that clouded their faces when she voiced caution, a complaint, another reminder. The fact that they could be close and their conversations long, that Nelson was good at knowing their daughter and she was not, was something that bothered Noor, but then again, all she ever wanted was for Lily to feel the irrepressible ripple of laughter.

# Twenty-Six

———◦◦◦◦———

Z od began to die in October. Time was short and now every hour seemed an hour from his death. A hush fell on the house, on the garden, on Noor and Lily and Naneh Goli, on Karim and Soli, on Hedi, Ala, and their customers. More than anything, Noor wanted to put her father's mind at ease that she and Lily would be all right, but Zod saw through any performance meant to please or assure him of this. It had taken her so long to understand that though Zod appreciated her attentions, he wasn't used to accepting care and it was best to anticipate his needs and not ask whether he was thirsty or needed an extra blanket. This, of course, was his gift; to know your desires before you said a word.

Noor did insist on the night shift (she practically arm wrestled Naneh Goli for the sofa) and would lay sleepless, conscious of every rise and fall of Zod's labored breath. He mostly dozed but stirred when the light first came in and she rushed to wash his face with a cool washcloth. Always tidy, he did not object to her shaving him. She would fill a bowl with warm water, tilt his head back, and put a hot towel over his face. Zod closed his eyes then and sighed with pleasure. Not once had he sat in Nezam's barber chair in the Hotel Leila lobby, yet in this seventh decade of his life, time stood still long enough for a proper shave. His daughter lathered shaving cream up to his temples and scraped the blade over his chin, gently pulling taut the loose skin and breathing in the clean scent that filled the air.

Such intimate work to sweep her fingers slowly over every line, every furrow engraved into the droopy folds of his jowls, stopping only to rinse the blade in the basin and resuming her delicate task. How long had it been since anyone had caressed this face? Traces of a handsome man still lurked in the sunken hollows of his eyes. He watched her without saying a word and it was impossible to know what he was thinking. All of a sudden he uttered, "A lot of the time I don't know if I've said something out loud or if I've just thought it."

"Well, you've been very quiet, so what were you thinking about?"

"Isn't it strange how our hair and nails keep growing even after we die? What practical purpose could it serve?"

If they all crowded into the room, Zod pretended to fall asleep. Oh, how they wore him out until Dr. Mehran suggested taking shifts, giving himself the longest hour. What comfort it was to have him in the house even if he sat birdlike and alert at Zod's bedside, twitching his beak nose to dismiss them and hardly looking up if they wandered in a minute early. "*Hanooz na, hanooz na!* (Not yet, not yet!)"

Sometimes Noor walked in to find Naneh Goli with her head on Zod's pillow and an arm draped over the skeleton beneath the sheets, twisted around him like a flame. If Zod spoke, a flicker of light would rise in her face, then quickly fade when he closed his eyes.

One afternoon, Naneh Goli was going through a pile of photos on Zod's nightstand and holding them up to his face one by one. Looking over her shoulders Noor saw a picture of her grandmother, a young mother of three boys: one lean, one burly, one angular. She recognized Uncle Morad, but her oldest uncle was rarely mentioned and when she glanced over at Zod, he drew in a deep raspy breath.

When she turned to go he said, "Aren't you staying?" *He wanted her there!*

"Yes," she said. "I'll stay right here," and pulled out a chair to sit on the other side of the bed.

Naneh Goli lifted another black-and-white image from the pile in her lap. Noor, maybe three years old, in a frilly bathing suit, holding Mehrdad's hand on the Caspian shore. Mehrdad looked away from the camera to the sky, with one arm raised and a finger pointing up and his little sister followed his gaze. What was he showing her? A seagull? It was his trick sometimes when she pestered and pestered him, just before frustration turned to fury, to distract her by pointing to something obscure in the sky—*Look, a bird! Look, a kite!* And if she resumed annoying him, testing his limits, he would make sure no one was looking and pinch her bottom, hard and mercilessly. She would shriek then, from the sudden, unexpected punishment, more surprised than in pain, and there was no end to her tears. It served her right. Being the older brother, he was forced to watch out for her and for the most part tolerated her wrecking a toy, running after his heels, but he didn't need her; she needed him.

Oh, Mehrdad. Suddenly, desperately, she wanted her brother. What time was it in California? It didn't matter. She got up.

"I have to make a phone call."

"Who are you going to call?" Zod asked.

"My brother."

"Is he here?"

"No, not yet," and she ran from the room to dial his number.

"Please come," she said. "Could you?"

THROUGH THE OPEN WINDOW Noor saw Lily and Ferry on the swing set in the garden, Karim pushing one, then the other, a hypnotic to-and-fro synchronized to the intervals of creaky metal chains. Their high voices carried upstairs to the bedroom. What did they chatter on about all day? How did they reach one another so easily? It seemed the bridge between them even diminished the distance between Noor and Lily.

That constant feeling that she was being endured was gone. For too long Noor had auditioned for motherhood, fun mom one day to authoritarian the next, careening from affectionate to cool, indulgent to critical, hands-off to hovering, and if Nelson was the arbiter, the easygoing dad, there to keep the peace and make their meals festive, it only heightened the pitch of her pendulum. It was exhausting being Noor, but she meant well. She always had meant well.

It was with the best of intentions that Noor had decided to pay a visit to the judge earlier that week. Yes, the one with the deranged nephew who burned Ferry. Maybe her father's rage had fueled her outrage. She'd been afraid for too long.

She borrowed Naneh Goli's black chador and sat on a hard chair outside the man's office for three days before he agreed to see her. Noor had refused to divulge the reason for her visit to anyone but him and eventually the clerks pretended she wasn't there. Noor rehearsed her story and prayed that her voice wouldn't waver in his presence.

When at last she was granted five minutes, a portly man in his sixties leaned over a cluttered desk and motioned to a chair across from him. Noor introduced herself and once again eighty years of the Yadegars' goodwill revealed that the judge had filled his ample belly more than once at her father's table. But she had not come for his "best wishes" and told him so. He assumed Noor needed a favor, offering "if there's anything I can do for you" and that's when she looked straight into his eyes, sweat dripping like a faucet from her armpits beneath the veil, said indeed there was, and came out with it, not leaving a shadow of a doubt in case he tried to dodge accountability.

"I had no idea," he said defensively, but of course you know when someone in your family is demented.

Noor couldn't make any viable threats and didn't want to put Ferry's family in peril, so she pleaded to his conscience. Leaving the adoption papers and the child's gruesome photos on his desk, she left quickly before her knees buckled. Ferry's mother had agreed, so all Noor needed was for it to become official: Fereshteh would become a member of the Yadegar family.

Now, through her bedroom window Noor watched the children through the tree branches. She saw Lily drop something. A Popsicle. Without missing a beat, Karim came from behind to offer his own. Even through the canopy of green leaves, even with his face half averted, Noor registered something in his stance. Karim stood before Lily, planted in the earth like the hundred-year-old mulberry tree, all shelter and shade, as if standing still to make a vow. Noor turned her head to the sky—the air was cooler now, and she could smell rain. All the small mannerisms, all the furtive glimpses, the color and light in his face when Lily came into the room. *How stupid can you be?* she thought. *Karim is in love with your daughter!*

She went downstairs to the kitchen and filled a pot with water, then carried it to the stove to cook the rice for dinner. She stood with folded arms, waiting for it to boil, then imagined her father's voice urging her to keep moving. So she took out plates and cutlery to set the table, dumped the tea leaves and rinsed the teapot, filled a pitcher of water and put it on the table with five glasses, washed lettuce for a salad, found a bowl, peeled cucumbers and chopped tomatoes until the lid shuddered on the pot, and she started the rice. She knew there was nothing she could do, nothing that would help Zod, and nothing that would help Karim. She couldn't change the conditions, she couldn't deny her awareness, and she couldn't stand in the way of death or love. The only thing to do was to keep moving, to do *something*, to show courage, to give everything she was capable of giving.

She turned the flame down, wrapped a dishcloth around the lid to trap the steam, and joined the children in the yard. Then all went quiet except for the crackle of tadig crust cooking beneath the rice.

"Dinner will be ready soon," she said.

"Good, I'm starving," said Lily.

"Anything I can help with?" asked Ferry.

"You three can clean up." And she squatted down to pick up a discarded Popsicle stick in the dirt.

# Twenty-Seven

They chose an overcast day, grayish and mild, to take Ferry to the pool. Bright sunlight was still irritating and the doctors advised her to stay mostly indoors. It was to be their first outing since she was attacked and Noor suppressed her apprehension, agreeing to accompany the girls. If only Karim could come, too, they lamented, and Lily teased that this time, "Cream can borrow my suit!"

They had just finished breakfast and Lily was biting off pieces of bread and mopping the remains of a fried egg. Karim was hanging around, his bright eyes glimmering and watching Noor expectantly. She took a swig of tea and looked at Lily's face, at Nelson's grin on her mouth and the laughing edges of Pari's eyes—his and her blood running through her veins. Lily gazed at Noor as if her mother could make things happen, as if she held the keys that opened doors Noor didn't know were shut. *Not a trace of fear in these children*, she thought. *They haven't seen anything, yet have seen so much, but oh, if they knew more, they wouldn't take on the world like this.*

At half past nine they left the house, walking through the quiet residential neighborhood with Ferry close between them and the wind swishing their scarves about. The curtains on the facade surrounding the entrance to the pool were drawn but the sound of women in water carried to the street and they linked arms to go inside.

The attendants were just sitting down to breakfast and the one with abundant loose black hair got up to sell them their passes while the other carried a teapot to the small round table wedged in the corner of the office, already laid with a floral tablecloth, a nice chunk of feta cheese, and a loaf of bread. It was only when the young woman looked up at Ferry's disfigured face that she gasped involuntarily. Ferry had not been around many people, she didn't know yet how to handle their gaze, their revulsion, their pity, or even their compassion.

Noor apologized for interrupting their meal, feeling sorry for the girl behind the counter who fumbled nervously with the tickets and change. Noor realized they were good people caught off guard and it was up to her to put this woman at ease, just as it was up to her to shepherd Ferry through these initial awkward encounters. Here is where her nursing skills came in handy and she quickly diffused the unpleasant air with a lucid explanation of Ferry's accident.

"You know this is not her fault," Noor added at length. "Come here, Ferry joon." She took Ferry's hand to bring her closer to the desk.

"This is Fereshteh. We call her Ferry for short. My name is Noor, and this is my daughter, Lily. And what's your name?"

"Soudabeh, but please call me Soodi," she lifted her eyes to peek once more, smoothing a creased bill before passing it to Noor. "Would you like three lockers or just one?"

They collected keys to adjacent lockers and Noor left her cell phone with Soodi, who smiled shyly and waited for them to turn the corner before sitting down at the table and dropping her head into her hands. Upstairs in the locker room they undressed quietly.

Lily was thinking back on the last time she was here, picturing Karim's anxious eyes darting back and forth. A pang of regret went through her for putting him in such danger. Ferry went inside herself the way she sometimes did. Noor draped their towels over one arm and gently put a hand on the girl's shoulder.

"Ferry, are you up for this?"

"Mhm." She shrugged.

"It isn't going to be easy, but it will get better," said Noor.

"Never. It will never get better," she cried. "The only three people I know who can stand to look at me are you, Lily, and Karim." Behind her dark glasses, tears welled up and trickled down her cheeks, soaking the gauze patch on her right eye.

They took a collective deep breath and opened the door to the pool, looking straight ahead. Five or six women sitting at a table in the café sipping tea stared with mouths agape until a sudden impulse made Noor look over to nod hello and they returned the greeting, lowering their eyes. She unloaded the towels to apply sunscreen to the girls' backs. Heads turned to look and one by one they averted their gaze, embarrassed when Noor acknowledged each with a friendly smile. *It's the only way*, she thought. *Exile is not a solution.*

"There you are, Mrs. Yadegar!" A voice cried from behind them. "Where have you been?" Bahar and her sister Sahar came towards them, suntanned arms outstretched.

"We were wondering when you'd be back," said Sahar.

"Hello! It's been too long!" said Noor, waiting for them to come closer. Lily took Ferry's hand.

"This is Ferry, *khahar koochooloo man* (she's my little sister)," Lily said in broken Persian.

There was a flicker of distress in their eyes. Then, "It's so good you're here. Bahar could really use another lesson!"

TWO DAYS EARLIER, AT around nine thirty in the evening, Mehrdad had called. Noor's first thought was that he couldn't get his passport renewed or he was too busy at work. Up until now, she had withheld information about Zod's demise, offering false hope in her flowery emails. Yet her most recent call came as no surprise. Mehrdad wasn't naive and was all too familiar with the Persian custom of keeping a true diagnosis from a dying patient or his kin to spare everyone unnecessary worry. Why ruin a life with bad news? But even in writing, Noor was a terrible actress and Mehrdad was prepared.

"Hey, Noor," he said. "It's me."

"Hi. Is something wrong?" She sat gripping the receiver.

"No, I just wanted to give you my flight number."

"Oh!" she cried, tears pooling in her eyes and falling like fat raindrops into her lap.

"Are you all right?" asked Mehrdad.

"Yes . . . yes, of course. I always cry. Let me write it down."

After hanging up, she searched for Naneh Goli and found her bent over the ironing board behind the yellow curtain that separated the linen closet from her bedroom. After sixty years of ironing, the smell of starch and rosewater saturated the walls, seeped into the carpet, and Naneh Goli carried that scent everywhere she went so it was never difficult to find her. How often had Noor snuck up behind her plump nanny and spooked her, Naneh Goli threatening to smack her bottom with a shoe. Even now she stood dauntless, though mostly shoulder blades and ribs beneath a thin housecoat.

Noor leaned in to hug the tiny, crooked woman who would iron paper towels if you let her.

"Naneh joon, you'll never guess who's coming."

"Doktor?"

"No. My brother."

"Tomorrow?"

"No, Saturday. Saturday night."

"We have to prepare a room."

"Yes, of course."

"Have you told your father?"

"No, I will right now." She breathed in Naneh Goli's perfume a moment longer before letting go.

All of a sudden, the house came alive as if light had only come through a keyhole before. She saw and heard everything, from particles of dust, to the mild fall weather, to the noise from the café, through Mehrdad's eyes and ears. She drifted from room to room, straightening objects, polishing furniture, peeping into bathrooms to check the soap, opening and closing the refrigerator door. What would Mehrdad like to eat? How much Scotch was left in the dumbwaiter? Naneh Goli circled the same rooms with a broom and a dustpan. Even Soli quit brooding—the prospect of another man in the house seemed to have softened the detachment that had taken him in its grip. He rubbed his hands together and set about peeling and chopping with new zeal.

The cuisine of Northern Iran, overlooked and underrated, is unlike most Persian food in that it's as unfussy and lighthearted as the people from that region. The fertile seaside villages of Mazandaran and Rasht, where Soli grew up before moving to the congested capital, were lush with orchards and rice fields. His father had cultivated citrus trees and the family was raised on the fruits and grains they harvested.

Alone in the kitchen, without Zod's supervision, he found himself turning to the wholesome food of his childhood, not only for the comfort the simple compositions offered, but because it was what he knew so well as he set about preparing a homecoming feast for Zod's only son. He pulled two kilos of fava beans from the freezer. Gathered last May, shucked and peeled on a quiet afternoon, they defrosted in a colander for a layered frittata his mother used to make with fistfuls of dill and sprinkled with sea salt. One flat of pale green figs and a bushel of new harvest walnuts were tied to the back of his scooter, along with two crates of pomegranates—half to squeeze for fresh morning juice and the other to split and seed for rice-and-meatball soup. Three fat chickens pecked in the yard, unaware of their destiny as he sharpened his cleaver. Tomorrow they would braise in a rich, tangy stew with sour red plums, their hearts and livers skewered and grilled, then wrapped in sheets of lavash with bouquets of tarragon and mint. Basmati rice soaked in salted water to be steamed with green garlic and mounds of finely chopped parsley and cilantro, then served with a whole roasted, eight kilo white fish stuffed with barberries, pistachios, and lime. On the farthest burner, whole bitter oranges bobbed in blossom syrup, to accompany rice pudding, next to a simmering pot of figs studded with cardamom pods for preserves. All night long Soli hummed in the kitchen.

SATURDAY BROUGHT RAIN, FINISHING what remained of their housekeeping so that even the cars and the streets shimmered. Anticipation took possession, bringing them back from the brink of despair and shifting attention away from sorrow to better attitudes and warmer feelings hitherto forgotten. Persians appreciate a proper welcoming party and didn't a native son's return call for one? Noor thought it would be a treat to eat a late dinner in the international terminal, remembering how often Zod had taken them there for a club sandwich to watch the planes land while waiting for Pari's arrival.

A trip to the airport was something Naneh Goli didn't want to miss—she never forgave Zod for leaving her behind the last time when Noor and Lily had arrived. Wedding gold was unearthed for the occasion and rouge applied carefully to her shriveled cheeks. Soli wore a cypress green hand-me-down sweater vest from Zod over a pressed white shirt to chauffer them to the airport.

With Ferry's help, Lily made a welcome banner, writing Mehrdad's name in Persian with colored markers and learning to write her own name, too—the sweeping rise and fall of the letters themselves more visual poetry than alphabet. She was quite fond of her uncle. Twice he had taken her to

Disneyland, and on his visits to San Francisco he rushed first to lift her off the ground in a whirling embrace, ignoring the adults and offering her tiny presents from his pocket.

Karim's eager pleas to Soli to accompany them were ignored. Stung by his uncle's cold refusal to take him, he hung back in their shared room, peering through the window across the narrow divide that separated the café from the old hotel. He jerked his head back when Noor stepped outside, pulling the hood of her parka against the drizzle. Watching them approach the car with their heads bent to avoid the rain, did he see Lily hesitating, craning around to look for him? No, she was only running back to grab the nearly forgotten bouquet Mr. Azizi had arranged earlier that day.

*Does she even know I'm here?* he thought. *Here I am, look up!* But then she was gone and he banged his forehead against the cold windowpane. How long would this last? He didn't think about the end of Lily's stay, but once he was reminded of it he couldn't help but hear the latch closing on the best days of his life. Fall was here, and with it a longer night. How many such empty hours had he before him?

A STEADY LAYER OF drizzle fell against the windows in the nearly empty restaurant where they had a perfect view of the runway. Lily pushed her forehead against the glass, watching the planes nose their way to the gates, wishing Karim and Ferry had come, too. Not so long ago, she had desperately wanted to be in a window seat on one of those planes taking off. That focused, inconsolable, anywhere-but-here hysteria driving her wild. How she had longed for her father, how she missed him still and wished she could tell him everything that happened. Looking back now, she could scarcely believe what the last days of August had brought her, how in one afternoon a world of unknown cruelty and unforeseen friendship opened to her, how suddenly she became a part of this everyday life. And it seemed like an immense span of time when in fact it had been only a few months.

After they had eaten and paid the bill, they walked to the waiting area where they watched through a glass panel as a stream of passengers entered the long hallway, pushing luggage carts and scanning faces for a familiar person. Lily unfurled her banner, filled with the simple hope of seeing her uncle.

"Looks as if his plane has landed," said Noor, rummaging in her purse for a mint. "Nice." Lily nodded and let her gaze wander to a little gathering of people a few feet away who were gesturing to get a passenger's attention. When she looked back her eyes grew wide and she let out a shout.

Nelson was surveying the crowd and spotted her just then.

"Lily!" he mouthed.

"Daddy!"

His eyes were shining. All the movement around him continued forward, but like an apparition he floated towards her, dropped his shoulder bag to the floor, and pressed his large palms against the glass. Forehead to forehead. Fingertip to fingertip. Voices and laughter growing distant around them. Nelson's face split into a huge grin. He crossed his eyes and stuck out his tongue. Lily, on tiptoes, glued to the glass, was afraid to move a muscle should he disappear. Noor stiffened, but then it was nearly impossible to be unmoved by the wonder of it. The others stood mystified. Someone, maybe Soli, picked up the banner Lily had let fall and held it up. Noor knew, didn't she, that Mehrdad would sense the direction of her thoughts and call Nelson. Until then, Mehrdad had not once meddled. Whether it was intuition or mutual understanding, she knew that her husband had come to take them home.

Naneh Goli inched her way to the front, digging bony elbows into paunches. She almost didn't recognize the two other passengers who came to stand next to Nelson: Mehrdad, tanned and slim, in jeans and a navy blue blazer, bent to say something to the small woman in a gray silk headscarf standing between him and Nelson. They looked up to smile warmly at their entourage waving wildly on the opposite side of the glass, waiting eagerly to flock around them.

"Farah joon . . . oh, Farah joon, I can't believe it!" cried Noor, turning to look at Lily to see if she had seen her aunt, too, and the utter shock in Lily's face confirmed that these three were real. The floodgates opened then and they wailed openly and without restraint. It's not something they had planned, but that's how it is when you come to a clearing. How else to let go of all that was inside them?

# Twenty-Eight

L ily would hardly let her father out of her sight. She waited for Nelson to wake up in the morning and brought him freshly squeezed pomegranate juice in bed to watch him gulp the cold, purple juice with loud exaggerated lip smacking. Inseparable those first few days, Nelson could hardly brush his teeth without an audience. He lifted Lily a few inches off the ground with feigned effort to express his wonder at how much she'd grown, grimacing under her weight before tossing her about, and their delight in this game rippled such that they all felt a little airborne.

*Ha ha ha!* Their laughter echoed through the house. His presence didn't fade Mehrdad's glory, not at all. In one day, they peeled back the sullen faces and reminded them how to laugh. *Ha ha ha!* The house itself seemed to flourish and flex its muscles, shutters sprung hinges to dappled sunlight, pipes rumbled, and lights shone in every window. Only Sheer, unaccustomed to the rich timbre of male voices, crawled under Zod's bed where she stayed until dinner smells lured her to the kitchen.

Aunt Farah had arrived in time to keep a tender vigil on the family and there was nothing in the world she wouldn't do to lift their heavy hearts. So petite, yet she filled the room when she appeared, always attentive and hugging them with her small arms. Her suitcases bulging with presents, she quickly endeared herself to everyone with intuition and small, thoughtful gestures, giving Naneh Goli a glittery cosmetics bag filled with shiny hairpins and satin bows, while Noor had lugged a fancy new iron across the ocean for her, which she didn't know how to use and had stored away.

In one afternoon Farah saw what had taken Noor three months to notice and she quietly took Karim under her wing, soothing the lovesick boy with affection.

"A thirteen-year-old boy needs a room of his own," she argued. "It's not as if there aren't enough bedrooms." Mehrdad and Noor, all too familiar with the twinkle in their aunt's eyes, agreed.

The next day, they moved Karim into Mehrdad's old bedroom, ignoring Soli's vehement objections. Karim carried his few possessions in a plastic grocery bag and sat on the bottom step with the bag at his feet until Farah took him upstairs and helped him settle in, rearranging the furniture, putting a poster of a soccer star above the bed, changing the faded duvet and threadbare towels, and taking him shopping for new clothes. He'd grown two inches and his pants were riding well above his ankles, but he blushed crimson when Lily complimented him on the new jeans.

In one week Farah became the person closest to the children, giving gifts of no occasion, and they took comfort in her dazzling presence like warmth from the sun. Noor wondered how Uncle Morad had never melted.

Mehrdad pulled the mattress off the bed Naneh Goli had prepared for him into the salon and slept on the floor beside Zod. Brother and sister camped out at his bedside, only leaving the room to use the toilet.

At night, he mumbled and gasped their mother's name, "Parvaneh, Pariroo, Parinaz." If they didn't know that he had always called for her this way, they may have wondered who all these women were, but this had been their parents' language—each name tied to the one before like precious stones on a string.

Mehrdad and Noor sat quietly on the sofa looking at photos of Cameron and Chloe on his iPad from their holiday in Costa Rica. Cameron, her fearless nephew, had surfed the enormous waves. Both were such a mix of their parents, but at ten, Cam reminded Noor so much of Mehrdad as a little boy—the same dimpled chin and that fantastic smile. Chloe, too, had Mehrdad's playful grin, but her mother's clear blue eyes looked up from under her long lashes, recalling Chrissy's candor.

Noor had never met anyone like her sister-in-law and she was admittedly a little afraid of her because Chrissy was incapable of *tarof* (a custom of self-deference exclusive to Iranians). She spoke frankly and without decorum. If she didn't like your chicken, she'd go in the kitchen and make herself a salad. If the flowers you brought made her sneeze, she'd tell you to put them on the porch. Once, she'd even taken half a German chocolate cake to a dinner party, admitting to the hostess that it was her favorite and she'd kept the other half. For months Mehrdad was too mortified to accept another invitation. Yet this very guilelessness is what Noor loved about her—you never had to wonder with Chrissy if *yes* meant *no*. This was her brother's life now: well-grounded, with a lovely family and a job he loved, and he was proud of that.

Nelson insisted that Noor stay in the room when he came to apologize to Zod. *Mr. Yadegar, I'm so sorry I hurt your daughter. I've come to take my family home. I promise to take very good care of them, etcetera.* Zod's eyes shone with gratitude as if this man alone understood him.

Later that night they found themselves alone in a rare moment of privacy when Noor walked into his room carrying fresh towels. Nelson closed the door, took her in his arms very slowly, and begged Noor to forgive him. It was like stepping inside a movie they had seen together, and she couldn't help but giggle at the cliché: jilted wife facing repentant husband. He kissed her tenderly and muttered a thousand apologies, pulling her to the floor, big hands caressing all her soft surfaces, almost reaching beneath her skirt, all the while begging *"please, please, come home"* in whispered remorse. Yes, his fingertips still burned a hole through her sleeves. Yes, her heart hammered in her chest and her legs parted ever so slightly. Noor sighed, took a deep breath and waited for it to settle. His scent of pine mingled with aftershave in the soft gully of his clavicle made her dizzy. Being virtuous was so very difficult. Didn't she deserve a wild and free moment? She trembled with the thought that maybe this would not be the last time they would make love together, glad, glad to have recovered what was lost. Yes, he'd come to take her home. What was she made of? Ice would melt in the glint of those eyes.

She placed a hand on his chest, feeling his heart pounding. He laid Noor down and kissed her neck, her ears, her mouth, cupped her bosom, and she kept her eyes open so she could see this magnificent man. He removed her skirt and rested his head on her stomach and she looked at him through eyes blurred with tears. *Oh, Nelson*, and she clung to him, wrapping him in her limbs. *My my my my my*. Nothing between them now but a wound, not forgotten, not even forgiven, but accepted.

Afterwards they lay close without speaking.

"I don't need anyone but you and Lily," he said at length. "I need nothing else."

"But what are we doing here, really?" she asked.

"Well . . . I think we are coming back to each other."

"Yes, but now I have to go." Dr. Mehran would be arriving any minute.

She stood up and fastened her skirt and smoothed back her hair. At that moment they heard Lily downstairs. "Dad? Dad!"

Lily reached the landing at the moment Noor closed the door behind her. Cheeks ablaze, Noor averted her eyes but her daughter had already noticed her untucked blouse and smiled knowingly.

"Is Daddy in his room, Mommy?" Mommy. When had Lily last called her "Mommy"?

"Sorry. Yes." Sorry for what, she didn't quite know, but she hurried past her daughter into the dim hallway of the house she knew, sailing past the bedrooms to the bathroom where she closed the door and leaned against the sink. Oh, what had she done? She had only herself to blame.

Downstairs, Noor noticed the kitchen clock had stopped at six twenty-five. She drank a glass of water from the tap and went to find her brother. Mehrdad, still a little jet-lagged, had woken from a nap upon hearing Zod call his name—or had he dreamed it? He rose to lean his cheek against the small pulse on the side of his father's neck. He and Zod resembled each other more now that Mehrdad's hair was graying, both with the same long, thin nose, the same shoulders, though Zod's had contracted considerably.

The pleats in Zod's eyelids fluttered and he opened them once to drink in the sight of his son, "*Pesaram* (my son)," and closed again.

"Baba?" said Mehrdad. "Baba joon?"

"Pesaram, pesaram," muttered Zod, reassuring Mehrdad that he hadn't left yet, that he was his father always and he lived inside him always.

Over and over they whispered back and forth, *Baba, pesaram, Baba, pesaram*, like a hymn. Even with his last breaths, Zod vowed his attachment to his son, so there would never be any doubt that he loved his children.

Dr. Mehran had told them that it would be soon. When? At most a day. Sheer, curled up on Zod's bed, yawned and went back to sleep, one crooked finger scratching behind her ear.

As Zod fell into sleep, he dreamed that he was flying a paper airplane. He was actually sitting in it and his brother was in the pilot's seat. Zod couldn't see his brother's face, of course, just the square back of his head and a voice, shouting like pilots do in old movies in the open-air cockpit, but he couldn't make out what Morad was saying. His brother was an idiot. He had always known it was best to keep away from him, so what was he doing here? Is this how he was going to die, with his brother throwing him out of a paper plane? Then the pilot looked back and Zod saw that it wasn't Morad at all, but his big brother, Davoud, yelling, "Are you hungry, Zod?"

"Starving."

And they flew like prayers through the clouds.

# Twenty-Nine

Z od was gone by the time Noor returned to his bedside with Lily and Nelson, and soon they were joined by Naneh Goli, Ferry and Aunt Farah, Soli and Karim, with Hedi and Ala close behind. Mehrdad choked back tears and held Lily, but Noor sobbed noisily into Nelson's chest, and before long they all wept together, resting their heads on one another's shoulders. When it subsided there was a moment of peace, a quiet interrupted only by the light scrape of the chair Soli brought for Naneh. Each one of them had already sat alone with Zod and said everything they wanted to say to him, and he had given each his last word like a keepsake. When Noor walked into the yard to call Dr. Mehran, she saw him asleep in the car with his mouth open. He'd never gone home from his last house call.

Poor Naneh Goli. She wondered if her sole purpose on this earth had been to keep a deathwatch. Will they all die before me? Haunted by the blurry vision of herself in the seasons ahead with too many ghosts, her eyes continued to fill with tears but she wasn't one to wail. Naneh had done enough of that, her scalp shone underneath what hair was left. She only longed to be alone with Zod before his soul left his body, and because they counted on her to get things done, Noor asked Naneh to prepare Zod. It's customary in Iran for a family member to wash the body of the deceased; there are no undertakers and no viewings, burial is swift, and in the Yadegars' case, there would be no clerics present at the funeral.

And so it was that Naneh Goli took soap and washcloths and a basin of warm water to bathe Zod in the salon, a ritual as familiar to her as the bare shoulders, limbs, and pale chest of this shrunken man who had once been her boy. Raising the rigid stalk of his right arm to lather it, then the left, she whispered to him to tell the others that she wouldn't be long now, that her days were numbered, too.

In the lamplight, moving with precision and utmost tenderness, she rinsed every inch of him, kissed and swabbed his eyes, ears, and nose with cotton balls dabbed in rosewater. She tweezed the wayward hairs of his earlobes, clipped his fingernails and toenails, buffing each nail to a fine gloss. Then she dried her hands to unfurl the shroud she had prepared days ago. It was the simple white cotton sheet Nina had once embroidered for Zod and Pari, ironed smooth and scented with rosewater. She wrapped Zod within it and stood beside him for what seemed to her a short time, when in fact the light from the rising sun lit the room and he glowed in his cocoon.

The aroma of toasted flour grew stronger as Noor came downstairs, and she opened the windows to let the smell of halvah drift into the streets and over the rooftops, heralding a funeral. This rich pudding of flour, butter, sugar, and rosewater was a salve to their grief. She found Soli alone in the kitchen bent over an enormous pot of syrup, his narrow shoulders slumped in sorrow. It would not be appropriate to touch him but she stood near the stove in solidarity.

"Is Naneh still asleep?" she inquired. Naneh Goli, parched from a night of ablutions, had gulped down some water and gone to bed at dawn.

"Yes," replied Soli, reticence under lock and key.

"Would you like some help with the halvah?"

"No, khanoom."

"May I prepare the dates, at least?" She wasn't giving up on consoling this lonely man.

He gestured to the platters of dates they would serve at the cemetery, already stuffed with walnuts and covered with plastic wrap. The man had only slept a few hours and was up long before dawn. Then he put the ladle down and faced her, his eyes shiny and round as coins, questioning her.

"What will become of us, khanoom?"

"Today. Let's just get through today and tomorrow, Soli," Noor replied, for the funeral was scheduled the following day and they still had much to do.

"But how? How will we manage without him?" It was like a wave breaking and Soli convulsed and crashed, heaving between sobs that shook his entire body. There was more going on inside that man than he let them believe.

"One foot in front of the other, that is the way we do it, Soli. One foot in front of the other," said Noor.

MEHRDAD, NELSON, HEDI, AND Soli carried Zod to Dr. Mehran's car. Some families choose to have the body transported to the cemetery in a limousine, but Dr. Mehran would not let a stranger drive his old friend to his grave and Karim had washed and polished the vehicle until it sparkled in the bright afternoon sun.

Noor and Aunt Farah followed with Naneh Goli and the children, all in black and their hair combed underneath their headscarves, in a minivan chauffeured by Aladdin. Wreaths filled every square inch of Mr. Azizi's pickup truck as he led the slow motorcade through town.

News of Zod's death had sent volts through the tight grid of neighborhoods, and one by one doors opened as people in their dark clothes locked their homes, pulled down the metal grates on their shops, and hurried to fall into a line behind cars and minibuses, motorcycles and bicycles. They poured into the street, their heads lowered, pressed to the backs of those before them, a procession that built and built like a line of dominoes. It was unlike anything Mehrdad or Noor had ever seen—car after car after car, shuttered shop windows, men and women weeping openly, mopping their faces with white handkerchiefs.

Noor peered around at the row of taxi hoods and the forlorn faces in the bus windows and all behind them, the rhythmic march of mourners bent under their grief, drawn forth by the single wish to say good-bye to a *yaar*, a constant and devoted companion. Along the sidewalks, policemen squinted to see, taking a second or two to realize what was going on, then pausing to touch the brim of their caps. For now, they tolerated the crowd and the wailing voices, held back by what was in their eyes, or rather, what was not—an unheeded indifference to their presence.

"Move along, now," they commanded in a half-hearted attempt to establish authority. But really, they knew that one ungenerous impulse and any one of these men, wracked by grief, would catch them by the throat, so they stood beneath the sparse trees clicking cigarette lighters in their palms, blithely observing a cortege the likes of which they had never seen but for martyrs and mullahs.

Noor turned in her seat to look back once more at the line that was growing longer still, ten, maybe twenty blocks, pressed together and tighter, moving forward in a slow pulse.

ARRIVING AT THE CEMETERY, fathers, brothers, and sons carried Zod on their shoulders to a freshly dug plot. And then the line broke and the volume of their cry rose like from a choir, wavering when they lowered him into the ground and crowded around his grave, utterly dependent on one another to bear this loss of the best in themselves. Gone was the slightly rigid mien of everyday, here their cheeks were wet, and everyone nodded and had a kind word for one another, whispered like involuntary prayers, some replacing the gravity with anecdotes about Zod, a connectedness between them he had fostered.

One by one they knelt to say good-bye, their eyes cast down upon their friend, only once more, then, no more, for before long the site was covered with flowers as if bulbs had bloomed all at once, and they rose with grass stains on their trousers and the scent of damp earth on their hands.

Naneh Goli, who held Ferry's hand until then, went to kneel as near to the pit as possible, her spine arched beneath a black veil, unaware of the crowd politely skirting her. Lily clung to Noor, for the wailing that erupted from the women frightened her, and Noor, overwhelmed by the sound herself, tried her best to reassure Lily that this was their way and she needn't be afraid. It was as moving as it was alarming, and the family huddled together to receive the mourners who came before them with fresh tears to utter "*may it be your last sorrow, may his soul be joyous*" while Karim and Soli passed around trays of dates and squares of halvah beneath a pink afternoon sky, the sun still warm on their backs.

Zod was buried in a shady spot next to Yanik and Nina. The government never having released her body, Pari's grave lay empty with a simple stone that read GIVEN TO US TOO BRIEFLY, PARVANEH YADEGAR *1943–1982*. Reading this, Noor felt a blow deep in her gut and her body coiled in reflex. There lay the Yadegars, side by side, deeper in the earth than the roots of trees they had planted. Maybe Zod had been right to keep the truth of her mother's death from her. Noor wondered how he stayed alive. The pain of keeping it to himself must have been more than his sorrow, greater than his loss. This thought filled Noor at once with profound gratitude and regret.

Ferry came to lightly grasp her elbow, propping her up, and she stood between her girls with a comforting arm around each, wondering how the story of her life would someday be etched into stone in the dash between two dates.

NIGHT CAME AT LAST and they returned to Café Leila, drawn and deafened from the noise, with adrenaline still surging through their bodies. In this house they had never known a day without work, so Noor followed Karim and Soli into the kitchen to prepare dinner, tying an apron around her waist. Traditionally, callers visit the bereaved family unannounced three days after a death to express their sympathy, so this evening was a gathering of family with a few close friends. Hedi and Ala pushed the tables close together on the marble floor and arranged the extra chairs and benches against the brown wood wainscoting. Naneh Goli ironed a thick white tablecloth and big square napkins with red scalloped edges. Aunt Farah polished Nina's silver and crystal goblets, arranging white lilies and hydrangeas with long tapered candles for the centerpiece.

Oh, how nice it looked. They had eaten here for decades, inside this wood-paneled room with its large windows through which the garden and its fruit trees were visible, but tonight, even with everyone in black, it gleamed in the flame of the candles Farah lit at dusk. What else to do, if not eat and drink? Bread, vodka, barley soup, roast beef, pickled cauliflower and beets, yogurt, dilled cucumbers, olives, bowls of spicy, warm, cold, red, green, and pink—a *buffet russe* as Yanik would have prepared.

At the head of the table, Mehrdad set a place for Zod with black bread over a shot glass of vodka, as they had done before at Yanik's, Nina's, and Davoud's wakes—a reversal of the Russian custom of breaking black bread when meeting someone for the first time.

In the salon where Dr. Mehran drank tea with Nelson while Lily and Ferry played with Sheer on the floor, Mr. Yazdan, one of Zod's oldest friends, sat on the piano bench and lifted the wing to test the keys. It wasn't tuned but you couldn't hold that against him when he tapped the first chords to "Mara Beboos"—a classic Persian ballad. These four notes brought the two doctors from the couch, two girls with their cat, three cooks from the kitchen, two elderly waiters, a kind auntie, a brother and his ancient nanny, into his aura. Shoja Yazdan wasn't naive, but there were songs everyone knew, which touch the most intimate raw emotions, songs that can turn you inside out.

One by one they detached themselves from tasks and slipped over to the piano, giving in to an overwhelming tide of sentiment. And Mr. Yazdan knew he would have to continue. They substituted prayer with music and circled the piano to sing the lyrics—for the first time, maybe ever, hearing one another sing. Even Nelson and Lily, who didn't know the words, swayed to the melody.

> Kiss me. Kiss me. For one last time.
> May God keep you safe. May God be with you.
> Our spring has passed. The past is past.
> I will arise and go now to my fate.

Noor didn't meet Nelson's eyes. She grew attentive instead to her surroundings, safeguarding the moment. Does this sort of thing really happen? Does it? Could they sing shoulder to shoulder with their eyes half closed? Did Zod have fellowship in mind when Pari sang? Was Café Leila a cloud cover above all their lonesome lives?

Noor felt protective, intertwined with the people who stood beside her. Dr. Mehran's hand on Karim's back, Sheer sheltered in the folds of Naneh's lap, Mehrdad's arm slung over Soli's shoulder, Ferry leaning into Lily, Lily's eyes regarding her parents, and Noor nearly undone by the glow of trust in them. Nothing would change the goodness within those around her. Nothing ever changed in their needs for security and affection. Minds changed. Bodies changed. Passions evolved. Nelson knew her in ways both joyful and bitter that the others never would, and she would keep that part of her past, their trysts and tussles, sealed in an envelope.

What diverted her thoughts was another envelope, hidden in her purse. It had arrived with the evening post from the adoption bureau. A letter sent cannot be unwritten.

*Maybe we don't really grow up until our parents die,* she thought. Maybe her infant memory was forever looking to Zod and Pari to make things better because they always did. Because if our parents didn't exalt us, we spend our adult lives blaming them—for not doing this, and not doing that, not being "supportive," not making an appearance at our first recital, being overprotective or aloof, damaging our self-esteem. Yet at our best or worst, who sees everything? Who knows us best? Who waits and waits to see what we yet may be? Then one day they're gone and it's just you, and there's nothing left to squeeze, no one to blame for the dismay over the course your life has taken.

Once the tears have stopped, it's just the here and now and the desire to do better, to be closer to the person you want to be. Noor didn't want to wish that she had been a better person. As a mother, she wanted to draw from Lily's trust in her to realize that whatever her own parents did or didn't do was nothing short of heroic and Noor couldn't hold up a candle to them. But she would try.

# Thirty

—⬳⬳⬳—

There was talk of closing the café in the days following Zod's funeral, but a steady stream of people wore the day out coming to sit with the family, ignoring their need for solitude because their need to be consoled in the intimacy of Café Leila was greater and to close the door on them was unthinkable. Pausing on the bleached steps to offer a bouquet, they filled the house with flowers and wreaths until it smelled like Mr. Azizi's shop and Karim was put in charge of refreshing the water in the dozens of vases and sweeping the petals into the yard.

Noor roused Naneh Goli's and Soli's spirits by recalling her father's desire to feed unannounced callers like fledging chicks and she saw that they trusted her, that a sense of security prevailed when there were tasks and expectations to keep the household running as it always had.

"Remember what my father used to say," she said. "'Nothing the cook can do is ever enough.'"

Thus Soli bolted to the market every morning, returning breathless, and before long they heard him shouting orders at Karim, pounding sorrow with his meat mallet, and resuming the familiar clatter of pots and pans. Grief could not seize them as long as they kept moving.

But by week's end Noor found Mehrdad and Nelson in the salon bent over their laptops making travel arrangements. There were crumbs and orange peels on the coffee table and when she bent to sweep them up with her hands, Nelson caught her wrist and winked at her. For a second she thought she might lean down and kiss his lips, to feel his rough cheek with her fingertips, but Mehrdad snapped his computer shut and said, "Well, that's that."

"What's that?" Noor turned to her brother.

"We booked our flights for Friday," said Mehrdad.

"Wait . . . already?" she gasped.

"Yep, your ticket to freedom, sis."

"We have to get back to work, *mi vida*," said Nelson. "I mean, what keeps us here?"

Noor bristled but said nothing. Up until that moment Nelson had been so kind, friendly to everyone, but in the week since Zod's death, the amicability slowly muted with talk of imminent departure. Both men became prickly and anxious to leave. They played cards to pass the time but had trouble concentrating. It was over, they said, no choice in the matter. They didn't want to wait another week.

Noor and Mehrdad, in the house together for the first time since they were teenagers, found it difficult not to fall back into their old roles. Not the adults they had become in America, but the needy sister and the exasperated older brother. They knew each other better than anyone, but it was as if he hadn't seen her yet and every time he met her gaze, she would feel the pressure of tears and look away. But Mehrdad sensed what was happening to Noor.

"You have to untangle yourself from all this, Noor," said Mehrdad. "Your life is not here—you know that. I've spoken to a lawyer about selling the café and he's confident that he can do it without our presence. Once he finds a buyer, I'll come back to sign the paperwork. It's valuable real estate, you know."

Noor felt like she was being shoved onto a moving walkway, a fierce tug against the soles of her feet.

"*Untangle?* How can we just turn our backs on Naneh and Soli? How can you hire a lawyer without even talking to me?" she screamed, for he knew exactly what to say to make her furious. Her hand flew up as if they were kids again, playing one moment, fists flying the next. Then he calmly took her hand and held it securely between his own.

"There are limits to what we can do for these people."

Nelson sat back and crossed his arms. "Lily has to go back to school, Noor, or she'll fall too far behind. We have to think about college soon. It's been a good adventure for her, and you, *pero* (but)—" He stood up to put his arms around her, pressed her close and rested his chin on her head.

*Here we are, entangled again*, thought Noor. And how good it felt. In the mirror above the piano, she could see their reflection, a portrait of a marriage becoming more vivid, forgiving all with her hand on his sleeve. It wasn't lost after all—here's a chance to have it back.

Of course he's right, how could you argue against it, the very things that mattered—keeping her family intact. Lily has to start school. Nelson has to work. She has a daughter. She has a husband. She had nursed and buried her father. Sooner or later she would get over the loss of Café Leila. Soon they could go back to live in their big, tidy house. They would ski at Lake Tahoe in the winter and spend summers in Spain. Soon she would have the simple pleasure of sleeping beside Nelson again and hearing Lily's voice singing in the shower from across the hall. Could she rely on Nelson's warmth, every day delivering the same smell and the same flare? How desperate she had been to put herself back together, and now here it was: a plane ticket and a safe place to go, even if she had left it once in despair.

Maybe Noor should have never come back to Iran, become so attached to these people. What had Mehrdad said? *There are limits to what we can do.* Who did she think she was? If only she had known about limits then, she would have spared Lily this voyage, spared her the torrent of tears in June and July, spared her the horror of August, and now the pain of having to leave her new friends behind. Her daughter was too young to know so much disappointment. Noor had imagined she could change, imagined she could comfort her father, or Naneh Goli, or Ferry, or Soli and Karim, imagined them waiting for her voice to tell them what to do next. She felt herself a poor substitute for her father.

Nobody would have to know about the envelope in her purse, yet unopened.

"We have to find a place for Ferry," she said quietly.

"No point in doing that . . . she can stay here for now with Naneh Goli, to help out," said Mehrdad, suddenly in command. "There's nowhere safer than here. When the time comes I'll deal with it, okay? I'll figure something out for her, and a home for Naneh Goli, too. I'm sure there's plenty of work for the boys." *Well, he's got it all figured out*, thought Noor bitterly.

"I'll talk to them, okay? Let me tell them," she said.

"Fine," he shrugged, "but we have to start packing."

From the café came the collective sound of hushed conversation—the usual thunder of laughter and boisterous goodwill, slapping tabletops, clinking glasses and cutlery was reduced to a pitter-patter. Murmuring was all the regulars could muster.

LATER THAT EVENING NOOR heard the children in the kitchen with Farah. Farah, who brought the fresh smell of her Beverly Hills home with her, had thought to pack Kit Kats and Goldfish and cereal boxes into her suitcase, thinking perhaps that Lily missed her candy and her sugary breakfast and Noor had to laugh when she found the three kids shuffling cards, sharing a bowl of Lucky Charms between them like peanuts.

Noor asked if Ferry could give her a hand with something. A brief rain had polished the path and she took Ferry outside to sit on the stone bench in the cool dusk, the days growing shorter now. Noor wiped the seat with her handkerchief and took Ferry's hand. Her skin was warm and they sat in comfortable silence like in a waiting room.

"What can I do for you, khanoom?" Ferry asked sweetly, still addressing Noor as "ma'am."

*What can she do for* me? thought Noor. She could not stand it. All the goodness in the world right here beside her. Ferry so painfully eager to please.

"Ferry joon," her voice cracked, "you're healing so nicely."

"Khanoom, do you think my face will always look like this?"

Noor turned to her then and stroked the crater that used to be Ferry's smooth right cheek with her fingertips, a slow, gentle examination of the wound that broke Noor's heart.

"Ferry, Ferry, look at me, *azizam* (dear one). Another few months and you'll have your surgery. I'll pay for it. You won't believe what they can do these days."

"Yes, you told me. Lots of times. But what about my old face, you know the face I didn't have to think about or feel . . . you know, like breathing?"

Noor nodded. "You mean like a habit."

"Yes, I suppose. I miss not thinking about it even more than I miss seeing."

Noor took Ferry in her arms. She couldn't put it off any longer.

"Ferry, I have to go back to America, but I want you to know that we're not leaving you on your own. You'll stay here with Naneh Goli and Karim. He's like a brother to you, no? Soon your left eye will be all healed and you'll have new eyebrows, too. And I will send for you. It might take some time, but I promise that I'll send for you and you'll go to school again."

Gripping her, Noor felt a young girl's strength in the small, firm back that somehow conveyed reassurance, and she found herself drawing from it to abate her own misgivings. *What can you do for me, indeed*, she thought.

ON THEIR LAST EVENING, Noor lit a few lanterns and spread out blankets for a picnic in their cherished place under the mulberry tree that had their names scratched into its bark. Soli prepared a feast but the children had no appetite for it. Neither Naneh Goli nor Soli were surprised so much as they were disappointed. They knew they would be left alone to fend for themselves, but the haste in departure seemed eager and disrespectful. They also knew that their opinions didn't matter.

It wasn't easy for Ferry and Karim to absorb the news of Lily's departure. It made almost everything and every moment with her so big that they could squeeze inside it, draw the drapes and tighten the knots. Lily joon was leaving. Lily-merci (for it had become her nickname), was packing her bags. Lily, who arrived only four months ago sulking in her hoodie. Lily, who spoke a little Farsi, with a twang, and could even write her name. Their minds were full of "the last this" and "the last that" and for their last meal, they baked a cake and cut it messily in three and let Sheer eat the crumbs from their palms.

It was Lily's idea to swap clothes.

"How do you say *shirt* again?" she asked Karim.

"Pi-ra-han."

"Give me your number six pi-ra-han and I'll give you my Cal hoodie . . . Ferry, you can have my high-tops." The shoes would be too big, of course, but Ferry would grow into them. The younger girl tugged on a gold bangle and nudged it onto Lily's wrist.

Everything that mattered to Karim was about to be lost, an ocean muscling its way between him and his first love, leaving nothing but a navy blue sweatshirt in his hands. But to Karim, it was laden with meaning. She pulled the shirt over her head, revealing the pale skin of her belly and he had to look away, still shy of Lily joon.

That night he opened to a clean page in his tattered notebook and started writing Lily a letter because his stammer had returned and when he tried to speak—"*no, don't go, stay, don't leave*"—the words shattered in his mouth. He wrote down what she meant to him. He wrote what he had felt that first morning in the kitchen and what he still felt, only more deeply. He wrote about the sound of her laughter like a tiny waterfall and how that sound alone could bring him to his knees. He wrote about how he loved the way she said his name, "Cream," like the word on the blue Nivea tin. He wrote that he didn't know what she would remember about him, but it didn't matter because he would love her forever and would remember her always. Lily moon. Lily sun. Lily, the light he held secret in his heart's very core. Then he turned off the lamp and fell back onto his new bed with that dark blue sweatshirt for a pillow, listening to the autumn wind shaking the tall trees.

TWO SHINY BLACK TAXIS were parked by the gate. *No need for an entourage*, Mehrdad insisted, and he called for cabs instead of letting Soli drive them to the airport—another affront that Soli accepted stoically. Huffing and puffing, Hedi helped the cabbies carry the bags outside. Both Noor and Farah had shopped for souvenirs, stuffed their suitcases with kilos of pistachios, *lavashak* (fruit leather), dried figs and barberries, spices and pomegranate paste.

The children were huddled under their tree, heads ducked and arms draped around each other's shoulders like before a match, exchanging their last-minute vows and promising to write. Naneh Goli wept into a napkin, so weary she was of love and the endless tug on her heart. Would it never stop, this coming and leaving? *I'm too old for this*, she thought. Had she not sent these children away once already? Why did they have to come back? "Good-bye, good-bye," they called, bending to kiss her hand and sniff her rosy scent once more.

Karim gave a short whistle and Sheer ran to leap into Lily's arms for a last nuzzle. Ala waited with a hose to spray the cars when they pulled away from the curb, no longer needing words but water to wash their sorrow and clear the path for a safe journey. Noor, in the backseat with Lily and Nelson, waved and waved until she lost sight of the six lonesome figures, feeling farther away than ever.

Lily sat between them, clutching the stem of a red carnation from Karim while Nelson teased, "Better not wear that jersey when we watch Messi."

"Dad, Iran held off Argentina till the very last minute!"

"Ha ha ha! Please, give me a break. Probably they ate kebab for lunch and were too sleepy to play *fútbol*." Lily punched him playfully and soon they were chuckling, the quivering lip gone, and Lily's face brightened as they left Tehran behind.

They both smiled at Noor. She smiled back, but she was silent. Her native city—bleak, savage, beautiful—retreated from her with a long sigh. *Well, go on then, go.* Fear and hurt and anger washed through her, reminding her that she was no more or less prudent, no more or less mature than she was at seventeen when her father had driven her to the airport. All that effort to open the world to her, only to see Noor return disheartened. And just when the idea of what she might do had started to form, the intensity of their time in Iran was diminished to an "adventure." Was the dawning of purpose so fleeting? She shouldn't be thinking any of this, but here it was.

They walked into the terminal building, checked their bags, and while Mehrdad suggested going to the kiosk for snacks, Noor excused herself to go to the bathroom. She looked at the clock. Another hour remained before boarding. When she returned to her family, Mehrdad was on Skype with a colleague, Lily was showing Farah a game on her phone, and Nelson handed her a cup of tea.

Her knees wobbling, Noor accepted the cup and sat beside him, taking his big hand between her own. Nelson saw that her eyes were watery and she was shaking.

"What's up? Why are you looking at me like that?" he asked.

"Nelson, I have adopted Ferry," she said, exhaling at last.

"*Qué?*" He looked alarmed.

"Mom, really? That's awesome!" cried Lily over Farah's shoulder.

Nelson blinked as if adapting to the bright light. "You are incredibly optimistic, Noor, to think we can bring her to *Estados Unidos*."

"I didn't say that." She met his gaze, his eyes a midnight black. Minutes ago, she had locked herself in the bathroom and read the letter confirming Ferry's adoption and the longer she held the envelope, the heavier it became—a pebble, then a stone, then a rock. A perfect rock.

"I'm not going back with you and Lily." Like the tide, the fear that had held her back for so long receded until she could not believe it once came up to her ears, and with newly found courage she hurried forward to reveal her thoughts—or rather her passion, fierce now for her people, for Café Leila and its patrons.

"I see," said Nelson, but he could not understand her divided heart.

"Lily joon, listen to me," and she reached over Nelson's lap, pulling Lily to her. "It isn't because I don't love you and you know I still love Daddy—but I've seen a look in your eyes I've never seen before, the way you've opened up to me, the way you look at me with joy and a tiny bit of awe, and more than anything, Lily, *more than anything*, I want to show you that our lives have meaning beyond the everyday things we dwell on. We play a part, however small, in the times in which we live—we are not here just for ourselves. You are *so* brave and all I've ever done is show you how to be afraid." Noor struggled to claim every word.

"Yes, okay, okay," Nelson interrupted. "It is different now . . . you are different, Lily is different, but this is something we carry with us, no? Noor, *mi vida . . . no dejes que nos separemos* (love of my life . . . don't let us be apart)," he pleaded. "I cannot understand how you could want to stay here, Noor. *You* cannot change anything." Noor caught the edge in his voice.

"Perhaps, but I mean to try," said Noor. She put a hand to his face, smoothed the ripple in his jawline. "I can't abandon them."

It was then that he lost patience with her and made a gathering gesture. "*Entonces, claro que pueden venir.* (Then, of course they can come.)" He shrugged. Nelson still thought that perhaps he could win by making a joke of it. "We will take them all—the whole lot . . . the girl, the boy, *la vieja* (old woman), *el gato* (the cat). I'll build an ark if you want!"

She expected sarcasm, but it hurt more that he didn't say their names.

"No, Nelson! What are you talking about?" she dropped her hand from his face. "Café Leila is *not* portable! The people are not portable. This is their home and I will do everything I can to preserve it. Everything I do will be to that end."

"And what about us?" he asked, shaking his head. "Are you leaving us then, Noor?"

Through it all, Mehrdad and Farah remained stupefied, her brother giving her long disapproving looks. Lily swallowed hard and tilted her head ever so slightly to gaze at her mother, mouth agape, though smiling a half-smile. Noor could see that she was trying to make sense of it. She remembered how her father had sent her away thirty years ago and the utter despair of parting, how Zod had pushed her into the stewardess's arms, reassuring her that she was a big girl now, how there was no end to her tears, and his. Oh no! Oh, her raggedy heart! How could this be? These—the worst moments of her life. Noor got to her feet and knelt before Lily, the pain in her chest unyielding.

"So, Mom . . . can I come back next summer?"

What? What could she give her daughter to carry so they would not stray too far apart? Noor reached into her purse, withdrew a small antique hand mirror that had belonged to Pari, and tucked it into Lily's backpack—a looking glass to see behind and to look forward.

Once, when Lily was learning to ride a bicycle, Noor had tripped while running behind and had broken her arm. Lily had squatted at her side and gently stroked her head until a neighbor called for help. For weeks she was helpless, not being able to lift or carry anything with her right arm, and Lily enjoyed taking charge of the household, playing mommy, insisting on washing Noor every night in a bathtub brimming with bubbles. She remembered sitting back and watching her daughter compete with Nelson in taking care of her. *I don't know what I would do without you*, she'd say, only to hear Lily sigh with pleasure.

Now she held on to Lily for dear life and with her other hand reached for Nelson, to lengthen the hour, to be close like this a little while longer. They used to sit for hours with the cradle between them, chatting about their baby girl—*she looks like my mother, no, mi vida, she looks like ju*—and here she was, a young woman, their excellent girl, with her chin raised quizzically. It was Nelson's gesture, and in her eyes, a glimpse of Pari.

Mehrdad, annoyed with his sister, pushed back his chair and walked away. Farah's eyes went from Nelson's blank face to Noor's, twisted in pain, and she rose to embrace her.

Moments later, when their flight was announced, Nelson gave Noor his arm, Lily gripped her hand, and she walked between them to the gate, and they cried through it all, as everyone seemed to do at this airport, at this hour of international flights taking fathers and sons and daughters away, parting sometimes for years.

# EPILOGUE

As I sit here writing this by the light of the stove, it has been nearly three months since my daughter left. Already darkness closes in by five o'clock and the only light is in the kitchen. Naneh Goli is asleep in the opposite chair, too stubborn to lie down. If her room is drafty, she would never say. Under the table, Sheer arches her back and rubs against my calf. I've become a cat person despite myself. I hear Ferry running a bath upstairs, all the pipes shuddering to tell me so.

Today we received a letter from Lily with a photo Nelson must have taken on Stinson Beach—a beautiful suntanned girl with spiky brown hair and the golden retriever she always desired at her side. It's still hard to believe she made Karim chop off her hair with my grandmother's left-handed scissors. Inside the folded note, she had tucked in some soccer cards for Karim and scented stickers for Ferry—it surprises me how at sixteen she still covets such things like a six-year-old. She had signed her name in Persian.

When my brother kissed me good-bye, he said, "Just promise me you won't turn sour." The Persian obsession with pickles and preserves serves not only as a condiment, but a metaphor. It is assumed that beneath a thick veil of loyalty or selflessness, a woman's deep discontent waits in brine. Perhaps Mehrdad was genuinely concerned—it's true that whenever I happened to catch a glimpse of myself in the mirror, I had a hurt look in my eyes, the droopy corners looking for sympathy— a preoccupied, pained look like I'd bitten the inside of my cheek.

These days I only look in the mirror to comb and pin up my hair. There's little time for reflection what with running the café, keeping Soli happy (stubborn and seething if a customer dare asks for salt), taking Ferry to her doctor visits, and homeschooling her for now.

"Don't worry," I told Mehrdad. "You, of all people, should know I'm more mouse than martyr."

It's strange sleeping in my parents' bedroom and finding remnants of them, like a strand of Baba's silver hair or a nail clipping, even though we scrubbed and polished and bought a new mattress.

At first Naneh Goli had stood by the door with her hands on her hips. "You can't sleep here!"

"Why not?" I edged back, sensing her outrage.

"It's not right!"

Then she turned and walked away. I didn't want to upset her. A few hours later she returned.

"Perhaps we should throw out the mattress."

I repainted, moved a few pieces around, and put a chair by the window where I like to sit in the early morning light when the house is still, my feet propped on the windowsill, and write a letter to my father giving him news of the café and his customers.

In a dresser drawer I found a bundle of my old letters from America tied together with kitchen string in chronological order. I will say first that it's embarrassing reading what I wrote so long ago—adrift, entangled with my faraway life and never quite maturing. I'm glad nobody else in the world will ever read them.

Initially it felt intrusive, that I was in their intimate space, but apart from a few sleepless nights, I've comforted myself with the thought that three generations have lived in this creaky old house and that it will remain standing with its doors open.

There isn't much certainty to anything, but this much I know, that the trees will bloom every spring and the rooms where we grew up will smell of clean sheets and furniture polish, that the pipes will rattle no matter who washes, and that someone will still buy groceries, light the stove, cook our meals, and we will never be short of company.

# Acknowledgments

GRATITUDE BEGINS AT HOME with my husband, Mitchell Johnson, and my son, Luca. You are my greatest love and the light of my eyes. Thank you for pulling me often and urgently into group hugs, for giving me the time I needed to write, and for your steadfast support. Without you, this would not exist.

If it weren't for my brilliant agent, Adam Chromy, this would have been a lesser book and it would not have found a good home in the hands of my wise and extraordinary editor, Andra Miller. I am grateful for your enthusiasm and proud to be represented by you. I would also like to thank Elisabeth Scharlatt, Brunson Hoole, Sasha Tropp, Anne Winslow, Lauren Moseley, Craig Popelars, Brooke Csuka, Debra Linn, and everyone at Algonquin who gave this book so much of their time and attention.

For the love my dearest friends gave and continue to give, I am very much indebted to Taraneh Razavi and Stuart Schlisserman for their medical expertise, to Faezeh Ghaffari and Noushie Ammari for sharing their funny hospital stories, and to Belen Byers for her swift translations. Special thank you to Peter Ovanessoff, whose mother's recipes were an inspiration, and to Nadi Ovanessoff, Jackie Espinosa, and Sia Sobhani, childhood friends and the best I ever had.

Those who believe they recognize any of my characters are mistaken, for they are all from my imagination except for Dr. Mehran, who is my father,

Dr. Bijan, beloved champion of his patients, gone before he could see how much I borrowed from his generosity. *Ti jan-e-man* . . .

A heartfelt thanks to my sisters, Shabnam Anderson and Sherry Bijan, for a lifetime of love and encouragement.

I reserve my most profound gratitude for my mother, Atefeh Bijan, who taught me the meaning of welcome, and home.